The
Private Revolution
of
Geoffrey Frost

Other Books by J. E. Fender

Easy Victories (Houghton Mifflin, 1973)
  Under the pseudonym of James Trowbridge

Hardscrabble Books—Fiction of New England

Laurie Alberts, *Lost Daughters*

Laurie Alberts, *The Price of Land in Shelby*

Thomas Bailey Aldrich, *The Story of a Bad Boy*

Robert J. Begiebing, *The Adventures of Allegra Fullerton;*
Or, A Memoir of Startling and Amusing Episodes from Itinerant Life

Anne Bernays, *Professor Romeo*

Chris Bohjalian, *Water Witches*

Dona Brown, ed., *A Tourist's New England: Travel Fiction, 1820–1920*

Joseph Bruchac, *The Waters Between: A Novel of the Dawn Land*

Joseph A. Citro, *The Gore*

Joseph A. Citro, *Guardian Angels*

Joseph A. Citro, *Lake Monsters*

Joseph A. Citro, *Shadow Child*

Sean Connolly, *A Great Place to Die*

J. E. Fender, *The Private Revolution of Geoffrey Frost: Being an Account*
of the Life and Times of Geoffrey Frost, Mariner, of Portsmoth, in New
Hampshire, as Faithfully Translated from the Ming Tsun Chronicles,
and Diligently Compared with Other Contemporary Histories

Dorothy Canfield Fisher (Mark J. Madigan, ed.), *Seasoned Timber*

Dorothy Canfield Fisher, *Understood Betsy*

Joseph Freda, *Suburban Guerrillas*

Castle Freeman, Jr., *Judgment Hill*

Frank Gaspar, *Leaving Pico*

Robert Harnum, *Exile in the Kingdom*

Ernest Hebert, *The Dogs of March*

Ernest Hebert, *Live Free or Die*

Ernest Hebert, *The Old American*

Sarah Orne Jewett (Sarah Way Sherman, ed.), *The Country of the Pointed Firs and Other Stories*

Lisa MacFarlane, ed., *This World Is Not Conclusion: Faith in Nineteenth-Century New England Fiction*

G. F. Michelsen, *Hard Bottom*

Anne Whitney Pierce, *Rain Line*

Kit Reed, *J. Eden*

Rowland E. Robinson (David Budbill, ed.), *Danvis Tales: Selected Stories*

Roxana Robinson, *Summer Light*

Rebecca Rule, *The Best Revenge: Short Stories*

Catharine Maria Sedgwick (Maria Karafilis, ed.), *The Linwoods; or, "Sixty Years Since" in America*

R. D. Skillings, *How Many Die*

R. D. Skillings, *Where the Time Goes*

Lynn Stegner, *Pipers at the Gates of Dawn: A Triptych*

Theodore Weesner, *Novemberfest*

W. D. Wetherell, *The Wisest Man in America*

Edith Wharton (Barbara A. White, ed.), *Wharton's New England: Seven Stories and* Ethan Frome

Thomas Williams, *The Hair of Harold Roux*

THE
Private Revolution
O F
Geoffrey Frost

Being an Account of the *Life and Times* of

Geoffrey Frost, Mariner, of Portsmouth,

in New Hampshire, as *Faithfully Translated*

from the Ming Tsun Chronicles, and

Diligently Compared with Other

Contemporary Histories

J. E. FENDER

University Press of New England

HANOVER AND LONDON

University Press of New England, Hanover, NH 03755
© 2002 by J. E. Fender
All rights reserved
Printed in the United States of America
5 4 3 2 1

Library of Congress Cataloging-in-Publication Data
Fender, J. E.
The private revolution of Geoffrey Frost : being an account of
the life and times of Geoffrey Frost, mariner, of Portsmouth, in
New Hampshire, as faithfully translated from the Ming Tsun chronicles,
and diligently compared with other contemporary histories / J. E. Fender.
p.   cm. — (Hardscrabble books)
ISBN 1-58465-212-8
1. United States—History—Revolution, 1775–1783—Fiction.
2. New Hampshire—History—Revolution, 1775–1783—Fiction.
3. Portsmouth (N.H.)—Fiction. 4. Sailors—Fiction. I. Title. II. Series.
PS3606.E53 P75 2002
813'.6—dc21   2001007121

To All Who Were—

And Are—

Involved in the Pursuit

of American Independence

and Freedoms

The
Private Revolution
of
Geoffrey Frost

HER LIST TO STARBOARD AND THE FACT THAT SHE WAS SUBSTANTIALLY DOWN BY THE BOWS WERE EASILY DISCERN- IBLE AS SHE CAME UP THE RIVER PON- derously, though with consummate dignity. She was helped along immeasurably more, perhaps, by the strong inflowing tide than by the ragged, hastily rigged lateen sail bent a-gun- dalow fashion on a poorly fished and gammoned yard slung from her stump of a foremast. The wretched vessel was the Frost Trading Company's square-rigged, four-hundred-ton armed merchantman, *Salmon*, possessing the second letter-of- marque issued by the House of Representatives of the Colony of New Hampshire. She was duly bonded by principals of the company and appointed and contracted by Continental Agent John Langdon to bring back cannons seized by Commodore Esek Hopkins in the Continental Navy's first amphibious as- sault upon the British Fort Montagu at the old pirate ren- dezvous of New Providence Island in the Bahamas. The vessel, like her namesake, was focused solely on seeing her long jour- ney completed and herself relieved of the burdens in her guts.

Geoffrey Frost balanced his telescope on an anxious Ming Tsun's shoulder, and in its erratic ellipse studied the activity at Fort William and Mary, the largest of the Piscataqua's three forts. "The fort intends to salute us, Slocum," Frost announced to his bosun standing two paces behind him.

"Then happily we'll take her salute, Captain, though we

don't have nothin' to answer her with, save perhaps a pop or two from a musket," replied the normally taciturn Slocum Plaisted in what was, for him, a lengthy speech. Frost reckoned that the blow to Plaisted's skull, which had been thick enough to turn the edge of a cutlass that had taken off only the better part of his right ear, occasioned his bosun's loquaciousness. Yet Plaisted was unique among bosuns, being widely read at a time when few bosuns were able to write, much less read. He particularly delighted in reading Shakespeare to the men in the fo'c'sle during long passages. Plaisted's head was swathed in a bloody bandage torn from Frost's last clean shirt. Except for Ming Tsun, Hannibal Bowditch (if you did not count that small but painful splinter scratch on his forehead) and Struan Ferguson, not one of *Salmon*'s crew had escaped some injury— or death, though the seriously wounded had already died, while those with light wounds such as Plaisted bore would live.

Frost spared a quick glance at the carnage on his deck, the great gaps blown in *Salmon*'s bulwarks, gouts and great swatches of dried blood amidst the fallen tackle and splintered spars, and the sad tumult of still, canvas-shrouded forms arrayed along both sides of *Salmon's* waist. Above the carnage rang the monotonous, lugubrious clanking of the pumps, which, judging by the increased sluggishness with which she responded to her helm, were not keeping pace with the water in her bowels despite the sailcloth fothered over the most obvious shot holes and seams hammered open by the shock of collision.

"I believe we shan't fall overly much behind the water if we pause the men at the pumps for a cheer." Frost traversed the telescope further inland and found the other flagpole rising from Bosun's Hill, the highest point on the New Castle bluff. Nothing was visible from its peak, and the chill breeze of this mid-April day of 1776 would have made a streamer of his house flag. Frost snapped the glass closed, pressing the objective lens against his body to offer the necessary resistance, then slid the glass into the long pocket of his faded and frayed tai-pan's coat, the snuff-colored one with the poorly mended rip in the sleeve.

The rip had been made by the blade of a drunken major of the British 49th Regiment of Foot, who had called him out in Macao for some obscure reason Frost had long forgotten. Frost disliked the coat, though a trader's frugality caused him to keep it, and it was the only coat Ming Tsun had been able to find in the bloody, water-soaked chaos of his cabin.

The doubts renewed their assault on Frost. Was he doing the right thing, running the Piscataqua with a sail plan suitable for the tributaries feeding into the Great Bay, but not for the fast currents of this treacherous river, in a vessel heavily down at the stem and balking at answering what relieving tackle steering he had been able to jury-rig?

The headache that had bedeviled him for thirty-six hours now pounded like a drum inside his skull, his teeth ached, and the acrid sulfur taste of gunpowder wadded at the back of his throat, defying all efforts to hawk it out. His ears still chirped like crickets from the concussions of the cannons. Frost wanted to be anywhere but here on the quarterdeck of his stricken vessel. Instead, he smiled at Slocum Plaisted. "That rag twisted around your noggin gives you a proper piratical look, Mister Bosun."

Salmon was reaching for the channel lying east of Great Island and Fort William and Mary; she had yet to round Fort Point and its grand light-tower, the one ordered built by John Wentworth, last royal governor of the British colony of New Hampshire, now ignominiously fled. Frost was immensely cheered that the log boom obstructing the channel at the narrows against a British warship's attempt to run the river had been temporarily shunted aside. There was still time to snub *Salmon* on a short cable, easy holding ground for an anchor in the ledges he knew were five fathoms under the keel, and wait for slack tide and a tow. Frost had no leadsman, not that he needed one, so well did he know the Piscataqua, but the spring flood tide was running near five knots . . .

"Prepare to haul round and hold her fair for midstream once we breast Fort Point, Mister Plaisted." This more formally: "Stand to your station. I'll handle the signal." Should he forgo the more dangerous branch of the Piscataqua around Pull-and-be-Damned Point and take the more sedate back channel of Crooked Lane behind Jenkins Island that the gundalow shipping generally used on the slack tide? Frost painfully hauled the telescope from his coat pocket, extended it, and swept Crooked Lane. He was startled to see the masts and spars of a vessel jutting above the channel just over Clark's Island, though he could spy no hull.

"Damme," Frost thought, instantly regretting the mild oath, "the New Hampshire Committee of Safety had the forethought to scuttle a vessel in the back channel." *Salmon* had Fort William and Mary behind and had taken a westerly heading as she raced toward the narrow gut of Pull-and-be-Damned Point, neatly splitting the two hundred yards of water between Seavey's Island, coming up sharp to starboard, and Pierce's Island, with the pitiful battery of Titus Salter's cannons poking out from the ramparts of the hastily thrown up Fort Washington to larboard, and Pull-and-be-Damned Point looming up. Was it possible Frost's vessel was nearly abreast the entrance to the Pool between Goat Island and the westernmost point of Great Island? Truly; Frost could see the masts of half a dozen vessels anchored in the Pool, including the two-hundred-ton brig *Prince George* taken the October before when the brig's captain had unluckily blundered into Portsmouth Harbor.

No! The *Prince George* was not in the Pool! Those were her masts and spars in the back channel, meaning that her hulk now effectively blocked Crooked Lane. The inflowing tide had been making for almost an hour, and would last another two. The greatest tidal influence would be around Pull-and-be-Damned Point, time enough to convey *Salmon* all the way to the Frost Trading Company's wharf without having to touch the pathetic scrap of sail—if the Great Buddha smiled and the Great God turned not away His head. Inshallah. Joss. Fate. Luck.

"Aye, Captain." In truth, Bosun Plaisted was busy enough. *Salmon*'s wheel had been shot away, and Plaisted was conning her by quietly giving orders to two teams of three more or less able-bodied seamen hunched in the wreck of Frost's cabin below, straining to keep a firm nip on the auxiliary steering cables —relieving tackle—leading around blocks to the rudder. A hole had been crudely mortised into the deck with axe, adze and saw, cutting out the small sky light, so that Plaisted could judge when to order more tension, first on the starboard, then the larboard cable.

Frost pocketed his telescope again, shook the flag Hopkins had given him at New Providence from its bag, and made his way, Ming Tsun following, to the short halyard at the stump of foremast from which fluttered the house flag of the Frost Trading Company, a black *F* in ornate French script inside a wreath of olive branches on a field of white, with the house motto, *Nil Desperandum,* surmounting the wreath. Frost reeved down his house flag using his left arm only, grunting against the pain the exertion caused. His right arm was bound tightly against his body; Ming Tsun had done that after applying a poultice and bandage to the deep wound in his right shoulder, and the other, lesser cutlass thrust and scrape to his ribs. Ming Tsun watched him now, fairly hissing like a goose tending an unruly gosling, and Frost studiously avoided his gaze.

With Ming Tsun's help Frost unbent his house flag, then bent on the dull yellow flag embroidered with the coiled rattlesnake and its legend "Don't Tread on Me," followed by the Royal Navy red ensign, its union flag in the upper staff quadrant, much soiled and stained by powder burns and smoke. In four quick pulls, using left hand to pull and teeth to hold the slack, Frost raised the flags the short distance to the stump's top. The mast was so short that the hem of the ensign would have touched the deck had not the breeze blown it into the belly of the lateen sail.

A cannon from Fort William and Mary coughed a deep, hollow boom, echoed almost immediately by another, and yet a third. "Damn fools," Frost muttered to himself, "don't they know powder's too dear to be shooting it off for display? With powder money being reckoned at two pence each registered ton of burthen, damned if I'll pay a penny or a pence more for

the forts." With a guilty start Frost realized he had used an oath
—again, even if no one had overheard.

The men on *Salmon*'s decks who could stand pulled off their
caps and at Frost's order dutifully uttered hoarse, weak cheers.
From astern came the answering roar of a cannon, and another,
then a third. With unseemly haste Frost ran back to his quarterdeck. The Royal Navy's late ship-rigged sloop-o-war, HM
Jaguar—its gilded figurehead of a panther, lithe yet muscular,
cunningly recumbent beneath the bowsprit and glinting dully
in the wan April sun—was following obediently two hundred
yards aft of *Salmon* and gathering in her unneeded top sails,
keeping jibs and driver only as she, like *Salmon* in front of her,
surrendered to the full tug of the inflowing tide.

Salmon had the light-tower at Fort Point abaft her larboard
rail now as the rattlesnake flag, followed by the Frost house
flag, and that atop a British Union Jack—that curious amalgam
of England's red cross of Saint George superimposed on Scot-
land's white cross of Saint Andrew, devised by the Scottish
James Six when he became king of England in 1603—soared to
the peak of Fort William and Mary's flagstaff. *Salmon*'s men
cheered again, though not so strongly that they could be heard
over the cheering from the warship behind.

"You have done a fine thing," Ming Tsun signed quickly
with his hands, trying to read his fate in Frost's eyes. Frost
responded with a quick nod. Fortunately, he was left-handed
and had taken the unexpected wound just below his right
shoulder blade. Great Buddha, but the matrosses at Fort Washington were also essaying a ragged, hesitant salute! Even with
cannon charged with shot, Titus' matrosses could not harm a
flounder. Had he but known the poor quality of their gunnery,
the *Prince George*'s captain easily could have evaded the capture
of his vessel laden with flour originally destined for Gage's
troops occupying Boston. And then two of the four cannons
on Seavey Island's Fort Sullivan spat out a welcoming salute.

The wharves of the town were lined with people, and on the
shores as well, on both the New Hampshire and the Maine side
of the Ports of Piscataqua, and they were cheering, and cheer-

ing. A number of boats were putting out from shore as *Salmon* rounded Pull-and-be-Damned Point, and they too were filled with cheering Piscataqua men.

Rindge's Wharf was still the better part of a mile upriver, though Frost could see the already planked hull of the *Raleigh* on the building ways. When the *Salmon* had cruised from Portsmouth barely six weeks before, the *Raleigh*'s keel had just been laid. "Cousin John is the Congress's agent, and he's a most impatient man when it comes to shipbuilding," Frost thought, marveling at the rapid progress of the work. "And Tommy Thompson, who wants command of her, is supervising her construction." Frost knew that command could be his, were he to accept the commission that John Langdon had strongly hinted would be in the offing should his cruise to New Providence be successful.

The blandishments of a commission in the Continental Navy were hardly tempting, for Geoffrey Frost was, first and foremost, a trader, and he fancied traders did not make particularly good naval officers. Frost spared not a moment's thought for the boats approaching from shore; he seized a hatchet in his left hand and stood ready to hack through the spring holding the best bower anchor in its trip should *Salmon* lose steering and threaten to run aground.

The fastest skiff hooked onto *Salmon*'s larboard foremast chains, paid off until the skiff was even with the great gashes in *Salmon*'s larboard waist, and one of the Piscataqua pilots, Reedy Stalker—universally known, and generally despised, on the river as "the stoat"—heaved himself aboard. He saluted Frost theatrically, grinning just long enough to show his rotted and mercury-blackened stumps of teeth—failed treatment for venereal disease—the grin quickly gone as Stalker wiped his ferret-like nose on a coat sleeve heavily slimed with mucus. "The morning's blessing to ye, Captain Frost, and not every morning it be that a Portsmouth merchantman fishes in a British man-o-war."

Frost almost gagged at the foulness of the man's breath. Stalker's clothes reeked of the punch house. "Thank you,

Mister Pilot, though as you ken I know the Piscataway well enough your pilotage is not required."

"God's witness, sir, I grant readily that ye know the river better than I, though ye'd allow it'd be five pound well spent, tide runnin' at such a moll and all. I was merely anxious to be first aboard to see if ye required assistance, and as ye know, there's always in-clearances which has to be writ."

Frost, despite knowing how dearly the stoat's help would come, almost accepted, for his men at the pumps could barely stand. But none of his crew would have wanted the stoat's assistance. "These are Portsmouth men, Eliot and Berwick men, Dover and Durham and Exeter men, Mister Pilot. They've just bested a British warship with five times our weight of guns, and almost thrice our number. They'll see the *Salmon* safely to her berth at my company wharf."

"Aye, but it seems this victory of yers came at some cost, eh?" The pilot glanced meaningfully at the still shapes beneath the sailcloth. "And a shameful waste of new sailcloth, yer cousin's *Raleigh* needin' it and all, when ye could have dropped them overboard wrapped in rumbowline with a few words from the Book, and naught to speak a'gin it. But 'spect ye be right a-bringin' 'em back, these boys died for a glorious cause."

Frost glared at the pilot, but Stalker affected not to see the contempt in Frost's eyes. "These men did not die for any glorious cause—they died for the *Salmon* and for me. Good day to you, Mister Pilot. I must be about preparing my ship for its berthing." Frost handed the hatchet to Ming Tsun and nodded stiffly. Reedy Stalker did likewise. Frost walked wearily back to his quarterdeck. *Salmon* had already drawn abreast of the town proper. He heard Slocum Plaisted give the helm commands that would keep *Salmon* in midstream to wear Noble's Island. The Pulpit was already in view, and just before the riverbank's curve toward the Pulpit, on Christian Shore, Frost could clearly see the warehouses and long wharf of the Frost Trading Company.

It was commonly accepted among New England sailors that their compatriots who died at sea would be buried at sea. Truly, no one in Portsmouth, nor any sailor's family, would have voiced complaint had Frost committed his dead to the sea off the Isles of Shoals, but Frost placed great value on those who had walked through the wall between life and death for him. *Salmon* was returning to Portsmouth with every crewman signed aboard for the cruise, the sick and lame he had taken aboard at New Providence because Hopkins' squadron did not want them, and as nearly as he could judge, all the British dead as well.

Frost awkwardly pulled the Bréquet watch with the delicate silver trellis of scrolled foliage on its silver case from his waist-coat pocket, the watch that their mother had given Jonathan to commemorate Jonathan's first voyage to China with Frost. Great Buddha, an hour had passed since *Salmon* had entered the Piscataqua channel: the tide was running slightly more than five knots! Almost to his warehouse and wharf, surely he could rest now, give the task over to Plaisted. Nobody could fault him . . . Frost snapped the cover of Jonathan's watch closed and pulled himself up to stand next to Slocum Plaisted.

Frost was beginning to recognize individuals on the shore now, and with his heavy stubble of beard, still tinged with a residue of burned powder and that had not seen a razor for well over a week, he wished that Ming Tsun could have shaved him. There had been time only to splash water on his face, club his hair and don his faded and frayed tai-pan's coat. A small hiss, a warning from Ming Tsun, brought Frost around: Reedy Stalker, thinking no one alert enough to pay him mind, was stealthily rifling the pockets of one of the corpses. In five rapid steps Frost laid the stoat by the collar and jerked Stalker upright.

"I've a mind you would filch the pennies from your own dear mother's eyes at her wake, Mister Pilot," Frost growled as he twisted the stoat to his feet.

"Naw, Captain, ye know these poor boys would naught object to their poor effects helpin' the poor still livin' . . ."

Frost hurled Stalker halfway across the main deck. "Ming Tsun, fetch the pilot's barge, if you please." Ming Tsun used the halberd he had recently wielded with such deadly ferocity, two feet of steel growing tonguelike from the mouth of a brass dragon that formed the tangs attaching the blade to its five-foot-long shaft, to hook the skiff's painter and draw it to the splintered waist. Frost tumbled Stalker into the barge, noting with approval that Ming Tsun had flicked the oars out of their locks with his halberd before parting the painter with a quick chop.

"Ye canna treat me this wise, no matter who ye be, Captain Frost," Stalker shouted, breaking off to lunge ineffectually for an oar floating just outside his reach. Stalker knelt in his skiff and shook his fist at Frost. "I'll see ye again, Captain Frost, when ye'll owe me far more than five pound for my pilotage fee, when ye wasn't be havin' yer heathern Chinee with ye!"

Frost thought no more about the Piscataqua pilot; from the sharp, stomach-churning agony in his right shoulder and Ming Tsun's sharp intake of breath, he knew that his exertions had opened the deeper wound. Damn that lieutenant who had pierced him unexpectedly from the rear after *Jaguar*'s dying captain had surrendered his sword and his ship.

Struan Ferguson, *Salmon*'s first mate, had wanted to kill the lieutenant there on the quarterdeck of the vanquished British warship, but Frost had forbade it. "That would be murder, Mister Ferguson. He must not have realized, in the excitements of the moment, that his ship had struck."

"He knew it well enough," Ferguson had retorted, shaking his head at Frost's obstinacy but knowing full well how obdurate his captain could be, "and he intended murder right enough. He'll do for ye again should he live."

Frost dismissed everything from his mind except the task of bringing *Salmon* to her final berth. Bosun Plaisted and the men laboring with the steering cables had long been spent past endurance, yet they kept to their tasks. Frost ascended from the waist to the quarterdeck to stand beside his bosun. "Well done, Mister Plaisted," he said, seeing the bustle of workers at the Frost warehouse, most of them, and a horde of town's people, gathering at the end of the long wharf jutting into the Piscataqua from Christian Shore. Frost was about to give up the vessel in which he made three round-trip voyages to China and which has been his home for ten years.

How old was the *Salmon?* Frost did the calculations, his mind slow and fogged from fatigue and sleeplessness. Half his age, so *Salmon* had been thirteen years off the stocks. "Signal Mister Ferguson that the British ship shall berth against the wharf. Let the good old *Salmon* take the beach. We have little cargo to shift, and she deserves her ease."

Plaisted gave orders through the mortise in the quarterdeck, and Frost turned away from the brief sight through the mortise of the shambles of his cabin, though the blood of poor Roger Green, mercifully, was hardly visible. "We can spare the men from the pumps now to take a line ashore over the larboard bow, then pass another through my cabin's larboard quarter badge. Bring cables aboard and hove the old *Salmon* down properly. Then dismiss the men. Men ashore who had the un-utterable luxury of lying asleep whilst we fought for our lives can unlade us."

Salmon thrust her bows into the muddy beach with an audible sigh. It was mean high tide, and *Salmon* would never stir from the Christian Shore again, at least not as a ship. Weary men, released from the pumps, their torn and bleeding hands still curled in the shape of the handles, clambered ashore with lines that were bent to heavier cables sent over to bowse the vessel. Silas Rutherford, Frost's warehouse superintendent, had somehow gotten aboard and was knuckling his forehead as he approached. "Good morrow to you, Captain Frost, I expect you'll be needing some yard workers."

"Truly, Silas, but first to remove our dead, then the dead aboard our captive." It was too difficult to think of the *Jaguar* as anything other than his captive; he hardly knew the vessel's name, much less the name of her late commander. "Every man is to have a coffin, made from our best lumber; the British dead without exception. Families may claim their dead once they are encoffined; those unclaimed because their families are too far away shall be buried in Portsmouth as soon as I have consulted a parson."

Rutherford nodded soberly. "A coffin for every man, of our finest wood, built before we shift *Salmon*'s cargo. And was your cruize to New Providence as successful, Captain Frost, as was your encounter with this British off the Isles of Shoals?"

Frost braced himself against the quarterdeck's fife rail to stave off the vertigo that suddenly seized him. A crow swooped low over the *Salmon*, gained altitude with a few wing beats, uttered several mocking, despairing croaks, and flew into the tall wineglass-shaped elm just beginning to leaf at the corner of the warehouse, joining the murder of crows that had solemnly and silently observed *Salmon*'s arrival. "We fetched away what Colonel Langdon commissioned *Salmon* to ship, the cannons Commodore Hopkins allowed, and some shot, and all of the powder. Not much powder, not upward of twenty barrels." Frost was too tired to tell Rutherford the fate of the cannons he had shipped, or of his planned use of the twenty barrels of gunpowder blocked in *Salmon*'s hold.

Salmon groaned slightly and listed imperceptibly to starboard. The tide had run past its peak, was already reversing, and Frost was more tired than he could ever remember in his life. But there was so much work to be done! Miraculously, Ming Tsun was at his side with a bowl of hot noodles. Where had Ming Tsun found the fire, much less the time, to cook? And wonder of wonders! Ming Tsun also held out half a lime! Frost took the bowl and lime eagerly, squeezing the lime juice onto the noodles as a condiment, then rubbing the pulp onto his forehead, a sovereign remedy for the headache that had plagued him since the desperate battle off the Isles of Shoals. Completely disregarding all his table manners, Frost tipped the contents into his mouth. When had he last eaten? The broth was thick with bits of chicken.

"Silas," Frost called to his warehouse superintendent, his voice a croak hardly different from that of the crow in the elm tree, "order food sent from the Widow Crockett's tavern, all she has, hot or cold, fetch it quickly, and bring out a hogshead of that sweet verdelho wine from the Western Isles. Our men to be fed first, then the British prisoners. Immediately *Salmon* be unladed, I wish all of the powder aboard the British sloop be shifted into the company's stone magazine—the powder aboard *Salmon* to be housed there as well, though both stores to be clearly marked as to their origins—and a guard set."

Frost eagerly drained the bowl of noodles, holding the hot bowl awkwardly with his left hand, and thought, guiltily and too late, to offer a portion to Ming Tsun. Frost glanced hastily around for his best friend in the world, but Ming Tsun had disappeared. As had Frost's headache. Frost, the now cooled bowl forgotten in his hand, turned to his bosun to give the next in a long series of orders that would unlade the mortally stricken vessel that had been his only home for the past ten years of his life.

❧ II ❧

❀❀❀❀❀ N THE EIGHT YEARS OF CLOSE AND
❀   ❀ INTIMATE CONTACT SINCE GEOFFREY
❀ I ❀ FROST HAD TAKEN HIM OFF THE BEACH
❀❀❀❀❀ AT THAT PESTILENTIAL JAVANESE PORT
of Batavia, where he had languished after the cheeseheads of
the Dutch *Vereenigde Oost-Indische Compagnie* had stranded
him there, Struan Ferguson had learned to anticipate his captain. Struan also was possessed of a fierce streak of highlander
independence, which had led him to take precautions, both
prudent and punitive, to prevent HM *Jaguar's* first lieutenant
from causing more trouble, by clamping Lithgow in bilboes
and chaining him to a ring-bolt on the cable tier of ex-HM
Jaguar without so much as a scrap of candle to disperse or even
hold the close, terrifying darkness at bay. For aboard a wooden
ship a candle could be an efficient weapon, and this Lithgow
was a dangerous, dangerous man. Struan knew full well that
Lithgow had tried his utmost to murder Geoffrey Frost; Lithgow had been fully aware that his captain had already surrendered his sword and thus his vessel. Struan distrusted the Royal
Navy lieutenant as only a highlander can distrust a lowlander,
and Lithgow was a Scot in the British service, which made him
doubly, nay, trebly suspect.

Indeed, the proper course, which Struan would have pur-
sued had the decision been his to make, would have been a
sharp rap on Lithgow's head with the hilt of the backsword
prised from his father's dead hand at Culloden, with the added

security of drawing the blade across the bastard's throat, then toppling the body overboard with a minimum of fuss and absolutely no ceremony.

Even now, wrapped in a heavy boat cloak as he supervised the careful hoisting up of the barrels of gunpowder aboard *Salmon*, the unlading of such explosive cargo only increased the strong craving for a pipe of tobacco or a cheroot, though of course a craving that had to be dutifully and rightly suppressed in the vicinity of the combustible gunpowder. Struan could not conceal a shudder as he ruminated over that battle off the Isles of Shoals. Damn, but it had been a truly close thing, the way Frost had engaged HM *Jaguar*. With a scratch crew of ploughmen and itinerant tinkers, cabinetmakers and close inshore fishermen, men who had never boarded an enemy ship—who had never ever remotely entertained such a ludicrous idea! Not the assault of a well-founded, well-manned, and well-fought Royal Navy sloop-o-war. But these ploughmen and artisans had done it for Geoffrey Frost, because of the discipline, fortitude, and, yes, belief in themselves that Frost had infused into these hopelessly unwarlike civilians in a mere six weeks of a pleasant cruise to and from New Providence in the Bahamas. It had seemed the most natural and matter-of-fact thing in the world for *Salmon*'s outmatched crew to board a hotly defended enemy warship, as if they were calmly taking some inoffensive merchant vessel a prize.

Not to speak of running this thin, crooked bastard of a river on an inflooding tide with his ship sinking beneath him, something that Struan Ferguson would not, could not, have done had he been in command of the *Salmon*. And Frost had actually been cheerful when going about it! Struan knew he could not have fought *Salmon* nearly half so well as had Geoffrey Frost. But he would not, could not have struck to a Britisher. Which meant that had he been in command of *Salmon* he would now be dead. Then he thought of Ming Tsun and his infernal machine, the eprouvette, and shuddered again. Struan Ferguson had been close to violence and death many times in his thirty-six years of life, but he fervently prayed to his ancient Scottish gods that he would never come as close to a violent death as he had when Geoffrey Frost so coolly laid *Salmon* alongside HM sloop-o-war *Jaguar*, as if it had been the most natural happening in the world.

After leaving Hopkins' squadron to beat into Long Island Sound, Frost had sailed the old bluff-bowed *Salmon* up to latitude 43 and twenty-five leagues offshore before altering course to the west-northwest. North of Massachusetts' Cape Ann, *Salmon's* lookout in the mainmast crosstrees sighted the topgallants of a patrolling British warship two hours before dusk. Within thirty minutes the other vessel's topgallants were visible from *Salmon's* quarterdeck.

" 'Tis not the *Scarborough*," Frost said as he trained his glass on the distant sail, "and certainly not the old *Canceaux* we've all come to know and love since Captain Mowat so courageously burned Falmouth and sank our inoffensive *Trout* and *Shad* lying peaceably to their anchors. It's another vessel Sammy Graves or Molly Shuldham—whoever commands now —has produced from the Royal Navy's bag of tricks." The rack and cut of the topmost sails he could see were typically British. Frost had seen the *Scarborough* and *Canceaux* often enough to know those vessels' sail plans, and he was particularly bitter about the loss of the Frost Trading Company's two merchantmen waiting at anchor in Falmouth harbor for crews and a favorable wind to Portsmouth. Mostly crews, for his brother-in-law, Marcus Whipple, earlier had taken his people to Boston to fight—and himself to be taken prisoner—at Breed's Hill.

"Most likely a vessel newly come from England to join the bonny admiral's forces in Boston," Ferguson had ventured, after studying the vessel at length through his own glass.

"I believe the British have left Boston," Frost said. " 'Twas tending so when we departed Portsmouth. They liked not the cannons Henry Knox hauled all that way from Ticonderoga. My brother, Joseph, helped Knox move sixty tons of dead metal all that way. Now Joseph fancies himself an artillery man as well as an iron monger."

"Whether the British are still in Boston matters not," Struan retorted, "there is a ship-rigged vessel of most warlike countenance squarely athwart the Portsmouth approaches, and belike, she has spied us."

Frost scowled at the strange sail with topgallants being trimmed toward them, which he knew in all certainty was British. "Any vessel come from England to join Graves or Shuldham would be of more help to the good admirals if she was in Boston loading troops and stores to go wherever it is General Howe desires to go." He ordered the third watch turned out to assist in the spreading of *Salmon*'s topgallants and stay sails, hands to the braces to bring *Salmon* around on a course to the east-southeast, with the wind largely behind them, *Salmon*'s best point of sailing.

Frost smiled as the increased canvas in the tack lay the *Salmon*'s lee rail almost on the water before she bounded onto her new course. Then he ordered the two helmsmen to make directly for a squall building to the south. Thirty minutes later, exceedingly grateful for the driving rain and sleet and the early darkness, Frost was content enough to leave the deck to Ferguson, with orders to return to *Salmon*'s original course two hours prior to midnight, and he went below to sleep. Attuned to every subtle nuance of his vessel, Frost roused once when Ferguson brought *Salmon* about, and again when *Salmon* ran out of the squall; otherwise he slept the night undisturbed.

But the British vessel's topgallants were visible to the northwest at dawn the next morning, the tenth of April, effectively blocking any attempt to run into Portsmouth.

"So we didn't lose our escort during the night," Frost said sourly when he came on deck in the chill of a clear morning, upon hearing the lookout's cry of sail in sight. "She was remarkably accurate in deducing where we would run."

Ming Tsun came aft from the galley with heavy glazed mugs of tea with generous dollops of honey stirred in for Frost and Ferguson, the *Salmon*'s best black tea freighted at Macao the year past, the sale of which, brokered by John Hancock of Boston, had brought the Frost Trading Company a handsome profit, and upon which no tax had been paid to the British

Crown. Frost had kept half a chest for his use aboard *Salmon*. He wrapped his chapped and chilled hands around the warmth of the cup and smiled his thanks to Ming Tsun before ordering *Salmon* brought directly before the wind. Ming Tsun signed to Frost. Frost thought about what Ming Tsun had signed, drained his mug of tea, handed the mug to Ferguson, and signed his response.

Ferguson could follow their sign language almost as well as Frost or Ming Tsun, though he never signed to Ming Tsun, since Ming Tsun understood everything he said perfectly well. Ming Tsun understood everything Frost said, for that matter, but long years together had caused them to appreciate and prefer silence whenever possible to audible communication.

"So Ming Tsun thinks the Britisher knew we were coming."

"Everyone on the Ports of Piscataway knew where our cruize would take us, Struan, and anyone with a pair of dividers and a nose for the wind could predict when we would be returning."

"And with one third of the people of New England of a Tory mind, and one third so apathetic they could bend either toward the Tories or toward a separate republic, any number of people could have given the British word of our cruize."

"That's unimportant," Frost said, as the warship's main course dipped momentarily into view. While he had always considered *Salmon* a comely vessel, she was after all built for transporting cargo, with a broad beam and bluff bows—a plough horse, not a racehorse. Her best turn of speed, even with the clean bottom *Salmon* currently enjoyed since Frost had ordered his vessel careened and cleaned of weed and barnacle while awaiting her cargo of cannons and powder in New Providence, would be perhaps two knots less than a British warship of comparable tonnage. "She means to give us a chace."

Indeed, the warship was giving chase. By the noon sight the warship was less than three miles away, and Frost spent an hour in the crosstrees of *Salmon*'s mainmast studying the details of the other vessel in the unsteady circle of his best telescope. When he descended to the deck, Struan Ferguson was chalking the last cast of the log on the board by the binnacle. Eight knots and a half; a good turn of speed in this breeze, but to have closed to three miles in half a day meant the Britisher was sailing a full knot faster than *Salmon*. And that calculation deeply worried Geoffrey Frost.

Several members of the off watches were gathered along the larboard rail in the waist, talking desultorily but now and again, with seeming nonchalance that fooled no one, gazing at the British vessel now virtually hull up, close enough to permit Frost to scrutinize her carefully.

"She's ship rigged," Frost mused, half to himself, half to confide in Struan. "Her size makes her not big enough to be a frigate, though the raised quarterdeck and fo'c'sle give her the ability to mount cannons on two levels. She could certainly pass for a frigate, though I make her for a sloop. Very sweet lines, somewhat akin to that French brig we spoke two days out of New Providence."

"No chance she could be French, ye ken?" Struan said wistfully.

"Not enough to cause me to haul my wind and wait for her to close near enough to speak. But she isn't carrying all sail she could set, which is passing strange. Only her mainsail is drawing, and that half-reefed; her main topsail and topgallants are still in the gaskets."

"Passing strange indeed," Struan opined, as he intently studied the trim of *Salmon*'s sails, and judged the weather. "But her fore sails be drawing suitable. She wants to catch us, right enough. It canna be that she toys with us as a cat would a mouse."

"Her mainmast is perhaps tender," Frost ventured as he glanced at the high clouds to the southeast, then pulled out Jonathan's watch and made several mental calculations. "Have the bonnets brought up and made ready, Struan. We'll have naught but light airs as night finds us, so we'll want every kerchief spread."

Ming Tsun's appearance on the quarterdeck reminded Frost that he was hungry. "Ask Cook Barnes to serve a hot dinner to all watches. I'm going to take mine now."

Frost had a few minutes to read while Ming Tsun readied the table and brought in his dinner, carefully marking his place in Livy and replacing the book in the rack beside his berth, latching the bar which held the books secure. He saw with pleasure the small bowl of sliced pineapple on the tray beside the boiled fish, rice and hot tea. Frost was partial to pineapple and glad that Ming Tsun had held back one from the small store they had taken aboard in New Providence. He lifted several pieces of the fish onto the bowl of rice and plied his chopsticks with gusto.

"The men wonder if you fight this pursuing dog," Ming Tsun signed after Frost had eaten the fish and rice and was enjoying the pineapple chunk by chunk. The pineapple was delightfully crisp and cool, and Frost savored each piece immensely before swallowing. He drank the juice in the bowl before answering.

"I am a trader. It is my preference not to fight," Frost signed. Ming Tsun moved among the crew easily, and they, grateful for the many small kindnesses he did them, talked candidly in the presence of the captain's servant and confidant, oblivious or uncaring, thinking that because he was unable to speak, and a foreigner to them, that he must therefore be unable to hear. Or, if he could hear, understand their words. A simple, good fellow, as good and simple as they, this inscrutable Chinaman in the crew's midst, who, amazingly enough if they had ever thought to remark it, could communicate with them when he chose with chalk and board, though his messages were, of necessity, brief.

Ming Tsun possessed four languages fluently, in addition to his Mandarin and Cantonese, and apprehended everything that he heard among the crew. Frost understood and appreciated this conduit into the character and morale of *Salmon*'s crew and used it to advantage.

"I wish to outrun this British, not fight him," Frost signed to Ming Tsun.

"Can we outrun this British?" Ming Tsun signed.

Frost was tempted to ask if there was more pineapple. The coming night would be a long one for him. But, if there was no more pineapple, he preferred not to know until later when he would ask for it. Frost pushed his chair back from the table and stood. "Only K'ung the Master knows," he signed. "But we shall offer the Master all possible assistance."

Ming Tsun was ready with his old canvas coat, heavy woolen scarf, and boat cloak, and, since he was shrugging into his coat, Frost spoke rather than signed: "K'ung the Master said that he who finds himself in circumstances of danger and difficulty acts according to what is required of a man under such circumstances. If the British warship leaves me no choice but to fight, we must win, or else all in *Salmon* will join Marcus in the prison hulks at Halifax." He knew this solemn reminder of his brother-in-law's fate would be passed to his crew.

But, as was usually the case, Ming Tsun had the last word, or rather, silent sign: "The Master also said that in all matters success depends on preparation; without preparation there will always be failure. When what is to be is previously determined, there will be no difficulty in its discharge."

"Deo Gratias," Frost said, reefing his scarf around his neck and smiling kindly at the man who was far more than his best friend in the world.

When Frost gained the deck, he did not glance astern but at the clouds ahead to gauge the weather. The wind was stronger than he wished for the maneuver he had planned, and it lacked at least three hours to dusk. "If you please, Mister Ferguson, lace on every bonnet our *Salmon* can set, aloft and alow, double seizings if you please, and hold her square before the wind."

Struan repeated the sail order to young Roger Green, cousin to the famous Doctor Ezrah Green of Dover, shipped as second mate, slowly recovering from the fever taken at New Providence, and the heading order to the two helmsmen. Young Green, barely sixteen years of age and who had tearfully been given into Frost's charge by his parents, instructed the duty watch with sufficient force of voice that the crew swarmed up the ratlines with alacrity, even enthusiasm. *Salmon* was carrying all normal canvas, and placing a hand on the leeward main brace Frost judged the strain on sails and riggings. *Salmon*'s protests —the protests of a living creature—came to him through the well-tarred brace, but they were muted, and she was willing enough. Frost knew the masts and standing rigging could bear the extra strain of the bonnets, but the temper of the bonnets themselves was a quality he could not gauge.

The duty topmen bent on the small triangular sails, normally used only in the lightest of airs, and Frost watched each man working aloft carefully. He knew and trusted every man who had sailed with him on previous voyages. But for the cruise to New Providence, and the expectation of taking a prize or two from the British, Frost had succeeded in almost doubling *Salmon*'s normal complement of forty able seamen, the number he shipped for a voyage to China. In addition, he had embarked a round dozen of Massachusetts men from near Boston, sickened in the tropics, and Hopkins unwilling to return them in his other vessels to New London.

If Frost had unknowingly shipped a Tory sympathizer who might seek to delay *Salmon* sufficiently for the British warship to close, Frost hoped the sympathizer would show himself now. Knowing in advance of Frost's plans to spread bonnets, it would be a simple matter for any topman desiring to slow the *Salmon* to reeve a gusset improperly, causing the sail to blow out, perhaps fouling another. However, all bonnets were bent on in record time, then double seized. Frost had not taken out Jonathan's watch to time the maneuver, but he had counted the seconds to himself, and he was pleased. "Our course, Mister Ferguson?"

"South, southeast by south, sir."

"And the last cast of the log?"

"Showed seven knots and a half, sir."

"You have enumerated our effectives?" Frost knew his own count, but wanted to know how his count compared to the count of his first mate.

"I ken we muster sixty and eight men who can fight. Eight of the Massachusetts men are too wasted to bear assistance. And there is no reason for them to fight for us being they not be enrolled aboard, save to avoid the prison hulks. Of course, Caleb Mansfield's ardor with that two-barrel rifle of his is such that I count him double. And I canna ascribe a value to Ming Tsun, having been the beneficiary of his efforts in the fight against those Dyak sea pirates in the Makassar Straits."

Yes, Struan Ferguson recalled that fight very well. It would have been his last, for two great brutes from the Borneo coast had him pinned against the foremast with a third wielding a monstrous great double axe ready to cleave his skull when Ming Tsun pierced the axe man squarely through the heart with an arrow from his Chinese longbow. And then bored in with his halberd and a fearful high-pitched ululating cry from his tortured throat frightful enough to give a saint the palsy, appalling and executing the two sea pirates pinning Struan with grim efficiency. Struan Ferguson had seen the usually gentle Ming Tsun infrequently aroused, but Struan placed no value on the life of anyone who threatened harm to Geoffrey Frost.

Frost ignored the latter of Struan's comments. "Sad testimony to the indulgence of ardent spirits found in New Providence, Struan."

"They should thank God on tremulous knee at the break of every morn that ye cruized to New Providence. Hopkins was all for abandoning them for their intemperance."

"It is not the men who should bear the reprimand, Struan, but their officers and mates for not caring for them properly."

Struan smiled one of the dazzling smiles that all too infrequently illuminated the Scotsman's handsome face. "I ken we have had this conversation before, Captain Frost. Ye find excuses for all who sin, save the sinner himself."

"We are all sinners, Struan, but to the men who serve my ship I owe a special duty." Frost paced to the larboard rail to lay hand on a brace slightly to weather to gauge its strain. *Salmon* was nearing the limits of her ability to carry sail.

"I calculate a British ship-rigged sloop-o-war would embark between one hundred twenty and one hundred forty men," Frost said, his hand moving to another iron-hard brace.

"Aye, and at least thirty, perhaps even forty marines," Struan replied in a voice so low that only Frost heard him. "Though 'tis mere conjecture on my part, knowing naught how long she's been out from England, where she touched, if a senior commander levied on this sloop for hands, or if she carries scurvey, or other disease."

" 'Tis best to calculate she carries at least twice our number, and men who are far more inured to a sea-fight than our lads." Frost silently assured his ship she would not have to endure the strain much longer. "If we must fight I shall speak to the Massachusetts men and they'll surely answer. Though Inshallah, and a benevolent God's willing, *Salmon* shan't have need to fight this cruize. If you'll be so kind, Struan, hands to the braces to trim sails for a course due south, south by one-half."

⊷ III ⊶

ROST KEPT *SALMON* ON THE SOUTH-ERLY COURSE UNTIL DUSK, WHEN F HE ORDERED ONE LAST HOT MEAL FOR THE CREW AND THEN ALL FIRES doused. Thirty minutes after dusk, Frost ordered all sails furled, which was smartly and quietly done; the helm rounded hard up into the wind so that *Salmon* quickly lost all way and actually began to drift slowly stern-first to the north, northwest, driven by the prevailing westerlies' force of wind against the yards and riggings. Frost walked both sides of his ship, making sure no off-watch seaman had kindled a pipe, and whispering to every man in his path how essential it was that no one made noise, that the men going off watch could lay below to their berths, for he wanted minimum company on deck as the *Salmon* lay hove-to, rolling sluggishly, bows on to building seas and winds from the southwest that Frost, drawing upon his almost twenty years of experience at sea in all types of weather, judged to be just in excess of fifteen knots.

The helmsmen had thrown a piece of canvas over the binnacle to shield even the slightest gleam of its gimbaled red-lensed whale oil lantern, and the glass was no longer turned. Every five minutes or so one of the helmsmen ducked under the canvas for a squint at the compass card. Frost continued his silent rounds of the deck, accompanied only by the low banshee's moan of the wind in the riggings and the sibilant, sharp slap of wave caps against *Salmon*'s hull.

When morning dawned and brought with it a diminution of the wind, Frost was in the mainmast crosstrees searching the horizon with eye and glass for the British sloop-o-war. He was relieved more than he could tell anyone that the sea's bosom carried no sail of any kind. With a sense of inner calmness he had not felt in many hours, he clambered down the ratlines lightly and ordered all plain sail spread: "Course west, south-west, Mister Ferguson, if you please, and carry her as close to the wind as she may ever bear." Their run and drift the previous day and night had taken *Salmon* more than one hundred sea miles northeast from the Piscataqua approaches, and Geoffrey Frost had cannons to deliver to John Langdon.

Salmon had beaten fifty sea miles on a larboard tack to wind-ward with sails trimmed on a westerly heading in modest airs, when, just after the noon sight, the lookout spied a sail to the west. Frost immediately wore ship to the south, knowing in-stinctively that the sail was the British warship, and without any real hope that the other vessel had not glimpsed the *Salmon*. The wind was slowly diminishing, and what little there was came in fitful cat's paws, leaving the *Salmon*'s sails slapping and only partially filling.

"'Twas a false hope, Captain Frost," Struan Ferguson said with all his Scot's dourness as he breathed into his chilled, cupped hands to warm them. "He's forewarned of our *Salmon*'s destination, and losing ye he need only lie athwart the ap-proaches and wait for ye."

Frost likewise breathed into his cupped hands. "But we shall anchor in the Pool, Struan, this knave not withstanding."

"Then muckle greeting give her, Captain Frost, for she has seen us sure, and certain she'll be sore from the slip ye gave her last night. I don't doubt but that she'll stretch every rag found in her sail lockers to catch up to us."

"We'll alter course to weather Cape Cod, then put into New London and see if this fellow is brave enough to bait Hopkins' squadron."

"Aye, but can we fetch New London?" Struan replied. "This breeze is fickle. I have not seen its like this time of year in these latitudes, but I fear the wind soon will lie." Which was true enough. "But this Britisher is newly arrived on the North American station. He knows not these waters, so we have naught to do but remain out of shot's throw."

"Unless yonder British vessel carries a Tory pilot with knowledge of these waters." Frost said. "In any case I thank you for ordering the watch aloft to wet down the sails for a better draw, since I collect yonder vessel is about to do the same, and in all that we do I must anticipate what her captain does before he knows to do it himself."

Wetted sails notwithstanding, by late afternoon the British vessel had gained half a mile, and by nightfall had lessened the distance between the two ships to less than two miles. "Shall we try the same trick of last night, Captain?" Second Mate Green asked. His question would have been presumptuous in the extreme had it been directed to a captain other than Geoffrey Frost.

"No, Mister Green, should we lose him this night again he'll but run to the Isles of Shoals and await us there. Once we stand in toward the Thames at New London he'll veer away."

"He must know we carry cannons for the vessel Colonel Langdon's a-building," the second mate offered.

Frost, concentrating on his study of the light overcast and southerly swell, saw no need to reply. He summoned Struan, who had been in the crosstrees with his telescope focused on the British warship. "I'm of a mind that what wind there is will lie at dusk. Ready two towing warps at the beak. As soon as we can no longer see the Britisher, launch the longboat and gig. We'll tow in two hour watches, spelling the longboat at the end of the first hour, at which time I'll pull oar."

"Ye have twigged to something amiss with her mainmast. Save for her main course and tops'ls, she spreads all sail she carries in this light air." Struan joined his captain in a study of the overcast sky. "And the moon . . . ," he began.

"Will be in the quarter after midnight, perhaps enough cloud to mask it. All hands to be fed and the off-duty watches below to rest. All fires to be doused as soon as the men have eaten."

"The night bids fair to be a long one."

"To the contrary," Frost said thinly, "the dawn will come all too early."

The longboat held ten oarsmen and the gig six. Both boats were launched to starboard, the side away from the British warship, and with oars muffled in old leather took up the laborious tow of the becalmed *Salmon* as soon as darkness settled over the placid ocean. The stout, ten inch in circumference hemp cables led over the beak wept sea water as they took the strain of *Salmon*'s four hundred tons burthen. Geoffrey Frost strained his ears in the engloomed dark, anxious to hear any chuckle of water under the counter but knowing there was small likelihood of it.

Frost paced by the six four-pounder cannons, three on either side of *Salmon*'s main deck. Fair armament, when his eight brass swivel guns were added, against Javanese pirates, but of small use against a ship with the armament of his pursuer. He sent for Caleb Mansfield and Ming Tsun.

There was not light enough to sign to Ming Tsun so Frost spoke. "Block over the lights in my cabin with old canvas," he said, just above a whisper. "Lathes in place as well, and rig the stay tackle to sway up a long nine-pounder and its carriage from the hold. Secure it in my cabin. An absolute minimum of noise. And take care to show no light. And when you have that gun secure in my cabin, sway up the same onto the quarterdeck."

When the longboat rowed back to the *Salmon* at the end of the first hour of towing, Frost estimated his vessel had covered half a sea mile in what was now an absolute calm. Young Roger Green, despite the cold, had great beads of perspiration standing on his forehead as he heaved himself up the short accommodation ladder swung abaft the bowsprit.

"Mister Green," Frost whispered, as they prepared to trade places in the longboat, "take a station aft whilst you rest. The Britisher ain't showing light, or making noise, but someone may cough or unmask a lantern for a second that betrays her position."

"Aye, sir," young Green whispered, unwinding the rags

which had protected his chaffed hands and stuffing the rags into pockets of his ragged great coat as he attempted to flex stiff fingers that still retained their curves formed by the oar handles.

The first thirty minutes of rowing were actually pleasurable, with Frost relishing the hard physical labor that replaced thought as he and the other nine oarsmen concentrated on the rhythm of lift, swing, dip and stroke in a silence broken only by the faint, muffled creak of an oar against a thole pin. The darkness suited Frost, and knowing the men were taking their cue from him, he put his back into his rowing, feet braced squarely against the stretcher, straining his knees, thighs, back, shoulders and arms with the repetitive toil of moving the fulcrum of oar through water that was molasses-like against *Salmon*'s resistance. Concentrating on pulling in a dead straight line, for it would be improvident in the extreme to veer ever so slightly to larboard or starboard and round down onto the pursing British warship in some fashion. The pain radiating through his thighs, shoulders and arms became an unbearable agony and then dulled into insensibility as he gave himself up to the mechanical repetition of lift, swing, dip and stroke, focusing upon the towing bridle brailed through ringbolts in the longboat's thwarts and chime, and keeping the wake, though puny in the extreme, at least straight on toward the bows of the *Salmon*.

Frost was aware of the gig's position by an occasional grunt or the labored breathing of someone in the other boat no more than twenty feet away. At the end of the hour the gig fell back to exchange crews. Frost sensed that his crew wanted to rest on their oars until the gig rejoined them on the tow, but he dared not lose momentum, now matter how tenuous.

"Keep your backs in it, lads," he whispered urgently. "Show the gig we can pull the old *Salmon* by ourselves."

"Gar, Capt'n," the rower sitting to Frost's right on the thwart, their knees touching, whispered in response, "I reckon ye can pull our old girl by ye ow'self, I do."

"Shush yore face, Slobber," the oarsman seated behind Frost whispered conspiratorially. "Ye need yore breath if yore to keep up to the Capt'n."

The banter pleased and warmed Frost. Slobber was old John Weliever, an able seaman from Exeter at least twice Frost's age. Scurvey had robbed him of his teeth years before, and the drool that frequently escaped his pinched and shriveled lips, which he was constantly wiping away on a dirty coat sleeve, had given him his nickname. The able seaman pulling a solid oar behind Frost was George Clancy from Rye. He had been with Frost on all three of *Salmon*'s voyages to Macao. These were good men, and Frost was curiously reticent to leave his bench in the longboat when his two hours at the oars ended.

Frost beat the kinks out of his arms and legs while he checked *Salmon*'s course on the shrouded binnacle. *Salmon* was still holding southerly. Then the muffled squeal of tackle and shadowy movements told him the second cannon was swaying up from the main hold. Frost found his knees unsteady as he groped for the scuttle and the ladder that led to his cabin. Ming Tsun had left a candle on his desk, and he saw with satisfaction the ton and a half bulk of the nine-pounder cannon on its carriage neatly triced to ringbolts newly augered into the sole of his cabin. He noted with equal satisfaction that the gun's tackle was neatly coiled on the deck on either side of the cannon and estimated there was enough distance in his cabin, just barely, to accommodate the gun's recoil. Soft, old canvas, double draped in the event of rents or holes and backed with lathes, covered the expanse of glass at the stern. Frost made his way to the trundle berth that pulled out from the massive storage chest against the starboard bulkhead, but first he paused to study the chessboard with its ivory pieces that was strapped to his desk.

Frost had watched the chessmen being carved from sperm whale ivory by a forecastle scrimshander during his first voyage to Macao as captain, and he had insisted upon a small dowel's being turned on the bottom of each piece to insert into a small gimlet hole pierced in the center of each square to hold all pieces steady despite a ship's movement. Frost had been playing against Ming Tsun teamed with Struan since leaving New Providence. He held the candle over the board for several minutes; he was playing white, and Ming Tsun and Struan were trying for a pin. Finally, Frost captured a pawn with a knight, positioning the knight to check on its next move, though he liked not the way black's remaining rook, bishop and knight were marshalling. Then Frost fell into the trundle berth and instantly was asleep.

Ming Tsun awakened Frost at four in the morning. Frost splashed water on his face from the ewer held in gimbals and brushed his teeth before collecting his night glass and going on deck. From the mainmast crosstrees the feeble light of a thin crescent moon, increasingly masked by a thickening overcast, was just sufficient for the night glass to reveal the British warship, closer than it had been at nightfall. Frost braced against the slow roll of the mainmast to study the dim image, inverted in the night glass. As he had anticipated, the British commander had swayed out three of his own boats to tow the sloop-o-war, though Frost wondered why the British vessel had not run out sweeps. A vessel of her type and size surely would carry sweeps. Several hours earlier Frost had ordered his carpenter to knock together some sweeps for *Salmon*.

The Britisher's gain during the night's calm had been about what Frost expected, and he calculated that by dawn the warship would be little more than a mile away. A long—very long—cannon shot.

Frost had ordered one cook fire started after the indifferent slice of moon filtered through the almost obscured sky, revealing the relative positions of the two vessels. Ming Tsun brought him a cup of steaming hot tea into which honey had been stirred, and, best of all, a small bowl of diced pineapple. Frost sent for Caleb and Roger Green and gave his orders while he savored the cool pineapple and hot, honey-sweetened tea. On the deck behind him the carpenter's mates were augering holes in the stern gunwales to affix ringbolts for the nine-pounder's breechings.

"Caleb," Frost said without preamble, "we've exercised our armament, but only for speed of loading and maintaining a hot fire. I've got no proper gun layers, so I am entrusting you to lay this long nine-pounder as well and true as you do that two-barrel rifle of yours. Concentrate first on the boats towing, then on her masts and riggings."

Caleb Mansfield scratched the scraggly beard on his chin with a torn, dirty thumbnail as he regarded the cannon dubiously, and then the warship that was just a darker shadow in the gloom behind *Salmon*. Frost knew he was asking for the impossible. The Britisher was directly astern more than a mile away, bow on. The towing boats, exceedingly small targets, were spread apart no more than fifty yards, not even visible except when both vessels rode up and crested identical swells at the same time—and then illuminated only as a faint phosphorescence stirred by an oar and scarcely visible over such a distance.

"Aye, have ye any idea how the ball throws?"

"Approximately one thousand feet in the first second."

"All respect, Capt'n, but I be askin' if this gun throws its ball direct on, or off-center like."

"There you have me, Caleb. We shipped this cannon at New Providence to outfit the *Raleigh* John Langdon's building in Portsmouth. What peculiarities this piece possesses are beyond the ken of any man aboard."

Caleb sighed. "Wal, then, the only difference a'tween Gideon and this 'ere piece is the size o' ball, and the fact I canna shoulder this one like. I make the true distance to yonder craft at two thousand long paces, though 'stimatin' distance over water whar ye can't step it off ain't as easy as figurin' how far across a valley the moose be."

"I estimate the same distance, Caleb," Frost said. He had been studying the swell since he first came on deck; the swell came from the southeast, and somewhere in that direction a storm of consequence was making. Frost estimated the *Salmon* would feel the storm's effects not later than nightfall. The storm might offer him and his vessel some succor, but first Frost and the *Salmon* had to live through the day that was about to break. "Your ball will take six, perhaps seven seconds to fly that distance."

Caleb sighed again and slapped his hands against the cold.

"Wal, I'll want to give her a wee bit more powder than's normal—if I knew what a normal charge wuz."

"Being a nine-pounder I'd suggest you use two of the powder charges we've already made up for the four-pounders," Frost said. He well knew that no one among his crew had ever shot a cannon this large before. "You shall have Hugh Eliot and his crew from our number two cannon to load and run out for you." Frost beckoned to Struan Ferguson. "Get some waisters up here to screen the gun whilst Caleb and Hugh load." Frost lapsed into typical New England frugality. "Have every man you send bring along a nine-pounder cannon ball with him." Then Frost gave the rest of his orders in a low voice to young Roger Green.

Behind Frost in the semidarkness Caleb Mansfield was feeling every nine-pounder ball brought up by the waisters with his hands to gauge the balls' roundness. "Gideon and I once shot a goose on the Pemigewasset. Don't collect how fur the shot; paddlin' around in an eddy this flock was, and I skipped the ball right into one. Rolled ol' Gideon's bottom barrel around and got another out of the flock when they rose."

Hugh Eliot gave a hoot of disbelief, and several of the waisters snickered.

"'Course, the Pemigewasset wuz smooth as a mill pond at the time, not goin' up and down and side'ers as she's a doin' now."

"We see there are doubters in our midst, Caleb," Struan Ferguson said. "Perhaps a wager with Eliot and his gun crew is in order."

"Naw, I took all their money at cards whiles we wuz at that island in the Caribee. They don't have nothin' left but paper New Hampshire scrip," Caleb scoffed.

Hugh Eliot bristled. "I'll have paying off money when we fetch Portsmouth. Two pounds says you can't come within half a cable of them boats."

Caleb stroked his beard reflectively. "Ye be talkin' paper or coin?"

"However the Captain will be paying us. If paper, then paper, if coin then coin. But you have to put up equal."

Caleb paused to rummage in his possibles bag, slung bandolier fashion over his left shoulder, and came up with a coin. He handed it to Slobber, who was number two and sponger on Hugh Eliot's gun crew. "Slobber kin hold the stakes. No need to put yer mark on a paper. Yer word's plenty for me."

Slobber held the coin aloft and squinted in the pre-dawn. "Five Spanish dollars I think it be," he announced, "in silver."

Frost was pleased at his men's banter. It was a good sign for the day's beginning. But it was going to be a very, very long day. Even if the storm from the southeast arrived by mid-afternoon. Frost looked to larboard, to the east, where a thin, anemic tendril of magenta was just giving tint to a bank of clouds. He knew the calm would last until an hour or so before the storm broke, though he would be very surprised if there were not some wind shortly after mid-day. If the *Salmon* were still afloat by then. He laid a hand on the stern cap rail and regarded the British warship, full hull up now. His hand warmed the rime ice coating the cap rail into a film of water. "Tell me when you are loaded and ready to run out, Caleb. Axes here, you two," Frost ordered, pointed to two waisters. "Mister Green, are you ready with the flag? And did you fetch my glass?"

"Aye, Captain," the second mate answered, appearing at Frost's elbow with the rattlesnake flag rolled into a ball, and Frost's best telescope.

"Please bend it to the mizzen peak halyard, Mister Green," and seeing the two waisters appearing with broadaxes, "you men lay into the stern counter timber with a will and carve a port for Caleb's and Hugh's cannon." Frost was careful to recognize both men's equity in the nine-pounder.

"A moment, Capt'n," Caleb was on his feet, silent in deerskin moccasins, beside Frost now, gazing back at the Britisher, gauging distance and wind and light. Caleb watched the warship intently, left forefinger pressed against the pulse of his right wrist, timing the swells. Caleb nodded. "Two four-pounder charges, right enough, and the distance be two thousand long paces to them boats—easy. That bein' when ye can see 'em, bobbin' about as they be." He turned his head slightly. "Hugh, ye got that slow match a-lit yet?"

"It's a-going, Caleb."

Just then Frost felt a touch of wind on his left cheek. A windlet rippled across the placid, oily swells of the ocean like a small school of flying fish in the tropics, and the sails hanging limp from their yards fluttered momentarily. Frost smelled the saltpeter from the sputtering slow match. "Cut away," he ordered, and nodded to the two seamen with axes.

Three feet of taff rail was gone in two strokes of the broad-axes, then the blades bit into the heavy oak of the stern gun-wale, great chips of wood flying as the two men wielded their axes with skill and enthusiasm. Frost strode to the binnacle and studied it intently so he would not have to look at the hideous wounds those broadaxes were inflicting on his beloved *Salmon*.

"Enough!" Caleb called. "Run her out for me, Hugh!" The crew tailed onto the gun's tackle and ran it, wooden trucks squealing and protesting, to the gun's snub at the stern gun-wale. Caleb had followed the gun, walking in a crouch, direct-ing Slobber in the employment of a quoin.

"Flag's running up, Captain," Second Mate Green cried.

Frost glanced up as the flag broke from its ball, momentum causing it to blossom momentarily, revealing the segmented rattlesnake, then fall limp in the still air.

Caleb sighted down the barrel of the long nine-pounder, eye just above the base ring, and called for another slight adjust-ment as Hugh Eliot pricked the cartridge through the vent. Hugh Eliot added a sprinkle of priming powder from a powder horn as a small swell passed under the keel, raising the stern perceptively, then falling back sluggishly. Caleb rechecked the cannon's alignment, timed two swells' lift and surge with his pulse, eyes constantly on the British warship, and muttered, "I wish this piece had a proper flintlock," then scampered out of the way. "Touch her, Hugh!"

Hugh Eliot stabbed downward with the linstock holding the slow match, into the touchhole. Frost, telescope already raised and focused, instinctively closed his eyes. The nine-pounder's muzzle blossomed into a flower of brilliant orange and red flame that would have blinded Frost at the same time the concussion of sound battered and deafened him, had he not prepared for the sudden illumination in the half light of dawn. Opening his eyes and trying to find a gap in the choking cloud of sulphurous grayish-black smoke that enveloped *Salmon*'s stern in the cold, still air, and finding one, Frost observed two rapid splashes, the ball's passage across the tops of two swells, directly in line with the foremast of the British warship. The boats towing were out of sight in the dip of a swell. Then the boats lifted into momentary view, blending almost completely into the shadow of the warship, and suddenly the ellipse of Frost's glass was filled with debris, some flying seemingly as high as the foremast yard.

"Search your piece! Serve the vent! Sponge and swab your piece!" Hugh Eliot shouted, covering the touchhole with his dirty, calloused thumb. Immediately the cannon recoiled, vicious as a rattlesnake, to the length of its breeching ropes. Slobber, as matross, dipped his sheepskin sponge into the bucket of sea water and ministered to the cannon, swabbing out any sparks or embers of charred flannel cartridge cloth. "Load with cartridge!" Slobber had his rammer ready as Tom Dreyer, another member of the gun crew, thrust the two bags of powder into the nine-pounder's muzzle. "Regard your shot! Put home the shot gently!"

Caleb was beside Frost, shouting into his ear to be heard. "If this cannon of yer's be like a proper rifle, she be needin' a touch more powder. That time she sounded a growl, not like the high bark a proper rifle has when her charge is sweet."

"Pass the word to augment the next charge, Mister Green," Frost shouted to his second mate. "The standard four-pounder charge is two pounds of powder. Make the next charge four and a half pounds, if you please. Carry on with this shot, Caleb." Frost had his watch out, timing the reload.

"What did we do with thet first shot?" Caleb asked. Frost realized the smoke had prevented anyone except him from seeing the shot's effect.

"Lay the next shot as well as you did that one, Caleb," Frost shouted to make himself heard over the ringing in his own ears, "and I'll add five silver Spanish dollars to the paying-off of every man in Hugh Eliot's gun crew!"

Struan Ferguson was at Frost's side now, his eyes wide in wonder. "God's truth, Captain, but that blast moved us a good ten feet through the water. The tension came off the tow warps and tumbled the men at oars into their boats' bilges."

"Please start our water now, Mister Ferguson. I would ask Mister Green to see the preparations underway, but directly he's overseeing the cutting of cartridge. Tell off some men with axes and have others stand to the pumps."

Consternation registered on Ferguson's face, but he recovered quickly. "Aye, Captain, starting our water immediately."

"Keep only the butt at the mainmast and any pannikin cook has filled. The crew's spirits and beer as well, do you ken?" Frost glanced down at Jonathan's watch as Hugh Eliot's gun crew tailed onto the nine-pounder's tackle and its carriage screeched forward to its snub. Frost made the reload two minutes and forty-five seconds. Not an exceptionally fast time for a well-trained gun crew, but admirable, very admirable, for a scratch crew that had never fired anything heavier than a four-pounder, and those occasions half a world away in the South China Sea and off Sumatra to repel pirates. Frost vowed, if he managed to elude the British warship, never to neglect gunnery again.

Caleb Mansfield was directing Slobber in minute, intricate adjustments with a handspike to the gun's lay. He was intensely concentrated on the warship a mile behind the *Salmon*. "Touch her again, Hugh!" Caleb shouted, as he leaped clear of the carriage.

The nine-pounder bellowed another sullen roar, and again Frost closed his eyes against the blossom of flame. When he opened his eyes he saw the skipping splashes of the ball *Salmon* had just fired, already a quarter of a mile away—and the skips of a ball coming toward his ship. Still focused on the course of his ball, Frost studiously ignored the ball fired by the Britisher.

Again a geyser of debris rose in the circumference of Frost's telescope lens. He consciously shut out of his mind the death and havoc the *Salmon*'s two cannon shot had just wrought. Impossible shots, both, the towing boats not even visible most times as *Salmon* and the British warship rose and fell in syncopated obedience to the subtle forces of the long swells. At a time when naval gunners swore that the first shot was for the Devil, the second for God, and only the third and afterward for the ship, two nine-pounder cannon balls in succession had smashed into kindling at least two, perhaps all three, of the small boats towing the British warship.

Perhaps God had directed the two cannon balls fired from the *Salmon*. Perhaps the Devil had directed the two balls.

Frost realized that he had been braced for the impact of the Britisher's cannon ball. Three seconds had passed; Frost concluded the shot had missed, though it could not have been by more than the barest whisker.

The nine-pounder was already being run up to its snub, and Caleb Mansfield was eagerly peering along the long nine's barrel. "Go to work on her riggings, Caleb," Frost ordered. "You struck boats with both shots." Hugh Eliot's gun crew, and the waisters standing about, all shouted and whooped in unison; backs were slapped; one waister danced an impromptu jig.

"Enough!" Frost snapped. "The Britisher has got at least one bow chaser in action! One ball into our rudder and we'll never see the Ports of Piscataway."

The men's spontaneous gaiety fled as quickly as it had gathered, and the gun crew resumed its careful attendance upon the nine-pounder. A moment later the cannon recoiled against its breeching tackle; this time the report of the cannon was a high, sharp crack. Frost stepped around a windrow of bitter smoke and focused his telescope on the British warship. No damage that he could see to her top hamper. Perhaps a ball somewhere through a sail, but he needed damage, major damage; a topmast carried away, stays parted, yards and spars coming down. Through his glass Frost observed the warship's bows slowly coming round to her larboard, and he saw the gleam of the gilded figurehead, far away and small, but in sharp relief. It looked for all the world like a cat crouched beneath the bowsprit. Strange that the cat would point toward the east, not the west where the land lay, Cape Cod, by Frost's rough calculations, not more than five leagues over the horizon. No, not so strange.

"Mister Ferguson!" Frost shouted.

"Aye," Struan replied, hurrying aft. "Water started, sir."

Frost stared at the gush of water through the canvas hose rigged on *Salmon*'s larboard side. Below decks, he knew, men were knocking in the heads of water and spirits barrels, letting the barrels' contents sluice into the bilges and thence to the pump wells where the pumps lifted the mix of liquids overside in steady gushes.

"The cat's turning, Struan, to the east. Caleb didn't get one boat. Her captain's readying a broadside from his starboard battery as soon as her bows are around."

"The cat, sir?" Struan was confused. "Yon vessel be not a cat-rig . . ."

"Ken that her figurehead is some sort of cat, stretched out beneath the bowsprit, a tiger or leopard or something. A cat. It's best we give our enemy a name." Frost spoke loudly enough for everyone nearby to hear. This battle had to be something personal: the cat and the fish, the *Salmon*. The enemy now had a name, perhaps a ludicrous one, but a name nevertheless.

"I had the carpenter knock together sweeps last night, stuns'l booms and barrel staves. Run them out through the gun ports and get three men on each sweep."

"Aye, Captain." Ferguson collected all the men at the stern not involved in the husbandry of the nine-pounder and sent them to the waist. Frost saw Roger Green supervising the filling of new cartridge bags with gunpowder in the shelter of the waist break—a singularly dangerous practice. Frost looked around quickly for any source of flame.

"Belay cutting new cartridge, Mister Green," Frost commanded. "The time for fine shooting is past. Assist Mister Ferguson in getting hands on the sweeps." Struan was already driving hands to the bulwarks, directing them to thrust the long, makeshift sweeps, stuns'l booms with barrel staves reinforced and nailed to them, through the gun ports, three sweeps to a side, with three men assigned to each crude, unwieldy sweep.

Struan walked the men through one evolution. Pivot the sweeps, keep the blades out of water, and move the blades as far forward as they would go by the simple expedient of walking the men two paces backwards toward the stern. Then dip the crude blades into the water and struggle forward, pushing against the awkward sweeps, half-sluggish step by half-sluggish step. Straun Ferguson evidently believed the men at the sweeps would obtain better purchase by pushing than by pulling the sweeps; the effect was far more like paddling than rowing. The first few strokes were uncoordinated; the hands at the sweeps grunted and strained against the weight of the ship. Frost very much doubted the sweeps would have any practical effect on a vessel of *Salmon*'s burthen. Sweeps were commonly employed on vessels, even warships, brigs, and larger, for maneuvering in calms or light airs. But sweeps were extremely awkward at best, and they lacked hydrodynamic efficiency on a vessel's standing as high above the water as *Salmon* stood.

Indeed, given her burthen and height, trying to propel *Salmon* with oversized oars was an exercise in futility, almost as futile as attempting to tow the *Salmon* with longboat and gig. Still, any distance gained was distance gained. Waiting passively while the British warship, the cat, made way was not an option.

The nine-pounder on *Salmon*'s quarterdeck bellowed famously and, satisfied that his waist crew was as profitably employed as possible, Frost bounded back to the quarterdeck. The Britisher's head was already around now, and Frost watched her starboard side grow a frieze of dirty grayish-black smoke. He judged the balls would arrive in six seconds. He counted one thousand three, one thousand four, one thousand five—and saw the spray hurled up by a ball twenty feet astern. Frost heard rather than saw the one ball that whistled harmlessly overhead, but then went sick inside as with a successive shudder three balls, at a minimum, struck *Salmon*'s stern at the waterline.

Three balls out of nine: tolerable gunnery given the distance. Frost raced to the taff rail and glanced down at *Salmon*'s rudder, his main concern. The rudder had not been hit. "Mister Ferguson, send the carpenter and a hand below to survey damage," he shouted to his first mate, and then to his bosun: "Mister Plaisted, I collect we did not find any great number of nine-pounder balls to ship in New Providence. I would appreciate an exact count."

Hugh Eliot heard Frost's order. "I have the count, Capt'n. We took aboard thirty."

"And we've fired away seven," Frost said.

"Aye."

"We've caused no damage to her riggings I can see, so work on her hull whilst she's broad on. Hold five balls in reserve, but continue firing. The recoil does move us away. If you do fire away eighteen balls, continue firing with powder only. We have plenty of powder, and the cat will just think our shots go wide." Frost had his telescope focused on the cat, and knew *Salmon* would receive another broadside in a minute or less. Was his better course to attempt turning the *Salmon*'s vulnerable stern away from the cat, or keep the stern's smaller profile toward the cat? Better to remain stern-on so his one pitiful cannon could bear.

Ming Tsun was at his elbow, gesturing. Frost jerked around, suddenly conscious that the lookout had been hailing him. "Deck, aye," Frost called. Who was at the masthead? A heavily pimpled young lad from a large family in Salem named Bowditch, Hannibal Bowditch. Frost knew the lad had a good pair of eyes.

"Sail due south! Topgallants are all I can see, but they be British cut!" A high-pitched young voice shrilled from the masthead.

◆ IV ❧

◉◉◉◉◉ ROST HEARD YOUNG BOWDITCH WELL
◉   ◉ ENOUGH THROUGH THE RINGING IN
◉   F   ◉ HIS EARS. "MISTER FERGUSON, ORDER
◉◉◉◉◉ THE BOATS TO ROUND US TO LARBOARD.
Vast heaving on the starboard sweeps, double up on the lar-
board sweeps. Mister Plaisted, tell me when the binnacle shows
our bows southeast by east."

The nine-pounder serving as a stern chaser bellowed most
satisfyingly. Frost felt the rush of air generated by a cannon
ball's passage overhead and heard a swift hiss like a hot iron's
first touch to a linen neck stock. A cannon ball fired by the
British warship had pierced ragged holes through several folds
of canvas hanging in the leach of *Salmon*'s main course.

"Caleb, Hugh, belay the nine-pounder. Hugh, attend to
your regular gun on the starboard side. Mister Green, all larboard cannons shall be served. Caleb, please assist with their
laying. Cannons may fire as they bear." Another swift, convul-
sive rush of air: the Britisher was firing high. Surprising. Frost
was no warship commander, but the few he had met were
emphatic that the gunners of the Royal Navy were drilled to
pummel the hull of an opponent. The French and the Spanish,
on the other hand, drilled their gunners to concentrate on an
enemy's top hamper and riggings with chain and bar shot.
Frost felt, rather than heard, two cannon balls strike the
Salmon's hull. The officer commanding the cat was evidently
a pragmatist.

Frost ran up the ratlines to join young Bowditch, blue from the cold. "Mister Bowditch, I've no doubt you have been cyphering your sums and paying attention to your geometry since we began our cruize from the Bahamas."

"Aye, sir," Hannibal Bowditch said through teeth whose chattering he could not still. "I'm most keen on geometry, sir, those sines and cosines and tangents are wondrous awful in their preciseness. I've finished the book on logarithms by Mister Napier, as well as the translation of Euclid, Captain, sir, and am so bold as to trouble you for another book of the same fare."

"You shall have it, Hannibal Bowditch. Repair to my cabin after you are dismissed from watch. I collect that I have a book by a chap named Newton who questions some of our dear Euclid's conclusions. I admit to being perplexed by some of Mister Newton's conclusions. The book should interest you, and I shall welcome your thoughts on some observations I made from time to time on the margins." Frost had long attempted to cultivate an interest in navigation among his crewmen, and on most voyages had scheduled the time to hold school at least thrice a week where he tutored any jack tar who sought enlightenment into language or mathematics.

Once, on a long passage from Macao and down through the Moçambique Channel, Frost had been laid low by dengue fever. For ten days *Salmon*'s navigation had been entrusted to a foretopman, since advanced to a master's mate on *Perch*, another vessel of the Frost Trading Company. The man, Tom Kent, had done a very creditable job of picking a way through the islands lying off Moçambique, else Geoffrey Frost would not now be tightening his legs around the comforting wood of the *Salmon*'s mainmast crosstrees.

Hannibal Bowditch was his brightest student ever, and during the interminable delays in the Bahamas while waiting for the cannons from Fort Montagu to be delivered to the *Salmon*, Frost had enjoyed sharing out his store of knowledge of mathematics and celestial navigation for Hannibal's benefit.

From his seat in the crosstrees eighty feet above *Salmon*'s main deck Frost could command a horizon of six miles in any direction. He focused his telescope on the barely visible smudge of dirty white on the southern horizon to which Hannibal Bowditch solemnly pointed. There was no mistaking the cut of those sails in the magnification of his glass: topgallants they were, and despite having seen the ship only once before, he knew it instantly. " 'Tis the *Roebuck*."

"The what, sir?" Hannibal asked politely.

"*Roebuck*," Frost said again, his heart sinking as he saw how the vessel's topgallants were drawing. The sails were now quite stark against the blackness of a squall line building on the southern horizon. "A British frigate, I believe she is the largest vessel the Royal Navy has on the North American station."

A wide-eyed Hannibal Bowditch had the temerity to ask his captain: "How large is large, sir?"

Frost had already hooked his feet into the heavily tarred ropes of the ratlines, but he paused to answer the youngster: "I believe *Roebuck* mounts forty-four great cannons." When he reached the deck, Frost realized he was perspiring freely despite the cold of the overcast day.

Brandon, the wizened carpenter, scuttled across the main deck to make his report. "Three balls hit amidships at the waterline, Capt'n, but praise be, naught pierced."

"Thank you, Mister Brandon, I'll ask you to assist Mister Ferguson begin swaying up the cannons in the hold." Then to Hugh Eliot: "Vast firing the four-pounders. Tip them overboard. All of 'em. Once done, back to the stern chaser and resume firing, two four-pounder cartridges of powder, no ball."

Struan Ferguson was hastening toward Frost, alarm and bewilderment broad on his face. "The deck cannons overboard as quickly as you can, Mister Ferguson," Frost snapped, forestalling Struan's protest. "Then all the cannons shipped at New Providence, save only our swivels, which are to stay below, though handy. After them, all cargo and stores we can jettison, saving only the powder."

"The sail to the south . . . ," Struan began.

"Is the *Roebuck*, and she has wind, with a devil of a blow directly behind her."

"Jesus wept," Struan said under his breath.

"John, chapter eleven, verse thirty-five," Frost said tersely. "A favorable outcome for Lazarus, though less so for He who summoned Lazarus from the tomb."

Struan turned and began shouting orders to cast off the breechings of the cannon carriages and truck them across the main deck to the entryway in the waist. The first four-pounder was over the side in less than one minute, and the *Salmon* was instantly lighter by twelve hundredweight of iron and three hundredweight of oak carriage.

Then Ming Tsun was at his side and Frost quickly assigned him and the cook the task of bringing up from his cabin personal trunks and possessions to jettison. He thought fleetingly of ordering Ming Tsun to break the glass and jettison the items in his cabin through the stern windows. But the solid line of black cloud he had glimpsed to the south told him he would need as sound a ship as possible, could he stave off *Salmon*'s capture or destruction until the squall arrived. And, if the stern windows were broken, the cat might in some wise twig to the other nine-pounder installed in his cabin. The thumping of another cannon ball into *Salmon* at her waterline brought Frost back to the more immediate problems he faced from the cat.

The nine-pounder on the quarterdeck bellowed sullenly and wreathed *Salmon*'s stern in a thick cloying cloud of smoke and sulfur stench. The cat was still fine on the larboard quarter with *Salmon*'s stern chaser not bearing, so that shot should have been powder only, no ball. And yes, the *Salmon* did hobbyhorse forward, throwing the hands at the makeshift sweeps offstroke. Frost trained his telescope on the cat as the last of *Salmon*'s deck cannons went overside. Struan Ferguson was already overseeing a gang tailing onto the stay tackle still in place from swaying up the two nine-pounders earlier. The deck was crowded with men, but they were going about their tasks with the efficiencies Frost had drilled into them.

Ming Tsun darted by with Frost's case of books. "Wait!"

Frost ordered, stepping over to the case. Ming Tsun paused, bookcase perched on the cap rail. Frost scanned the books, trying not to think about Livy, Shakespeare, Hobbes, the other authors who were his friends and companions; he flinched away the case's wooden locking bar and drew out his tattered and much thumbed copy of Moore's *Practical Navigator*. "I've noted numerous errors in Mister Moore's calculations, and I fancy other mariners would be pleased to know of them." He plucked out Messier's *Memoires de l'Academie* with its astronomical catalogue, and Abbe de la Caille's *Observations from the Cape of Good Hope* as well.

Frost turned away in order not to see the bookcase go overside. Cook Barnes hustled up with Frost's toilet case and other personals clutched in his arms and anchored with the hook strapped on his left wrist. Frost's chess set and the *wei chi* board were balanced precariously atop a pair of boots, a chamber pot into which, incongruously, Frost's dressing gown and slippers were stuffed, and a tarpaulin jacket. Frost swept the chess set and *wei chi* board off Barnes' load and handed them and the *Practical Navigator*, as well as the *Observations*, to Ming Tsun. "We have not finished our chess game. I collect I was besting you and Mister Ferguson."

Ming Tsun smiled and signed quickly, "Thank you, but you have never bested me in *wei chi*," before hustling away for another load.

"Sweeps, both sides!" Frost ordered. The nine-pounder cracked again. There was no answering broadside from the British warship. A quick glance at the cat showed the sloop-o-war struggling to bring her bows around to starboard to lie on the same southwest by west course as *Salmon*. The British captain had ceased trying to disable *Salmon* with a broadside and was resuming the chase. But the British captain's initial turn to larboard had cost him dearly in time and effort, particularly with only one boat towing, and that with what had to be a fagged crew. Would the British captain pause the precious few minutes necessary to replace the fatigued oarsmen in the towing boat with fresh hands? Did he have a fourth boat to commit to the tow? Frost hurried back to the quarterdeck. "Caleb! Hugh! The cat's towing 'round! Her boat should bear directly. Make it three boats with three balls!"

Caleb wiped his smoke-begrimed face and nodded. Despite the enveloping cold, Hugh Eliot, Slobber, and the rest of the gun crew had stripped off their coats and shirts. Their pastry-white torsos were dripping perspiration from their exertions in serving the nine-pounder. Behind Frost on the main deck a cannon taken from Fort Montagu, just lifted from the hold, was walked across the deck and the slings undone overside. The cannon fell into the sea, cascabel first, hardly raising a splash. *Salmon*'s progress was agonizingly slow; she had barely moved past the flotsam of barrel staves and empty provision barrels thrown overboard from the waist. Another cannon emerged from the hold.

As Frost began to hoist himself into the mainmast shrouds, Cook Barnes, bearing two wheels of cheese, hurried toward the starboard rail with all the enthusiasm the joy of destruction brings. Frost stopped him. "Better to feed us than the fishes, Mister Barnes. Serve that out to the men." Chagrined, the cook dropped the wheels of cheese to the deck, anchored one with his hook, fumbled out his jackknife, and thumbed open the blade with his right hand with the ease born of long experience. Cook Barnes carved a large slice of cheese and presented it to Frost with a flourish. Frost thrust the piece of cheese into a coat pocket, and jumped into the ratlines.

Young Bowditch had been relieved by a brawny topman named John Nason, a quiet, competent hand from York who had been with Frost on two China voyages. Frost remembered that Nason had aspirations to be a minister. He had never heard the man curse. During Nason's first voyage Frost had taught the man to read, and later had given him a copy of a four-shilling Tyndale Bible. Once he had settled in the main crosstrees, Frost broke the piece of cheese in half and shared it with Nason.

"Grateful to you, Captain. I had watched old Barnes throw two good wheels of cheese overside before you crossed his bows."

"Men do strange things when the excitement comes on them," Frost said. "I doubt not that you have marked the same yourself."

The *Roebuck*'s topgallants were clearly visible in Frost's glass, though not yet the tops of her courses. He judged the *Roebuck* had covered the better part of a mile since he had observed her last. Her sails were drawing well and she lay heavily on a starboard tack, so the wind, when it came, would come from the southeast, as Frost expected. The forward edge of the squall was sharper, more pronounced, akin to a gigantic cliff; Frost called to mind the wall of Table Mountain at the Cape of Storms, though this squall rose until it was absorbed into the gray, lowering sky. The *Roebuck*'s sails were virtually lost, no more than an insignificant speck against the building squall on the southern horizon.

The fact that *Roebuck* had not reefed her topgallants to prepare for the approaching storm told Frost that her commander was driving his ship as hard as he could, gambling that he could close with and identify the sails on his northern horizon before the storm overtook him. Perhaps the *Roebuck*'s commander had been patrolling in concert with the cat and recognized her as pursuing a prize.

Frost chewed absently on a mouthful of cheese as he turned his glass on the cat. The nine-pounder on *Salmon*'s quarterdeck coughed its deadly ball as he refocused the telescope's tube for the shorter focus. The scope of tow had been increased to provide slightly greater leverage as the remaining boat struggled to haul round the cat's bows. The boat towing was at an acute angle to the cat's bows, almost invisible against the hull of the sloop-o-war. Frost saw one long, thin furrow cut by the nine-pound ball across the top of a swell in the telescope's periphery, passing just aft of the towing boat and striking somewhere in the British warship's hull. The towing boat still swam, yes, but something was amiss, for the boat surged forward momentarily. The boat was veering, no, turning around, and with a speed that showed there was no longer any strain on the tow cable.

Ha! The ball had missed the boat but had severed the tow

cable! A fluke well enough, an extra fluke at such a range, just as hitting the two other small boats with the nine-pounder had been flukes. But luckier for this boat's crew than the other two. That should delay the cat, and Frost doubted if the crew of the remaining boat cared much for pressing their duties.

Frost gave John Nason the cheese he had not eaten. "You are to hail me the moment this southerly vessel takes in sail," he said and slid down to *Salmon*'s main deck. On his way aft to his quarterdeck Frost saw Ming Tsun and signed for him to lay below to Frost's cabin and bring him the barometer reading.

Frost described to Caleb and Hugh the results of their last shot, then conferred with Struan, who came after to report that all the cannons, so laboriously loaded in New Providence, had been jettisoned. A glance overside showed that the *Salmon* had pulled away from the majority of debris floating on the oily swell, though the distance traveled was less than one hundred fathoms. A shockingly hard-won hundred fathoms, Frost noted, when he looked at the bleeding palms of some of the men at the sweeps. Hardened men these sailors were, with well-calloused hands, but walking the sweeps was hard, grim work.

Frost took Struan by his elbow and led him to the starboard rail, glancing back at the cat wallowing, sails flapping, in a long swell, expecting to see at any moment a billow of smoke from her bow chaser. "The *Roebuck* is just ahead of a line squall, likely of most fierce intensity, though I know not its speed of travel. Her captain has not shortened sail. I think he is peeling his onions mighty thin."

"Should we begin to take in sail, Captain?" Struan said with some anxiety, straining his eyes southward, though from the deck the *Roebuck* was not visible.

"No, the cat cannot be blind to *Roebuck*'s presence, but in all the confusion we've caused with their tow, mayhap the cat's captain has not given due consideration to the squall."

The cat's bow chaser was in action again. Frost felt the ball thud into *Salmon*'s stern before he heard the cannon's report.

"Caleb! Hugh! Silence that bow chaser!" Should he unmask the second gun? The cat could bring only one of its bow chasers to bear at one time. Frost could bring two stern chasers into action. No. He had no crew who could serve the second gun as ably as Caleb and Hugh, with the precision requisite at this range, and he wanted to conceal from the cat the fact that he had preserved two cannon as long as possible. Frost pulled out Jonathan's watch; one hour past noon. Great Buddha, how the time had passed so fast and yet so slow! He resumed talking to Struan. "I collect we'll have wind within the hour, and shortly after that more than we could want. I've seen this approaching squall's like only thrice before, and all in the Southern Ocean. A calm like this, and then a devil of a squall striking fiercely, though in the Southern Ocean the squalls would come from the north. You'll recall once, south of St. Helena, our *Salmon* was almost pitch-poled, and we were lucky not to have lost her masts."

"I ken that occasion, sir. We came within a shade of turnin' the turtle, and yes, the conditions be markedly similar, this increasing swell and all."

There! Frost felt a faint caress of wind on his left cheek. The mainsail slathered and crackled against its mast; *Salmon* surged forward eagerly as an exceedingly heavy swell from the southeast began lifting her. "Secure the tow and get our people aboard immediately, Mister Ferguson. Have the sweeps run in, we shan't need them presently."

The long swell flowed on and lifted *Salmon*'s stern directly into the path of the cannon ball fired six seconds earlier from the cat's bow chaser. The ball struck the larboard quarter of the stern on a level with the muzzle of the nine-pounder, exploded the dry oak of the gunwale into a mist of splinters and dust, and ricocheted off the heavy elm carriage, overturning the carriage instantly. The ball spent itself by striking the driver boom an oblique blow that almost snapped the boom.

Something large and heavy slammed into Frost's back and threw him to the deck. He instantly regained his feet, rising at the same time as Slobber struggled away from the overturned cannon, a great, yard-long splinter of oak torn from the stern bulwark, as thick as a belaying pin, protruding from his bare torso six inches above his belt. Frost caught the man as Slobber's knees buckled, easing him back to the deck, feeling as he did so the bloody tip of the splinter poking through the torn flesh of the man's back.

Frost frantically scanned the quarterdeck for the rest of the gun crew. Hugh Eliot's body, which had struck Frost, lay against the binnacle like a discarded doll. Half of Hugh's face and forehead had been neatly nipped away by the cannon ball, a trail of pinkish-gray brain matter and bone fragments marking the path of his body's slide. Frost's peripheral vision scanned a body pinned beneath the overturned nine-pounder. From a long distance, Frost faintly heard himself shouting: "Topmen at the sweeps! Aloft to reef topsails! The rest of you, bear a hand to shift this cannon!"

Slobber was strangely still, though Frost could feel the man's heart beating fiercely. Slobber was bleeding profusely from his nose, and his eyes were wild, staring, unfocused. Then Slobber's arms flapped with all the aimless ferocity of a chicken whose neck had just been wrung, steadied, and fastened upon the hideous splinter. Frost cradled the man, left arm around Slobber's shoulders, while his right arm pinioned the man's arms gently. "There, there, John Weliever, it's naught but a scratch you have, less than a bee sting, surely."

Slobber opened his mouth, but all that came out was a thick bubble of blood, dark in the light from the sullen sky. Struan Ferguson had run the length of deck from the bows, where he had gone to direct the recovery of longboat and gig. Struan grasped the overturned cannon by its barrel and heaved vainly, trying to move it off the body beneath.

Frost snarled at two members of the gun crew who hung back, open-mouthed, terrified. "Bear a hand! Use that rammer as a lever! Shift that cannon!" He turned to shout at the horrified men who still stood, rooted to their sweeps. Slobber moaned; his lower jaw worked feebly as he coughed, his shriveled, toothless mouth trying to form words. Frost held his ear against the man's mouth. "Ah, Capt'n, does our dear *Salmon* yet swim?"

Frost did not trust himself to speak for several moments; then he mastered himself and spoke in a normal tone. "Yes, John Weliever, our *Salmon* yet swims."

"Ah," Slobber breathed, and his grotesque, bloated face arranged itself into the semblance of a smile. "Ah," he breathed again, as he turned his head into Frost's chest.

Frost was immediately on his feet, rushing to the pitiful remainder of the taff rail, raising his fists in the direction of the cat and screaming at the top of his lungs: "Damn you, God Damn you, cat, God Damn you and all your spawn to hell!" Then a massive slug of wind struck the *Salmon*'s sails without warning and threw Frost across the nine-pounder, which some hands, under Struan's direction, had just levered upright. Briefly, Frost was face to face with Caleb Mansfield, who had two of the blackest and most bloodshot eyes Frost had ever seen.

As soon as Caleb had been extricated, Struan ordered more topmen aloft. Frost grabbed his speaking trumpet from its rack by the binnacle and shouted aloft: "Masthead there!"

"Masthead, aye!" John Nason shouted back, his voice barely audible above the wind's whine and the ringing in Frost's ears.

"How fares the *Roebuck*?"

"Deck, she was swallowed into the gale a few moments past," and divining his captain's real question, Nason added: "She had not shortened sail when I lost her from sight."

Frost turned aft, just in time to see a mighty fist of wind roil the cat almost on her starboard beam, and the sea, which moments before had been placid beneath its swell, was now frothing in four-foot wave crests. Aghast, Frost saw two of the men who had come aft to lever the cannon off Caleb had lifted Hugh Eliot under his armpits and by his legs and were struggling with their burden toward the lee rail. They were Massachusetts men he hardly knew. "Belay that!" he shouted, "No man of our ship's company shall ever be dumped unceremoniously overside like so much offal! Strike Hugh Eliot and John Weliever below to the steerage!"

Ming Tsun was beside Frost trying to wrestle a tarpaulin jacket over his shoulders. But where had Ming Tsun gotten a

tarpaulin jacket? Frost had seen his only tarpaulin jacket jettisoned. No, it was only a shawl of light canvas. He started to
protest, but then the first blinding gust of sleet arrived; he
wrapped the canvas around himself gratefully, then signed to
Ming Tsun: "Make sure the dead are taken below."

Ming Tsun handed Frost a scrap of paper upon which he
had written the barometer's reading. Frost had rarely seen such
a reading in the North Atlantic this early in the year; it was a
reading he associated with hurricanes and typhoons. Caleb
Mansfield blundered into him, dazed. "Take Caleb with you,"
Frost signed, "I won't be needing him for awhile." Then,
to the men who still clustered around the overturned nine-
pounder and its smashed carriage: "Secure the cannon. Don't
try to remount it, just snug it down. Get a canvas over it if you
can't find the tampion."

The sleet was now mixed with snow, and was almost contin-
uous; Frost marveled at the rapidity with which the squall had
arrived. It was a true snow squall, and he had never known a
snow squall to move so quickly. But then, Frost reflected
grimly, there was still a great deal the sea had yet to teach him.
All he had to do was remain alive long enough to absorb the
lessons. Frost looked again in disbelief at the scrap of paper
Ming Tsun had given him. A blast of wind and sleet whipped it
from his hand and swirled it away.

"Helm alee," Frost commanded the helmsmen as soon as
the topmen had somehow gotten two reefs into main and
mizzen topsails. He cursed himself for a fool for not taking in
sail sooner, then reflected that had he done so, he would have
alerted the cat to his judgment of the squall's ferocity, a ferocity that had already wrapped the *Salmon* into such a dense cloak
of freezing sleet and wind that Frost could see but a dozen fathoms ahead of *Salmon*'s bowsprit, plunging into waves now
surging well over six feet. No, regardless of what warning his
taking in sail might have given the cat, for the safety of his ship
and crew he should have ordered it done sooner. Frost spared
a thought for the *Roebuck*; he much doubted there would be
anything to fear from her for some time. Her captain had mis-

judged the rapidity of the snow squall's approach even more than Frost.

Struan Ferguson reported all the men from the gig and longboat safely aboard, though they were having the devil's own time of recovering the boats. Frost heard Struan shouting virtually simultaneous orders: brace around the yards; ensure all hatches were properly battened down; hands to the pumps. A knot of men in the waist succeeded in hauling the longboat over the larboard rail by dint of muscle, given the lack of time to rig lifting tackle. The gig was already wrestled aboard. Frost shivered inside his sodden wrap of rumbowline canvas, judged the need to reef main courses, and calculated back to the onset of the squall, disbelieving that less than five minutes earlier the random surge of an unexpectedly long swell had lifted *Salmon*'s stern into the path of an enemy cannon ball. Save for that swell, the ball would have passed harmlessly five feet above the heads of the two men who now lay dead in *Salmon*'s steerage. Joss.

"Mister Ferguson! Double reefs in the main and fore courses! Rig the small fore staysail, and when you can spare the hands, I wish the topgallant yards and masts sent down!"

Struan's reply was snatched away by the wind, but Frost saw Struan's vigorous, affirmative nod. Frost worked a quick plot in his head. When the snow squall struck, he calculated *Salmon* was fifteen leagues off Cape Cod, the land just over the horizon, and what could well be a lee shore, depending if the wind veered easterly from the southeast. He fought the initial urge to run for sea room: too great a chance he might blunder into the cat. Or the *Roebuck*. Despite the barometer's abrupt fall, Frost hoped that, as quickly and violently as the squall had struck, its ferocity would soon be spent, perhaps even before dusk. He intended to run up the Massachusetts coast, keeping roughly this same distance off the land through the evening, to raise the Isles of Shoals toward morning, and immediately stand in for Portsmouth.

ᴇᴅ V ᴅᴇ

B UT THE SNOW SQUALL WAS NOT ABAT-ING, AND WELL BEFORE DUSK FROST KNEW HE WAS CONTENDING WITH A MA-JOR NORTH ATLANTIC WINTER STORM, with the winds oscillating between southeast and east. He ordered lifelines laced and reluctantly sent topmen into the treacherous, ice-coated riggings to take in courses to the last reef points and shorten the fore staysail until it was little more than a handkerchief, just enough to provide heading control and a solid bite for the rudder. He briefly considered unreefing a point of the fore course to bring up *Salmon*'s bows but rejected that sail plan as too dangerous, both to ship and to crew. Then, ever so cautiously, Frost brought his *Salmon* onto a hull-pounding starboard tack.

Frost remained on *Salmon*'s pitching, rolling quarterdeck throughout the night, going below only once when Ming Tsun and Struan convinced him to shift his sodden, ice-glazed clothes for garments less waterlogged and wash down a mouthful of moldy cornbread with half a cup of cold, bitter tea. Once enough feeling had returned to his hands to hold a quill, Frost wedged himself into the settee along the starboard bulwark and brought out *Salmon*'s log from the desk, which had been displaced and stood on its side in a corner to accommodate the menacing bulk of the nine-pounder cannon now sharing his cabin. By the erratic light of the one candle lantern constantly swinging on its gimble, Frost rested the log book on the cannon and wrote the date, 10 April 1776, and then:

Cape Cod NW_N, 20 leagues, calm seas, swell from SE_S. Towed and swept. Chaced all day until the mid-forenoon by a British sloop-o-war with a cat figurehead, whose last ball coming on bd, before a fast gale rising from the SSE, took the lives of Hugh Eliot, bosun's mate and gunner, from the town in Maine by the same name, and John Weliever, able seaman, of Exeter in New Hampshire. They served their ship well, and their souls are commended to their Deity.

Frost returned the logbook to its proper drawer in the desk and turned his tired face toward Ming Tsun, who stood across from him.

The feeble light was enough for Frost to read Ming Tsun's signing: "You must rest. Ferguson has the deck."

"My soul is heavy, I cannot rest. Those who left us this day are beyond our help, but not our sympathy," Frost signed. "It is you who must rest. I shall have need of your strength presently."

"As you wish it," Ming Tsun signed, "but you must have another pair of stockings." He brought the stockings and anxiously watched as Frost slowly drew them on, then thrust his feet into his boots.

"They bind. I am as apt to get the black-toe with these stockings as I am without them." Frost laid a hand briefly on Ming Tsun's shoulder as he crossed the small cabin and enfolded himself in the rectangle of rumbowline canvas Ming Tsun had earlier provided. "Thank you for the wrap. It is as snug as a tarpaulin jacket," Frost signed, before drawing on his woolen gloves. He checked the barometer as he left the cabin, glad to note a slight, a very slight rise in the mercury.

As soon as he appeared on the frigid, sleet-swept quarterdeck, Struan loosened the lifeline securing him to the binnacle sufficiently to shout into Frost's ear the course, weather, and condition of the ship. Frost nodded as he adjusted to the pitch and roll on *Salmon*'s quarterdeck, which differed from the pitch and roll below decks, and the blackness of the night. "Very good, Struan. Please pass the word to continue relieving the helm and lookouts every half-hour. The deck is mine 'til dawn."

Struan helped Frost lash his lifeline around his waist, and with a hesitant glance over his shoulder tumbled down the aft companionway, leaving the *Salmon* to Frost, Nathan Adams and Lynch McManus, helmsmen, and the two lookouts in the bows. Frost checked the course in the dim illumination of the small oil lamp reflecting onto the binnacle card. Northeast by north: not nearly the margin for sea room he would have steered under ordinary circumstances, but present circumstances were far from ordinary. Though he sorely regretted the lack of a noon sight, Frost was fairly confident of *Salmon*'s position, placing her some fifteen leagues northeast of Cape Cod's northernmost point, the set of the offshore current, more than the storm, giving *Salmon* her present course. Frost wanted to stay as far away from any vessels in the Boston approaches as he could without running due east, for reports of the British evacuation of Boston had been contradictory. Frost believed that all of General Howe's troops had enshipped for Halifax, leaving General Washington in possession of the city. But he was not prepared to bet his ship's life on that belief by standing in too close, where *Salmon* might encounter yet another picquet vessel.

Frost paced three steps either side of the helm, the scope of his lifeline, clinging to the earrings laced about the quarterdeck to keep from being swept away by the occasional towering roller of dark water, which broke when divided by the bows and raced *Salmon*'s length to dash against the quarterdeck. There was much he had to regret this day past. He had not judged the swiftness or the ferocity of the storm accurately. If he had done so, he would not have jettisoned the cannons, the precious cannons from New Providence that John Langdon was counting on to arm the *Raleigh*. The *Raleigh* was set for launching in late May, and she must have cannons. Now the cannons intended for the Continental Navy's vessel—named for the feckless adventurer who had attempted to settle a colony in Virginia, far to the south of New Hampshire—lay irretrievable somewhere in *Salmon*'s wake. Had Frost more accurately gauged the arrival of the storm, those cannons would still be comfortable ballast low in *Salmon*'s holds.

And the deaths of John Weliever and Hugh Eliot. Surely there was something he could have done to have seen them elsewhere on the *Salmon* when the cannon ball struck; some way he could have arrested the stern's rise in that deadly swell . . .

The helmsmen changed; Herbert Collingwood and Shad Billingslee relieved Nathan Adams and Lynch McManus, who did not speak to their reliefs but indicated their captain's presence with a quick nod of head toward Frost, who stood taking the sleet's force full on, the men leaving Frost to wrestle with his personal demons. Throughout the subsequent changes of helmsmen and watch Frost retained his place on the quarterdeck, his face long frozen into a mask by the constant whip and sting of the sleet, eyes shuttered into slits though brain still worked furiously, whirring with myriad thoughts within thoughts while at the same time noting all that wind and sleet-laden sky and sea and intuition were telling him.

Toward dawn the seas and winds began to lay somewhat, short, jerky, hobbyhorse surges and dips rather than the previous poundings and crashing through heavy waves. The sleet turned to rain that fell in a curtain, though not a curtain so thick it concealed the tendrils of a cold sea fog and sea smoke setting in, and Frost finally achieved a semblance of peace within himself.

❧ VI ❧

❀❀❀❀❀ TRUAN FERGUSON WAS ON DECK BE-
❀　S　❀ FORE FIRST LIGHT, DARK POUCHES
❀　　❀ BENEATH HIS EYES ANNOUNCING THAT
❀❀❀❀❀ EVEN IF HE HAD BEEN BELOW IN THE
relative warmth of his cabin he had not slept any more than
his captain.

"This wind should moderate within the hour, the sea as well,
though the weather will remain much unsettled, possibly with
sleet again toward the forenoon. I expect the fog to thicken as
the wind abates. When the wind settles inform Cook Barnes
that he may start fires and prepare a hot meal for all hands."
Frost glanced up at *Salmon*'s lower masts. "It was trouble
enough to strike down the topgallant masts and yards, so leave
them be for the present. Keep the lookouts fresh. In this fog we
can overrun another vessel—or a shoal—before we know to
down helm." Frost was incredibly tired, but he resisted the
yawn that would have showed Struan how tired he was. "You
have the deck. Please call me before any sail change, or the sight
of any vessel."

But Frost slept little in his cabin and was on deck in the early
noon, appreciatively sniffing the air. After a few moments
studying the weather Frost fancied that he knew *Salmon*'s
position to within two leagues despite the fog. "Please break
out the hundred-fathom line," he ordered Struan, "and muster
enough men to serve it, but quietly. I ken it to be a laborious

chore, but I believe we are in soundings, and I should like to have the weight armed."

Angus Wyeth, dragging the coil of hundred-fathom line, and Troy Giddings, able seamen from Portsmouth, worked their way along the lee rail to the foremast lee chains, where both men tied themselves off, Giddings holding tightly to Wyeth's shoulder. Struan organized the extra haul-men into a team ranged along the lee side as Angus Wyeth buckled himself into the breastband and tied off the breastrope, which two seamen held to steady him. Wyeth clambered over the bulwark onto the lee chains, got his balance, and heaved the line. Frost followed the curving downward path of the weight and saw the bit of flotsam flash on a curling wave crest so quickly he was not certain he had actually glimpsed it. Frost untied his lifeline and hastened forward as fast as he could.

"Do not call out the mark," Frost told Angus Wyeth in a low voice. "Tell me the depth in a voice no higher than my own." And to Struan, who had followed him: "Keep the men below for the moment. No one to speak or make any noise, no iron shall strike iron, or wood strike wood."

Mystified, Struan hurried away to do his captain's bidding. The lead line stopped running through Wyeth's cold, calloused fingers. "Fifty-five fathom, Capt'n Frost," Wyeth said in a voice barely audible above the wind's soft twang in the riggings of the living ship.

"Pass me the lead," Frost commanded, as Wyeth and the haul-men put their arms and shoulders into the task of handing up the long scope of line and the fifty-pound *dipsy led*. The weight passed from Wyeth to Giddings to Frost as soon as it broke from the water. In the poor light of the rainy, fog-shrouded early noon Frost peered at the snatch of small stones and a piece of shell stamped into the soft tallow at the lead's bottom.

Frost thumbed the gravel and shell piece out of the weight's hollow. "Favor me by casting the lead yet again," he said. "I'll wager five New Hampshire dollars of script you'll find bottom between fifty and fifty-two fathoms, but no stone; most-like a fine sand the color of the sand off Sable Island." There were no takers for his wager. The lead was thrown in silence and ran through Wyeth's calloused, rope-burned palms to a sudden slackness.

"The mark is fifty fathom, Capt'n," Wyeth announced respectfully, and two minutes later when the team of haul-men had handed up the line he glanced quickly at the tallow before passing the lead to Frost. Giddings and Ferguson stared at the grains of wheat-colored sand without saying anything.

Frost turned to Roger Green, who had joined Struan and Giddings. "I reckon us between five and seven leagues directly south of the Shoals." Frost ordered Wyeth and Giddings out of the chains. "You have done your jobs." Glad that the fog appeared to be thickening, Frost paced back to his quarter-deck, followed by the very mystified Struan Ferguson and Roger Green.

"With the loss of two men, I reckon our effectives to be sixty and six, that is not counting the eight sick Massachusetts men as well enough to serve swivel guns," Frost said, smiling at the incredulous looks on the faces of his first and second mates. At least he believed his face contorted into a smile, though his cheeks and forehead were still so frozen he could not tell for sure. "Mister Ferguson, you shall have Caleb Mansfield take great care to load each of our eight swivel guns below deck. Load them with as much langrage as Caleb considers they can throw at short range. You shall serve out the small arms and pikes to all the men and hold them in readiness on the berth deck. Caleb is to appoint whomever he wishes to assist in the loading of muskets and pistols, though no arm is to be primed without my signal. I shall address the men presently."

Turning to Roger Green: "Mister Green, have Hugh Eliot —no, his help to us now must come from another quarter— you carefully, under cover of canvas, charge the nine-pounder here with as much langrage as you consider proper." Frost inclined his head toward the stern. "Then do the same with the cannon in my cabin. You shall have charge of that cannon whilst I tend this one. I stress to you both that the swivels and cannons and small arms must give fire when summoned."

Confident in the full knowledge that his orders would be obeyed to the letter, and with dispatch and without need for further explanation, Frost reflected momentarily upon the disturbing significance of the British marine's shako he had glimpsed on the wave crest. He made for his cabin to prepare for the approaching battle, and to tell Ming Tsun what he must do.

But Ming Tsun most assuredly did not wish to accommodate himself to Frost's order. "You fight this British. I must fight with you," he signed frantically as Frost opened the locker where his cutlass and pistols were kept, drew out the walnut case that contained the brace of pistols and their accouterments, and bent to the task of unscrewing the barrels of the turn-off-fire, double-barreled pistols manufactured by John Bass of London.

Frost was very, very tired, though not so tired he could not admire the ingenuity of the single-trigger, single-hammer design of the Bass pistols, with the frizzen extending across the barrels in front of the rectangular pan, nor forget the man who had made them a gift. Captaine Albert Tonneau, of the French East Indiaman *Ponte de Noyon*, philosophically drinking champagne on the quarterdeck of his mortally wounded ship when Frost had found the vessel impaled on a reef north of Madagascar during a voyage to China, whose captain, crew, and some cargo he had taken off to Mauritius. When had that been? '71? Frost could not be sure, though the Bass pistols had been comforts, coming in quite handy several times since. He had idly wondered on more than one occasion how a Frenchman had come to be in possession of this marvelous pair of British pistols.

"You shall obey my orders," Frost signed impatiently. He was proceeding with the loading of the double-barreled pistols very methodically, reflecting as he did so that he held the lives of four men in his hands. At least four men. The heavy, lightly engraved brass knobs on the butts made excellent clubs. The engraving on one butt was mildly distorted from a fierce blow of some nature. Frost could not recall how that had happened.

"I know no place in battle but with you," Ming Tsun signed in agitated protest.

"No more!" Frost gestured angrily. "If we prevail, the honor is yours for your constancy as if it were mine." He paused, searching carefully for the right combination of signs, the right expression: "If we do not prevail, we shall be taken prisoners, those who do not die in the engagement. And rather than be prisoners and share the fate of Marcus Whipple, it becomes us to die. If we are to die, it is meet that the Britisher shall likewise die. The Britisher knows our business. Therefore he knows the business of all that comes to the River Piscataqua."

Frost thought briefly of the letter from a Lieutenant Barker, John Barker, of the King's Own Regiment, the 4th, describing the British retreat from Lexington and Concord on the 19th April—scarce a year ago. The letter to Barker's family had been reprinted in a dog-eared copy of the *Gentleman's Magazine* dated in late 1775 that Frost had found in Fort Montagu. He recalled a particular passage vividly: "We were now obliged to force almost every house on the road, for the Rebels had taken possession of them and galled us exceedingly. All that were found in the houses were put to death."

"My place . . ." Ming Tsun began signing fiercely.

"Is where I tell you your place is!" Frost shouted, instantly sorry, crossing hurriedly to Ming Tsun's side, placing a hand on the man's shoulder. "It is joss."

"Yes," Ming Tsun signed, reluctantly, "it is joss."

Frost finished the careful loading of the powder and ball into their chambers, screwed in the barrels to their witness marks, and placed the muzzle wrench back in the walnut case. Loading the Bass double-barreled pistols took such a long time that reloading in the thick of a battle was out of the question. But these gifts from Captaine A. Tonneau were as near proof against the wet as pistols could be. Frost was thinking of Caleb Mansfield and the double-barreled rifle he called Gideon. It was going to be a desperate set-to. Frost hoped the commander of the British sloop-o-war did not foresee it. "Please fetch my sword," he signed to Ming Tsun.

Actually, it was not a true sword, but a common stirrup-hilted sea service hanger with a twenty-nine-inch single-fullered blade Frost had purchased in Mombasa when the threat of a typhoon had found him too close inshore to run for sea room and forced him to seek shelter for *Salmon* in that ancient Portuguese and Arab harbor. The crabby old armorer, from the north of Portugal, who would never again lay eyes on Trans os Montes in this life, had soldered and pinned a thin strip of brass from the ricasso down the top and sides of the blade to the point where the concave blade was sharpened. An opponent's blade would catch, not slide, in the softer brass, giving Frost a greater purchase to parry or deflect an opposing blade.

Frost settled the cutlass carriage over his shoulder and opened another drawer to lift out the eprouvette, a powder tester that resembled a pistol though it had no barrel, only a small cylinder with a spring-loaded, toothed wheel. He cocked the hammer and snapped the piece; the flint sheared a satisfying shower of sparks off the frizzen steel. Incongruously, the shower of sparks brought to mind a line from the *Iliad*. Frost frowned in concentration, trying to recall the gist of it. Yes, he recalled the phrase now. It was Hector addressing his wife, Andromache, on the eve of Hector's foreordained battle with Achilles: "The painful thought of you, when some bronze-armed Achaean leads you off weeping, robbing your day of freedom; and in Argos you weave at the loom of another." Like Hector, Frost's own fate weighed less heavily on him than the fate of his ship and all its company.

Frost handed the eprouvette to Ming Tsun, who took it reluctantly. "You shall go to the magazine before the cannons fire," he signed, the sharp jerk of his hands making a statement, not a question.

"Yes," Ming Tsun signed submissively.

There was nothing more to be said, so Frost carefully put the Bass pistols back in their case, glanced at the barometer, and went to the berth deck by way of the quarterdeck so he could verify the weather. The wind that had moderated to eight knots when Frost had gone below earlier had increased to above ten knots and was still out of the southeast. He judged visibility was a quarter of a mile.

The berth deck was dimly lighted by two whale oil lanterns; Frost stooped his head and shoulders in the cramped 'tween decks. Struan Ferguson had crowded in all the crew, even the eight sick Massachusetts men. "The British sloop is little more than a mile in front of us," Frost said without preamble. "She is unaware of our presence, though she has run back to her picquet to keep vessels from entering or leaving the Piscataway. I intend to engage her within the hour."

The men standing shoulder-to-shoulder in the berth deck were too surprised to say anything.

"This fight is not of our making. I would heartily leave it for another but am forced to it whilst the Britisher is the stopper in our river." Frost continued hurriedly so that no man could interrupt. " 'Tis plain some Tory has shared out our cruize, and this fellow would like nothing better than to see us all in irons and the prison hulks in Halifax. But more to our notion is the fact the Britisher strangles our families' livelihoods whilst this vessel advances so grave a threat."

No one had found his voice yet, so Frost continued in a rush, his voice rising: "He outnumbers us two to one—at least two to one." He did not say that Struan's and his best guess was the odds were more akin to three to one. "But he expects us not, cannons bowsed, no slow match alight, so we fall upon him like the veritable furies and overwhelm!"

There were several slow, affirmative nods of heads, and Frost continued: "No one here misdoubts that a New Hampshire man, a Massachusetts man, a Maine man," Frost paused and looked at the two freed black men standing uneasily in the second rank, Cato and Scripio Africanus, who had come to him from the rag-tag of Massachusetts men rejected by Commodore Esek Hopkins, "and freed men can outfight a dozen Britishers . . ."

A hoot from somewhere in the dim recesses of the berth deck: "What be of Verdmont men . . . ?"

"Of course Verdmont men, I was just coming to them," Frost shouted thankfully, putting the name to the voice: "John Cavendish. You would not let me finish, though I, by all rights, should have named Verdmont men first since we all know what Ethan Allen and his boys did at Fort Ty." Appreciative chuckles from a few men, and Frost knew he was beginning to get the crew behind him. "Now, we crack on some sail, our advantage in this southeast breeze, come up behind the Britisher, at the last moment wear ship, rake her decks from astern with our two long nines, fall back on his quarter, board, and she strikes as easily as kiss my hand! By tomorrow night you'll all be home, feet under your own tables, with your darling ones close around, planning how to spend the money this prize'll bring!"

"All respect, Capt'n," from a voice Frost did not recognize, "but since this British fella is a'headin' to the Piscataway, why don't we come about and head where he ain't? What's fer the need to fight this fella?" The anonymous voice was not disrespectful, but it held fear. Frost guessed the voice belonged to one of the Massachusetts men.

"A fair question," Frost responded. "Coming up hard on us from the south is the British frigate *Roebuck*, with double the men and metal of this sloop-o-war with the cat's figurehead . . ."

"Aye," another anonymous voice broke in, "that be the sail to southard seen afore the squall struck."

"Yes," Frost said quickly to capitalize on the advantage the second anonymous voice had unknowingly provided, "the two British warships have been seeking to pinch us between them. The choice is ours. We can fight the cat or we can fight the frigate *Roebuck*. Or if we delay getting into the Piscataway, we could find ourselves fighting both of them. What is your pleasure, gentlemen? Fight a frigate of forty-four guns when she has had time to clear and make ready to engage us, or fall upon a sloop-o-war unprepared to receive us? For fight the one or the other we must!"

Young Hannibal Bowditch stepped out of the gaggle of men, doffing his cap: "Three cheers for Capt'n Frost!"

Frost threw up his hands in quick protest: "Nay, I beg you. We are so close to the British a cheer could carry to them. Morning watch on deck to increase sail as the first mate calls. Everyone else remains on this deck. See to the careful loading of your pieces. Arms and cutlasses will be served out immediately. No priming, however. I believe Carpenter Brandon or one of his mates can find a whetstone for those wishing to touch up the edge of a cutlass. Mister Plaisted!"

"Sir!" Slocum Plaisted spoke, identifying where he stood among the men.

"You and the sailmaker cut yard-long ribbands of sailcloth, sufficient for every man to make several turns around his right arm to identify our band. Massachusetts men! I intend sending every able seaman onto the decks of the Britisher! Immediately prior to boarding we shall sweep her decks with our swivels. What say you, may I count on you to serve the swivel guns?"

"Aye, aye," a few muffled voices responded. "We shan't be left out!"

"Right! Mister Ferguson, your morning watch on deck, shake out two reefs in the tops'ls, maintain this tack and we'll run right up the sternpost of the Britisher! Caleb, get the swivels on deck, under canvas carefully, but first instruct the Massachusetts men in their loading. Mind you all the strip of cloth that identifies us!"

"A tot of rum, Capt'n, a gill, no more?" someone called from the rear ranks. Frost placed the name by the voice.

"Solomon Bright, supposing your dear mother from Berwick were to hear you pleading for a dram when you might meet your Maker with the reek of rum on your breath, and knowing that a tot might mean a misjudgment in your aim; would she be proud of you or no?"

"No, I reckon not, Capt'n," answered an abased Bright.

"But strong tots all around once you've taken the British, Solomon. From the stores of Jamaica rum the British carries! My word on it!"

And this time Frost could not stop the men from cheering. No one had asked how he could possibly know the Britisher was a mile or so ahead of the *Salmon*. Had he been asked, Frost could not have answered. But he *knew*.

✸ ✸ ✸ ✸ ✸ ROST AND STRUAN FERGUSON WERE
✸ F ✸ ON DECK, PEERING ANXIOUSLY INTO
✸   ✸ THE SEA FOG. TOPMEN HAD SHAKEN
✸ ✸ ✸ ✸ ✸ OUT TWO REEFS IN THE MAIN AND
fore topsails, and *Salmon* was fairly protesting as she ploughed
through the wave crests, shouldering them aside, spray flying
high enough to touch the leech of the fore mainsail. She was
rolling heavily, her headway close on to five knots as nearly as
Frost could judge. Frost grabbed Hannibal Bowditch by his
collar as the youth, attempting to give Frost a wide berth, scurried past. "Mister Bowditch, you shall take the helm with me,
and we shall put our *Salmon* fair against the British cat. Once
our hulls touch you are to lay below to my cabin and there assist Mister Green. Do you ken?"

"I can heft a cutlass, sir! I beg to go with you onto the British decks." The lad was crestfallen.

"The long nine in my cabin will assist our *Salmon* more,
Mister Bowditch. She will need to add her voice to the din as
oft as possible. Mister Green will require your assistance to
swab out, load and fire. I shall depend upon you."

"Aye, sir!" Hannibal said with more enthusiasm. "I'm to repair below to assist Mister Green in keeping up a hot fire once
you and I lay our *Salmon* against this British fellow."

Frost marked the youngster's proud use of the phrase "you
and I" and tried not to smile. The safest place for the lad was
below the waterline, even in the steerage, though Frost did not

want to send Hannibal there with the corpses of Hugh Eliot and John Weliever. Frost had already forgotten Weliever's nickname. John Weliever, not someone named "Slobber," had died for Geoffrey Frost, the *Salmon*, and the Frost Trading Company. He had not died for any abstract theory such as liberty or freedom from unjust taxation.

And young Bowditch might twig to the fact that Frost was trying to secure him a place of safety if ordered to the lowest deck, though in truth there was no place of safety on the *Salmon*, not with Ming Tsun dispatched to the makeshift magazine stacked with the few precious barrels of powder brought away from New Providence. Inside the hour all that might still swim of the *Salmon*, and the cat also, could well be shattered, burned planks, wadded, waterlogged sails, cordage and corpses.

Better a swift death and natural burial in the cold, clean sea than the bleak prospect of years in prison hulks as an ungrateful, detestable rebel against his sovereign in the eyes of his captors, with no hope of exchange. Frost reminded himself of the carnage wrought on helpless Falmouth by Mowat and HM *Canceaux* and quietly acknowledged his willingness to die before being taken prisoner and following his brother-in-law to the living death of the Halifax prison hulks. Of course, Frost also acknowledged that he would be taking the lives of his own crew, and he had not consulted them. Joss. If his had been the iron command of a duly commissioned naval vessel, Frost would not have had to cajole, even shame, his crew, his uneducated, trusting, suspicious, superstitious, untrained, and mostly untried crew, into fighting. He would have given the necessary commands and expected to be obeyed. Frost shrugged. Whether he achieved his ends by an aura of invincible authority or an appeal to the practical self-interests of his crew, the result would be the same.

Frost had no way of knowing where the *Roebuck* was, or what condition she was in after being ravaged by the squall. Perhaps the *Roebuck* no longer swam. Frost had seen more than one vessel carrying too much sail driven under during a blow. But lacking knowledge of her position and condition, Frost had to assume *Roebuck* was near and ready to engage.

No one in his crew, Frost included, had any experience fighting the well-drilled and seasoned crew of a heavily armed warship. Fending off Dyak pirates in the South China Sea was an encounter of a vastly different nature. His was a desperate plan, but it was a plan, and Frost intended to carry it through. Given the fact that they would come upon the British warship suddenly when she was unprepared for an engagement, Frost would have opted to fight the *Roebuck* were she the vessel ahead of them. The thought caused Frost's heart to constrict. Suppose the shako he had seen momentarily on the crest of a wave had been that of a marine aboard the *Roebuck*? He shrugged the thought aside.

"Mister Ferguson, you may order up the swivels, if you please. Please distribute the sailcloth ribbands Mister Plaisted has obtained from the sailmaker." Frost searched the deck for Ming Tsun. His best friend was nowhere in sight. Good! Ming Tsun, the only person Frost could entirely depend upon to carry out his order, was at his appointed place.

"Mister Green, I would be obliged if you would fetch me the pistols from the case in my cabin. Then return to my cabin, where you may knock out the stern lights.

"Caleb! You and Gideon to the mainmast cap. You will doubtlessly observe the cat's officers on her quarterdeck. If they have the scope of their sovereign's desires, no man of New England would ever walk free in our forests with a fine flintlock rifle, nay, even a crude musket, in his hand. Which means that no man could really be free of the king's displeasure. You ken how the British General Gage sequestered all civilian arms when the lobsterbacks invested Boston! Over two thousand firelocks of divers kinds, even the ancient blunderbuss, all deposited in Faneuil Hall and forfeited to the Crown! Select her officers, and may your aim be true."

"I 'spect it'll be, 'cuz me 'n' Gideon got scores to settle for Hugh and Slobber." Caleb Mansfield carefully wrapped a protective strip of soft, well-tanned buckskin around the locks of his double-barreled rifle.

"His name was John Weliever," Frost said softly.

"Aye," Caleb said, "that it wuz. I had forgotten it, but alus ol' John wanted wuz a pipe against a warm fireside after the end of a cruize, a wife he alus gabbed about, though probably never appreciated . . ." Caleb broke off, shrugged, and spat to leeward. "He wuz such a bad hand at cards that I wuz goin' to give him back the twenty Spanish dollars I won off him. No so fer Hugh. He wuz a right cove, he wuz, played his cards well."

Roger Green was at Frost's elbow, with the two double-barreled pistols, butts extended. Frost took them and thrust them into his belt. "Mister Ferguson, without her fore starboard truck, this long nine is going to buck worse than Parson Whipple's mule when we lay fire to her, but no matter, we shall be within fifty feet of the cat when we fire. Mister Green! As soon as you hear my shot, discharge your cannon loaded with langrage upward as high as the piece can be elevated into the Britisher's riggings—mind you stay well clear of the carriage's vicious recoil—then sponge out and reload with langrage so long as you can. I regret that I cannot provide you with a crew other than Mister Bowditch, so of necessity your fire will be slow."

Roger Green smiled happily as he said "Aye, sir" and turned away. Frost did not smile, but at least young Green had not twigged to the fact that by the time he and Hannibal Bowditch could possibly reload the long nine and tug the carriage back into battery, a task they might accomplish in ten minutes, the *Salmon* and the cat would have been held side against side almost that length of time by grapples. There was no way the aft-facing long nine in his cabin could possibly be brought to bear on any part of the British warship. And before that ten minutes had elapsed, the fates of both vessels and the men who sailed in them would be determined.

Frost had fleetingly thought of detailing Cook Barnes to keep an eye on the two boys, but Barnes was keen to board the cat, and he was a prodigious scrapper despite the loss of his left hand. He had lost it in a long forgotten and unremarked sea fight. And Frost needed every man he could put aboard the cat. He thought of Ming Tsun: as Struan had said, it was impossible to ascribe a value to Ming Tsun as a fighter. Was he doing the right thing by ordering Ming Tsun to stand by in the powder magazine? Would not Ming Tsun's skills be better utilized in the boarding party? Frost knew the first terrible gnawing of doubt. "No!" he told himself fiercely, "Ming Tsun is the only person on this planet I can trust to do the difficult task I have set him." Joss.

"Mister Ferguson, I trust you won't mind leading the first party aboard the cat from our waist. I'll handle the helm until we are fair alongside, though at least four men in the starboard bow with grapples to throw across and tie off would be much appreciated. Discharge the swivel guns into the British on the foredeck and waist. In·truct the Massachusetts men who shall serve the swivels to direct their fire accordingly. With any luck, every jack soul on the quarterdeck will have departed this life with our cannon fire. I shall join you over the taff rail. When we meet on her quarterdeck, the cat will be ours!"

Struan Ferguson shifted his grip on his targe, like the backsword his only legacy from his father, and pulled the massive, thirty-eight-inch blade from its sheath to slice the air in quick, massive strokes. The air fairly moaned with the sword's vicious passage. Struan had told Frost the history of the backsword only once. His father had been isolated on the rain- and grapeshot-swept, bloody moor, back against a tumble of rocks from the thrown-down Culloden Park enclosures, his only armament the targe and great double-handed claymore handed down through three generations of Fergusons, as he fought to preserve his clan colors from capture by Cumberland's highlander allies.

Only after the seventh bayonet had pierced his body had Struan's father fallen dead, but not before he had broken the great blade between two stones to prevent its capture intact— and skewered two highlander traitors with the bit of shattered blade still attached to the hilt. After Struan's sister had fetched the targe and broken blade from the battlefield at the price of her maidenhead and then her life, Struan had a Scottish armorer grind down one edge and fit a fishtail grip with a basket hilt. A portion of the name of the ancient Venetian blacksmith who had wrought the blade, *Andrea Ferara*, was still visible.

"My father's blade has nae tasted English blood since '46; it thirsts for English blood as I thirst for vengeance. It is a good plan, Captain. Isolate the quarterdeck, seize it, and the cat must strike to us. We carry surprise as great an asset as our arms!"

"Aye," Frost thought grimly to himself. "Just to happen fortuitously upon the British warship in this sea and this fog, your only peg that she's even near a British marine's shako, perhaps lost when a seasick marine vomited overside, glimpsed quickly, mayhap too quickly, atop a wave's crest. Which, soon waterlogged, should have sunk within ten minutes of the shako's being whipped from the hapless marine aboard the cat, but which you saw and upon which, intuitively, you staked all." He hoped devoutly that his judgment was wrong, that the British warship was nowhere near the Isles of Shoals, and that the approaches to the Ports of Piscataqua were open and unguarded. He did not, in truth, relish going up against a sloop-o-war mounting at least eighteen six-pounder cannons and a veteran crew.

Frost's attention wandered as his peripheral vision caught Caleb Mansfield climbing the mainmast ratlines toward the mast cap. "God, Jesus and Mary, El Senhor, the Great Buddha —may I be wrong and the cat a dozen and more leagues away and a quick run from the Shoals as I've done many and many a time square for the Piscataqua, and by midnight, depending on the tide, my feet under a proper table which doesn't pitch and smite the dishes." And just as Frost dared hope he might indeed gain home as easy as kiss my hand, the lookout in the mainmast crosstrees called down loudly and excitedly: "There! Comin' up in the fog! That dam' Britisher!"

And there was the cat, a ghost vessel just visible in the fog's heavy vapors, little more than a quarter mile away. "Mister Ferguson! Reefs out of mizzen, main and fore tops'ls, jib sheeted home!" Courses brailed up for better visibility from the deck;

never mind if the tops'ls and jib blew out—Frost needed a quick burst of speed, for no matter how unexpected, *Salmon*'s sudden appearance would galvanize the cat's sea-hardened crew into immediate action. Or had the cat's captain somehow deduced *Salmon*'s nearness, or taken the precautions of having cannons loaded and ready to run out, slow match alight, even if it meant tedium and fatigue for a crew long standing-to? In any event, the cat's captain would expect *Salmon* to flee, not fly directly toward him.

Topmen already aloft shook out reef points on the tops'ls, and *Salmon* surged faster, vehemently protesting this unkind and most unusual treatment, heeling to larboard, the lee rail driving under momentarily and a great wall of greenish-gray water curling, rolling, exploding toward the quarterdeck, which broke it and shrugged it off in a fine, high shower of spray. Then the old *Salmon* steadied, sails straining to the edge of endurance, cracking like cannon shots momentarily as the rushes of turbulent air snapped them into full draw.

Frost ordered his bosun, who had relieved the two helmsmen, to steer directly for the cat's stern post. He hazarded a quick glance at the cat through his telescope and saw nothing but confusion on the British quarterdeck as the cat's lookout shrilled *Salmon*'s sudden appearance. The gap between *Salmon* and the cat was narrowing rapidly, much more rapidly than Frost preferred. *Salmon* had gone from a laboring four knots, accelerated through five, and now was exceeding six knots in the bare half minute since her unreefed tops'ls bellied taut. Judging when to put the helm up or down, and whether it should be lee helm or weather helm, were difficult equations calling for immediate solutions.

Young Bowditch had joined Slocum Plaisted at the helm. A sudden spate of half sleet, half rain slanted in from the southeast, drumming against taut canvas. "Mind your linstocks!" Frost shouted. If he guessed correctly, no slow match was glowing anywhere on the British, and no broadside could bear on him at this approach. Deciding, as the gap between the vessels narrowed to one hundred yards, Frost shouted: "Up helm!

Give her a good rap full!" Plaisted and young Bowditch spun the wheel smartly, rudder biting firmly into the turbulent, sleet-laced sea. At the same time, hands let go the weather breast backstays, and the sheets on the mizzenmast driver were hauled taut, pulling *Salmon*'s bows violently to starboard as she pivoted abruptly on her rudder. The wind from the southeast collapsed the starboard clews and leeches of tops'ls, flailing them against their masts, the sudden torque forcing their yards around in a quarter-circle as *Salmon* continued to pivot, though slower now, around her rudder until she fell off, bows directly into the wind, sails slanting, protesting, then partially filling from the front, driving *Salmon* backward.

Frost faintly heard the shatter of glass, a chair through the stern lights of his cabin. He hoped it had not been the ivory and ebony chair purchased on his first voyage to China as *Salmon*'s master. He crouched with Angus Wyeth, who held the smoldering slow match, sighting down the long nine as the wind continued to push *Salmon* stern-to.

"Center helm!" Frost called, frantically directing Wyeth to make a few adjustments with his handspike. *Salmon* was not thirty yards from the cat's larboard side. "Stand clear the gun—fire!" and Angus Wyeth stabbed the slow match onto the touchhole, which had been covered with its leather apron, now whipped aside, and the long nine recoiled as viciously as the rattlesnake on the flag that *Salmon* flew. The carriage overturned violently for lack of a starboard truck on the forward axle, but the breeching rope snubbed the cannon. Frost never heard the muzzle's blast. "Down helm!" Frost shouted, and as the bows continued their turn to starboard in obedience to the rudder and the *Salmon*'s considerable momentum, the foresails filled with a rush, followed by the tops'ls' yards ratcheting around as they began to draw again.

"Mister Bowditch! Lay below to your station!" Frost commanded, and jumped to assist Slocum Plaisted at the wheel. A glance at the cat showed furrows gouged out of the quarter-deck bulwark, no helmsmen standing to her wheel, and the mizzen plainly wounded, but altogether less damage than Frost had hoped. "Helm up smartly," Frost said to Plaisted, and the obedient rudder acted as the fulcrum around which *Salmon*'s stern began to rotate slowly to starboard. The deck beneath Frost's feet trembled as the nine-pounder in his cabin bellowed, but Frost could not see where that shot struck the cat.

"Struan! Swivels to fire as they bear!" From above, Frost heard Gideon's sharp crack and saw a sailor running for the British warship's wheel fall in midstride. All eight swivel guns fired, langrage flicking like whips along the cat's gun deck, and then *Salmon*'s starboard stern quarter touched heavily with a crunch and heavy jarring impact of timbers just forward of the cat's larboard stern quarter light. Struan Ferguson and fifteen men were on the lee rail, poised, then leaped the four feet and slightly down onto the British gun deck. The shock of their contact forced *Salmon*'s stern to rebound quickly away from the cat; the gap between the ships widening quickly so that additional boarders could not follow Struan.

"Helm up! Helm up!" Frost shouted across the wheel to Plaisted, hoping the rudder had not been damaged. "Grapples there!" And a few grapples flew across the ten feet of water between *Salmon* and the cat, one of them catching in the cat's weather shrouds and pulling free when strain came on the line, the others draping across the cat's larboard bulwark. A British sailor brandishing an axe charged one grapple, and Frost, sighting hastily, discharged one barrel, noting as from a great distance the sailor's tarpaulin hat falling away at the sudden jerk of the man's head.

Salmon's starboard quarter was pivoting away from the cat, tug of wind and the hull's momentum stretching the grapple lines, then snapping them like so much thread. Over the fifteen feet of water now separating the two vessels Frost saw a gunner at one of the six-pounders on the cat's raised quarterdeck, muzzle pointing directly toward him, lowering a linstock. He fired the second barrel from the Bass pistol and the gunner fell back, though another man seized the linstock and scarce a second later a cannon ball smashed through the *Salmon*'s mizzen-mast's sixteen inches of stout New Hampshire pine three feet above the deck in a shower of splinters. Frost had thrown himself on the deck, pulling Angus Wyeth and Slocum Plaisted down with him as soon as he saw the linstock descend the second time. The shower of deadly splinters blown out of the mast at the ball's impact passed just over them.

"Axes! Broadaxes here!" Frost shouted, regaining his feet. The mizzen was sorely wounded but shrouds and stays resolutely held it upright. The wind had pivoted the vessels by their sterns like weathercocks and the cat's sails now blanketed *Salmon*'s, preventing their draw, though the cat was turning hard to starboard and the gap between the vessels was widening. Frost glimpsed Struan Ferguson's mighty backsword flashing, blade well bloodied, and knew Struan was keening a fierce Scot's war cry, though Frost did not hear it because at least two, perhaps three, of the six-pounders in the cat's larboard waist discharged into the *Salmon*'s starboard stern quarter.

"Axes! Axes here!" Frost shouted again, and men with broadaxes were beside him now on *Salmon*'s quarterdeck. "Cut away the mizzen, fell it onto the cat's deck!" Somehow the *Salmon*'s mainsail's starboard yard had tangled in lines flailing from the cat's riggings, momentarily keeping the gap between vessels from widening, slightly pulling down what was now the cat's lee rail. Other six-pounders in the cat's waist fired, their barrels raised to maximum elevation to account for the angle, and *Salmon*'s starboard rail disappeared in a massive gout of flung balks of timber and splinters. The man wielding an axe beside Frost, Mather Goodell from York, fell across the shattered pedestal, all that was left of the wheel. Frost caught up the axe and attacked the tottering mizzenmast.

There! The mizzenmast, with mizzen topmast yard and gaff yard and sails furled and unfurled, its weight taking its main and mizzen topmast length of seventy-two feet wrenching through the protest of standing riggings, angling down onto the cat between her fore and mainmasts, catching in the spider's web of riggings, holding. Two more of the cat's waist cannons fired, converging, striking the *Salmon*'s mainmast and buckling it. Frost glanced up, searching for Caleb. Caleb, braced securely against the doubling, one foot pressing against the futtock shrouds through the lubber hole, was calmly reloading his rifle, shoulders hunched to protect his powder from a fresh blast of rain and sleet.

Eyes stinging from the sleet, Frost attacked the tangled cordage of *Salmon*'s starboard mizzen shrouds with the axe, wanting the broken mizzenmast to settle more. A musket ball struck the side of the axe, knocking it from Frost's grasp, the blow temporarily stinging and numbing his wrists and elbows. Slowly, grudgingly, the cat's riggings tore and parted under the mast's weight, and the mast settled heavily across the cat's larboard rail. With his unfired double-barreled pistol thrust in his belt and his cutlass gripped in his left hand, Frost jumped up onto the slippery mizzen and began working his way through the tangle of riggings and sailcloth, the round, sixteen-inch-diameter mast rolling and sawing backward and forward as the two vessels wallowed and tossed on the sleet-filled sea.

Frost was dimly aware of a marine on the cat's deck not ten feet away now aiming a musket at him. Frost felt his testicles withering, shrinking into his groin, and the eel of abject fear slithering in his belly—"I have to go on," he reminded himself fiercely, "I don't have to come back"—as he waited, seemingly forever, for the shock of the bullet that would topple him off the mast. He pushed on against the fear, despite the fear—then the snap of hammer, the puff of smoke from the priming pan, something plucking swiftly at the shoulder of his coat, almost knocking him from the mast, and then gone, and he turned briefly to shout back to his own deck, "*Salmon*s! With me!" Slashing with his cutlass at a tangle of rope that impeded his progress, again almost falling from the slippery mast, he caught himself on the gaff spar, then leapt down onto the cat's gun deck between two six-pounders, hands groping and tearing at him.

The cat's men were everywhere, densely crowded together, and there was scarcely room to employ a weapon. He came down savagely with the hilt of his cutlass against one hand, smashing the hand against the cold, wet, hard barrel of a cannon, and then he pivoted his blade ninety degrees and thrust at the throat of another nameless, faceless sailor, and the blade went in—seemingly effortlessly, though it took a fierce backward jerk to pull the blade free.

An overpowering presence, foul breath and body stench sharp and rank above the stink of burned powder, assaulted Frost as the tip of a marine's bayonet thrust toward him. He parried it aside with his cutlass and brought up the double-barreled pistol in his right hand, cocking the lock with his thumb and thanking his joss for the well-corned French powder in the priming pan as the flint sparked and the indistinct face behind the bayonetted musket, mouth forming an "O" and indistinct obscenities, snapped back. The heavy, malleable lead slug entered between the marine's eyes, flattened with the soft tissues' contact, and carried away the rear of the his skull in a brief, bright fountain of gore.

Another marine behind Frost dropped a musket over Frost's head, hauling it taut in both hands against Frost's chest, pinning his arms so that he was unable to raise either cutlass or pistol as another marine, indistinguishable from the one he had just killed, drew back his bayonetted musket for a murderous stroke. Knowing the thrust was coming, Frost focused on the mainmast, splinted with sweeps and gammoned with chain, behind the marine, comprehending for the first time why the cat could not be driven to her capabilities. Her mainmast was sore! Cocking his knee to propel himself backward, but also steeling himself for the bayonet's thrust into his chest, which would end his life in a few short, blood-foamed seconds if he could not outrace it, he saw an arrow bury itself to its fletching in the marine's throat just below the Adam's apple. The musket was cast away as the marine's hands flew to his throat in an instinctive, futile, spasmodic reaction, to fumble at the slender shaft of wood that had severed his spinal cord and purchased his death before his body collapsed to the cat's deck.

The momentum from Frost's cocked knee carried the marine who gripped him backward sharply against the bulwark. The marine grunted as his grip was broken and ducked as

Frost brought his right elbow up into the marine's windpipe, wrenched the musket askew and thrust his cutlass blade into the man's torso, smelling what the man had eaten for breakfast. Frost levered the still living, quivering body aside with the flat of his blade, sucking the blade free and keening his own war song, the blood lust upon him as it had last been in the Sunda Strait, when the Javanese pirates had attacked *Salmon* at night. Though there were considerably more British now than there had been Javanese then, or so it seemed as Frost threw up his pistol, remembering to slide the button that uncovered the right pan, and shot a gunner charging at him with a rammer. He turned to face another seaman with a pike, though this seaman had dropped the pike and was staring helplessly at the arrow that blossomed like a deadly flower from his chest.

Struan's cry, "Geoffrey—for the love of God!" galvanized Frost as he parried a bayonet's thrust with his cutlass, then slashed the marine behind the musket with the knob of his pistol, followed by a slash to the side of the man's head. He bulled into the back of another British, thrusting him forward with his blade to gain a moment of respite in the maelstrom of noise, sleet, smoke and fear.

"Struan!"

"Here!"

Frost easily blocked an ill-aimed pike, grasped the staff of the pike and drew the pikeman, screaming, onto the point of his cutlass. And then, above the insane hubbub of noise, Frost heard a voice roaring, booming, a north country voice that could only be Caleb Mansfield's: "*Salmon*s! Down!" Frost immediately went to deck, grasping the man he had just gutted by the collar as he twisted out his cutlass, the man's body partially draped over Frost, as two or three of *Salmon*'s swivel guns fired simultaneously into the writhing mass of men struggling on the cat's gun deck. A vicious scythe of langrage bowled over anyone standing upright in the confined space between fore and mainmasts, including, Frost realized when he pushed the dead pikeman aside and staggered to his feet, one George Adams, a Kittery man whom Frost recalled to be above average deaf. He lay dead on the deck in front of Frost, his head and torso pocked with multiple red craters.

"Struan!"

"Here!" The voice came from less than ten feet away, though the press of bodies that had appeared quickly in front of and around Frost was so dense it seemed to form an impenetrable palisade. He was treading on a fallen marine whose hands still clutched a musket; Frost stuck the point of his cutlass in the deck and fumbled up the musket, the press of bodies so dense against him he could not extend the musket but fired with the lock under his arm, the man immediately in front of him falling away in a horrible slow motion, but no time to see; he reversed the musket and used it as a club, laying about him with the savagery of blood lust. Frost's lips formed a keening that he knew, though he could not hear it, was consonant with Struan's own war cry. He struck, battering with the musket until the stock went splintering away from the barrel, propelling the barrel behind him with a quick thrust into what he knew instinctively had to be the belly of a sailor ready to cut him down, feeling the barrel's muzzle jab deeply into flesh, but not bothering, not daring to take the time to look behind him.

Frost plucked his cutlass from the deck and wielded it double-handed, doing grim execution on the press of men around Struan, until he broke through their circle just as another swivel from *Salmon* poured an evil sleet of musket balls and chopped nails into the cat's crew gathered around the mainmast.

God and the Sweet Infant and the Holy Apostles and Allah All Great, but Frost was weary; his arms weighed more than lead and his coat sleeves to the elbows were dull red with blood. His palms were slippery with the lives of the half-dozen British sailors and marines he had slain in less than two minutes, but then he was leaping over the last sailor his cutlass had struck down, partially decapitated, to stand with Struan Ferguson. Suddenly almost everyone's arm paused in whatever deadly work was within its compass as a despairing keen—like nothing on earth, a cry ululating from a throat with no tongue, and whose despair was all the more poignant for it—rang out, and a fearsome cannon ball of a man leaped off *Salmon*'s shattered mizzenmast into the carnage on the cat's deck. The man immediately laid about him with a short, terribly sharp and wicked halberd.

Ming Tsun! Ming Tsun began clearing a path toward Frost using the graceful, seemingly slow but nevertheless swift, almost choreographed strokes and parries of the classic *wu dang* Chinese swordfighting art that Frost so admired and that Ming Tsun had tried to teach him, though to no avail. Frost's peripheral vision deciphered movement, and he turned to deflect the sword blade of a Royal Navy lieutenant, or so the man's blue coat, with its white facings and cuffs, white waistcoat and breeches, proclaimed him to be; the man's bright red hair, unrestrained by a tricorne, shone startlingly bright against the pallor of his face. Frost looked directly into the man's small and lusterless eyes, did not mistake the intense hatred and guile pooled there, and bore the lieutenant's rapier to the deck. He trod upon the blade, snapping it, and then viciously, with all his strength, smashed his cutlass's hilt into the lieutenant's face. Another sailor rushed at him; Frost clubbed him down with the side of his cutlass, then two marines wielding muskets pressed him backwards, the marines treading heavily upon the bodies of the lieutenant and the sailor.

Ming Tsun had joined Struan, and they attacked the two marines from behind, both falling instantly, decapitated, by strokes from Ming Tsun's halberd and Struan's backsword. A musket, no, a pistol discharged close to Frost's head, further deafening him, though he still heard a cannon fire behind him —another cannon ball into his *Salmon*; at least one of the cat's cannons was still in action.

John Nason was drawn into their small company, and Struan plucked a dazed topman, John Olson from Eliot, out of the tangle of bodies on which they were treading. A British sailor armed with a cocked pistol appeared behind Ming Tsun, aiming at his unprotected back, and Frost cried a warning, the knowledge dismal in the pit of his stomach that it would come too late, but the pistol never discharged, the sailor sagging, neatly skewered in the throat by a well-aimed thrust from Slocum Plaisted's pike. Frost prised the unfired pistol from the sailor's hand and shot a marine five paces away who was just bringing a musket to shoulder.

Frost heard the faint bang of a swivel gun, followed by the bellow of a cat's waist gun, and then a slight noise, barely perceptible through the ringing and chirping in his ears, but enough to cause him to glance upward for a moment, a slash of rain streaking the blood and softening the spittle caked on his lips—the cat's mainsail yard was falling, caught momentarily in a tangle of fouled cordage, but dropping . . .

"Charge the quarterdeck!" Frost shouted, amazed at the dim hoarseness, the faraway sound of his voice as he forced Struan and Ming Tsun, Plaisted and Nason against the wall of sailors between them and the quarterdeck, moving from beneath the falling yard by half a breath, the shock of the yard's fall scattering British sailors and marines, momentarily fencing them from the cat's company save for the dozen or so sailors between them and the quarterdeck. These dozen quailed before Frost and his four men; two sailors were cut down by Ming Tsun's halberd as he rushed them; another, a young lad, a very young lad, no more than ten or twelve, barefooted, dressed in a tattered jerkin and ragged duck trousers, fell to his knees and held up his hands.

Frost diverted the downward stroke of his cutlass, narrowly avoiding cleaving the youth's skull, but leaving himself open and defenseless to the cutlass thrust of a sailor. The sailor's cutlass blade grated against ribs, though, curiously, Frost felt no pain. Frost's cutlass dropped from his hand.

Struan's backsword severed the sailor's arm above the elbow. Frost grabbed the sailor by his hair and tumbled him to the deck, sprawling him atop the terrified lad. "Don't move from this spot if you value your life," he shouted at the boy as he grabbed up his fallen cutlass in his right hand. Keening his war cry, Ming Tsun's ululating war cry, even more horrible than his own, joined his, both rising above the din of bodies clashing against other bodies, the pop-pop of muskets and pistols, the shrill rasp and clang of steel against steel, and the incongruous, impartial rattle of sleet against sailcloth and wood.

Slocum Plaisted speared the last man guarding the ladder to the quarterdeck, heaving the sailor overboard when the pike stuck in the man's body and would not pull free, the pike going overside as well. He caught the cutlass Frost threw him as Plaisted flew up the ladder and immediately jumped into a lively engagement with a marine wielding a bayonetted musket with a remarkable degree of dexterity. A British sailor, a quartermaster, slashed with a cutlass at Plaisted's head, and Frost, conscious of a great froth of blood spraying around Plaisted, grabbed the marine's musket, falling backward with it. As the marine, still grasping his musket, came up to him, Frost kicked him mightily in the groin, then wrenched away the musket and clubbed him, the shock of the blow tingling up his arms.

Just ahead of him now an officer: blue coat with blue facings, cuffs and collar, trimmed with silver buttons, each bearing the proud stamp of crown and anchor; tight, drawn face framed by loose blonde hair streaming in the rain and sleet; left hand tightly pressed into his waistcoat, through which spread a horrific crimson stain; right hand, trembling right hand, extending an ivory-hilted sword toward Frost. Frost stepped over the prostrate body of the marine, reversing the musket so that the bayonet pointed at the officer. The cat's captain!

"Do you yield?" Frost shouted, staring incredulously at the man. Save for the color of the man's hair, the cat's captain was Frost's virtual twin in appearance, same height, same weight, same nose, jaw, full lips, same facial features. The man in front of him nodded faintly, not speaking. "Order your men to stop fighting," Frost commanded. The captain nodded, still proffering his sword, and Frost stepped to receive it as the captain's knees buckled, Frost moving forward to catch the man, bending at the waist, and then something sharp and hot and long lanced into his back, transfixing him with shock. The captain's ivory-hilted sword clattered to the deck and Frost fell over it, looking into the captain's sightless gaze, knowing that the man was dead, rolling over against the pain to see Ming Tsun jabbing the butt of his halberd into the belly of the lieutenant whom Frost had earlier knocked senseless, sending him to the deck.

Struan and Nason had cut down the Royal Navy's red ensign, and Ming Tsun, reversing his halberd, was poised to slash the lieutenant's throat. "No!" Frost ordered. "The Britisher has surrendered! We fight only if force is offered!"

But most of the cat's company had seen the British colors come down, and the fight, what little remained, drained out of them. Two or three isolated clashes continued for another minute or so, one cat's sailor being felled by a belaying pin accurately thrown by Hanson Nelson, an able seaman from Little Harbor. Reuben Howard, foretopman from Durham, was pinked in the arm by a marine's bayonet. But the cat's men were dropping their arms and gathering in small, sullen groups about their ship.

Slocum Plaisted bent over Frost, Plaisted's face greatly bruised and blood matting in his hair, streaking his face. Frost gained his feet, kicked away the stub of rapier with which the lieutenant had pierced him, and grabbed up the musket, thrusting its bayonet downward and through the collar of the lieutenant's coat deeply into the planking of the quarterdeck, pinning the man. He turned to face Ming Tsun, deep concern in Ming Tsun's eyes, a hand reaching out toward Frost. Frost shrugged the hand aside.

"You disobeyed my order," he said flatly, fighting the pain writhing like a serpent just below his right shoulder blade, the grimness and fire in his eyes forcing Ming Tsun to drop his arm and turn away in the sleet and rain.

"Mister Ferguson! Take command of this vessel! Relieve those men of their weapons! Get them below decks! Discover if there is a surgeon aboard!" Frost's eyes fell on Slocum Plaisted. "Mister Plaisted, transfer all weapons to our *Salmon*!" Frost pulled Slocum aside and spoke in a lower voice: "Bring our *Salmon* alongside; get every able body on *Salmon* aboard this vessel. See our men are well armed, the rest to begin clearing ship." And in a whisper, even more urgently: "Slocum, we cannot let the British know how few we are."

Something pulled on his coat, the movement of wool cloth across his wounded and scoured ribs inflaming them anew. Frost looked down into the dirty face of the waif whose life he had earlier spared.

"Beggin' pardon, sir, but surgeon's ain't no use, he's drunk in the cockpit."

"The sailor whose arm was severed . . ."

"He was my mate, sir, he be dead, sir." The urchin shrugged, his tattered jerkin smeared with his mate's blood.

"Hark you, then. Lend this fellow a hand," Frost indicated John Nason, "getting the wounded out of this weather, your company below, first deck down; mine returned to my vessel. No need carting your fellows all the way to the cockpit if your surgeon fails of assistance. Make your fellows as comfortable as you can. Rum, water if they call for it. Do you understand?"

The lad's lips quivered. "Yes, sir."

"Be there any tincture of opium on this ship?"

"Tincture . . ." the lad said uncertainly.

"Laudanum you may have heard it called." Frost replied impatiently. He had much work to see about, but duty and humanity obliged him to assist the crew of his captive as much as his own.

"There be if surgeon and his mate have not drunk all," the boy said.

"If there is a sailor you trust, send to get it. You are as able to dispense it as anyone." And then Frost stumbled his way through the barrier of horrors and deaths at the cat's waist to the tenuous bridge of *Salmon*'s fallen mizzenmast. He lacked the strength to clamber onto the mast, but then Ming Tsun was with him, and Frost allowed himself to be helped across the slippery, pitching, sleet-sheened mast and stepped wearily onto his own deck. How long ago had he left it? Ten minutes perhaps. Ten lifetimes.

Frost leaned heavily on Ming Tsun, knew he had to rest, and half sat, half reclined on a massive tangle of cordage, his back to the wind and sleet, unable to resist the weariness welling from deep within his soul, eyes closing involuntarily, then opening with a start to find himself face to face with young Bowditch.

The lad's eyes were red and swollen, and the moisture beneath his eyes came not from the sleet or rain. His forehead bore a long but shallow gash cut by a flying splinter, blood just beginning to coagulate in the corners of the wound. "Mister Green, sir," young Bowditch said through sobs. "He's dead, sir, a cannon ball coming through the hull smashed his leg. He bled out as I held his hand, but he never cried, just smiled at me, sir. He died so beautiful."

Frost laid a hand as gently as he could on the boy's shoulder. "Thank you for telling me, Mister Bowditch." He tried to feel some semblance of greater loss, of extra grief for the death of his second mate. But the loss of so many other men from *Salmon*'s company had numbed him beyond all feeling. To his certain knowledge, no one had ever died beautiful. "Mister Green died in good company," Frost said simply.

Then harshly to Ming Tsun as another gust of sleet snapped across *Salmon*'s ruined and chaotic main deck: "Bind Mister Bowditch's wounds, and then mine."

❧ VIII ❧

⚜⚜⚜⚜⚜ OMEONE WAS CALLING FROST'S NAME
⚜   ⚜ INCESSANTLY AS HE FOUGHT HIS RE-
⚜ S ⚜ LUCTANT, TROUBLED WAY UP THROUGH
⚜⚜⚜⚜⚜ THE VARIOUS DEPTHS OF SLEEP, UN-
willing to awaken, turning away sluggishly, drawing the bedclothes up to his head, trying to shut out, hide from the nagging voice. Compounding the injury, the injustice, someone
was shaking him, the movement banishing all further sleep.
Frost rolled over reluctantly, struggling to lift his right hand
toward his forehead to shield against the uncommonly piercing
light, but something entrapped his arm. A shift of weight to
throw off the covers brought twin stabs of pain, sharp and hot
as needles, in ribs and shoulder. The bedclothes were twisted
around his body, trapping his right arm—no, some cloth securely bound him.

At least his left hand was free, so Frost shaded his eyes with
his left palm, only to have his hand seized, nauseous pain radiating from Frost's shoulder, to draw him upright in bed, where
he gazed into the joyous face of his younger brother, Joseph.
"Geoff, I bear grand news! Marcus and the other New Hampshire men seized prisoners by the detestable British after the
battle on Breed's Hill have been moved from the prison hulk in
Halifax to Louisbourg!"

Frost wrested his left hand free of Joseph's grip and sank
back on the goose feather mattress, the contracting and move-

ment of muscles bringing even more pain to the area below his right shoulder blade, and then he remembered.

"Infernal joss! What am I doing abed when my ship is still unladed, and I have men to bury, men to pay off, a thousand matters held at bay which neither Rutherford nor Ferguson can ken, words with John Langdon . . ." Frost ran out of breath and coughed, the coughs rekindling the fire in his wounds. Something welled and grew thick in the back of his throat, and he hastily sought a handkerchief, hawking up a cast of dark blood, knowing that the stub of a sword blade had touched a lung.

Joseph looked at him pityingly. "Geoff, you'll not be burying men today. John Nason handled that task for you admirably —yesterday. As you know, he has aspirations to be a minister— faith, so he is, for he preached a monstrous great service about sacrifice and laying down one's life for one's brother, even though the brother was not by blood but by burden, so as he described. He preached them all right into Heaven. Reverend Nason's service was monstrously wonderful to all who heard it, and that was the whole of Portsmouth and most of Dover, Kittery, Durham and Exeter."

"What is today?" Frost asked, struggling to his feet.

"The sixteenth," Joseph answered.

"Then I have been asleep for over twenty-four hours."

"More like thirty-six. Ming Tsun gave you a potion to salve your extreme fatigue, though you have no recollection of my talking to you within one hour of your bringing the honorable old *Salmon* to our wharf."

Frost, strength fleeing, sat on the edge of the bed and rested his head in his hand. "Truth, I remember nothing . . . no, I lie, I remember Struan coming to me and telling of Ming Tsun's infernal device . . . but what is this you say of Marcus?"

"Geoff! Marcus has been moved from Halifax where naught could contemplate his rescue, to Louisbourg, a much more sanguine place for rescue, and rescue Marcus you shall!"

Frost hooked his left hand onto the bedpost and heaved himself to his feet, changing the subject warily. "You say my men are buried?"

"Aye, and the British too, including the indomitable young captain Hugh Stuart, whose likeness to our lineage many gazing upon his composed countenance before being lowered into the ground have commented upon, saying that he was the very image, grown to size, of . . ."

"Enough!" Frost shouted, the sound ringing and reverberating in the small room, which he now recognized as the superintendent's quarters in the company warehouse, which he appropriated for his own use whenever he was in Portsmouth, seeing that he had neither rooms nor welcome in his father's house.

"Yes, enough, Geoff, but Marcus is alive, that we know, and Charity has confided her absolute knowledge you can effect his rescue."

"With what?" Frost asked bitterly. "I have neither vessel nor crew, having buried fifteen of my complement . . ."

"Seventeen," Joseph said quietly, "your men Tompkins, a cook's helper I believe, and Clifford Watson, a foretopman, brother-in-law to John Weliever, succumbed to their wounds and were given into the ground by John Nason's eloquent words."

"Jesus wept," Frost said.

"But you have the *Jaguar* . . ."

"The what?"

"The British vessel, His Britannic Majesty's sloop-o-war *Jaguar*."

"Which shall be condemned by a prize court and paid out to my crew."

"But there are thrice a hundred men in Portsmouth this day willing to be led by the most audacious captain of the age . . ."

"Ha! Joseph, you jest! Who would follow someone who brings back a quarter of his shipped crew to be encompassed by pine and heralded only by a scant piece of slate?" Frost looked desperately around the room, and Joseph, knowing his needs born of thirty-six hours of sleep, quickly fetched the chamber pot.

Joseph continued as Frost relieved himself: "Geoff, your

victory complements a victory won by Hopkins in Long Island Sound, a smaller victory it's true, but one which nevertheless signals the United Colonies need not retreat before the British Navy."

"Good, let Hopkins lay siege to Louisbourg and fetch away Marcus. I would be obliged if you would fetch hot water and help me wash myself." Frost shrugged out of his night shirt and turned to survey his back in the mirror over the chest-of-drawers, his neck stiff and crank from the hard pull to look over his shoulder. He was frustrated to see nothing but a heavy bandage flemished neatly from just beneath his armpits to his waist. Frost raised his eyes to scan the face that peered back at him from the glass, scarce believing the gaunt, hollow-eyed scarecrow with a heavy fringe of whiskers and tousled hair that glared back from the silvered glass was Geoffrey Frost, mariner and trader.

Joseph was back bearing a heavy porcelain bowl and pitcher, followed closely by Ming Tsun with a tray holding a bowl of noodles and a pot of tea. Ming Tsun placed the tray on the chest-of-drawers and left the room quickly, without glancing at Frost.

Joseph unrolled Frost's toilet articles as his older brother raised the bowl of noodles to his lips and sipped the hot broth. "I can shave you if you wish."

"With my right arm bound as it is, your assistance will be gratefully received," Frost said, amazed to find that he had already finished the bowl of noodles. He poured a cup of tea, the sharp, astringent taste of gingerroot and dried ginkgo leaves mingling with the tea.

Joseph helped Frost sponge bathe all of Frost's body not hidden beneath the bandages. Then he made his brother lie back in the room's only chair, face covered with a hot towel to soften his whiskers, while Joseph industriously beat soap into lather and, whipping away the towel, began enthusiastically brushing the lather onto Frost's face.

"Geoff, you simply must be still whilst I have this razor in my hand," Joseph cautioned his brother, "otherwise I cannot answer for the safety of your nose." Knowing that his brother could not, at least for the few minutes that he plied the razor, argue with him, Joseph again repeated his entreaty. "Marcus and the other Portsmouth men captured at Breed's Hill were removed to Louisbourg from Halifax over a month ago to give over more room for the British fleet preparing another invasion. We shall have a far easier time of investing Louisbourg than Uncle Pepperrell had in '45."

"Thirteen years before you were born," Frost snapped irritably, wincing under the scrap of blade. He collected that Joseph would be eighteen in July. Joseph was unfamiliar with the softness of his skin, the special contours of his face, unlike Ming Tsun. "And it took Uncle Pepperrell a considerable army and siege train to conquer. You will doubtlessly recall that the British restored Louisbourg to His Most Christian Majesty following the Treaty of Aix-la-Chapelle, compelling Amherst and Boscowen to spend even more lives and treasure in '58."

"Bah! The British have their intentions focused elsewhere; they are knocking vessels apart in the Saint Laurence to transport them to the Champlain headwaters. A wondrously adept plan, I must acknowledge, and frightening in its import to our prospects of holding the Lake. Howe is marshalling forces for New York, so Cousin John is reliably informed, to strike up the Hudson and, meeting with forces driving southward through the Champlain, to isolate our northern United Colonies from the southern colonies. What better time to strike against Louisbourg?"

"What better time for you to be making cannon balls at Saugus, Joseph? It appears there is and always shall be a good market for such fruit. And whilst you are at it, you could learn to pour cannons."

"Aye, cannons the United Colonies can sorely use." Joseph said, cutting off his brother's further speech as he tweaked Frost's nose to one side and brought razor against upper lip. "I can tell you truly it was a near thing, the way Knox brought those cannons from Tyonderoga which His Excellency General Washington employed to such excellent effect that Howe was forced to quit Boston. And John Langdon was quite put out, the account I heard, that you gave those cannons, so dearly won at New Providence, to the sea's tender care." Joseph modestly did not bore his brother further with mention of the rôle he had played as a member of Knox's complement in fetching those cannons from Fort Ticonderoga.

Frost stiffened but made no reply; he could not without risking a slice being taken from his upper lip by the razor Joseph was plying so happily. Frost realized his younger brother was enjoying his temporary helplessness.

"Of course, bringing in such a prize as the *Jaguar* did much to assuage Cousin John's ill humour at losing the New Providence cannons. When we conversed briefly at the funerals— yes, Cousin John took time away from his heavy duties as Continental Agent to see our men, and the British too, delivered into a far happier life by the eloquent words of Parson Nason— and he has stopped by once to inquire of you—John mentioned that his intent was to stop work on the *Raleigh* to repair the *Jaguar*. That way Thompson can be away on a fine capital ship . . ."

This was too much for Frost. He seized Joseph's hand manipulating the razor and angrily thrust it away. "Tommy Thompson shall never command a vessel I won!" Frost got to his feet, momentarily giddy from the sudden rise; three paces and he was across the room, throwing open the door, looking out into the greater room adjoining which was the kitchen. His father's slave, Juby, outfitted as always in the incongruous, stiff, white-powdered peruque, sky blue, high-collared, swallow-tail coat with gold buttons, buff waistcoat, white trousers and stockings, was sitting with his back to the bed chamber on a pine bench near the fire in the kitchen's red brick hearth, companionably talking to Ming Tsun, sitting nearby mending shirts, who could, of course, make no reply.

Juby got to his feet when he heard the bed chamber door open, his broad, honest black face drawing into a wide smile of great pleasure. "I see you, Tai-pan."

"I see you, Baba," Frost said. The towel was still around his shoulders; he scrubbed his face with one corner, then folded the fingers of his left hand around Juby's clasped hands. "You look more the mariner than any captain in the house of Frost."

"I bring news of your parents, Tai-pan."

"First of you, Juby, and Cinnamon. I find you both well?"

"Well, Tai-pan, and give you joy for your victory over the British. It has been occasioned by the Savior this happy Easter season."

"Truly as you say, a hard won victory as you ken, regardless of the season." Frost was startled with the realization that his savage battle with the cat had taken place during Easter's Holy Week. Inshallah. "What of my parents now?"

"Your father demands you send your servant with his trunnels and spikes to relieve the pains in his feets and knees. Your Mother, Lady Thérèse, sends for her son."

Frost slowly released his clasp on the warm, ebony-colored fingers gripping his. "If my father eschewed rich food and drink, he would vanquish the gout which cripples him. And my servant is not his to command. If Marlborough Frost wishes access to the healing which lies in Ming Tsun's needles, he must apply directly to Ming Tsun." He paused, dreading the answer to his next question: "And for which of her sons does my mother pine?"

"She pines for her son Jonathan," Juby said sadly, avoiding Frost's eyes.

"Yes," Frost said, "as ever it were. Directly she shall see him, though for now tell her Jonathan has much remaining to undertake, and mayhap a day must pass before her dutiful and obedient son can pay homage to the fair Thérèse."

Juby smiled: "This was the message I was certain I would convey, so certain that I have already made the particulars known to the Lady Thérèse."

"And others ask for one of the brothers Frost?" Frost had spied a scone warming on a brick by the hearth and, his hunger still very much unassuaged, stepped over the bench to scoop it up, juggling it briefly for fear of scorching his hand, then biting into it quickly. A raisin scone, the kind he liked best. He saw a pan covered with a damp cloth and knew other scones lay beneath, their dough rising.

"The fair Mistress Charity. Still more beautiful than any lady of Portsmouth despite her anguish over her husband's captive state. Her only joys in life are her children, now just weaned."

"Never fear, Juby, nor Charity either. Geoff will deliver her husband to her arms soon enough."

Joseph was at Frost's side, bending over the hearth, sniffing appreciatively as he lifted pot lids. Ming Tsun placed two more scones on the brick hearth to warm. Joseph cocked an eye at his older brother, who nodded, and five seconds later Joseph had devoured the first scone and was making great headway on the second.

"It would be better if you waited for them to warm and melted butter atop them," Frost said kindly. "No one in all the world can bake scones like Ming Tsun. It is a gift." Ming Tsun was bent over a pan, stirring furiously, and Frost could not see the man's face.

"Have you a carriage without?" Frost asked.

"It is so, Tai-pan. Your father's small landau and the two matched bays."

"Then wait without, I pray. Fifteen minutes, no more, and you must drive me to John Langdon at the State House. Joseph, I beg you attend Rutherford and return with a summary of the *Salmon*'s condition. Ming Tsun shall finish shaving me."

Juby bowed, gravely, and he and the irrepressible Joseph were through the main door, jostling and bantering with each other, leaving Frost and Ming Tsun alone.

"You disobeyed my order," Frost said. Ming Tsun turned just long enough to sign in the affirmative before going back to his dishes.

Frost thought about the discipline of life at sea, the unquestioning discipline and authority to which he had always been subject, and to which he held others. A command given was to be obeyed for the lives of others, yes, veritably the life of the ship depended upon obedience. He had disobeyed and had in turn been punished, just as he had punished others for their disobedience, punishments that still rankled and pricked his conscience after lo these many years. Still, Ming Tsun's disobedience had saved his life at least thrice during the desperate battle for the cat.

"I am glad you disobeyed. Though, as you have known me these many years, such words come with the greatest difficulty," Frost said evenly, marveling that he could actually say the words, though he knew they were true.

Frost gazed steadily at Ming Tsun's gaunt, ravaged face, this direct lineal descendant of Yang Shen, the greatest scholar-official of the Ming Dynasty, who had dared criticize his emperors and been persecuted and exiled for his honesty. This Ming Tsun whose family later had been welcomed warmly as advisors into the Chun-chi Ch'u, the Grand Council of the Ch'ing reformist emperor Yung-cheng. Only to be cruelly cast down by the successor emperor, Ch'ien-lung, for the family's temerity, though devout Buddhists, to shelter Jesuit missionaries who had carried on the propagation of their faith years after the K'ang-hsi emperor had banned Christianity in China.

The family had been forced into hiding and the young scholar Ming Tsun, arrested as he studied the Confucian Rules of Virtue with the great academic Tai Chen, having already supplemented the literature of herbal concoctions and the healing needles, was tortured in a vain effort to discover where his family had fled. A younger sister, less able to resist her torture, had named the family's hiding place in the southeastern coastal city of Kuang-chou—Canton. While being transported to Kuang-chou for the mass execution of his entire family, Ming Tsun had somehow escaped down the Chu Chiang—the Pearl River—to the Portuguese enclave of Macao. Ming Tsun had never commented on that harrowing journey; perhaps he recalled nothing. But he had been plucked, feverish and incoherent due to the fiendish, crude excision of his tongue, from the river by Geoffrey Frost just as *Salmon*, concluding her first voyage to China, was weighing anchor for her circuitous, lengthy passage to North America. Thus had fate and providence intertwined the lives of the highborn scholar bereft of all family and connections in China and the mariner Geoffrey Frost.

"I did not so much disobey," Ming Tsun signed fiercely, "as I did what you would have wished me to do, had you but known all that I knew."

"You are my best friend in this or any other life," Frost said. "I know my words and actions have caused you pain, and for that I ask your forgiveness, for you knew better than I."

"The result would have been the same," Ming Tsun signed quickly, "whether I snapped the flint directly, or the next person to the magazine. The force of the powder would have taken both vessels, you and me and all the British and our men with them." There was no mix of gestures in their sign language for "explosion," though of course Frost knew what Ming Tsun meant by the more awkward signs "force of the powder."

"Struan told me the device was most cunning."

"A small thing," Ming Tsun signed, "easily done."

"Yet we live and the British cat is ours. You must finish shaving me; my brother came near to cutting my throat, and there is much to be done if we are to be at sea the next two weeks, at the maximum three weeks." Frost allowed his hand to rest, briefly, on Ming Tsun's arm.

"We speak no more of this," Ming Tsun signed.

"Only to say I owe you my life," Frost said simply.

Ming Tsun bustled from the kitchen, returning quickly with the razor and the shaving bowl. He refilled the bowl with hot water from a kettle gurgling gently beside the fire. "More lives than I can ever repay you," he signed.

"Truly this ends the matter," Frost said, moving to the ladder-backed chair near the hearth as Ming Tsun approached him with a freshly whipped cup of lather. He thought: "Discipline and command are truly interesting counterpoises to the phenomenon of a man's true sense of duty upon occasion," as he surrendered gratefully to Ming Tsun's skilled ministrations.

Fifteen minutes later, neatly shaved, hair queued, bandages changed, a fresh compress of herbs bound against the wound in his back, buttoned loosely into a trader's coat of grayish-green wool that Ming Tsun had somehow unearthed, his right arm bound to his waist by a wrap of muslin, several cups of tea to his benefit, and carrying the paper Ming Tsun had written at his direction, Geoffrey Frost strode out of his warehouse into the subdued glare of a soft mid-April sun.

A woman, shrunken, virtually toothless, a ragged brown scarf covering her head, detached herself from the shadow of the warehouse where she had been keeping watch and stopped Frost with desperate hands on his right arm, the sudden pain causing him to falter while his dimmed vision was shot through with electric sparks. "Pardon, sir, but ye be Captain Frost, can ye tell me of my son, Quentin, Quentin Fowle?"

Frost gently detached his arm from the woman's grasp, keeping her hands gathered in his left hand. "Aye, mother, Quentin Fowle served me faithfully aboard the *Salmon*, he was a good and true carpenter's mate."

"Then tell me, sir, where he be."

"Good mother, he had a slight wound in the shoulder, scarce worth the binding, but I know not where he is now, save to say with certainly that he does not repose beneath the ground as do so many of his shipmates."

"But he has not been home these two nights, sir, and I am at my wits' ends with worry."

Frost had a very good idea indeed where Quentin Fowle was at this very instant, but he did not think it appropriate to inform his mother of her son's whereabouts. "Good mother, Quentin is indeed remiss if he visited not your hearth immediately upon his return." He saw a way to occupy Joseph at the same time. "Good mother, if you will but return to your dwelling, giving first my brother your address, he shall locate your son and bring him there forthwith."

"And shall he have prize money?" the woman demanded.

"He will have his wages, yes, good mother. And there will be prize money later, of which he shall unfailingly receive his share." Frost rummaged in a pocket of his waistcoat with his left hand and drew out several coins, small Spanish silver, and handed her a Spanish five-dollar piece. "This be not an advance on his wages, nor prize money, but gratitude for the woman who bore such a fine son to serve his ship so well." He bowed to the old woman, not thinking in his heart to condemn her lack of subtlety, for times were dear.

Frost beckoned Joseph to attend: "Find her son, a likely fellow, twenty years, perhaps twenty-two, fair hair, smallpox scars on his forehead, a tattoo of a mermaid on his right forearm, souvenir of Jamaica as I recall. He associates with Caleb Mansfield when ashore, so wherever Caleb is, Quentin won't be too far away. Dead drunk, most likely, but sober him before taking him home to his good mother." Juby stood ready to hand him into the landau. "And Joseph," Frost said in a whisper, "give Master Fowle to understand that if he wishes to remain part of my crew in future, he is always to repair first to his mother's abode upon return to Portsmouth."

Joseph nodded cheerfully. "Aye, brother. Do you think this Fowle fellow will be accompanying us to Louisbourg?"

"Louisbourg is a far piece away, Joseph, well fortified by the British, against whom I have absolutely no stomach for fighting." Frost swung himself into the landau quickly to avoid his brother's shocked, mouth-agape stare.

The streets of Portsmouth were narrow and muddy, and a pig rooted forlornly in the midden heap near the Widow Crockett's boarding house. A maid in a second-story window yapped the customary warning, "Gardez de l'eau!" before throwing a chamber pot's contents into the street. Juby cracked the matched bays into quickstep to avoid the unexpected shower. A fishmonger yelled his wares, the best cod caught that morning off the Shoals, from the next street corner. Frost lay back on the satin cushions of the landau and smiled with satisfaction. Yes, he was back in Portsmouth, dear, dear Portsmouth, the town he loved best in all the world.

Juby halted the bays before the State House, and Frost dismounted from the landau before Juby could jump down from the driver's seat. "I can make my way back to the warehouse from here, Baba. Rather than give my father further offense, please return to Ming Tsun and tell him I would count it a personal favor if he would attend my father. Marlborough will demand cupping, but Ming Tsun's needles will prove more efficacious than any amount of blood which may be drawn from my father's veins."

Juby eyed Frost dubiously. "You are not well, Tai-pan. I should remain nearby . . ."

"Baba, be gone! It is my wish. My sister will doubtlessly inquire of me, but I can see her only after Jonathan has visited our mother."

"Yes, Tai-pan," Juby said resignedly. "I am sure the lady Charity will understand." He chirruped to the bays, and they started off, carriage wheels squishing in the mud.

"No," Frost thought with equal resignation, "Charity will not understand, nor will my mother, not that she is capable of understanding, nor would anyone else in Portsmouth be capable of understanding, for that matter." But Geoffrey Frost had much to do, and little time, very little precious time, the greatest, most valuable commodity of all, to accomplish all which demanded to be done as he had just resolved.

IX

ONE OF JOHN LANGDON'S SLAVES, PROSPEROUS, AS APPROPRIATELY AND LAVISHLY OUTFITTED AS HIS NAME, WITH PLUM-COLORED LIVery and a powdered peruque equal to—no, even more elaborate than—that which Juby wore, admitted him to John Langdon's presence in the corner office of the State House overlooking the main square.

"Cousin!" John Langdon cried heartily upon hearing Frost's name announced, emerging from his office to greet Frost at his office's wide, imposing door. "I salute you with all joy at your most audacious victory! All the more poignant occurring during this Easter season! I've waited for you patiently these past two days, not calling upon you directly since I had been given to understand you were incommunicado, recovering from your wounds, as it were, sustained in valiant defense of the land of your nativity." Langdon swept his arm around the large, well-lighted room, books and maps everywhere, ledgers, lists, a half-hull model of a ship propped against the desk from which he had risen to greet Geoffrey Frost with such great enthusiasm.

"Though it does go hard for me to admit, the exploits of a Portsmouth man have been obscured, most unfortunately, by all the gaggle about Hopkins' action with HM *Glasgow* after you parted company outside Long Island's Sound."

Frost met Langdon's hearty clasp with his left hand, wishing to avoid further harm to his right. He was completely unconcerned about the fact that news of Hopkins' small fleet's running fight with HM *Glasgow* had totally eclipsed his single ship victory over HM *Jaguar*; in fact, Geoffrey Frost vastly preferred being spared the notoriety. During Joseph's abortive attempts to shave him, Frost had quietly digested the brief, flabbergasted accounts Joseph had imparted concerning Hopkins' half-hearted and piecemeal efforts to marshal his overwhelming force of seven vessels to deal with one nondescript twenty-gun British demi-frigate bearing dispatches to Charleston. In truth, though, Frost had no idea how he would have met the ill-conceived affair, so he refrained from criticizing Hopkins, just as he refrained from criticizing all other sea captains.

Langdon took due note of Frost's infirmities and pulled out a chair for him. "I trust you brought back no one from New Providence who was suffering from the yellow jack?"

Frost smiled. "Hopkins and his captains may have embarked some men so suffering, but the Massachusetts men I shipped for home were suffering nothing more than surfeit of the strong drink which proliferated on that sunny isle."

"Cousin, Elizabeth was absolutely beside herself with joy when she unwrapped the pearls you so generously sent as a wedding present. They must have graced the throat of an Oriental princess! And I cannot tell you how delighted I was to find the gold snuffbox you bestowed upon me. Look! I have it here!" Langdon produced a small, ornate snuffbox from his waistcoat pocket and thumbed open the lid.

"May I offer you a pinch of especial snuff? A blend concocted by our mutual friend, Henry Knox, a most improvident bookseller but an extraordinarily brilliant cannoneer, as His Excellency George Washington avows, and a bosom companion of your dear brother Joseph. Henry swears that his concoction of snuff will cure deafness, blindness, the ague, improve memory and cleanse the breath." Langdon thrust the snuffbox eagerly toward Frost.

Frost declined. "My thanks, Cousin, but I've never acquired the habit. I am glad to know that Elizabeth appreciates the

pearls. I had kept them for her over twenty thousand sea miles."
And yes, Frost acknowledged to himself, those pearls had once
adorned the throat of a most beautiful Oriental princess, one
fully the equal of the beautiful Elizabeth Sherburne, recently
taken to wife by his cousin, John Langdon. Ming Tsun had
restrung the pearls.

The only woman Frost had ever known who exceeded Elizabeth Sherburne's beauty was his sister, Charity, Jonathan's
twin, happily, and unhappily, married to Marcus Whipple. And
of course, his mother, before . . .

"Some brandy? Perhaps some excellent Madeira? I have a
stock that you provided some months ago from Funchal itself.
Or perhaps that delightful wine from the Western Islands, a
cask of which you presented me—when was it, a voyage ago?
I understand that the majority of it was destined for the Czar
of Russia. Lucky fellow!" Langdon allowed his voice to fall:
"And faith, dear cousin, there is little of consequence landed in
Portsmouth which has not made its way here save through the
agency of the Frost Trading Company."

"I would be happy if you could command a pot of tea,"
Frost said. "My wounds are inconsequential; still, my physician
recommends tea over spirits for the convalescing."

"By physician you mean the Chinee," Langdon said: a statement rather than a question. Frost nodded.

"God, cousin! If we could be fathom what nature his medicines have, and replicate them, what a fortune we could make!"

"They are efficacious, as I've long maintained with my father,
only if we believe in their sanguinity," Frost said.

"Tea, of course! I have half a chest from you. The very best
from Canton, I warrant, though you never shared with me its
source." John Langdon pulled a bell; Prosperous entered and
was given instructions as to the tea.

John Langdon seated himself behind his desk, seized a quill,
and rotated it reflectively between his right thumb and forefinger. The light hovering over his shoulder through the tiny
panes illuminated his handsome features, momentarily turned
in frown. "Damned shame about losing all those cannons. The

United Colonies, the Continental Congress needs cannons now in the worst way."

Frost did not bother to remind his cousin that Langdon had left a fort full of cannons at William and Mary after seizing the fort in December of '74, cannons that the British had subsequently removed, though the one hundred barrels of precious powder had been gotten safely away to Exeter and Concord. It was to Concord to retrieve the powder cached there that the British had gone one year ago, virtually to the day, and the ensuing skirmish with a group of armed farmers had precipitated this War for Independence. No, that would be unkind.

"The *Jaguar* is a handsome vessel, and I have written the Congress for permission to purchase her into the Continental Navy."

Frost sat forward on his chair and regarded his cousin steadily. "The cat, for that is what I call her, is my purchase, the purchase of my crew both living and seventeen beneath the earth. I, and no one else, shall employ her."

John Langdon could not have been more startled, for he dropped the quill. "Faith, Cousin, I had not ascribed to you so much martial ardor," he said to mask his surprise.

"My psyche is totally lacking in ardor of any martial sort. My sole desire is to employ the sloop in ways which shall assist in the conclusion of the present hostilities as quickly as possible on terms favorable to these United Colonies, so that I can return to my trade." Frost sat back, virtually exhausted, dismayed that the simple act of talking had taken so much of his strength.

John Langdon picked up the quill he had dropped and stroked his chin with the feather's tip. "It will take some time to condemn *Jaguar* in a prize court. She is the second prize brought into Portsmouth this fortnight. Your colleague, John Manley, brought in the brig *Elizabeth*, taken off Cape Ann, a vessel most adroitly laded by the Tories with plunder from Boston. And a wasp's nest of Tories, lead by that despicable fellow, Crean Brush, all most prudently marched off to Boston gaol." Langdon gazed at Frost with intensity. "Of course, the United Colonies as yet have no mechanisms, no courts, for condemning prizes, so Manley and Joshua Wentworth—you'll remember Joshua, I'm sure, from your voyages to the Antilles —I succeeded him as Continental Agent, and he is now prize agent—have gone off to consult His Excellency in Cambridge about the matter."

"A prize court is not necessary, John. You wish to purchase her into the Continental Navy, therefore you have already established a very good estimate of her value. In fact, you would be remiss in your duties as Continental Agent had you not already, perhaps in consultation with Messrs. Paul, Hackett, and Hill, pegged her value to the Colonies' Naval Service."

Prosperous threw open the door to the office with a ceremonial flair. He was followed by another slave, a young lad of fourteen or fifteen, awkward and uncomfortable in his livery, bearing the tea tray. The lad held the tray before Frost. Frost was acutely conscious of the fact that the young man was perspiring heavily. It could not be the temperature; this April morning was still quite cool. Doubtless the lad was ill at ease at being togged out so. Frost poured with his left hand, nodded that he would require neither milk nor sugar, lifted the cup from the tray, and shifted it to the exquisitely delicate Queen Anne mahogany candleslide tea table beside him.

"It is true that I have had a conversation touching upon the value of the *Jaguar* with the good yeomen Hackett and Hill," John Langdon said quickly. "And you need have no concern for the fragility of that table. It is stoutly made."

"A conversation which established a value to the United Colonies of—let me postulate—fifteen thousand pounds for the sloop, her tackle, and all her appurtenances, of which sum you are prepared to take a discount for specie." Frost sipped from his cup. The tea was badly made. How could anyone not make an adequate pot of tea, when all that was necessary was the elementary skill of boiling water?

"The value thus calculated upon the sloop I accept as the monies to be shared out among my crew, though as you ken, I shall of necessity have to deduct from that amount the costs of contracting incurred when you chartered *Salmon* to follow

Hopkins' fleet to the Bahamas and lade the arms and munitions."

John Langdon laid aside the quill, rose to his feet, and began pacing the strip of floor behind his desk. He waved Prosperous and the other slave away, then stood with his hands clasped behind his back, staring out the tiny panes of glass into the square. He spoke without turning to face his cousin.

"I confess a value of fifteen thousand pounds for the British HM sloop *Jaguar* lately conveyed into the harbor of Portsmouth, in the colony of New Hampshire, as a lawful prize taken by the Frost Trading Company's *Salmon*, Captain Geoffrey Frost." John Langdon rested his knuckles on his desk and looked directly at Frost. "But I know not where this conversation is trending."

"Which amount is discounted to eleven thousand pounds, immediately payable in specie, such discount also recognizing the contract of one thousand pounds which the Continental Congress need not now lay out," Frost said calmly and amiably.

Langdon raised one hand to stroke his cheek reflectively, shrugged his shoulders, and turned to glance out into the square. "I shall have a broadside published to that effect . . ."

"With application to be made directly to me at my warehouse on Christian Shore by all who were crew upon my *Salmon*, their heirs and assigns." Frost removed from his coat pocket the broadside Ming Tsun had prepared for him earlier. "Perhaps you may find the language of this draft sufficient. I believe all it requires is to be set in type. I beg your indulgence for disrupting your schedule of construction for the *Raleigh*, though it shan't be for long. I shall move the sloop to your yard on Rising Island on tomorrow's first outgoing tide. The cat requires a new mainmast, repairs to hull, topside, rigging, some new spars, and divers other particulars. I intend to be aweigh not later than tenth May. I shall be paying in specie, of course, and you shall receive six percent commission on the labor rather than your set five percent since my requirements disrupt your schedule for *Raleigh*."

John Langdon was incredulous, almost angry. "Cousin, you

enter my office where I receive you with the utmost civility, only to order me about as if I were Prosperous' git . . ."

Frost raised his hand. "Nay, cousin, I enter your office in a great hurry to be southeast of the Açores in a capital ship by the first part of July."

Langdon's face stiffened. "What marks the first part of July?"

Frost knew his cousin was an accomplished mariner, though one who had engaged only in the lumber, dried fish, rum and sugar trade with the West Indies. In fact, Frost recalled that his cousin had run afoul of British trade regulations on one or more occasions, including having a cargo of rum seized and condemned. "The Honorable John Company's vessels which left Calcutta in late February will be approaching those waters, and an East Indiaman laden with teas, spices, silks, and porcelains will make a grand prize."

Langdon resumed his pacing. "I see," he said thoughtfully. "I had thought for a moment that your haste to regain the sea was motivated by some desire to rescue Marcus Whipple and other New Hampshire men languishing in Louisbourg gaol."

"I weep for my brother-in-law." Frost chose his words carefully. "I weep even more for my sister, and my nephew and niece who have never seen their father. But I have seen Louisbourg, impregnable Louisbourg, even though the fortifications were thrown down in '59. Louisbourg is bare fifty leagues distance from Halifax, and by Halifax you must pass to gain Louisbourg. All the Royal Navy's warships not at sea or in New York are to be found at anchor in Halifax harbor. Faith, Marcus is shut away in Louisbourg gaol even tighter than were he still in the Halifax prison hulks. To put my ship across the breakers benefits neither Marcus, Charity, the cause of the United Colonies, nor me."

Langdon hurled his big body into his desk chair and drummed his fingers on an opened ledger. "Yes, you are quite right, Geoffrey. The fate of every Portsmouth man in harsh imprisonment weighs heavily upon us all. I had hoped . . . yet reality is a cold douche to hope."

"A quick end to this dispute with our overlords will be the

greatest aid to Marcus and all other prisoners. The weight of the British Navy and Army is greatly against us. But clip the London, Bath, Bristol merchants in their purses, drain away the Royal Navy's warships on convoy duty . . ." Fine words, brave words, smooth words: Frost could almost believe them when spoken so convincingly. In his heart he knew they were lies.

And John Langdon, Frost was sure, did not really believe them, either. Doubtless his cousin was disappointed in him. So be it. Frost struggled to his feet; he had been sitting too long. "I'll take no more of your time today . . ."

"A long way for a private man-o-war to venture, Geoffrey. The privateers thus far authorized, and His Excellency's schooners, have enjoyed marked successes in nearby waters. It may prove difficult to entice men to serve with you on such a long cruize."

The office door was thrown open unannounced and with an uncommon degree of force. "John, I say John, you must take action at once; there has been most wretched treatment visited upon a king's serving officer . . . ," someone declaimed in a loud, pompous voice, and Geoffrey Frost did not have to turn around to identify the speaker. He did so anyway, extending his left hand in greeting.

"Hello, cousin Woodbury, what's this about wretched treatment of a king's officer? The only king's officers presently in Portsmouth, to my certain knowledge, are those officers conveyed hither aboard the sloop-of-war *Jaguar*, late of His Britannic Majesty's Navy."

Woodbury Langdon, John's older brother, and Frost's cousin also, stopped short, attempted to ignore Frost's proffered hand, then, seeing that he could not, shook Frost's hand perfunctorily, not bothering to remove his tricorne, which was crushed down on his untidy hair. "Cousin Geoffrey, I give you joy on your prize, but surely, cousin, you should grant parole to that poor wretch, Lieutenant Lithgow, whom I have released from purgatory."

Frost heard the name for the first time. "Doubtless you

mean the cat's first lieutenant. My first mate, Ferguson, in-formed me that he had this person under close arrest."

"Close arrest!" Woodbury waved both arms excitedly. His nose, despite some judiciously applied finely ground rice pow-der, was still the bulbous red associated with intimate and prolonged contact with the spirits bottle. "Your man Ferguson had this poor devil short-chained to a bolt-ring on the *Jaguar*'s cable tier, where he languished in his own filth until I, hearing of his plight, like any Christian took pity upon him."

Frost inclined his head slightly and became aware that the young slave had entered the room and was scooping up the tea tray. "What is your name, lad?" Frost asked.

"Darius, sir," the slave answered hesitantly, unaccustomed to being addressed directly by anyone outside the Langdon family.

"Good morning to you, Darius. Would like to trade the con-fines of Portsmouth for the broader expanse of the ocean?"

Darius stood stiff, face frozen into a blank, unreadable mask, without speech or comprehension. Frost smiled and turned back to Woodbury. He trusted John Langdon as much as he trusted any man who had not fought shoulder to shoulder with him in the dozen or so savage, desperate life-or-death combats incident to four voyages to and from the Orient, but Wood-bury was suspected of pro-British sympathies, and Frost most definitely did not trust this particular cousin. Still, Frost never antagonized anyone if he could possibly avoid it.

"My dear cousin, I know aught of this lieutenant, save that he pierced me from the back with his stub of a sword . . . after his captain was in the process of surrendering his vessel to me, a matter of which this lieutenant was plainly acquainted. His blade touched a lung and has given me much pain. Still, I am willing to forgive a man much for what happens on a ship's deck in the smoke and confusion of battle when one fights for one's honor, and one's life."

Woodbury fairly beamed. "There you have it! A capital fel-low you are, Geoffrey! I knew you wouldn't object to my hav-ing Lieutenant Lithgow's chains struck off."

Frost kept his expression neutral. Struan must have been

occupied elsewhere, else Woodbury would never have dared even the attempt to free the British lieutenant. And of course, an application, some inquiry to some civil or military authority, should have been made before so cavalierly releasing the British lieutenant.

John Langdon faced his brother and demanded harshly: "And where waits this paragon whose virtues obviously blinded you to the fact that as Congress' Agent I should have been consulted on any matter touching the prize now in our harbor?"

Woodbury averted his gaze but at least had the decency to blush. "He is presently within my house, where I conveyed him with leave to bathe and shift into a fresh uniform."

"Then convey him hither as soon as he is presentable, so I can determine if it is acceptable to offer him parole. I forewarn you, Woodbury, should, following my interview, I deem it not prudent to offer this British lieutenant parole, I shall have him clapped in more irons than abound in Cousin Geoffrey's warehouse and marched off to New London, the destination of the *Jaguar*'s crew once I have secured the necessary guard force."

"But surely, John, if Geoffrey has not objected . . ."

"And surely, Woodbury, it strikes you that Geoffrey had no chance to object to any offer of parole."

"Well, it was an insufferable way to treat a Royal Navy officer, given that these petty differences which divide us will soon be resolved, and peace reconcile us."

"Remove your hat, Woodbury. I may be your brother, but I am also the United Colonies representative in New Hampshire and entitled to a measure of respect, even from my brother."

"Of course, John, I meant no disrespect, you ken that. My thoughts were preoccupied once I found Lieutenant Lithgow so unjustly detained." Woodbury Langdon quickly whipped off his tricorne.

John Langdon eased his bulk into his desk chair. "Have you any observations to make on this matter, cousin Geoffrey?"

"As Congress' Agent I leave the matter of parole strictly to you, John, though my observation to us all is that Marcus Whipple certainly did not consider the differences dividing the

American people and George the Third to be petty or amenable to being soon resolved."

John Langdon nodded emphatically. "Well said, cousin." Then his gaze shifted to Woodbury: "Tell me, brother, how came you to know that Lieutenant Lithgow had been clapped in irons? To my knowledge, you are not a frequenter of the cable tier of any vessel, much less a British sloop-o-war."

"Why, John, I went aboard the *Jaguar* at the express invitation of the port pilot, Mister Reedy Stalker, a man much oppressed with the thought of any human suffering, and who had acquainted himself with Lieutenant Lithgow's sufferings."

John Langdon frowned, turning his head away so his brother would not see his chagrin. "I ken. Nothing escapes the benevolent attention of our esteemed port stoat."

"Parole matters are not of mine, but of yours, cousin. I bid you both farewell." Frost winked at the young slave who had stood, unmoving, throughout the three men's conversations. "You may do me the kindness of showing me out, young Darius."

"A moment, cousin." John Langdon held up his hand. "It comes to mind that you may welcome some additional capital to assist in your venture."

"At present, no, cousin. This venture after East Indiamen is too speculative to involve a relative. However, should it prove as successful as I hope, I shall be amenable to assistance in fitting out other ventures." He bowed politely to both his cousins and followed Darius out of John Langdon's office.

Once in the street the enormity of the task he had set for himself momentarily appalled him, but then Frost set a course back to his warehouse with a purposeful detour by way of the Widow Crockett's, where he knew he would find Caleb Mansfield, and like as not, Struan Ferguson.

❦ X ❧

ROST WAS WORKING AT HIS STAND-UP WRITING DESK, HIS BACK TO THE WINDOW LOOKING OUT ONTO THE PISCATAQUA THROUGH WHICH MILD April sun was pouring. his right arm was no longer bound to his body but worn in a loose sling. As long as Frost moved the arm slowly, the motion did not pluck and tear at the wound in his back. A pot of Ming Tsun's best tea and three scones on a plate rested atop the desk, and Frost had put aside the nagging knowledge that he still owed his mother a visit, and that Joseph had left for Saugus in a huff when Frost had told him pointedly that he was not going to engage in anything as quixotic as trying to steal Marcus Whipple out of Louisbourg with the ill-disciplined crew that would be the lot of any privateer and the hundreds of demands upon his time that preparing the cat for sea required.

The cat: Frost turned and walked to the heavy brass and ebony telescope on its oak tripod standing in the nave of the garret window facing the river and Langdon's Rising Island shipyard. Struan Ferguson had careened her on the island's northeastern shore, and through the telescope Frost could see workers scraping away the growth on the cat's coppered bottom.

Copper applied to a ship's hull all the way from water line to keel: Frost had heard about such a wonder, but he had never actually seen it. Yet there it was, the copper gleaming dully in

the steady circle (how marvelously steady the warehouse floor was as compared to a ship's deck even in the most gentle of seas) as men wielding mats of woven sea grass impregnated with sand scoured away the sea's growth.

Frost calculated that he needed at least two hundred men for the cat. By a grand stroke of joss, young Roger Green's cousin, Doctor Ezrah Green, no doubt mourning his loss, which a physician's service might have prevented, had volunteered as the cat's surgeon. Ezrah Green was even now at Rising Island, where the cat had been moved, and was examining each recruit individually. No men with venereals, no men with ruptures, all men to have been previously delivered safely from the sweats and fevers of the smallpox or else sent to the hospital on Pest Island where Ezrah Green, at Frost's command, together with Continental Army Surgeon Hall Jackson, had established a variolation hospital. However, Frost had ordered the two week "cooling regime" advised by Dr. John Morgan's treatise *Recommendation of Inoculation According to Baron Dimsdale's Method*, as well as the dosing with antimony and mercury, to be eliminated. He would ship the men who recovered from their smallpox variolations by the time he sailed. Those still suffering the "innocent disease" would have to be left behind. Frost intended to introduce into his ship no man who was not proof against the smallpox, for as Doctor Hall Jackson had told him, "men dread the disease more than the horrors of war."

Frost knew his demands were rigorous but believed that the number of men he needed could be raised without relaxing the standards he sought—they were nothing more than the physical standards he had insisted upon for his crews in voyages to the Orient. Nevertheless, he grimaced at the tortured doggerel of the recruiting broadside that Struan had penned and circulated throughout the towns of Portsmouth and Kittery. A copy had been slipped under Frost's bedroom door during the night.

> Come, ye young lads, of currage so bold,
> Come, and enter ye abord, and good Capt Frost
> will cloth ye in gold.

Repair ye to Portsmouth, which towne ye shall find,
a Sloop late the *Jaguar*, now called the Cat.

She be neatly riged, her sails neatly trimed,
She be comely shaped, and sails faster than wind.
She be fit for our design, so God prosper the Cat,
For she sails faster than bullet or wind.

Capt Frost, he commands Hur, and calls Hur his own,
He will Cruize Hur to sou'ards, 'fore turning home,
The bane of the British, especially the Honorable John.
Many John ships shall the cat's prises be,
so enter ye abord, and take up ye share.

Frost smiled in spite of himself, then sighed, laying the cheap
paper aside to take up his latest petition to the Continental
Congress.

Petition Geof Frost, Esqr
    The Petition of the Subscriber, Humbly Sheweth that your
Petitioner is Fitting Out a Sloop lately of the Royal Navy, duly
taken as a Prize by the Petitioner, Libeled and Condemned before the Piscataqua Continental Agent according to the Ancient
Law Maritime, for a Private Vessel-of-War of these United Colonies, that the Petitioner hath acquired all Materials for that Purpose. And Whereas, the Business of Privateering appears the
most likely Means by which these United Colonies may hope to
Annoy our Ruthless Enemies, Arm Ourselves with the Weapons
necessary to procure the Liberty We so earnestly Seek, Supply
Ourselves with the Foreign Necessities of Life, and Discipline a
Nursery of Seamen, by which means we may acquit Ourselves a
formidable Nation at Sea as well as Land.
    Therefore, your Petitioner Humbly Prayeth your Honors in
Congress assembled shall grant Him the necessary Licenses for
a Private vessel-of-war according to the Ancient Law Maritime,
as your Honors in your Great Wisdom shall think fit. Your Petitioner, Duly Bound, shall ever Pray, on behalf of Himself and
Crew of the Sloop . . .

There was a knock at the office door as Frost lifted his quill and reflected upon the inane bureaucracy of having to petition the Congress for a privateer's license when he already possessed a perfectly valid letter of marque and reprisal issued to *Salmon* by the New Hampshire Legislature. It should have been a simple matter to transfer that letter to the cat, but John Langdon had been adamant that the cat required a privateer's warrant granted from the Congress, not a letter of marque from the Colony of New Hampshire's Legislature. The British Government would not acknowledge a letter of marque issued by a breakaway colony, and in the case of capture at sea—yet, Frost had thought irritably when he discussed the matter with his cousin John, it was hardly likely that a privateer's license issued by the Congress of the United Colonies would receive any greater deference by the Royal Navy or the British Ministerial Government.

A glance out the garret window showed the messenger, mount unsaddled, seated at the bench beneath the elm tree across the road from the warehouse, flirting with Mrs. Rutherford's twelve-year-old daughter, evidently in no hurry for the letter of request to be entrusted to him so that he might ride post-haste to Philadelphia, where it would wait the pleasure of the Continental Congress. The expense of the post rider, plus John Langdon's 6 percent commission, had already been entered in the ledger of general accounts, which Frost annotated and Ming Tsun meticulously audited.

This jumped-up Continental Congress was already showing itself to be as irksome as any government bureaucracy of any stripe where he had traded. He also had to make judicious references to the Continental Agent, since the Continental Congress had not gotten around to establishing any sort of courts for the libeling and condemnation of prizes. "Enter," Frost said, staring once again with distaste at the petition, which he had already blotted several times, though Ming Tsun's excellent script would frame the fair draft.

The door duly opened and closed. Frost looked up from the petition, the sun's glow on the foolscap momentarily dazzling him as he glanced into the room's shadow and saw no one. Puzzled, still clutching the quill, he stepped to one side of the tall writing desk. No one . . . no, his scan caught a small shape, directing his surprised eyes downward.

A small urchin dressed in the shabbiest clothes Frost had ever seen covering human nakedness, save for the piteous wretches of the Slave Coasts, stood at rigid attention in front of the writing desk. "Permission to speak to the Commanding Officer," the urchin spoke in a thin, shrill pipe.

Frost stepped back behind his desk. The urchin disappeared in the desk's shadow. "Your business?"

"Volunteering to serve yer next commission, sir."

"You are?"

"Nathaniel Dance, sir, nipper 'n' powder monkey on the old *Jaguar*."

"How came you to be out of the stockade, Mister Dance, where the *Jaguar*'s crew, save Lieutenant Lithgow whose parole has been arranged, is confined?"

"Nobody pays attention to Nathaniel, sir, bein' small, ye see. I goes through a crack in the logs 'n' nobody pays me never mind, sir. Same wise I got in here, sir."

Frost emerged again from behind the desk to examine the urchin more closely. Though the boy stood straight, hands curled into tight fists along his thighs, eyes unblinking, lips drawn into a line as tight and thin as a scar, his bowed legs showed the lack of nourishment needed for a youth his age, and he was obviously very frightened, though controlling his fright exceedingly well. It was also obvious that his calloused and cracked bare feet had never known shoes.

"Just why do you wish to volunteer for service in my next commission, Mister Dance, and why should I trust a British subject?"

The boy fidgeted. "Well, sir, I don't think of me'self as rightly a British subject, as ye calls it. I was taken from a foundling home 'n' sold into the Navy for a shilling. Seems like a British subject, as ye calls it, would naught been sold out of a foundling home. Ye catch my drift, sir?" the urchin said urgently.

Frost recognized the boy now. "When did you last have something to eat, Mister Dance?"

"Can't right recall, sir; nothing save a few potato peelings too moldy for my mates' liking since ye brought the old *Jaguar* into port."

Frost swept the plate of scones off the writing desk and motioned the urchin to the trestle table that groaned under a load of ledgers. He pushed several books away and put the plate of scones in the cleared space. "Kindly eat these scones, Mister Dance, and excuse me for a minute."

Frost left his office, going downstairs to the kitchen where Ming Tsun sat with his abacus, ciphering the shares and portions of shares due for disbursement to *Salmon*'s crew, or, for those who had died, their survivors. At his elbow was the worn leather portfolio that contained many odd-shaped scraps of paper covered with small, fine calligraphy. Ming Tsun used the script for recording his chronicles when he found the infrequent moment to pen notes in a precise, backward-written code combining elements of Chinese characters and the Portuguese alphabet for which not even Geoffrey Frost possessed the cipher. Ming Tsun looked up from his abacus and accounts as Frost entered the kitchen.

"Fine guardian you are," Frost signed. "A person quite capable of slitting my throat entered this kitchen and walked brazenly up the stairs and into my office without you so much as marking an assassin's presence."

Ming Tsun was alarmed. The long kris always strapped to his left arm inside his tunic miraculously appeared in his hand, and he plunged it into the kitchen table. "I am shamed," he signed abjectly, avoiding Frost's eyes.

Frost smiled and spoke rather than signed. "In this case the 'assassin' is so weak from hunger that he would be hard pressed to lift that kris, though he is having no difficulties in battening down a cargo of your scones. I know Mrs. Rutherford keeps a cow. Please see if she can spare a pitcher of milk, and fetch along to my office a bowl of that soup you have simmering in the caldron, and a hunk of bread, as well as some cheese, when you bring the milk." Frost climbed the stairs back to his office in time to see Nathaniel Dance licking the plate that had contained the scones.

"There will be more breakfast presently, Mister Dance. In the meantime I recommend a cup of tea."

"It be all drunk, sir," Nathaniel said, "mighty good it was."

"And just why do you wish to join my next cruize, Mister Dance? You've no idea where I sail, though doubtless you ken that this sorry business between George Three and the United Colonies may put me to the necessity of dealing harshly with your countrymen, or they with me. In such event anyone among my crew who hails from a British man-o-war can hope only for a quick death at the end of a rope, though the more likely result will be a flogging 'round the fleet."

"Yes sir, I seen one fleet floggin'. T'weren't pretty, not by a long sight. But without my mess mate to look after me, I'll be buggered for sure, sir, should I stay with the *Jaguar* men."

Ming Tsun bustled in with a tray covered by a napkin. His eyes registered surprise at the slight Nathaniel Dance, recognizing the youth instantly as he placed the tray on the table.

"Mister Dance, this is Ming Tsun. He is my best friend in life."

"I be 'ware of that, sir. He cut *Jaguar* men down like they wus reeds, sir. I saw half a dozen *Jaguar* men drop out of the fight rather than face Mister Ming Tsun, sir." Nathaniel Dance's eyes were fixed longingly on the tray. Frost whipped off the napkin with his good hand, exposing a jug of milk, a loaf of bread, a bowl of steaming soup, a rasher of freshly fried bacon that Ming Tsun had somehow procured, and a large cut of cheese.

Ming Tsun lifted the teapot to refresh Frost's cup. Frost winked. "I would appreciate another pot of tea please, Ming Tsun." Ming Tsun nodded and left the office.

Frost poured the lad a cup of milk. "What is this, sir?"

"Milk, Mister Dance. From a cow. Surely you have drunk milk before."

Nathaniel raised the cup and sipped tentatively. "Never

tasted the like, sir." He took a larger sip. "But it be better than grog, sir, so it be." Nathaniel tore a sizeable piece from the bread loaf and pulled the bowl of soup toward him.

"I caution against eating too rapidly, Mister Dance," Frost said as the lad attacked the soup. The lad hesitated, then began eating more slowly, and Frost waited until the lad had consumed almost the entire bowl. "I would be correct in my assumption that your mess mate was the man who pinked me in the ribs?"

Nathaniel wiped his lips on the back of his arm and attacked the handsome piece of cheese and rasher of bacon. Frost noted that the cup of milk had been half-drained in one gulp. "Yes, sir. Townsend Hewlett. A gentler man never lived, sir. He never knowed ye had stopped yer blow agin me, sir. Things happen quick in a fight, ye know, sir. Townsend, he thought ye was guttin' me for sure, sir. So he rushed in waving a cutlass, which he had never had in his hand before, sir, God's truth."

Frost massaged the cuts on his ribs. Thankfully the cuts were healing rapidly. Ming Tsun came in with a fresh pot of tea. Frost accepted his cup's refill gratefully. Ming Tsun took a seat at the far end of the trestle table.

"So you no longer have a mess mate to protect you."

"No, sir. Townsend keep the men away from me, he did. Laid out Jack Catton with a rammer, he did, when Jack had me caught fair 'n' was pullin' down my breeks."

"And this Townsend Hewlett bled to death as a result of the wound my first mate gave him," Frost said.

"Yes, sir. Though 'fore he died he kenned ye never intended to harm me."

Frost took his teacup and began to pace the room. He did not like being reminded of the deaths he had caused. "Why should I enlist you in the cause of the United Colonies' liberty from George Three and his ministers, Mister Dance?"

Nathaniel was applying himself industriously to sopping up the dregs of soup with a piece of bread. "'Cuz I kin bring ye between twenty 'n' thirty prize hands from the old *Jaguar*, sir, hands who been to sea since Noah, who can reef, hand 'n' steer."

"And who would swing from rope's end if they were taken by a Royal Navy warship and the treacherous nature of their change of allegiances discovered. Is that not correct, Mister Dance?"

"Yes sir," Nathaniel said, oblivious to the use of the napkin as he sucked his fingers clean.

"Or men who would conspire to retake the cat at the first opportunity."

"The cat, sir?"

"My name for the *Jaguar*. A jaguar is a cat, a big cat. From the jungles of Amazonia." Seeing Nathaniel's blank stare, Frost continued: "A region on the continent of South America."

"Yes sir," Nathaniel said dubiously. "But ken ye, sir, that these hands never would hae been in the old *Jaguar* on their free will, 'n' they likes even less the thought of yer prison hulks."

Frost poured himself another cup of tea. He was more than a little hungry himself and for an instant wished he had saved aside one scone. "We have no prison hulks. His Excellency, General Washington, has commanded that all British prisoners be treated with the utmost civility."

Nathaniel Dance tried to disguise the snorting sound he made deep in his throat, returning to his cup of milk with renewed interest. "Yes sir, but when it come to prisoners, they be prisoners 'n' they be prisoners, if ye catch my drift, sir. Officers 'n' such like, they have terms, 'n' are 'changed, whilst common seamen, like, wait their turns, like as not years. 'N' I seen our hulks in Halifax."

"Would these prime hands of which you speak be willing to become citizens of New Hampshire, committing themselves so irrevocably to a new master that recapture by their old would mean their most painful and ultimate death?"

"I kin ask them," Nathaniel said, some doubt in his voice. "Some will, some willn't."

"You may inquire of those you believe sincerely would cruize with me. Any British sailor who petitions for New Hampshire citizenship will receive equally the pay and shares apportioned to any man in my crew. Come tomorrow at this time; bring me a list of their names."

"I kin't write, sir."

"There will be one among your fellows who does."

"Likely not, sir, leastwise all's I'd trust to hold their word can make their mark, 'n' naught else." Nathaniel brightened. "But I can remember their names, sir, 'n' their birth towns."

Frost paced to the office window and gazed across the Piscataqua to Rising Island. He could see the sheers slowly, imperceptibly raising the new mainmast of the finest New Hampshire pine alongside the cat. He turned to catch Ming Tsun's eye and slowly signed, taking care not to flex his right arm too quickly. Ming Tsun signed his understanding and left the office.

Nathaniel's head turned to follow Ming Tsun's leaving, and his gaze fell on the chess set at the other end of the trestle table. He walked over and regarded it intensely. "Pardon, sir, but ye plays white?"

Frost had turned back to his petition to the Continental Congress. "What? No, I'm playing black."

"Ye be due check in two moves, sir, and mate after two more."

"And where did you learn your game, Mister Dance?"

"My mess mate, Townsend, sir. A prodigious learned man he was. Knew a wonder of Greek words, and Latin ones too. Leastwise, Townsend said they wuz Greek and Latin words. I'd never heard them anyways, before. Had been a parson, sir, though somehow he fell from grace. Most like it was strong drink. Reason he first brightened to me was 'cuz I gave him my grog ration."

"And this Townsend taught you to play chess," Frost said, interested despite himself.

"Yes sir, had a little board, metal it was, with tiny pieces on magnets. Once, when he weren't exactly sober, Townsend clapped a piece under the binnacle on the old *Jaguar*. Bowlixed the compass somethin' wonderful. Mister Lithgow was all for taking the hide off poor Townsend, but Captain Stuart, he knew there weren't no guile in Townsend when he done it. All Captain Stuart did was take away the board. Captain Stuart said he'd give it back to Townsend if Townsend would keep his head clear."

Frost walked over to the chessboard. "Pray, tell me where you see my danger." In truth, Frost was quite pleased with his positions on the board, especially since Ming Tsun and Struan were teamed against him, and he thought the advantage lay with him.

"It be clear, sir, see?" Nathaniel pointed to the more advanced of black's knights. "I ken ye have the next move?"

Frost nodded. Nathaniel placed a dirty finger beside white's bishop threatened by black's advanced knight. "This be the move ye favor, since by takin' the bishop ye have only one more move to check the king?" Frost nodded again. "So ye capture the bishop, but movin' the knight opens a path for this rook to threaten yer king. Then yer knight retreats to cover that danger, 'n' then white's queen checks yer king on the diagonal, yer king retreats, and white's remainin' bishop comes up this diagonal to make the pin and mate."

XI

FROST HAD TRIED TO IGNORE JUBY, BUT OF COURSE HIS FATHER'S SLAVE COULD NOT, WOULD NOT, BE IGNORED. JUBY HAD SHIFTED THE MATCHED BAYS, Willow and Birch, out of their traces and tethered them beneath the great elm, just beginning to leaf, at the edge of the roadside across from the Frost Trading Company's warehouse.

From his loft office, which occupied the entire garret, Frost could look out the garret window and see the portly black man patiently combing the bays again and again until their already brilliant coats shown even more brightly. Juby had moved on to buffing the coach work of the landau when Frost, dressed in his best tai-pan's coat, the bottle-green one, and carrying his tai-pan's cane, but bare-headed, strode purposefully out of the warehouse.

Juby acknowledged his presence by backing Willow and Birch into their traces. "It is time, Tai-pan," he said simply.

"Yes, Baba, it is time." Frost waited for the hitching to be completed, savoring the mild late-April breeze; from the east, which would be foul for any vessel outbound from the Piscataqua, though he knew the wind would veer sharply in another week or less. By which time he intended to be standing well off the Isles of Shoals.

"That son of Prosperous, Darius, is a likely lad," Frost spoke as he companionably pulled himself up to join Juby, who was stiff on the driver's seat of the landau, as Juby clucked to the bays. "Think you that he might entertain a desire to follow the sea?"

"Many black peoples be of a mind to follow the sea, Tai-pan, would that be possible."

"And you, Juby, would you follow the sea?" The landau's wheels threw mud against the gleaming coach work recently so meticulously polished by Juby, who looked upon the desecration with equanimity as he set the bays on the post road toward Dover Point. The landau overtook the Reverend Claude Devon astride his gray mule. Reverend Devon moved out of the ruts onto the muddy verge. Recognizing Frost, he tipped his tricorne.

"A fine day it would be, young Captain Frost."

Frost saw no need to comment on the obvious, or respond to a statement. "Good day to you, Parson," he said in as civil a tone as he could muster.

"God's blessings on your venture to the southern Atlantic, young Captain Frost!" Reverend Devon called after the hurrying carriage. "I'll be purchasing the first chest of tea after Joshua Wentworth condemns your East Indiaman and its cargo. May you sweep the entire November fleet into the Piscataqua!"

Frost heard and mused, but did not reply.

"The parson, your father no like," Juby said as soon as the landau had passed beyond the good reverend's hearing.

"He means well, I'm sure."

Juby laughed. "Your father, or parson?"

"Both, Juby, the parson in particular, even when he tried to console my mother, papist though she be, and the parson bred out of judgmentally pure puritan stock."

Juby tugged on the reins to steer the bays onto the fork of the post road leading toward the heights above the Great Bay. "Parson know how to count the wealth of the Frost Trading Company, better'n your own father. Parson's got a daughter, fact be, he's got three daughters, but the one, the one with the most age, she likes Master Joseph abundantly." Juby sighed. "But for your Mother Lady Thérèse, there be no consolin' her, not in this life."

Frost scowled: "Joseph ain't got the time for 'abundantly' liking women, whether they be parson's daughters or no, or whether they like him 'abundantly' or no. He's cast in the rôle . . ."—Frost was rather pleased with his play on words—". . . of casting iron balls for cannons, and mayhap learning how to cast cannons as well."

"I just be reportin' what us folks who serve the quality have occasion to observe," Juby said slyly. " 'Abundantly' be the word used by parson's Gabriel to describe the way Miss Hannah does carrry on over Master Joseph. 'Course, what we folks think be no nevermind to the quality, just like we be part of the walls, or somethin'."

Frost considered it particularly abhorrent that a man of the cloth, supposedly, was a slave owner. But he ignored Juby's comments and returned to his earlier theme. "But were it possible, Juby, would you follow the sea?"

"If God made it possible, dogs could fly and pigs would bark, Tai-pan, but since God has not made it possible, it is not so."

"Then would you like to follow the sea? Juby, you ken the difference between the desire and the actual."

"No, Tai-pan, I would not follow the sea, not now, even if God made it possible. My responsibilities are heavy. But there be many other black peoples who would follow the sea. I think the peoples Mister Wentworth has closed in the Portsmouth gaol would follow the sea, that for sure."

"I know of no black people in gaol," Frost said. He had been quietly exercising his right arm, stretching and flexing the muscles to a greater extent than at any time since taking his wound. Physically, Frost felt good; he had not hawked up any blood for a week, and the bandage around his chest had grown smaller in proportion to the strength of the soups Ming Tsun had fed him.

"When your friend, Captain Manley, brought in the *Elizabeth* prize, there be black peoples in her. Mister Wentworth close them in gaol 'cause they be prize property."

"How many black people, Juby?"

"Two mens and two womens."

"I'll have them released."

Juby was doubtful. "Captain Manley and Mister Wentworth, they goes to Cambridge to asks Mister Washington who gets the properties."

"Yes," Frost said. The landau was almost ready to swing into the long lane lined on either side with fifty-year-old elms that led to Jonathanwood, or *Bois de Jonathan*, the name his mother chose for her house when she had elected to live apart from Marlborough.

As his cousin John Langdon had told him, there were no prize courts yet established in the United Colonies. Frost heartily detested the whole idea of privateering and prize courts. Admiralty courts, yes; they were necessary to sort out rights to insurance and claims for salvage. But he was heartily against financing a war through the greed that seized an enemy's vessels, condemned and sold them, to the vast profits of a large number of people—piracy done under color of governance.

This went against all his instincts as a trader. Yet he, Geoffrey Frost, was preparing to engage in this nefarious practice which he abhorred—just as he had once engaged in the even greater greed and horrific evil that was slavery.

But now the landau was starting around the ornate high fountain, the water not yet flowing from it due to the threat of a late spring freeze, the fountain his mother had brought all the way from her native Martinique. They went left around the wide courtyard paved with pea gravel—ships' ballast—and Frost, catching sight of that small, dear, dear white-coiffed head peering from the second-floor bedroom window, vaulted off the seat and jumped, legs moving in synchronization with the speed of the carriage, across the driveway in three long strides, through the door held open by Cinnamon, Juby's woman, past the long sitting room looking out over the Great Bay, with its gaunt loom's frame holding the half-finished, no, quarter-finished heroic tapestry of all the Frost Trading Company's ships and the ports into which they traded, shouting as he ran up the staircase, "Maman, c'est Jonathan, ton fils, qui revient des mers pour Êntre À nouveau avec toi!"

☙ XII ❧

MING TSUN ROWED FROST IN A SMALL SKIFF TO LANGDON'S SHIPYARD ON RISING ISLAND AT THE FIRST SLACK TIDE OF MORNING. FROST HAD DE-liberately remained away from his cousin's building ways, entrusting oversight for all the repairs to Struan Ferguson and Slocum Plaisted, busy enough himself with winnowing the best and sufficient hands anxious to join. He had studiously ignored the jealousies of his fellow privateer captains who watched him taking their best hands. And Frost had had quite enough of the interminable correspondence with the New Hampshire Legislature and the Continental Congress, and the ordering and payment of provisions, and not least, arranging the transfer of money of account in various drafts for the cat's purchase into the Frost Trading Company accounts.

The skiff passed under the bowsprit and Frost stared up for several thoughtful moments at the large, exceedingly graceful and gilded feline form stretched full-length as a figurehead, arrested forever in mid-pounce, its gaze not so ferocious as intent and purposeful, eyes fixed straight ahead at some object in the middle distance, startlingly lifelike. Frost would never know his identity, but he acknowledged that some unknown carver had put a bit of the carver's soul into this figurehead.

An extremely weary Struan Ferguson met Frost at the rise of the wharf against which the cat, swarming with workmen, carpenters, caulkers, rope wrights, sailmakers, joiners and fitters, and buzzing with the raucous cacophony of saws and mallets, was berthed. A glance at the *Raleigh* showed no work of any nature going forward on that vessel. All of John Langdon's craftsmen were lavishing their skills on the *Jaguar*. The new mainmast had been stepped, and all standing rigging had been rove, though not a yard had yet been crossed. The *Jaguar* appeared a long, long way from being ready for a cruise.

Frost stood for a moment on the wharf, taking immense pleasure in the vessel that was now his to command, breathing in the sensuous blend of aromas: tar, paint, oakum, sawdust, wood shavings, sweat, strong glue, the sizing of sailcloth. Geoffrey Frost had every intention of being well at sea five days hence, and he noted with satisfaction the six-pounder cannon that had been swung out of the *Jaguar* and mounted against a makeshift bulwark on the dock. The master gunner he had hired, overseer of the cannon of Fort William and Mary, a Nutmegger with the improbable name of Roderick Rawbone whose shrewd, angular features gave the appearance of having been constructed from cast-off barrel staves, was exercising a muster of would-be matrosses anxious to be enrolled aboard the cat.

A hundred yards up from the wharf Caleb Mansfield and two of the ten *coureuse des bois*—woods-cruisers—he had recruited were instructing a gaggle of landsmen in the intricacies of musketry. Their target, a large plank of wood propped against a dirt bank fifty yards away, bore the grotesque silhouette of a crowned man with an abundant, exaggerated derriere that had been peppered with bullets.

"I want only men who are not put off by the work and weight of cannons, Mister Rawbone," Frost said as he walked behind the sweating scratch crew, sizing up the men. By constructing a faux gundeck and sweating men through the agony of serving a gun, running it in and out innumerable times, he was fulfilling his promise never again to neglect gunnery. "I've volunteers enough already for this cruize, and no one ships aboard the cat unless he likes the sniff of slow match and the honest exercise of snubbing a gun's been fired."

"This be a groat of matrosses," Rawbone, a tall, morose man of indeterminate age with a prominent red nose and scanty hair, said sourly and inordinately loudly. Like all who husbanded the heavy cannons, Rawbone was partially deaf, so he spoke loudly to compensate for his loss of hearing. "Farmers with hands shaped to the plough, and never havin' seen a cannon, would be better than these dainty maids who dinna a linstock from a cartridge bag, Capt'n Frost. I've a mind to put the lot in a snow, run them up to Halifax and sell them to the British. Payin' these maids to cruize with ye be the same as throwin' pearls 'fore swine, as it says in the Good Book, mark my words, Capt'n Frost."

"If there be anyone in New Hampshire and Massachusetts who can show these men how to work a gun, it be you, Mister Rawbone," Frost said amicably. In truth, he was appalled by the uncoordinated efforts of the hands making an ineffectual shambles of trying to run the six-pounder up to the makeshift gun port after simulating the reloading of the gun. Still, his resolve for departure five days hence was unmoved. "Keep them sweating, Mister Rawbone," Frost said as he walked behind the gun crew. "The more they sweat learning how to be husband and wife to the cannons, the less they'll bleed in battle."

One of the men heaving on the tackle had somehow gotten a bight of rope looped around his right ankle. As the cannon was hauled forward with its blocks, the rope tightened, pulling the man off balance and caroming him into his mates, which brought the maneuver to an abrupt halt in a tangle of sawdust-smeared bodies.

"Watch that one closely, Mister Rawbone," Frost snapped. "If he blunders again so, dismiss him. He may better serve on one of His Excellency's schooners under the command of John Manley or John Ayres now in port and looking for crew." Frost walked on without pausing and did not see the look of unadulterated malevolence the man sent in his direction as he got clumsily to his feet.

Ferguson conducted Frost to the commodious and bright captain's cabin, somewhat quieter than the rest of the ship, where Frost marveled at the taut, black and white checkered canvas on the cabin sole, all neatly boned into one smooth surface; the ceiling height sufficient and more for him to stand anywhere in the cabin without stooping—at least six feet, two inches of head room; the wooden rails bolted into the overhead, convenient to grasp for a brace in a running sea; the bookcases fitted into larboard and starboard bulkheads, even more bookcases tastefully set on either side of the efficient-looking, tall iron stove with heavy, beveled-glass eyelets, bookcases similar to those Frost had on the *Salmon*, with wooden locking bars to keep the books from spilling out, but designed in sections that could be struck below when clearing the sloop for action, and so many more of them.

And the titles! So many old friends, dear acquaintances on four long voyages—lo! Here was Thucydides even! And yet so many newcomers whose names he knew, but to whom he had not been properly introduced. Dios! Was that a copy of More's *Utopia*? He had lost his when his cabin was flooded by a typhoon that had almost demasted the old *Salmon* in the Moçambique Channel. And by the Golden Buddha! There on the bottom shelf of books on the larboard side, in leather-bound glory, was the three volume set of *A Dictionary of the Arts and Sciences Compiled Upon a New Plan,* or, as Bell and Macfarquhar, printers, preferred to call the set, the *Encyclopædia Britannica*. Frost had heard of this marvel, but this set of books was the first he had ever seen. What joy awaited!

The cold light of the first day of May was warmed in passage through the stern windows and quarter badges. Frost sat gingerly in the solid and elegant chair, the ebony and ivory one that Struan had thoughtfully salvaged from Frost's cabin in the old *Salmon* and placed behind the captain's desk. Struan gave Frost the sloop's history and inventory, reading from a list he had painstakingly compiled. "*Jaguar* was specially commissioned by John Stuart, Earl of Bute, most likely as an attempt to ingratiate his way back into the good graces of George Three, for whom he had once been Secretary of State and Chief Minister. She was built at Port Glasgow, her lines taken off

Le Corsair, a demi-frigate of recent design from the draughting table of one of the best French naval architects of this age or any other, Alain Derrez. The stoutest Scot's oak went into her ribs, knees and planks, and good elm into her keel, but the supply of good masts being stopped from New Hampshire and Maine meant that she was fitted with masts from the Baltic upon her launch barely this year past."

Struan turned a sheet of paper from the sheaf in his hand face down on the desk, and held up another sheet. "We know the outcome of relying upon those Baltic masts, thank God. Had good sound Piscataway sticks been in her, that for which the Admiralty pays one hundred and fifty pounds delivered to the dockyard, we would nae be standing here now."

Frost nodded noncommittally. This cabin was much more elegant than what his brother, Joseph, had once derisively termed his "monk's cell" aboard *Salmon*, but an elegance that spoke of quiet good breeding and a refined, restrained, deliberately understated taste.

"Her length overall is one hundred and twenty-five feet; on the water line she is one hundred and five feet. Her gun deck is eighty-six feet, with a beam of thirty-four feet. Depth of hold is fourteen feet, and her registered Thames tunnage is three hundred and fifty. She bears, as we know, eighteen six-pounders."

"And her powder we know, Struan, is fifteen ton of the best corned English less than a year from the mill."

"Yes," Struan swallowed before continuing, "and most wondrous of all, as ye know, her bottom is coppered against the cirripeda, something I've never heard of, but upon reflection it makes excellent sense."

Frost smiled. "I've heard of it, though as a retardant against marine growth. In addition to stanching such growth, the copper makes cleaning a foul bottom much easier. Think of it, Struan, how much easier it will be to scrub barnacles and limpets which do adhere off copper rather than heavily tarred wood when we careen."

Struan Ferguson nodded. "Maylike, such a simple thing, so obvious and yet so unobvious. How many ships' designers, masters, dockmen may have thought of such a simple thing but did not act upon it. And seeing how the growth comes off the copper so wonderfully, at her careen it took less than two days to clean her complete to the keel."

Frost moved to the cabinet attached to the starboard bulkhead and opened several drawers. He drew out a heavy walnut case, knowing full well what the case would contain. "Tell me what you have divined about her captain."

"Hugh Stuart, second son of John Stuart, Third Earl of Bute, a Scots," Struan said with great bitterness: "a close adviser of George Three when George was still the Prince of Wales. Still favored by George, I'm reliably informed, but fell afoul of Grenville and banished. Being as Hugh Stuart was a second son, he was destined to be either clergy or a military man since he stood not to inherit. By all accounts, he came to his captaincy by merit."

Frost smiled thinly as he opened the walnut case. "As much as I keep you at sea, Struan, I do not know how you ken these matters."

Struan put down a sheet of paper with its inventory. "In almost every port where we touch there'll likely be a Scot or two. If they're highlanders, we be a small, quite small, fraternity, I can talk with them, but if they're from the lowlands I listen only, though I buy the liquor to ensure their tongues are loosened."

"I have heard of this marque," Frost said as he lifted one of the slim, all-metal pistols from its velvet nest. "But what can you tell me of Andrew Strachan?"

"A Scot of the last century, from around Edsell. By all reports he made wondrous pistols. His family continued the tradition. I know some were at Culloden. A bit long in the barrel for most tastes now, though ye'll note that pistol, known as a lemon butt, has a vent pricker screwed into the butt."

Frost cocked the pistol he had lifted from the case, after first running the ramrod down the barrel to make sure it contained no charge, and blowing into the pan to ensure no stray grain of powder was lodged there. The pistol, though overly long for his preference, as Struan had opined, had a balance that was steady and exact in his hand, a marvel, though he was somewhat discomfited by the lack of a trigger guard and the round knob at the base of the trigger. Frost aimed the pistol toward a port light. The cock struck a satisfying, though transient, shower of sparks from the frizzen, the majority of which fell into the uncovered pan. Frost savored the pyrite scent, akin to that left in the air following a near overhead flash of lightning, then put the pistol back in its case, closed it, and held out the case to Struan.

"It would pleasure me, Struan, if you would accept these pistols."

Struan Ferguson hesitated. "I dinna know if it be right, dividing up the property of a dead man thus. But they be good pistols, Scot's made, not those bastardized clumps being made now in London or Birmingham."

Frost clasped his hands behind his back and paced the cabin. Although the checkered sole and airiness make it appear large, it was, after all, a small cabin, the size expected on a three-masted, square-rigged sloop-o-war. He managed three full paces from the desk to the forward bulkhead. "I have purchased the cat, all her tackle and appurtenances, for the appraised and agreed upon sum of eleven thousand pounds in money of account. This amount has already been delivered to my father's bank, with due deduction to my cousin, John Langdon, of his six percent commission. The Frost Trading Company has been paid five thousand pounds, money of account, as compensation for the loss of *Salmon*. Of the remainder, as owner and captain, I am entitled to one half or fifty shares. Such amount, and more, I am applying against the cat's refitting.

"Officers and mates of the *Salmon*, carpenter, cooper, bosun, are due twenty shares, to be divided equally among them. The portion due our poor Roger Green has already been paid to his bereaved parents. Perhaps that act did as much to entice his cousin, Ezrah, to ship as our surgeon, as did a desire to spare others poor Roger's horrific and agonizing death. I do not know."

"And thirty shares apportioned among those shipped afore the mast," Struan said, "handsome indeed!"

Frost paced the width of the cabin, not even having to alter his stride to avoid the coal stove secured against the forward bulkhead. Almost four long paces, and he stopped to peer into the cubby where the captain's bunk was. His eye fell on the small but exquisite miniature of a young woman affixed on the bulkhead at the foot of the bunk. Mother? Sister? Wife? Friend? Mistress? He noted with satisfaction, though no surprise, the tell-tale compass mounted in the overhead above the bunk. It was a duplicate of the tell-tale compass he had already noted mounted over the captain's desk. Hugh Stuart could track his vessel's course from his desk or his bed.

"You have been too driven of late preparing the cat for sea, Struan, to reflect upon these matters. Your share amounts to one thousand twenty-five pounds, which sum, in specie, not those new Continental dollars, is on deposit with Rutherford, payable as you wish. All subordinate shares had been adjudged and paid out, even to the last shilling to the last widow." Frost paused to inspect the clock that reposed in a special gimbeled box. He expected Struan would tell him about this clock presently.

"The cat, and all that is in her, is mine, as much as any mortal in this life can command a vessel subject always to the vagaries of winds and tides. My cousin doubtlessly thinks I've the better of the bargain we struck, particularly now that he's had intelligence of her coppered bottom and sturdy construction—facts he could have ascertained before we concluded our negotiations for her price to be paid out to the *Salmon*'s crew, seeing as how it would affect the amount of his commission."

Struan coughed drily. "Yer cousin John has a masterful knowledge of cost plus a percentage of cost. I ken yer bold attack by offering him a high amount at the opening of negotiations gave rise to greed which caused him to accept handily for fear ye would change yer mind."

Frost returned to the desk and sat once again in the ivory and ebony chair. "My cousin thought we had fetched in a Royal

Navy vessel which had been hard used and sea-worn for two years, rather than a vessel scarce a year off the stocks. But the Scottish pistols are undoubtedly mine to gift." Frost held out the walnut case again.

Struan Ferguson took the pistol case hesitantly. "That gimbeled case contains a clock, a most wondrous exact clock, a clock so exact it is called a chronometer. A clockmaker named Harrison came up with the design. Supposedly he won some sort of prize the British Admiralty had long offered. Someone named Larcum Kendall made this one. There is a special procedure for winding, and I have been keeping it. With it you need never work a lunar to calculate longitude."

Frost's eyebrows shot up: "You may recall a Royal Navy vessel we met in Batavia which had a clock such as this you describe," but before he could say more a knock sounded at the door. "Enter," Frost commanded. Nathaniel Dance, his face immeasurably brightened by several scrubbings with lye soap personally administered by Mrs. Rutherford in her wash pot, peered around the door. "Beg pardon, sir, but a barge with some sort of dignity aboard just shoved off from the Portsmouth shore, and Bosun thinks it be someone ye should attend." His voice was almost drowned out by a burst of hammering.

"Ah, Mister Dance, have you enumerated your colleagues anxious to become New Hampshire citizens to Ming Tsun?"

"Yes sir, Mister Ming Tsun has a clear copy already made."

"And you furnished Ming Tsun only the names of the twenty men in which you repose the greatest confidence?"

"There be more than twenty, thirty-three more like, but as ye ordered I gave the names of the twenty I felt surest of."

"The prayers of the other thirteen shan't go unanswered, Mister Dance. Enumerate that list to Ming Tsun immediately, and I'll forward it to Captain John Manley of the Colonial schooner *Hancock*, who'll appear here shortly. He will likely winnow among those thirteen as he sees fit for his command. Though I value your judgments of men's characters most highly, you ken that I'm reluctant to ship more former king's men than a bare ten percent of my force, lest they conspire to rebellion."

"Just so, Captain Frost, sir. But Bosun desires yer presence on deck, should ye be so pleased. This dignity is approachin' at a wondrous rate."

Frost nodded, hand already at the door. "Shift those pistols to your cabin, Struan, and depart the ship the remainder of the day. Confirm with Rutherford where you wish your share deposited and discharge any local affairs you must, because we stand to sea prior to this week's end."

"I canna leave the ship now, sir. Whatever share may accrue to me, I shall be happy to entrust to yer father's bank, for I know him to be a man of punctilious honesty, though I could find . . ." Struan flushed, knowing where the sentence would end, and did not finish it. "I thankee for the pistols, Captain Frost," Struan said formally, clasping the walnut case to his breast and waiting until Frost had gone through the door.

Frost paused. "You are sure you want no liberty, Struan?"

"Plaisted fetched my chest from the *Salmon*, sir. Else I require, may I ask Nathaniel Dance to procure?"

"So be it, Struan. Your berth, of course, is the cabin once the province of Lieutenant Lithgow, now the darling of Portsmouth society, thanks to my cousin, Woodbury Langdon."

"Aye sir, and fear not on that account, for I have had it fumigated and repainted to rid the cabin of the lieutenant's stench."

"I wonder who this 'dignity' is whom Mister Dance reports comes at such a wondrous pace," Frost mused as he sought his way through the cat's unfamiliar passages to the deck, though once he had walked the passages he would recall them again unerringly.

Slocum Plaisted guided Frost through the buzz of workmen to the quarterdeck and pointed toward the barge partially shaded by a purple canopy with silver fringe being rowed by two smartly attired black men. Frost recognized Darius and his father, Prosperous. "Unless I be much mistook, Captain, that be your cousin, Mister Langdon, and pardon if I say it, sir, but he looks none too happy."

John Langdon's barge touched the owner's floating steps, and Langdon, surprisingly nimble for so large a man, stepped onto the float and came up the stairs with alacrity. Once on the wharf he scanned the bulwarks of the *Jaguar*. Frost walked to the side of the quarterdeck and lifted an arm. "Do you seek me, John?"

"Indeed I do, Geoffrey, I have your warrant as a private man-o-war, received within the hour by dedicated post from Philadelphia, and I desire to have a word with you—in private."

Frost nodded to Nathaniel Dance, who raced away to the stern brow spanning the *Jaguar* and the wharf. "The lad will show you to my cabin," he said. The words gave him a special thrill. He had been aboard the *Jaguar* for less than an hour, but the vessel was already as familiar to him as the *Salmon* had been.

⟶ XIII ⟵

"**IN** GOD'S NAME, GEOFFREY," JOHN LANGDON EXPLODED WHEN THE TWO OF THEM WERE ALONE IN THE CAP- TAIN'S CABIN OF EX-HM *JAGUAR*; alone except for the din of sawing and hammering, which made a virtual necessity of shouting. "What possesses you to think that you can purchase every slave in Portsmouth?"

Frost had taken the chair behind the desk for himself as soon as he and his cousin had entered the cabin. He would, out of simple courtesy, have offered the chair to his cousin, but John Langdon was accustomed to pacing, a trait common to most men who had commanded at sea. So Frost had taken the ivory and ebony chair as John Langdon began pacing the width of the cabin in quick, hurried steps. "Male slaves mostly, and only of a certain age, though I did purchase from our esteemed friend, Joshua Wentworth, or more accurately I paid into an escrow account pending his establishment of a prize court, with a commission for him, naturally, the four people languish- ing in gaol who had been taken from the *Elizabeth*."

"Slaves, Geoffrey," Langdon snapped irritably, "slaves, you purchased slaves, not people."

Frost was not really following the conversation. He had noted during his brief tour of inspection that the taff rail still re- quired repairs where his puny broadside had struck during his desperate fight off the Isles of Shoals. He was scheming out a way to protect that weak point of the sloop. "As you say, cousin."

"But to give them their freedom, and solicit others . . ."

"Their freedom, is it?" Frost said mildly. "I took the women to my mother who engaged them for wages. The two men I afforded the option of engaging with my mother for wages or entering my crew. Either way, they exchange their labor for argent; I am not sure that is freedom."

"But you engaged these slaves at the same wages you pay laborers and crew . . ."

"Then they cannot be slaves if they are compensated for their labors at the same rate as others, cousin, so why not refer to them as people, for such they surely are."

John Langdon stopped in mid-stride: "Geoffrey, cease mocking me this instant, this is a preposterously serious matter."

"Yes, working for wages certainly is," Frost said, allowing his gaze to wander toward the small sleeping cabin and wondering again at the identity of the woman in the miniature—she was almighty pretty. "Whereas I, who labor not for wages but the increase of my profits, bear a burden greater than slavery, for the fortunes, nay, the lives, of so many depend upon me."

"Geoffrey!" John Langdon flung out in desperation, "let us not jest, there is talk in the town . . ."

"As you know, cousin, I am neither interested in nor influenced by gossip; nay, I eschew it assiduously."

"But you are purchasing slaves in order to augment them into your crew . . ."

"I have paid the manumission price for ten people total," Frost said in an even tone of voice, "including the assistant to Tempel Bennington, who largely runs Tempel's grist mill on his own. He has the makings of a prodigious carpenter's mate." The woman in the miniature had to be either mother or sister to the late Hugh Stuart. He would ask Dance. Nathaniel Dance was a rare 'un; hard to believe the lad was only twelve years upon this earth. He possessed knowledge that learned men stooped with age, honors and prestige could never hope to attain. Nathaniel Dance would know. The youngster had filled out wondrously with Mrs. Rutherford's and Ming Tsun's attentions. "I have given the men the choice of working ashore or following the sea. As you remark, cousin, for those who work for wages there is little to distinguish between slavery and freedom. The men have opined that the sea is their true vocation."

"But Geoffrey, dear, these are men of a different stamp, as the Bible decrees—drawers of water and hewers of wood."

"I cannot tell you how glad I am you attend just now, cousin, for I was to wait upon you tonight. I wished to gaze once more upon your fair Elizabeth before I cruize; also, I collect a bauble, a ring to match the necklace of pearls, which Ming Tsun found among my tumbled effects and which should be a handsome complement. And for you I've noted a few bottles, a case or so, of especial port wine."

John Langdon gathered the tails of his coat into his lap and reclined on the larboard settee. "So you are set to cruize. I marvel that you have accomplished so much in two weeks' time."

Frost smiled and focused his gaze first on the polished brass of the chronometer and then on the equally polished rim of the tell-tale compass overhead. He and Ming Tsun had computed to the shilling what John Langdon's commission on the three weeks total labor of his cousin's yard workers would be. It was substantial. "I am always anxious to ship good men, and I wished to speak with you about Prosperous' son, Darius. He's a likely lad who, when manumitted, would doubtless wish to follow the sea as have Scipio Africanus and Cato Calite, men who have cruized with me in the old *Salmon*."

Langdon sat up quickly. "You say 'when manumitted,' cousin, as if the manumission of my property was an assumed end. And, pray, who are these Scipio and Cato you just enumerated?"

"Two Massachusetts men, freedmen for whom Hopkins had no use at New Providence, so I took them into my crew. They fought exceedingly well when we fought this *Jaguar* for our lives. As for the *Elizabeth* men, their enthusiasm for the sea is keen, but alas, whilst I see aptitude there, they have no practical knowledge of reefing, handing, and steering, so I have rated them landsmen against their sure education."

"Welcome to them, then, but Darius is issue of Prosperous and therefore my slave; my household has need of him."

Frost got to his feet, paced over and laid his hand on John Langdon's shoulder. "Forgive me, cousin, I prattle on about your property, when I just now collect that Darius is property of your wife. My manners are inexcusable. I cannot offer you a glass of spirit. I do not wish to victual until the cat is warped against my own wharf and powder has been stowed, a process which begins tomorrow. However, I can offer you tea. Ming Tsun!" Frost shouted.

The cabin door opened and Nathaniel Dance peered around. "Ye be calling for Mister Ming Tsun, sir?"

"Please pass the word for Ming Tsun and tea, Mister Dance. You have only to say the word 'tea' and he will understand."

"Yes sir, very good, sir," and Dance was gone.

"Who was that?" John Langdon asked. "Seems hardly old enough to be weaned."

"Cousin, are you forgetting that both you and I were apprenticed to the sea ere we were ten years of age?"

"All very well, Geoffrey, but who is he? He's not native to Portsmouth."

"Our namesake city in Hampshire, perhaps? He was aboard the cat and has come over to the colonies' side, along with a score of other former *Jaguars*. Think of it, John, British subjects who have foresworn their king and now enroll with us!"

"Yes," Langdon snapped. "Slaves to a tyrannic sovereign, who take up arms against their former sovereign. This is an analogy I wish to spare our nascent nation, Geoffrey . . ."

"All the more reason to enlist men of all persuasions, John! No tyrants we!"

"Geoffrey, mock me not!" John Langdon said fiercely. "Freedom is not a business for slaves . . ."

"There you have it, John! If we enlist men in freedom's . . . in justice's cause, they must not be slaves; at least they must be men able to sell their labor on their own volition where they will."

"A slave has no say in determining where his labor shall be

directed, Geoffrey; that decision is made for him, and I dare say, he is the better for it. A slave cannot comprehend the weighty issues of resistance to tyranny, a determination to rule one's self, a desire to shape one's own destiny . . ." John Langdon, highly agitated, had gotten to his feet and resumed a fierce pacing.

"And why not, cousin?" Frost asked gently.

"Because it flies in the face of common sense," Langdon said hotly. "Some are born to lead, some are born to follow, and there are others who are born to serve. It is all a matter of station."

"An accident of birth, then?" Frost interjected quickly.

"Geoffrey," Langdon said with exasperation, "a slave is a horse is a dog is a cow, to be directed to his duties and content with his lot. I tell you, it is the natural order of things." Langdon did not cease his pacing. "All as sanctified by Holy Scriptures and the clergy, Geoffrey. Consult the tax lists for Boston. You will see that over half of Boston's clergy—and there by a power of 'em—enumerated on the lists as slave keepers."

There was a knock at the door, followed by a squeaky voice: "Beg pardon, sir." Nathaniel Dance threw open the door, standing aside to make way for Ming Tsun who was carrying a tray.

"Please, there," Frost signed, and Ming Tsun put the tray on the desk. Ming Tsun thrust his hands into the sleeves of his tunic and retreated to stand beside the door. He was joined by Dance, who, having no flowing sleeves into which to thrust his hands, made do by clasping his hands into fists and standing to wooden attention.

"John, you will take tea with me? No one knows how to brew this remarkable infusion better than Ming Tsun, my companion for many a weary sea-mile."

"I do savor the aroma," Langdon said, doubtfully, his nose twitching. He did not object while Frost poured two cups and handed one to him. "Now why can't I get Prosperous to make tea the equal of this?" Langdon exploded after he had lifted his cup to lip. "Damn it, Geoffrey, this goes too far. You must have your Ming Tsun instruct my Prosperous on the correct way to infuse tea."

Frost set down his cup after swallowing a deep draft, a deeply satisfying draft. "I shall be happy to sign on Prosperous as a cook on the Frost Trading Company's first voyage to China once this current but long-simmering unpleasantness with the British has ended, John. But only on the condition that he has a writ of manumission in his pocket and decides of his own free will to sell his labor in such wise."

John Langdon also put down his cup, but it was empty, so Frost refilled it. "A slave has no will of the slave's own, but only the will of the master."

"Indeed?" Frost cocked an incredulous eye: "What say we send for Darius and ask him if he would—assuming his manumission—be lief to ship with this vessel as a landsman, or whether he would remain in your employ."

"A slave . . ." John Langdon began, but Frost cut him off.

"Mister Dance, favor me by inviting the young black gentleman waiting in the barge beside to present himself in my cabin as soon as he may find it convenient."

"Geoffrey, you do play too much the fool," Langdon remonstrated, but Frost was already pressing a third cup of tea upon him. "Damned fine tea," Langdon said with an air of resignation. "I don't suppose you could entice your servant to instruct my Prosperous with the secret of its making."

"You've asked that question already, cousin. Such instruction comes only at sea, when one has ample time to contemplate the stigmata of heaven and the stench of hell—and contemplate the brewing of the perfect cup of tea—on a six months' passage. But I think our young man comes."

Indeed, there was a clatter of heels on the companionway outside, and in a moment young Darius, all flustered and rigged out in his preposterous, plum-colored suit, miniature peruque, and tricorne trimmed all round with ostrich feathers, stood in their presence.

"Now see here, Geoffrey . . ." John Langdon began, but Frost interrupted.

"How old are you, Darius?"

Darius, still flustered, stood even more stiffly and moved his fingers in a futile effort to count his years. "I can't say, Captain. I know I was born in the year of the big snow."

"That was the year '61," Langdon snapped. "The boy is fifteen."

"If you are fifteen, then you are old enough to know your own mind, is that not true, Darius?"

"Oh yes, Captain, I knows my mind. Captain, I sure do."

"Then are you of a mind to cruize with me and follow the sea, Darius?" Frost looked keenly at the young man, whose face was bathed in perspiration.

"I be of such mind, Captain, but Masta John, he got the say what I be."

"There, John," Frost said triumphantly. "The lad knows his mind, and his mind compels him to follow the sea."

"Back to the barge, Darius," Langdon said brusquely. "I'll be returning to Portsmouth presently." Then to Frost, as the youth bowed stiffly and left through the door that Nathaniel Dance opened: "He's just a boy, Geoffrey."

"But he knows his mind, cousin."

"But I am his owner."

"Technically your wife is his owner, but of course our laws provide you with the ability to dispose of your wife's property, or else I should apply directly to her. What price do you name to no longer be his owner, then, John?"

"Sell him to you?" Langdon mused. "I had not thought on it."

"Not sell him to me, John," Frost said loudly, indicating to Dance and Ming Tsun that their presence was no longer necessary. "I can see no merit in this life or the next in owning another human's body. I wish merely to pay the price you set upon his manumission. Darius shall choose his own path, but if he chooses to follow the sea I shall gladly employ him."

John Langdon carefully placed his empty cup on its saucer. "I shall think on it. Perhaps I shall give you my decision tonight, but truth, cousin, I am loath to give up such a likeable and bright boy, and truth to say, he is Elizabeth's property, not mine. I gifted Darius to her shortly after our wedding."

"Even to fight for the freedoms of the United Colonies?" Frost asked.

Langdon did not note the irony. "The commission for your private vessel of war is complete, Cousin, save only her name. You may add that yourself once you have determined a name."

"The *Cat* will suffice for the moment, John."

"Elizabeth and I shall wish you every joy on your cruize, Geoffrey, though why you cruize so far when there are British prizes so much closer than the coast of Africa is beyond me."

"There be richer prizes, cousin," Frost said. "Faith, captains like Manley will leave but lean pickings in close waters."

"Tonight, then. Fashionable seven, thereabouts, I believe is the time Elizabeth has set."

"It shall be." Frost escorted John Langdon down to the floating wharf and handed him safely into his canopied barge. He returned to his ship and threaded his way through the press of workmen to the cat's bows, where he stood watching the barge's progress toward Portsmouth.

Nathaniel Dance joined him but said nothing, waiting a pace behind his elbow until Frost shot a quizzical glance at Dance to acknowledge the youth's presence. "There be two people telescopin' ye, Captain, from the far shore."

"My father and my brother, most likely."

Nathaniel Dance digested that information for a moment, then piped: "Ye be standin' where he stood when he cussed ye."

"Who was standing here, Mister Dance?" Frost said distractedly. So his father, Marlborough, and his brother, Joseph, were watching him. He had hoped Joseph would have remained at his iron works, casting cannon balls for the United Colonies.

"Captain Stuart, sir. He was planted right where ye be when he waved his fist and cussed ye somethin' awful for havin' killed his men. I had just brought up cartridges for the f'ard starb'd battery and I heard everything he said."

"The men at the oars of the two boats?" Frost conjured,

unbidden, the violence and deaths the two cannon balls laid by Caleb Mansfield had wrought.

"Yes, sir. Captain Stuart was wondrously wrought."

"You have an elegant turn of phrase, Mister Dance. Courtesy of your mess mate Mister Hewlett?"

"Yes, sir, Townsend, he studied me much as he could. He knew more than the master when he studied the young gentlemen, the midshipmen, sir. He was wondrous to hear talk, Townsend was. Many a forecastle jack would offer him a swig of their rum just to hear him recite stuff, poetry, he said, and by the way he talked about him, Townsend had a high regard for some chap named Shaky Staff."

"I likewise cursed your captain and your cat, Mister Dance," Frost said heavily, "when a ball from the cat came aboard my vessel and killed two of my men."

"Yes, sir. I heard ye did. Ye and Captain Stuart be much of the same stamp—beggin' yer pardon, Captain, sir, if ye appreciate not the comparison, it was not said in disrespect—for when ye loomed over me with yer cutlass I thought ye was Captain Stuart to strike me dead for not fightin' harder."

Frost searched the Portsmouth shore, wondering from which vantage point Marlborough and Joseph were watching him. Were they watching him even now? He unconsciously massaged his right arm against a vestige of lameness, then clasped his hands behind his back and began an inspection tour of the cat's standing rigging, which was being roved.

"Not taken as disrespect, Mister Dance," Frost said to the urchin, who walked a discreet pace behind him, consciously or unconsciously emulating Frost's stance of clasped hands. "Unlike a number of Englishmen met in my voyages, I believe I would have enjoyed Captain Stuart's company. More's the pity that we have been thrown into this killing of each other over restraint of trade, grossly unfair taxes—and no say in the governing of ourselves." Frost paused to murmur a word of encouragement to Slocum Plaisted, who was stripped to the waist as he assisted half a dozen heavily perspiring yard workers sway a six-pounder from the wharf onto the main deck.

"Captain Stuart, he wasn't no Englishman, sir, he was a right Scot."

"Yes, Mister Ferguson has often explained the vast gulf separating Scots from English," Frost said, barely restraining a smile. Indeed, he spied Struan Ferguson just now on the quarterdeck directing a quartet of carpenters measuring out repairs to the after rail. "You seem to know Captain Stuart well, Mister Dance," Frost said suddenly, laying hand to a ratline and testing it for proper impregnation of tar.

"No, sir. I never had a word with Captain Stuart at all, but I was near him oft enough and heard his talk with others. Heard him once talk to Lieutenant Lithgow about what would happen if he, Captain Stuart, fell in battle, how Lieutenant Lithgow was to follow Captain Stuart's standing orders for fightin' the ship. He even gave orders for his burial, he did, sir. Captain Stuart thought of most everything. He was a wondrous thinker."

"I suppose his desire was to be buried at sea," Frost said idly, having proved to his satisfaction that the rope was properly tarred and looking around for a scrap of cloth or a cup's worth of sawdust to cleanse his fingers.

"As ye say, sir. Captain Stuart spoke once of a strong dislike for being put under the ground, 'less he died an admiral of the blue, of old age ashore ashore, full of dignity, age and honors, I believe I heard him say." Nathaniel Dance obligingly found a handful of oak shavings with which Frost cleaned his fingers of tar.

"Mister Dance, please find Ming Tsun and tell him that I am ready to return to the warehouse. You shall remain here to assist Mister Ferguson, though I would take it with the greatest kindness if you could prevail upon Mister Ferguson to get some sleep in his cabin tonight. I know for a fact that he has not put head to pillow for the past three nights. Like all I hold in high regard, Nathaniel Dance, his health be precious to me." Frost paused, gazing at the swarming knots of workmen, whose toils seemed so uncoordinated, but whose toils were, in fact, as closely orchestrated as an opera; the cannons yet to be brought aboard, the balks of timber yet to be fitted, the piles of ropes and canvas yet to be rove and spread. From the direction of the makeshift target butts came the pop of musketry.

"Mister Ferguson has need of his sleep, Mister Dance, for tomorrow the cat must be shifted to my wharf, her powder and stores to be laded. Please remind Mister Ferguson and Mister Plaisted of my order that all crew be thoroughly bathed, barbered and deloused before they bring their effects aboard."

Late that night, after he had returned to his garret from the enviable and refreshing company of Elizabeth Langdon, Frost stood at his eastward-facing window, watching the braziers illuminating the cat and the activities aboard her, then silently pacing, pacing up and down the long room. Unable to sleep, he lighted another candle and cast once again the lists of men who would be embarked under him, the stores, water, rum, powder, sailcloth. If not all could be laded in three days' time, what could the cat most conveniently forego? No. If not all could be laded in the three days he had allotted, what could be deleted from the cat's manifest without putting her unduly at risk? Time and again he blotted what he had tallied, pulled a fresh page of foolscap from the pile in the center of his work table and began his tally anew.

Toward morning, Frost crept downstairs on stocking feet, small taper in hand, hoping not to awaken Ming Tsun; a forlorn hope as he well knew, since Ming Tsun, asleep on a pallet athwart the entry, was instantly awake as soon as Frost touched a kettle hanging near the dull coals in the fireplace to determine if the water it held was hot enough to brew tea. There was nothing for it then but to mull over his plan while Ming Tsun stirred up the fire and began to prepare Frost's breakfast.

Frost brushed aside both the breakfast preparations and all his instincts, which counseled that his plan was rash, quixotic; while he sipped a cup of tea, he calmly signed to Ming Tsun in great detail all that he expected Ming Tsun and Nathaniel Dance to accomplish before the setting of this day's sun. There was a great deal to be done before the full dawn. Frost signed with great emphasis that Ming Tsun was to exercise especial care that no one took notice of him or the boy at the graveyard.

☙ XIV ❧

☼☼☼☼☼ HE FIFTH DAY OF MAY 1776 BROKE
☼ ☼ QUIETLY. THERE WAS HARDLY ANY
☼ T ☼ WIND AT DAYBREAK, BUT BY SEVEN
☼☼☼☼☼ O'CLOCK GEOFFREY FROST, WHO HAD
been aboard the cat since midnight, felt a knot or two of wind
brush his left cheek as he gave the order to cast off the lines
holding the cat to the Frost Trading Company's wharf.

"Now see here, Geoffrey," John Langdon remonstrated at
Frost's elbow, "you cannot keep my workers aboard this vessel.
It—it is kidnapping."

Frost ignored his cousin. "Mister Ferguson, tops'ls on her,
gently, fore and main only, brace to larboard. Just enough to
keep steerage on her; the current will do the rest of our work."
From the corner of his eye Frost saw Caleb Mansfield emerge
from the press of people crowded onto the wharf. Caleb carried
a deerskin-wrapped bundle in his arms; hesitating on the edge
of the wharf and then seeing that the tide and the wind's
meager push had not yet taken the cat more than five feet into
the channel, he crouched and sprang like a veritable catamount
himself, launching himself successfully into a knot of landsmen
gathered at the waist, who cushioned his landing though falling
like so many bowling pins.

Caleb hastened up the break from waist to quarterdeck and
thrust the parcel into Ming Tsun's hands. "Here be yore arraws.
Took me a power of persuasion and a pile of skins, including
my last bear—all my deer and beaver, too, save that one yore

holdin'. But I got ever arraw the Abenaquis at Durham had, so help me."

Ming Tsun threw aside the deerskin cover, drew one arrow out of the large birchbark container, and examined it minutely. Ming Tsun scowled at the obsidian head, and Caleb interjected: "No ind'un ever knapped a knife after they seed a white man's metal blade. Precious few still knapp arraws, not if they kin get 'hold of a musket. I know they ain't as long as your arraws, and they've turkey rather than goose fletches, but the Abenaquis still make arraws as good as they come."

Ming Tsun balanced an arrow on his forefinger, then twirled it for concentricity; finding the balance of the arrow as it swayed on his finger to be acceptable, he nodded and smiled at Caleb.

"Cousin," John Langdon plucked Frost's coat hesitantly, "my workmen . . ."

"Any workman who attempts to leave my vessel before his task be discharged, John, shall be shot," Frost said quietly. "You should pass that word to them for their sakes. Mayhap it will add strength to their arms, more power to their saws, more precision to their hammers."

"But I am aboard also," John Langdon said, his voice uncertain, for he had not trod his own quarterdeck for at least ten years, and he knew he was subservient in that respect to Frost.

"By your choice, Cousin John," Frost said, not allowing himself to relish Langdon's discomfort. "You ken the boats I tow behind. Your workmen may depart—if their tasks be fairly done—once we fetch the booms. If not, they shall remain aboard until their tasks be finished, and I'll put them ashore somewhere in Massachusetts, or perhaps Maine."

"But what of me, cousin?" John Langdon said plaintively. "How shall I get ashore?"

"Have you written out the manumission for Darius?"

"Yes, damn you, I have it here." John Langdon quickly drew a piece of rolled foolscap from the tail pocket of his coat.

"John," Frost said kindly but softly so no one else could

hear, "a barge awaits you at the light tower. I'll touch just long enough to transfer you, and your workmen—though as you perceive, they bend to their tasks wondrously, for they truly believe I shall ship them with me."

"Faith, you had me believing it, cousin," John Langdon said crossly. "You have extorted the manumission from me."

"Only after paying full value to the most beautiful woman in Portsmouth, John, to whom you had so gallantly made Darius a present shortly after your exchange of wedding vows." Frost was frantically busy, his eyes darting quickly from sails to wind to current to tide, to crew to the people on shore. He was also mulling the ironic conventions of the times, which forbade a married woman control over her property and finances so long as she was married and required her husband's approval for virtually every expenditure.

Frost was not surprised to see his father's landau at the foot of Market Street, though he was mildly surprised to see Woodbury Langdon seated beside his father. Frost was more than mildly surprised to see Lieutenant Lithgow standing at the landau's side, conversing amiably with Woodbury and his father. Marlborough Frost should credit Ming Tsun's knowledge of the healing needles for his current mobility and freedom from gout's pain, Frost reflected as he searched the crowd for his brother, but if Joseph was there in the throng he was not with his father.

"Surely he is now in Saugus concentrating on ways to cast cannons, though such has not been successfully done before in these colonies. Like enough, it will be a Frost who first twigs the method," Frost said to himself. He glanced aloft at the taut canvas of the topsails. Great God, Great Zeus, Blessed Buddha, the Mighty Allah, but he was taking to sea an unknown vessel and an untried crew. He suspected that most of the men who had signed aboard for twelve Continental dollars per month had joined the cat because of Frost's feat of having defeated her in a single-ship duel; considering him a lucky captain, they were already counting their prize money. What he would not give for two months to whip this lot into shape.

"You are still bound on this quest of yours for the John Company's East Indiamen, cousin?"

Frost stared a moment at the rolled piece of paper that represented Darius' freedom before thrusting it toward Ming Tsun for safekeeping. "There be prizes, and there be prizes, John. An East Indiaman brought here as prize may easily yield a value of one hundred thousand pounds in specie."

"But suppose you cannot bring her all this way?" The avarice was hopeful in John Langdon's voice.

"Then into a French port surely, where the United Colonies have prize agents, cousin. But be not overly concerned as to the nature of prizes. The ocean is large and holds its mysteries and secrets dear. If the seas bear the fruits of India and China as I hope . . . well, I would much prefer bringing any prizes back to these shores." The current was increasing its pull, and Struan Ferguson and Slocum Plaisted, both standing near the helm, were gazing expectantly at Frost.

"Let fall the spritsail, Mister Ferguson, and haul taut." The spritsail was out of fashion with many captains and rarely used, but Frost had always found this scrap of canvas, spread on its absurd yard beneath the bowsprit, to be an excellent way to enhance a vessel's agility, especially when instant helm response was necessary, as in the straited, tortuous, dangerous channel of the Piscataqua on a swift outgoing tide. Knowing his captain's predilections, Struan Ferguson had stationed two old *Salmon* hands in the bows to hand the spritsail sheets.

Then in a much larger voice Frost shouted, "And cut those launches we are towing free immediately if this gaggle of pampered yard workers, who have scarce a callus among the lot, don't finish their carpentry tasks! Careful there at the braces!" Frost shouted, "Veer not a line more!" Then to the helm: "Steady and meet her, hold fair for Pull-and-be-Damned Point, then helm up at my word." The pull of the tide, the excitement of taking the cat to sea, the clean bottom that accelerated the cat's speed, the furious hammering and sawing of the yard workers laboring mightily to finish the last details for which Frost had so exorbitantly paid were a tonic to counteract the three weeks Frost had spent ashore readying the cat for this day.

Behind him a carpenter was demonstrating to Struan Ferguson how the heavy rectangular plugs in the stern bulwarks were lifted to open firing ports for the nine-pounders. "Mister Ferguson, why haven't those plugs been painted? John," Frost said urgently, turning to his cousin, "this man's work remains undone, so I am shipping him until his tasks be completed. I'll land him on the first civilized shore I touch, though his carpentry skills are so few, by all rights I should rate him landsman and augment him into my crew." Frost heard the carpenter's sudden wail of terror. "Mister Ferguson! Keep that man at his job or he'll likely rate no more than helper to Barnes the cook."

"Now, Geoffrey," John Langdon said soothingly, "this man, Sumner Morris, is a capital shipwright, and I have much need of him in my yard . . ."

"Cousin!" Frost said sharply to stop the conversation, gazing aloft to gauge whether he should order a reef in the topsails for a slight slackening of speed before the sharp change of course necessary to keep to the middle of the channel. By God, no! Frost was awed, as he always was upon the first unfurling of a sail, by the mystery and the miracle that puny man could entrap the wind, control it, though never tame it, momentarily harnessing something ephemeral as breath to move something so ponderous as a vessel across and through the element of water.

The cat was abreast the Pool and the dozen vessels at anchor there. Frost saw John Ayres standing near the tiller of His Excellency's schooner *Lynch*, named for a South Carolina delegate to the Continental Congress; Ayres was examining the cat through his telescope. *Lynch*, with its incongruous four small two-pounder pop guns! But Ayres was an able and brave captain whom Frost respected, and he would have given much to have Ayres as a ship's officer. But once a man had trod the planks of his own quarterdeck he would never, willingly, serve as a ship's officer under another. Command, no matter how small the vessel, was a powerful tonic.

Frost was eager to gain the sea, and the flow of speed down the Piscataqua was as intoxicating as the inward pull of tide and wind that had sped the *Salmon* so rapidly up the river a bare three weeks before. The lure of performing an intricate feat of seamanship with panache and nonchalance before an audience of his peers was as strong as the tide that pulled the cat seaward. Shamelessly, Frost yielded to the lure.

"Mister Ferguson, please to shake out the reef remaining in the fore topgallant," then the quick thrust of guilt striking to the core of his being, the sudden acute awareness of his own hubris and vulnerability. The cat had awakened beneath his feet a bare fifteen minutes before, and he was already risking her life in a restricted, hazardous channel for the momentary glow of showing off in front of one of Washington's captains and others of his peer. Doubtless they would think him an idiot instead.

Frost thought of the *Salmon*, already a hulk, everything of possible value removed from her, the rest destined to be reduced to firewood. Frost was glad he would not be ashore to watch the final humiliation and destruction of the vessel that had been his only home for nigh onto ten years. How he loved the *Salmon*! Could he ever love this cat so?

But Frost had committed himself and his ship. He turned to John Langdon and continued in a more even, though quite loud, tone: "Cousin, the barge which will take you off is less than fifteen minutes away. If you have anything you wish to say to these workers before you take your leave of them, the moment may be appropriate."

"But Geoffrey," John Langdon said, hardly heard over a rising chorus of terrified, dismayed wails from the nearest yard workers.

"Damn it, John!" Frost fairly screamed. It was a proper theatrical scream, and Frost was quite proud of it. "These men, though no fault of your own, of course, dragged out a simple outfitting job which should have taken no more than one week into thrice that length. I can't imagine how they'll ever complete your *Raleigh* when their only concerns are their own indolence and sloth." Frost was enjoying himself hugely.

John Langdon appeared on the verge of apoplexy. "Cousin . . ."

Frost moderated his tone. "All right, John, your men may accompany you ashore, but only because of my esteem for you. Should I ever have need of these men again, I truly expect they shall willingly redouble their efforts for my forbearance."

Then quickly to the helmsmen: "Up helm!" And the cat turned smartly on her rudder, water boiling beneath the bows and flinging as high as the bobstay as the cat shoved her counter toward the Pull-and-be-Damned rocks, then straightened and shot past them. Frost ordered the helm almost due east. The cat was even with Fort William and Mary, the light tower plainly visible a point or two off the starboard bow and a barge with the rowers resting on their oars scarce half a cable's length off the light.

"You must now take your leave, John," Frost said quickly. "I'm hauling my wind only long enough to put you and your workmen over the side. A British warship is likely cruising offshore, and should she come hull up whilst we are discharging picnic-fashion, it would go ill for us."

"Quite," John Langdon agreed readily. "I think my workmen will need no urging to fall into their boats and pull for shore. I am thinking to give them a day's rest on the Sabbath, on full pay, since they have served you wondrous well with their labor."

"I could not agree more, cousin," Frost said, "so long as their wages for the day come from your six per centum. My generosity has long since been strained." Frost hesitated. "Still, we both concede that the cat has profited by a swift and thorough refit, so if you be pleased to give your workmen a day of paid rest, I shall go halves with you for their wages of the day."

"Splendidly said." John Langdon grasped Frost's right hand and pumped it enthusiastically. "You cannot deny that my men have done well by your ship."

Yes, Frost reflected, the refit had been done in an impossible three weeks, but he still had an untested ship and an unknown, green crew. And he did not like the greenish-gray tint of the sky to the south and east.

Struan Ferguson cleared his throat to gain Frost's attention. "I believe we are about to greet an old shipmate, sir."

Frost glanced quickly at the barge, then ordered all sails backed. The cat fell off handsomely and came to a gentle halt, slightly rolling in the chop of the open bay a bare three oar strokes from the barge. The barge was alongside in a trice, and a youth, leading an elderly gentleman, was shortly aboard.

Frost met them at the waist entry. "I bid you welcome, Mister Bowditch," he said by way of greeting to young Hannibal Bowditch. "Do I take it rightly this be your father?"

"Please you, Captain, yes," the elderly man said, peering at Frost with rheumy eyes. "I be Habakkuk Bowditch of Salem, proud to be father to young Hannibal here, but Mary and I have four mouths at home to feed, his brother, Nathaniel, bare three years old, and me, after the disastrous loss of the ship of which I was master, employed now as a cooper. So I came all this way from Salem to ask you to ship young Hannibal for your current cruize."

Frost shook Habakkuk's hand warmly. "Your son has proved his valor and worth, Mister Bowditch. Truth, I have already looked for him among the crew, and heartily glad I am to see him. I know it is a long way to Salem and back, and hard to give up the lad after so brief a stay at home." Frost was anxious to shake out more sail and be on his way, but Struan and Rawbone, the gunner, were making the yard workers walk between them one at a time before clambering down into the boats, to ensure the yard workers were taking only their tools and not absconding with any of the cat's stores.

"May I suggest that once landed you make your way to my warehouse at Christian Shore and inquire for Mister Rutherford? Young Hannibal has some hundreds of dollars of wages and prize money to his account, and if he approve, you should have part of it."

"Joy at meeting with you again, Captain Frost," young Hannibal Bowditch said demurely, "and happy to ship with you again. My family shall have all in my account, if you could make the proper paper for me to sign."

"Surely," Frost said, begrudging the precious seconds he had to snatch away from his ship's management, not liking the southern sky at all, and keenly aware that the wind could shift at any moment, perhaps even embay the cat in the Piscataqua estuary. But he was glad to see Hannibal Bowditch once again. He and Nathaniel Dance would complement each other splendidly. Then again, he thought, they might not. No, they would complement each other, or he would have the hides off both of them. Ming Tsun was at his elbow with a portable secretary, a sheet of paper already on the platen, and on a sidepiece the sum owing to Hannibal Bowditch written in.

"Mister Bowditch, I find you have six hundred and fifty-five Continental dollars as your share of the capture of this prize. Wish you to keep no part of it?"

Young Bowditch whistled under his breath, and his father's eyes widened at the announcement of such a magnificent sum. As a cooper, Frost doubted that Habakkuk Bowditch would see half that much in a year, though there was little likelihood that the Continental Congress would ever make good on its promises to redeem dollars, which were nothing more than optimistic draughts on an empty Continental Treasury. "All of it to my family, sir," young Bowditch answered confidently.

Frost scratched a few words on the paper, grateful that Ming Tsun had trimmed the quill for a left-hander and had let no one else use the quill to wear the nub. He knelt down on the quarterdeck and held out the paper for Hannibal's inspection. "Your signature on this paper ensures the payment of six hundred and fifty-five Continental dollars to your father as your agent."

"I sign gladly, Father," Hannibal Bowditch said as he grasped the quill Ming Tsun held out for him, one cut and shaped for a right-hander. "Cruizing with Captain Frost, I am assured of far more."

The boy's confident words smote Frost like a physical blow. He turned to John Langdon, who had just noisily cleared his throat, a not-so-subtle hint that he wished to take his leave. "Cousin, kindly remember me to la belle Elizabeth."

"She went this day to commiserate with Charity."

"I am truly sorry that my haste to ready this vessel for sea spared me no time to visit my sister, John," Frost said, choosing his words carefully to forestall more from Langdon. "But Charity knows full well that this war we have had thrust upon us is fraught with great perils and dangers. At least she possesses the luxury of knowing that her husband is alive. Of the seventeen men who cruised with me to New Providence and then walked through the wall between life and death on my behalf, John, ten left widows and I reckon twenty-four orphans, though at least one widow is springing with child and shortly will bring an infant into this world who shall never know its father."

Frost then shook Langdon's hand heartily. "Your yard workers did a superb job on the cat, John." Frost swept his hand around, taking in the entire ship. "And we drove them harshly, I acknowledge. Upon your return to Rising Island at the tide's changing, you will find my man Rutherford has delivered two pipes of best Jamaica rum to your yard, and for the men enumerated on this list, whose diligences are attested by Struan Ferguson and Slocum Plaisted," Frost handed Langdon a letter, "there waits a Spanish silver five-dollar piece from the cat in appreciation."

John Langdon cleared his throat several times, searching for words. "You'll spoil my yard men, Geoffrey. They'll be hard pressed to return to work on the *Raleigh* after such largess."

"Hopefully, they'll soon be employed building merchantmen rather than ships of war, John." And then his cousin was over the side, and with a perfunctory wave to Langdon and Habakkuk Bowditch, Frost surveyed his ship and saw with immense satisfaction that Struan Ferguson had hands already prepared to execute his next command.

"Mainsail haul, Mister Ferguson!" And to the helmsman: "Our course be southeast by east."

✥ XV ✥

HE STORM—IT WAS NOT REALLY A STORM, BUT RATHER A BLUSTERY, PRO-LONGED SQUALL—LASTED THE BETTER PART OF TWO NIGHTS AND INTO THE early morning of the third day. Frost had sailed directly into the squall at first, to get away from any coasting British frigate, to get as far offshore as he could, and to observe his crew. Frost had gone over the names of the men enrolled aboard the cat, making a tic by the names he knew either personally or by reputation. He knew so few of them out of the 227 signed aboard. As he cast the figures a second time to make certain of the reckoning, Frost reflected that he had only fifty men less that the number Magellan had crowded into his five ships that late September day in 1519 when those incredibly small vessels had cleared the mouth of the Guadalquivir.

Frost was under no illusions about the overall quality of the men he had enlisted and fully anticipated that his raw crew would present as much a challenge to his leadership as Magellan's rabble of adventurers had presented to that worthy. He kept the cat under storm canvas, weighing his crew closely as they changed the fair weather sails for the heavier sailcloth, keeping the cat mostly on a larboard tack in winds that gusted to twenty knots and seas that crested as high as six feet.

Frost was pleased to find the cat a dry and weatherly vessel, one that tracked a steady course without the adverse roll, almost a wallow, that had been the bane of every merchantman he had ever commanded. At the end of the second day Frost knew that the cat was a glorious ship, a miraculous sailor. He heartily wished his crew met the cat's measure. The cat, as a British sloop-o-war, could accommodate 120 to 150 people within the compass of her 125 feet. She was severely cramped now with 227 souls since the arrival of young Hannibal Bowditch.

During all his years in the China trade, Frost had settled on three watches as the most efficient way to utilize his crew; one third of his complement on duty, one third off watch, and one third sleeping. From long custom and usage, men expected eight hours of sleep, and the system of three watches, with four hours on beginning with the evening watch, continuing through the afternoon watch, then two dog watches of two hours each between four in the afternoon and eight in the evening, provided it.

And he had never had any high regard for strict adherence to the ship's bell for keeping his crew informed of the passage of time. Frost himself had a keen regard for time and the mathematical beauty and exactness of a celestial observation. But a bell thirty minutes prior to the changing of the watch, and a double bell to summon the off-duty watches, and such of the duty watch as could be spared, to meals, had proven sufficient for his merchantman crews.

So he formed the cat's company into three divisions, one under Struan Ferguson, another under Slocum Plaisted, now advanced to second mate, and the third temporarily under John Nason, the same John Nason who had designs upon a minister's pulpit but who had shipped with Geoffrey Frost since the times were not accommodating to a course in divinity. Frost reckoned that if the cat were actually a commissioned war vessel he would be the captain as well as master, Struan would be the first lieutenant, Slocum the second lieutenant, and Nason the third lieutenant.

Now that Hannibal Bowditch had rejoined, all of the old *Salmon*s whose wounds had not been disabling had signed aboard for the cruise. Caleb Mansfield has recruited ten woodscruisers supremely confident in their skills with rifle, knife and hatchet, so Caleb was a lieutenant of marines. Frost half smiled at the thought: Caleb would have been incredulous at the mad idea of his being an officer, or even a non-commissioned officer for that matter. The boy, Nathaniel Dance, had brought aboard twenty former *Jaguar*s, whose applications for New Hampshire citizenship were pending before the legislature. Frost did not doubt but that half the ex-*Jaguar*'s crew would have been amenable to cruising with him, but he had drawn the line at accepting more than twenty, at that almost one tenth of his crew. If others wanted to escape the uncertainties of waiting for an exchange that might never come, or mayhap even found the idea of fighting for the United Colonies appealing, then they could volunteer for other privateer captains. For the men he had brought, rate Nathaniel Dance as master's mate.

Frost believed he had stumbled onto a real treasure in the taciturn Rawbone: if Knox—now so infatuated with cannon that His Excellency, Mister Washington, had designated the former bookseller as his ordnance master—had known about the man, Knox would have given a great cartload of his favorite snuff to employ him; so rate Rawbone master gunner. And Frost knew he also was fortunate, extremely fortunate, to have Ezrah Green aboard as surgeon.

So the cat had the nucleus of an efficient crew that any privateer captain or naval commander would gladly have sold his soul to the devil to possess. But there was the matter of the crew: the ex-*Jaguar* men, the farmers, the men who claimed to be seamen, able to reef, steer and hand, but whose qualities were completely unknown to Frost or any of his officers, who had been so occupied with repairing and victualling the cat for her cruise that it had been impossible to form any opinion as to their individual capabilities or their reasons for shipping aboard the cat.

If asked, certain of the men would cite a desire to fight for the freedom of the United Colonies against the tyranny of the ministerial government of England. And that was a load of codswallop. Men like John Langdon, Benjamin Franklin, and John Adams were astute enough to cherish concepts such as liberty and self-determination; but these were abstract concepts to most Americans, who were resolutely apolitical. In that, Frost knew, they were no different from the vast majority of Englishmen. He reckoned the vast majority of men born in the United Colonies had signed aboard the cat for the twelve dollars a month and the potential prize money he offered.

So, as with all his crews, Frost had to give his men something to believe in, something to work for. That "something" was not an amorphous concept of liberty and freedom that did not ring well with landsmen more concerned with their crops or animals than hyperbole they could not comprehend. But to identify with and believe in a known quantity to believe in a known quantity—that is, his vessel—aye, that was the key to getting men to work, and to fight. Not for the United Colonies, but for a smaller universe, the universe populated by a ship's crew. That was his next order of business. But first, there were certain solemnities to be observed.

At six o'clock on the morning of 8 May 1776, Frost appeared on deck to gauge the weather and was pleased to note that the sun was coming up gloriously strong to easy seas and light winds out of the southwest that were, as the chalk board verified, pushing the cat along at a steady six knots. "Mister Ferguson, I would appreciate your ordering the ship rigged for chapel services, and I would appreciate your swaying up the coffin stowed in the cable tier."

"Aye, sir," Struan Ferguson replied, the thought of questioning his captain's unusual request never once crossing his mind. "Rig chapel and sway up the coffin from the cable tier." And he at once began bellowing the necessary orders to a surprised crew.

❧ XVI ❧

GEOFFREY FROST HAD SHIFTED INTO HIS BEST TAI-PAN'S COAT, THE GREEN-ISH-GRAY ONE, WHICH MRS. RUTHER-FORD HAD ASSIDUOUSLY BRUSHED TO clean and raise the nap before Ming Tsun had packed it in Frost's sea chest. He was studying the service for burial at sea contained in the Royal Navy's *Book of Regulations* when a hurried knock resounded on his cabin's door. He looked up and nodded to Ming Tsun, who drew open the door to reveal an agitated Struan Ferguson.

"Sir," Struan took one hesitant step into the cabin, "beg yer pardon, sir, but there be two coffins on the cable tier. I was not able to divine yer intentions about which one to sway up, they being coffins and all, and not wanting to disturb whoever be inside . . ."

But Frost, glimpsing the truth, the awful truth, because he knew, he absolutely *knew*, had slammed down the Royal Navy's book of regulations and was bolting for the door. He brushed past Struan Ferguson, who had drawn himself into an inconspicuous width. "Struan, please locate Doctor Green, my respects to him, and would he be kind enough to join Ming Tsun and me on the cable tier with whatever medicines he deems fit to revive a living corpse."

Frost, followed by an equally frantic Ming Tsun, pounded away toward the cable tier, scarcely aware that the cat was heaving to, her speed slowing as sheets were slackened and way came

164

off her, scuttling doubled over along the passageway next to the hull, breath coming in labored gasps, hurtling down more ladders than he could recall until he stood in the cable tier, in the circle of fitful light cast by a phoebe lamp held by a white-lipped Nathaniel Dance.

Frost stood for a second, lungs laboring, taking in the two coffins, both weighed down by massive bights of ropes and hawsers yet to be stowed in their proper places. He looked carefully at both coffins, one of whose planks bore evident traces of earth attesting to the fact that it had been interred in the ground, the other's clean exterior mute evidence that it had never nestled in a muddy grave.

He bent close to the mud-encrusted coffin that was nearer and took an exploratory sniff, catching only a faint—very faint —cadaverine aroma of corruption. "When we's dug him out, he was fair preserved, sir," Nathaniel Dance quavered. "The ground, it was cold and all, so it weren't like he was already worms. We took him to yer warehouse, like ye ordered, and wrapped him in the sheets, spirits-soaked, and he was right proper for another funeral . . ."

Frost signed furiously to Ming Tsun, then snapped: "Mister Dance, give Ming Tsun a hand in clearing those hawsers off the second coffin, quickly now!" He turned to the noise of foot-steps hurrying along the passageway against the cat's hull. "There you are, Ezrah! God bless your speed! Pray you and Ming Tsun attend my brother who lies in yonder coffin, never dreaming that he could not, like Lazarus at the voice of Jesus, rise easily from the tomb . . . nor anticipate that his coffin would be stored on this cable tier with hundreds of pounds of hawsers and cables atop."

Frost watched with increasing anxiety as Ming Tsun, Na-thaniel, and Struan feverishly tugged away the heavy cables and hawsers piled on the second coffin, heedlessly covering them-selves with tar and Portsmouth Harbor's foul mud, until the last coil slid aside and they stared at the bare coffin in the light of the phoebe lamp that Frost now held. Ming Tsun had pro-duced the kris from inside his tunic's sleeve and was preparing to insert the blade into a slight gap between side and lid of the coffin at one corner.

"Yes, Ming Tsun, unless my surmise be wrong, you need only start the lid: those screws do not go through." And surely enough, Ming Tsun's blade, pried upward, popped the lid off the coffin, and Geoffrey Frost, leaning anxiously forward, saw what he knew he would see—the still, pale, hideously contorted and desiccated features of his brother, Joseph.

A very shaken Geoffrey Frost returned to his cabin to compose himself while Struan Ferguson took charge of bringing up the coffin containing the body of Hugh Stuart, and Ezrah Green and Ming Tsun labored mightily on the cable tier to preserve the faint spark of life glimmering in the breast of Joseph Frost.

The knock at the cabin door was followed by a soft, low cough that Frost recognized as Nathaniel's. Frost crossed to the door, his own somewhat tattered Bible and the Royal Navy's *Book of Regulations* under his right arm and his tricorne in his hand, noting with approval as he opened the door that Nathaniel Dance had cleaned himself of mud and tar remarkably in so short a time.

Nathaniel held himself rigid, eyes straight ahead. "Chapel rigged, sir. Coffin at the waist, covered proper with the ensign and all. I dinna think the Americans in our crew was acquainted with the procedures, so I asked the *Jaguar*s to assist, and to a man they was."

Frost mounted the companionway with a calm, even pace belying his inner turmoil, Nathaniel Dance a respectful step behind him. "Thank you, Mister Dance. I knew without doubt that I could depend upon you." He clapped tricorne to head as he paused at the head of the companionway before stepping out upon his quarterdeck, looking around at the calm sea upon whose bosom the cat rolled slightly, the azure mid-Spring sky above, a tidy bank of white clouds to the north, and the crew of the cat, in a polyglot of mismatched landsmen's clothes, drawn up in uneven ranks on the waist.

The coffin, draped with the Royal Navy's red ensign that Hugh Stuart had so proudly flown above his *Jaguar*, and that he had been in the reluctant process of hauling down to spare his men further death and maiming when life had left him, lay on a grating placed at the starboard waist entry. Frost recalled something about the protocol of a Royal Navy vessel of war, the captain always returning and departing by the starboard entry, and appropriate honors rendered, et cetera. He solemnly descended the short ladder to the main deck, hearing nothing but the soft murmur of wind in the rigging, so silent was the crew; even the working of the ship could not be heard. A day fair enough for a funeral, Frost decided.

Eight men, ex-*Jaguars*, stood, four along either side of the grating; a pipe twittered somewhere as Frost's right foot touched the main deck and the eight men braced to attention. The pipe was a thoughtful touch: doubtlessly he had Nathaniel Dance to thank for that courtesy. Frost paced solemnly to the waist entry, turned with his back to the entry, removed his tricorne and handed it to Nathaniel. He surveyed the assembled crew, noting John Nason at the head of his division, tufts of bristle on cheeks and chin showing the recent attention of a razor. "You prayed him, his crew and ours, directly into Heaven," Frost thought to himself as he looked at the expressionless Nason, "but it is up to me to commit his body to its rightful owner."

Frost opened the *Book of Regulations* to the burial service at sea and nodded to Struan Ferguson: "Mister Ferguson, please ask the men to uncover." Struan shouted the order, and those of the crew who possessed hats and caps, though unsure of what would happen next, promptly whipped them off. Frost began reading the ancient words: "Man, who is born of woman, hath but a brief time to live upon this earth . . ."

He continued through the solemn service, giving each word eloquence and meaning, marveling at how still the sea was, how silent the ship, and how indecipherable to mortal man the workings of the God, the Great Buddha, El Senhor, Allah, the Almighty One. Frost closed the *Book of Regulations*; the remainder of the service so clear that he did not need to refer to the printed page.

"And we therefore commit the mortal body of our comrade, Captain Hugh Stuart, fallen gallantly and with great honor in the defense of His Britannic Majesty's sloop-o-war *Jaguar*, to the deep, to be turned into corruption, looking for the resurrection of the body, when the Sea shall give up Its dead, and the life of the world to come, through Our Lord Jesus Christ; who at His coming shall change his vile body, that it may be like His glorious Body, according to the mighty working, whereby He is able to subdue all things to Himself, in the sure and certain knowledge that the immortal spirit of Captain Hugh Stuart, who having done his duty in this life, shall be numbered among the Elect of Heaven in the Life Everlasting."

And under his breath: "Inshallah." He was faintly envious. "You are out of it now," Frost thought. "You did your duty. You don't have to go on any further."

Frost nodded to the eight sailors and saluted the ensign; the hidden pipe twittered, the sailors raised the grating smartly to a sixty-degree angle, and the coffin slipped smoothly from beneath its draped Royal Navy ensign, dropping, with scarcely a splash, into the sea. Frost was reminded of the cannons he had consigned overboard during the *Salmon*'s chase by the *Jaguar*.

Frost handed his Bible and the Royal Navy's *Book of Regulations* to Nathaniel Dance. "Command the crew to stand easy, Mister Ferguson. I desire to address them." Behind him the eight ex-*Jaguar*s were solemnly folding the red ensign. Frost paced in front of his crew after Struan Ferguson had given the order to stand easy, peering intently into the face of each man he passed.

"The business of this ship is to capture prizes, to harass and deny the ministerial government of Great Britain the benefits of its lucrative trade. Mayhap the denial of trade will cause the ministerial government to think anew its unscrupulous declaration of war against our lands in the colonies, where we, through hard labor and the sweat of our brows, had built our lives unaided by the ministerial government, nay, challenged by the ministerial government at every turn."

The men were paying him polite attention, mostly, though

he saw queries in the eyes of some, and there was one man—where had he seen him before?—whose smirk indicated his attention was elsewhere. "But our business is to capture prizes." He paused for dramatic effect. "It is given to us the privilege of gaining prizes and doing great work for our United Colonies at the same time. We have shaped a course for Louisbourg, where the British government has gathered a large fleet of wealthy prizes for our taking—-and where a number of our countrymen lie prisoners ashore."

Frost willingly spoke half a lie, perhaps a full lie, and he detested himself for it. He had absolutely no intelligence, or even a hint of intuition, that any British vessels worthy to be taken as prizes, nay, any vessels at all, lay at anchor in Louisbourg Harbor. And all he had in the line of credible proof—if Joseph's enthusiasm could be credited as evidence—that his brother-in-law, Marcus Whipple, and an unknown number of other New England folk were imprisoned in the old fortress was the unsubstantiated word of one escaped prisoner from Halifax. "We shall set our fellow countrymen imprisoned there at liberty whilst, at the same time, snapping up vessels whose cargoes are valued at a minimum ten thousand pounds." The cat rolled softly, and Frost willed the vessel to be still, held in place on the surface of the sea by the tightness of his overly taut stomach muscles. "Ten thousand pounds each," he said for emphasis.

"We have a staunch vessel, a fine crew, and naught shall prevail against us. You shall return to Portsmouth as heroes. Wealthy heroes." Frost turned abruptly and nodded at Struan Ferguson. "Please dismiss the men, Mister Ferguson, then ease off and put the cat before the wind," and Frost strode back to his quarterdeck.

The crew dispersed, but slowly, and Frost marked the furtive way small clumps of men coalesced, exchanged a few words, then split apart. "What I wouldn't give for a right crew of men who had been with me ten years in the China trade," Frost said to himself as he checked the cat's course against both binnacles. He had brought aboard the cat the *Salmon*'s binnacle, knowing it to be exceedingly accurate, but more perhaps as a talisman, a link to a vessel that had served Geoffrey Frost well, even to the extent of surrendering its life for him.

Frost paced the weather side of his quarterdeck while Struan ordered several minor sail changes and ranged around the main deck to check tension and haul on stays and sheets. From the corner of his eye, Frost saw Hannibal Bowditch emerge from the fo'c'sle scuttle close beneath which Ezrah Green had established his sick bay, threading his way between the cannons and knots of men, clumping up the waist ladder for all the world as loud as a herd of cattle anxious for their barn, to stand breathless before his captain.

"Compliments of Doctor Green and Mister Ming Tsun, Captain sir, they wish to inform you that the gentleman lives!"

Frost did not check his steady pace down the weather rail. "I'm pleased to hear it, Mister Bowditch. Our United Colonies can scare abide the loss of even one man in these crucial times." Frost peered aloft to gauge the effects of the wind that was now striking his cheek at a slightly different angle. "Even one who willingly brings his own coffin to war," he said to himself.

"Doctor Green says the gentleman is wondrous resilient, filled with 'jug de vie,' I think them's the words he said, Captain sir, though I never heard them before."

"Please ask Doctor Green to spare Ming Tsun as soon as convenient, Mister Bowditch. I have work for him."

"Yes, Captain sir, but Doctor Green asks where shall the young gentleman berth once he's regained his strength. Doctor Green is quite willing to surrender his berth and shift elsewhere."

Frost turned sharply and fixed the youth with an icy stare: "Mister Bowditch, the young gentleman whom Doctor Green attends is a stowaway, and once the good doctor discharges him from care, he shall be turned forward. I doubt if he can be rated more than a landsman, more's the pity when we need men acquainted with ship-keeping." He cocked an eyebrow when Hannibal Bowditch stood seemingly rooted to the quarterdeck, his mouth agape. "Was there something else, Mister Bowditch?"

Geoffrey Frost was now responsible for the lives and wellbeing of 228 people, himself included.

"No, Captain sir," young Bowditch stammered. "The young gentleman to be turned forward in the fo'c's'le, once he's able. Very good, Captain sir." And Hannibal Bowditch turned and was gone.

Frost did not see the youth go. He was staring fixedly astern at a wondrously large albatross that was following in the cat's wake, though he could not see the albatross very well through his tears, which fortunately were hidden from the helmsmen until the passage of time and the stiffening breeze astern dried them.

❧ XVII ❧

CALEB MANSFIELD AND TWO OF HIS WOODS-CRUISERS, PAUL LIBBY AND HOMER CLARK, SAT ACROSS FROM GEOFFREY FROST IN FROST'S DAY cabin as he ate a bowl of rice garnished with chunks of boiled pumpkin, the last of the noble, orange-colored, firm-rinded winter squashes brought away from Mrs. Rutherford's capacious root cellar. The cat was two leagues off Louisbourg in the early evening, wrapped in dense fog, five days following the sea burial of Hugh Stuart, having passed one hundred leagues well southeast of Halifax and raising only one sail in that time: a British vessel surely, at so high a latitude, but passing it hull down, on opposite tacks, an hour before sunset.

All three woods-cruisers reeked of tobacco smoke, but they knew better than to bring their pipes into Frost's cabin. "A Mi'kmaq will smell you two cable-lengths away," Frost said, laying aside his chopsticks, which two of the three woods-cruisers had been watching with surreptitious wonder, never having seen chopsticks employed before. "Any British picquet without a head cold can wind you at a hundred yards. Your ripeness will panic any game you cross into headlong flight."

"Now, Capt'n," Caleb said placatingly, "this cold fog and a little honest sweat will wash off this 'bacca, and soon's we're ashore we'll rub down good with spruce boughs." Caleb raised his hand to smite a ladybug that was crawling across a corner of the map spread open on Frost's desk.

"Spare the creature!" Frost commanded, seizing a goose-quill pen and carefully stroking the ladybug to safety with the feather's tip. "Ladybugs are harbingers of good luck."

Caleb moved his suspended hand upward to scratch his beard reflectively. "I collect hearin' somethin' about ladybugs and good luck, aye," he said grudgingly.

Frost watched the ladybug take flight and gyrate away toward his sleeping cabin, then tapped the quill against the map. "This map was brought back from Louisbourg by my Uncle William Pepperrell, who commanded the '45 Louisbourg expedition. The British returned the fortress to the French by the Treaty of Aix-la-Chapelle three years later, forcing Amherst to take it again in the summer of '58. The French lost Canada when Wolfe bested Montcalm before Quebec City." His explanation of Canadian history was lost on the three woods-cruisers, who were uniformly contemplating their cups of rum, well-watered, at Frost's direction. "It is, as you see, a most excellent chart rendered by Monsieur Morpain, the port captain."

Struan Ferguson knocked and Ming Tsun admitted him into the cabin in time for Struan to hear Frost's last remarks. "Mister Rawbone has the hands standing to their cannons, Captain. All loaded and run out to Mister Rawbone's satisfaction, with slow match alight." Struan peered over Caleb's shoulder at the map. "The year of the risin', '45: the year before Culloden. Pity the British weren't engaged in more places around their empire. They mightn't have had the troops, time or inclination to murther my poor da and rape my sister." His voice was bleak and bitter.

Ming Tsun refreshed Frost's cup of tea. Caleb, Libby and Clark slurped their rum. "There is some of your Scot's whisky in a decanter in the larboard cupboard. Ming Tsun, please measure Mister Ferguson a glass of *uisge beatha*, the water-of-life, distilled by Mister Ferguson's ancestors to comfort them through their long, dark winters."

"Aye," Struan said appreciatively, eyes following Ming Tsun to Frost's spirit cabinet, "and if the winter past is as harsh as reports I've heard, muckle a Scot will be forsaking the auld sod."

Frost refocused everyone's attention onto the map. "I cannot vouch for any soundings in Gabarus Bay, though they are plain enough in the South West Arm of Louisbourg Harbor. This fortuitous fog will shield our approach. Presently we are creeping in toward shore under headsails only until we plumb twenty fathom, at which time I judge we'll be one sea mile off the shore. By my reckoning, a course of west-northwest will fetch you ashore in the gig just to the south of Coromandiere Cove. You'll know it, Caleb, by two rocks south of the cove which you shall see and hear. One hundred, two hundred yards beyond the rocks will be the shore."

Caleb continued to scratch his beard. "How far southard of Loo-e-burg do ye think we'll fetch?"

"Three sea miles, five English miles. I could not risk putting you so close to Louisbourg were it not for the fog. The shore is quite flat, and the spires of the town are easily seen from Coromandiere Cove."

"The fog is handy," Homer Clark opined. Frost did not elaborate that fog was a common enough occurrence this time of year at these latitudes and along this coast—as were the easterly winds prevailing, and their perils of a lee shore.

"Your schedule of reconnaissance is ambitious, Caleb," Frost continued, sweeping the tip of his quill northward and then east from Gabarus Bay, around Louisbourg. "And one which you must accomplish in four days, since we must enter the harbor with the crescent moon, which will provide just enough light to identify and keep clear of charted rocks. Fog then will make for an interesting entrance."

"By dang!" Caleb expostulated. "If ye expect me to trot from this 'ere Garabus Bay all around Loo-e-burg to Lighthouse Point with a little meander to check on the number of cannons pointing yore way from the Grand Battery 'n' Battery Island, ye'd better cut me more slack'n that!"

"Four days, Caleb," Frost said firmly. "Fates and tides allow no more. Depending upon your estimate of distance to cover,

I can take you off south of Louisbourg, at the same place where you go ashore, or two leagues northeast of Lighthouse Point."

"That be close to forty mile!" Paul Libby muttered. "Ain't no way under God's green earth we can cover that kind of distance in four days!"

"Wall, only if'n we stop to dally with the Mi'kmaq," Caleb Mansfield retorted. "Ye forget we've got kith and kin shet up in that fortress."

"A hard task, surely, Caleb," Frost said soothingly. "An impossible task for anyone but you, Paul and Homer." He did not glance up but knew that both Libby and Clark were fair swelling with pride.

"How much time ye reckon 'fore we fetch this twenty fathom line of yor'n?" Caleb asked.

"Less than twenty minutes. I've two men in the chains casting lead. Presently we have bottom at forty fathom."

"Homer, ye and Paul skettle fo'w'rd and get yore traps. If ye'd fetch my blanket what's got a rasher of pemmican rolled in it, and my hatchet, I'd be obliged." Caleb nodded toward his double-barreled flintlock that he had earlier placed on Frost's settee. "Gideon's already here, and I've got horn and possibles bag. I wants to study this 'ere map of the Capt'n's uncle . . . what ye say his name be, Capt'n?" Clark and Libby tossed down the dregs of their rum and went out the cabin door that Ming Tsun held open for them.

"Pepperrell."

"Had a big slave with one of them high Latin names, belike? This slave of his'n drove a carriage so big it took four hosses to pull it?"

"Sounds like Uncle William," Frost said. "He had a slave who answered to the name Pompey."

Caleb sniffed. "I collect I once had to skettle mightily to get out of the way of that big carriage 'fore bein' run down."

"Uncle William's been dead these seventeen years," Frost said, "but I know this map is sound."

Caleb reached for his cup and saw Struan looking at him. "Don't think I know how to cypher a map, do ye, Mister

Ferguson? Wall, I maybe kin't read and all, but this 'ere map is as clear to me as one of them moose hides with pitchers the Five Tribes make."

"I meant naught of criticism, Caleb," Struan protested. "I was marveling that ye could traverse such a vast shore in four days."

"Wall, I ain't sayin' it won't be hard goin', but like I said afore, we've got kith and kin inside Loo-e-burg, which don't leave us much choice, now do it?"

"I want to hear the reports of the leadsmen," Frost said, standing up. Ming Tsun hurried over with his cloak, and Struan put down his cup of whisky. "Nay, tarry here, Struan. You relieve Slocum Plaisted soon enough."

"The gig is ready at the larboard waist entry, Captain," Struan said, "though Stowell, the coxswain I had in mind, stumbled against the stove scarce an hour ago and suffered a thumpin' great burn."

"I hope not great harm," Frost said, for he needed every one of the 228 odd men and boys aboard the cat.

"No sir, but Ezrah . . . Doctor Green gave him a dollop of laudanum and don't believe he should conn the gig this night."

"I'll appoint an alternate coxswain, Struan. The most important member of the gig's crew is our Mister Bowditch, who has revealed a singular ability for navigation, and who shall take my boat compass. Please answer any questions Caleb has, and the two of you arrange a signal for the rendezvous point. Is there anything remaining you would like from me, Caleb?"

Caleb scratched his beard. "I'd admire to have a stem or two of that 'loe plant Ming Tsun raises 'mong yore vegitables. It's powerful soothin' on cuts, scratches and such like."

Frost glanced at Ming Tsun, who gestured quickly. "Ming Tsun will be glad to share two stems of aloe from his garden with you, Caleb." He opened a drawer in the desk and drew out a small, brass-rimmed spyglass. "Here is a glass I found in the trunk with Uncle Pepperrell's maps of Louisbourg. He may have used it to gaze upon Louisbourg in '45. May it serve you well."

Obviously pleased, Caleb Mansfield accepted the spyglass eagerly. "Thank'ee, Capt'n Frost, I'll care for it, same as for Gideon."

On deck Frost spoke briefly with Slocum Plaisted, who stood with the helmsman, and a pinched-faced Nathaniel Dance, barely visible in the very faint light of the binnacle. "Wind's light and from the northeast. Mister Rawbone's making rounds of the cannons. Two men in the crosstrees as precautions was this fog to lift, and two runners have been relaying the soundings to me. Your orders was to call you when we sounded thirty fathom, but we're still touching forty fathom."

"The next cast from the larboard will measure thirty fathom, Slocum," Frost said with assurance, glancing forward in a futile effort to see the leadsmen. Faith, the world of dark, dense, cloying fog in which he found himself stopped a virtual hand's breadth away. He could not even see the glow of the lantern in the bow that the leadsmen were using to count their lines. Still, he could smell the land, even above the brimstone odor of slow match, and he knew the land was a mile, no more, to the northwest. Frost checked the ship's course, first in the red-shaded lamp of the cat's own binnacle, and then in the Judas binnacle he had brought from the *Salmon*.

Frost noted their agreement with satisfaction as the hand stationed near the mainmast groped his way up the quarterdeck ladder and whispered in a loud voice to Plaisted: "Larboard leadsman reports bottom at thirty fathom, Mister Plaisted."

"The state of the tide, Mister Plaisted?" Frost asked.

"Should be on the rise . . ." Slocum saw Frost's quickly raised eyebrow even in the dense fog: "Tide's on the rise, Captain."

"Very good, Mister Plaisted. You may wish to order headsails taken in, spritsail and main jib hauled, all quietly as possible. Is Mister Nason standing by in the bows? We'll trip the bower when we touch twenty fathom. All way will be off her by then." By the Almighty, but this cat was a sweet vessel! A week's hard sailing had given Frost tantalizing glimpses of her abilities. Orders to topmen were passed in hushed voices, and Frost felt the cat obediently slowing as the jib was gathered in.

"Aye, sir, Mister Nason standing by in the bow," Slocum whispered.

Frost spoke to the messenger: "O'Buck, isn't it? From Epping?"

The messenger smiled, though it went largely unnoticed in the fog. "Yes, Captain, Daniel O'Buck from Epping, sure enough."

"Do you know the state of the gig which will take our woods-cruizers ashore?"

"No sir," O'Buck answered honestly. "But a moment's query will give me the answer."

"You've sailed with Captain Whipple, I recall, Daniel O'Buck. He spoke highly of your seamanship."

"Yes sir, I was with Captain Whipple when the British and a foul wind had us blockaded in Falmouth, so we quitted Falmouth in order for Captain Whipple to march south to Boston. The British later burned the poor ol' *Trout* and other vessels found there. Wanted to accompany Captain Whipple to Boston, too, but my wife was about to birth, and he wouldn't hear of it. Mayhap if I'd been with him at Breed's Hill . . ."

"Mayhap if the sea freezes over we'll walk to Louisbourg," Frost said harshly, then, more kindly, "never blame yourself for the misfortune of another, Daniel O'Buck, less you actually caused it. That way lies madness." Yes, Frost reflected, he knew quite a lot about madness. "You're a good stroke oar, I collect my brother-in-law saying. I've got a navigator, but the coxswain I named ran afoul of Cook Barnes' fire-breathing stove. Think you up to being coxswain tonight?"

"Yes sir!" O'Buck said, too loudly, then in a much lower voice, so low that Frost had to strain to hear him. "I'll see the woods-cruizers safe ashore, Captain Frost. I've sailed these waters afore with Captain Whipple."

Caleb Mansfield joined Frost on the quarterdeck, his buck-skin moccasins soundless on the fog-dewed planking. From the smell of his breath Frost knew that Struan had given Caleb a stiff jolt of the Scot's whisky. "Caleb, if you haven't met Daniel

O'Buck, shake hands with him now. He's the coxswain who'll see you, Homer and Paul safe ashore."

"Ye much given to the playin' of cards?" Caleb asked as the two men shook hands.

"I had a lesson once, in the French Islands," O'Buck said, "but I couldn't cypher the Frenchies' way of doing things. I'd be obliged if you could advise me in a language I understand."

Another runner hurried up. "Larboard leadsman 'ports eighteen fathom last cast, Mister Plaisted," said the runner, Nathaniel Dance, to Slocum Plaisted rather than to Frost directly, as the best British Royal Navy tradition demanded.

"Report forward, Mister Dance," Frost said, completely oblivious to British Royal Navy tradition, "with my compliments to Mister Nason, and my desire to trip the bower as quietly as possible. Enough scope to hold us in position against this tide, but no more." Then to Caleb and O'Buck: "Follow me, gentlemen. You can discuss gaming when you, Homer, Paul and Gideon have returned safe, Caleb."

"Old Gideon 'n' me, we'll bring Homer and Paul back safe, though I misdoubt we'll fire a single ball."

"Yourselves, and the intelligence we need, Caleb." Ming Tsun was at his side now, the small mahogany box that contained Frost's best boat compass clasped firmly in his hands. Frost slowly led the way to the larboard waist entry. "Mister O'Buck," he said softly, "you have command of this gig, a staunch crew, and a wondrous navigator in the form of Mister Bowditch, whose tender age should not beguile you. Hannibal Bowditch, you have studied the Morpain chart, and my plot of position. Here is my boat compass. What course will take you ashore?"

"Due west-northwest, sir," Hannibal Bowditch said without hesitation.

"And the return to this vessel, Mister Bowditch?"

"The reciprocal, which is to say east-southeast, Captain Frost. Though there be much to cypher in, such as the set of the tide, what current there be here 'bouts, the drift of the wind, such as it be . . ." The pimpled, white-faced youth stared up unhesitatingly at Frost. "I comprehend how to return to the cat, sir, disregarding the fog and the night and all."

Frost allowed himself a slight smile. "Very well, Mister Bowditch. And how much time will you run?"

"For one sea mile, sir?"

"For one sea mile."

"Tide running us in, with fair rowing we'll fetch the shore in half an hour, but coming back against the set of the tide will be closer to an hour."

"And how shall you measure that time, Hannibal Bowditch, seeing that you have no clock?"

"I have this thirty-minute sand glass, sir," Hannibal said, producing the phial from a pocket. "I estimate one glass, and twice that returning."

"Hard to extrapolate minutes with the running of sand through a glass, Mister Bowditch. My watch will serve you better, though have a care with it; it was a gift from my mother many years ago."

Hannibal gulped. "Yes sir, your clock, sir. That would be much handier, sir."

Frost pulled the watch from his waistcoat's pocket and handed it to Hannibal. "Good. Now, here's Caleb and his colleagues. Remember, lad, the faster you get them ashore, the sooner you can be breathing uncloyed air again."

"Nah, Captain Frost," Caleb Mansfield, bristling, said warily, "this noble odor keeps the agues at bay, that it does."

"Stay downwind of any picquets then, Caleb," Frost said, seizing the man's right hand in his own and giving it a mighty squeeze. "And if that be rum in Homer Clark's canteen, give it now to Mister Dance so he can change it for one with water." Homer Clark grinned sheepishly and handed his canteen to Nathaniel Dance. "You may as well take Mister Libby's canteen also, Mister Dance; the contents overboard and replenish from the butt at the mainmast." Then to Caleb: "You and Struan have agreed on a rendezvous point and a signal?"

"Landing Cove east of Lighthouse Point four nights hence. Lights as he knows."

The launch was away and Frost had nothing to do but pace several times the length of the main deck, both sides, scrutinizing his crew and their attention to their cannons. He was not particularly pleased with what he saw. Rawbone joined him unobtrusively and followed Frost through the damp, cloying fog back to his quarterdeck. "We have our work cut out for us, Mister Rawbone."

"Aye, sir, that we have. Though I ken your brother takes to cannons right enough."

"He should. He went with Knox to Ticonderoga. Both legs of the fatiguing journey. I had wished him safe in Saugus, casting ball to feed these beasts." Since he was concealed adequately by the fog, Frost felt safe in peering anxiously toward the number six cannon, where he had observed a grimly determined Joseph crouched beside his iron charge. His attitude told Rawbone that Frost wished no further conversation as he began pacing his quarterdeck, so Rawbone turned and groped his way back to the main deck, where he made yet another tour of the cat's cannons and crews.

Frost was left alone on his quarterdeck, except for the two helmsmen, and Slocum Plaisted and Nathaniel Dance. From long experience, he could estimate the passage of time well enough that he did not need to go below to check the Kendall chronometer in his cabin. One hour after Struan Ferguson had quietly relieved Plaisted, Frost heard the faint stroke of an oar to larboard. He estimated that dawn was less than fifteen minutes away.

"Our young Hannibal Bowditch is a most punctual navigator, Struan," Frost whispered to Ferguson. "He has used the ebb of tide to good advantage. Pass the word to Nason to weigh the anchor, softly, ever so softly, as soon as O'Buck, Hannibal and the gig's crew are safely aboard. Both jib and foremast topsail let go, softly, softly. Bring her stern-to as the tide ebbs, then lay us on a gentle starboard tack. We'll bear south-southeast." He heard the gig bump the cat's hull. A glance to the east revealed a slight, very slight attenuation of the opaque darkness. He groped his way to the larboard waist entry in time to see a very tired Hannibal Bowditch being greeted by Nathaniel Dance.

"Here be your time-piece, Captain Frost, safe and all. Thank'ee for its use."

"Caleb and the others safely ashore?"

"Yes sir, a wondrous accurate compass this, sir," Hannibal said, handing Frost his boat compass. "Ran in straight; heard the breakers on the rocks but missed them handily. Mister Caleb and his friends got ashore in water no deeper than their knees, then we backed water and used the tide to bring us back to the cat, sir."

"A handy piece of navigation, Mister Bowditch. I reckon a slight current setting from northeast, which could not have assisted you."

"Yes sir, it was confusing at first, but I cyphered its compensation," Hannibal Bowditch said, swallowing nervously, unaccustomed to the praise.

"If I may say so, Captain Frost," O'Buck said in a low voice, materializing out of the fog, "Mister Bowditch did a right proper job. Calm he was, as if we was on a mill pond in bright day. I'll be coxswain for Mister Bowditch anytime you need me, Captain."

Frost heard the windlass pawl stop and knew the anchor was aweigh, then the gentle tug of headsails as the cat's bows swung slowly in a half-circle. There was sunlight somewhere, for the fog has a faint luminescence to the east. Frost could not identify the first faint snap he heard, but the second he could. Long behind the cat to the westward, but sound carried well, even in heavy fog. The third snap left no doubt: three shots from a long rifle or a musket.

☙ XVIII ❧

☀☀☀☀☀ HE FOG LIFTED TWO HOURS AFTER
☀   T   ☀ FULL SUNRISE. FROST ORDERED TAM-
☀   ☀ PIONS IN THE CANNONS' MUZZLES AS
☀☀☀☀☀ HE KEPT THE CAT ON A LARBOARD
tack to clear all the Cape Breton headlands. But he drilled the
crew through a variety of sail changes, furling and unfurling,
hauling down the topsails, unbending them and bending on
the heavy storm sails. Drilled them so thoroughly that by noon
time, under a mostly overcast and somewhat chilly day, most
of the hands, though hardened to the plough and axe, were visibly fatigued with the constant movement around the decks,
the hauling out of new sails from the sail room, passing them
up, bending them on, and no sooner than they were bent and
unfurled, hauling them down again.

Frost carefully plotted his noon sight and calculated that
the cat was now thirty miles east of Cape Breton, with the
lookouts reporting no sail in sight. "Bring up an empty flour
barrel, Mister Dance," he ordered as he handed Ming Tsun his
sextant. Then in his sternest voice to the group of his officers
gathered in a loose knot immediately below his quarterdeck:
"Mister Ferguson, as soon as the flour barrel is thrown overboard, I'd like the vessel to come onto the starboard tack as
quickly as you can manage, then swing her through the wind
to reverse course, and bring us back on the reciprocal for the
barrel. The course reversal should take no more than five
minutes, which is ample time for Mister Rawbone to clear his

cannons and be ready to take the barrel under fire with the larboard battery."

Both Struan Ferguson and Roderick Rawbone turned to stare at Frost with mouths agape, saw the flint-like set to Frost's jaw, then closed their mouths and began bawling the orders to their respective contingents of the cat's crew. Nathaniel Dance popped out of the companionway leading from the galley, followed by two men lugging a cumbersome flour barrel. "Over the side with that barrel, lively now! Then back to Cook Barnes and order the galley fire doused," Frost shouted as he watched the pandemonium, no, the confusion of men rushing to pluck tampions from cannon muzzles, bring one slow match in its linstock touched to the galley stove to set the others a-smolder. Two matrosses were tripped as hands raced to brace the yards around, and one hand, scurrying aloft, missed his footing on a ratline, and almost his grip, but caught himself in time and continued upward toward his station in the fore top.

The barrel was bobbing in the cat's wake, and Frost had given his watch to Hannibal Bowditch, who was standing by with a slate. "Mark which of the larboard cannons won't fire, and I wish a tally of the times from course reversal to when the first cannon engages the target, as well as the times each gun crew requires to reload." Frost glimpsed Ezrah Green poking his head up from the larboard companionway, for all the world like a marmot peering out of its den on a pasture's hillside, to see what all the bustle was about. "Surgeon Green!" Frost shouted. "Lay below to your lazarette, parcel out your knives and tourniquets, and be ready to receive the wounded!" The doctor disappeared down the companionway with alacrity.

Struan Ferguson's threats and imprecations had the sails trimmed and the cat through the wind and on a reciprocal in a reasonably efficient manner, though far too slowly for Frost's liking. Clearing the cannons was a different matter—most of the crews were still struggling with tampions and tailing tackle as the cat established herself on her new course and in a light breeze bore down on the barrel.

"A broadside upon my order, Mister Rawbone," Frost

shouted through his speaking trumpet. "There is plenty of time for every gun to train upon the target. Every gun to reload and make ready for another broadside." Frost withheld his order until the barrel was a hundred yards away, beginning to rise on a moderate swell. He guessed that of the nine six-pounders on the larboard no more than five would fire. He was pleasantly surprised when six of the nine cannon fired, though as he peered through the smoke he saw that his brother, Joseph, who had been assigned to a gun on the starboard side, had left his cannon to assist the matrosses at the number three gun on the larboard side. As he had expected, watching the splash of shot, no ball had come nearer that twenty yards to the floating barrel.

"Mister Ferguson," Frost shouted through his speaking trumpet, "lay her about so we can compare the marksmanship of the starboard cannons with the accomplishments of the larboard cannons." The standing rigging fairly hummed as yards were braced around, parrels grating smoothly, heavy canvas drawing well one moment, deflated and flogging momentarily the next, then bellying again, the cat turning quickly in a new direction as obediently as a well-trained water spaniel cast for a duck, and the sweet, oh so sweet, kiss of the spray against the black hull knifing so smoothly through the gray North Atlantic swells.

Frost curtly noted for Hannibal Bowditch's benefit the larboard side cannons that were experiencing difficulties in reloading and was gratified to see Rawbone descending like a wraith upon the crew of a cannon that had not fired. The confused matrosses had started to load another charge without first drawing the wet charge.

And now the cat had turned and was bearing down on the floating barrel, a faint mark on the sea. "Hold her off one hundred yards, same as for the larboard crews." Then through his speaking trumpet: "Mister Rawbone, by my order, a broadside from the starboard cannons, if you please." Frost glanced aloft at the well-filled canvas; at least Struan's foretopmen and deck hands were keen to their tasks. The gunners were another story.

"Fire!" Frost shouted when the cat was abreast the barrel, and this time only four six-pounders spat their balls at the bobbing target, which chose the precise moment the cannons fired to duck behind a wave crest. "Mister Ferguson, about as quickly as you can," adding ironically, "we must not let the barrel escape."

The gun crews of the cat drilled through their maneuvers twice more, the barrel still tantalizingly unscathed, though at least, once their wet charges had been drawn, all of the cannons were firing. The wind sweeping in from the northeast was chill, but their furious activity had caused the majority of the matrosses to shed their jackets and shirts. Rawbone had shouted himself virtually hoarse, and Frost had quickly determined that he would have to form the gun crews into divisions of some sort. It was demanding too much of one man to coordinate the operations of all the cannons.

"Mister Dance," Frost said to the youngster who had stationed himself by Frost's side to relay orders, "I'd be obliged if Cook Barnes could serve up bread and cold meats, with cheese and one mug of small beer, to all the hands. No more than one mug, mind." He waited fifteen minutes until a frugal dinner was being served to all the cat's men before striding down the main deck, peering closely at each gun crew as he passed. The main deck stank of sweat, sulphur, slow match and not a little bit of fear—which was a good thing—as the men continued to serve their cannons while snatching at their food when they could.

"Mister Rawbone," Frost said, using his speaking trumpet to single out a man. "This man has just been killed by a nine-pounder shot fired from the flour barrel. Have him report to the belfrey to await his resurrection." Frost beckoned to Nathaniel Dance. "Mister Dance, when ten 'bodies' join you at the belfry, break out the sweeps. Mister Ferguson, prepare to strike all sail!" Frost continued to pace the length of the main deck, pausing to select two more men at random.

"Wounded by a splinter in the right arm," Frost shouted, pointing his speaking trumpet at a black man. It was not Colossus Bennington, the man was nowhere near Colossus' size. What was his name? "God help me," Frost said to himself, "I've got to do better tying names to faces." The man looked first at Frost with unspeakable horror, then at his right arm, as if expecting to see a foot-long splinter of oak transfixing the limb.

Darius! How the youth had fleshed out and grown! Frost had been too busy to mark the lad among the crew. "Strike him below to Doctor Green's lazarette! Have a care! His right leg is broken also. It will take two men to carry him. Look lively there, you two! Seize your mate as tenderly as you would wish to be treated and hasten him down to the lazarette. Then return to your gun crews!" The two men Frost indicated nodded dumbly and began escorting the putatively injured Darius away.

"No, No! He is wounded! Take him beneath the arms, you there! And you! Seize your mate by his legs. Thank God that his guts are not spilled out like tripes to trip you on the deck! Be careful of that tender arm! Below with you, and back to your stations as quickly as you can!" Frost took a second to wink at Darius as the youth was lifted from his feet, far more gently and capably than Frost had thought possible. A startled Darius winked back.

Frost found himself standing a few feet from Joseph, shirt wound turban-fashion around his head, face and upper body well-begrimed with powder. Joseph caught his brother's eye and winked. Grudgingly, against his will, Frost returned the wink, hoping that no one else saw their brief exchange of familiarity.

He rounded on two gun crews who were hopelessly tangled in their cannons' tackle. "Mister Rawbone, this is not a cotillion where rustic, lovesick swains sit idly about as young women primp and pout! Set them to their duties!"

Rawbone drew himself up to his full, not inconsiderable height, tricorne long since lost, his face contorted almost in apoplexy as he turned first one way, and then another, surveying the chaos that reigned on the cat's gun deck. "And pray, sir," Rawbone cried, his voice breaking in despair, "what is their duty?"

"To put iron on target, Mister Rawbone," Frost said happily, reveling in the glorious confusion he had created. "That is their duty, so long as the cat swims and the enemy has not struck."

Something tugged at his sleeve and Frost, carried along by events, momentarily thought that an enemy bullet had grazed his arm; but the tug came from Nathaniel Dance. "Please, sir, I have ten 'bodies' gathered at the belfry. What am I to do with them?"

"You have broken out sweeps, have you not, Mister Dance?"

"Sweeps in hand, sir, awaiting yer orders, sir."

Frost glanced aloft; all the sail had come off the cat smartly. The foretop hands were good. Pity the deck crew was not their equal. "But what if a chance cannon ball has left naught of me but a pair of legs drumming against the deck, Mister Dance. To whom would you look for orders?"

"Mister Ferguson, sir."

"Mister Ferguson was killed two minutes ago when a broadside fired from the flour barrel left the quarterdeck in bloody shambles. You are the senior person of this ship's complement left standing, Mister Dance. All top hamper is shot away. What orders do you give?"

Nathaniel Dance stared up at his captain, his hat almost tumbling off as the blast of a six-pounder swept over them.

"Well, Mister Dance?" Frost said, impatiently tapping his fingers against the shell of his speaking trumpet.

"Out sweeps and sweep down on the enemy, sir, keeping up a hot fire as we go."

"Make it so, Mister Dance. If any 'body' lags in his duty, he is to be cast overboard to make room at the sweeps for those whose spirits still live. Mister Rawbone! Take instruction and inspiration from the child whose honor obliges him to close with the enemy!"

"Aye, sir," Rawbone shouted, joining in, no, abandoning himself to the enthusiasm of mock combat, "my boys will have reduced her to kindling a'fore we close! Mary's oath, mark it!"

Frost's gaze turned toward the waist, and he saw Ezrah Green staring from a scuttle. "Doctor!" Frost shouted in exasperation, "You have had ample time to shear off a dozen limbs. The only mission which would bring you on deck is to cast the bucket of limbs into the sea, a task better left to your loblolly boy!"

Just then a ragged cheer went up from the matrosses, and Frost turned quickly to see a shower of staves raining down upon the crest of a wave. Some gun had finally struck home. A glance along the gun deck saw Joseph hopping in a victory shuffle with two other matrosses at the cannon that he had laid.

"More sweeps," Frost called savagely. "All cannons reloaded and ready to fire. Muskets on deck!" He ran through the names of the woods-cruisers on board now that Caleb Mansfield, Paul Libby and Homer Clark were ashore—or were they already dead or captured? "Singleton Quire! How many muskets were shipped aboard the cat?" The manifest in his cabin listed two hundred stand of long arms, one hundred small arms, three hundred cutlasses. Frost did not wait for an answer. "Twenty muskets to be loaded under your direction. First man to hit one of the barrel staves shall have an extra ration of rum this day— as shall the crew of the six-pounder first to strike the flour cask fair! The rest of you, sweep as if your lives depend upon your rowing, for indeed they do!"

Struan Ferguson joined him as Frost went below to make his rounds of perspiring, grunting men heaving on the sweeps. "I dinna think the lads understand what ye do be for their benefit," Ferguson said softly.

"It matters not what they think, or whether they applaud," Frost responded beneath his breath. "I lost good men on the old *Salmon* because I neglected gunnery. Passing the Malacca straits, yes, I was prepared to deal with Malay pirates, but off the Isles of Shoals I had no idea how this war between cousins would be fought. Now I find that a ball from a British cannon kills as deadly as a ball from a Malay skirl."

"So the men must learn their trade is not a delicate one," Struan said.

"We have, of necessity, shipped a gaggle of ploughmen,

Struan. To throw them against well-trained British soldiers or seamen would be tantamount to murder."

"They think they are signed on to chase British merchant tubs into a Yankee port, there to be condemned and their fat profits be shared out."

"I'm not above self-interest," Frost said, "far from it," pausing to glare at a hand on the sweeps who was evidently malingering. The hand immediately picked up the stroke from his mates. "Enlightened self-interest and patriotism are not incompatible. But to have a chance at achieving the benefits of either self-interest or patriotism, certain skills must be acquired, skills which come not but at great cost."

"Yes," Struan said, nodding his head at his captain's remarks. He waited until a spatter of musketry had died out before continuing, "It is necessary to nurture and husband both of these concepts, which, I wager, none of these ploughmen can articulate, fixated as they are upon prize money."

"In order to live long enough to enjoy their prize money, they first must possess certain skills," Frost replied. "But prize money is a far cousin to the task of bringing our kindren from gaol in Louisbourg."

"Aye, but none are likely to enjoy the acquisition of their skills."

"Mark you, no," Frost agreed. "But such skills they have, for repetition is the mother of skill, and years hence they who live shall boast of themselves as patriots."

"But of the nonce . . . ?"

"They shall truly hate me in a way they have never hated anyone before," Frost said, pacing forward to scrutinize another trio of men at a sweep. "For they have just begun to acquire those skills which shall guarantee them both profits and the right to call themselves patriots—and the long life to enjoy both. The more they sweat now in these drills . . ." Frost broke off; Struan had heard this homily often.

"Yes sir," Struan said, grinning, "the less they'll bleed in battle."

"And the crew may bleed a bit later today, after the men

have all had a chance to enjoy the exhilaration of pulling a sweep, Mr. Ferguson, for you are to take them by divisions and begin their tuition in employing cutlasses and pikes to best advantage."

And Frost, true to his word, intensified the drills with the cat's cannon, small arms, sail changes, and most of all, sweeping, over the next three days and nights.

❧ XIX ❧

MING TSUN AWAKENED HIM QUIETLY, THEN FROST HEARD HIS CABIN DOOR SQUEAK SOFTLY ON ITS HINGES, OPEN-ING AND CLOSING IN THE DARKNESS. Frost sensed Struan Ferguson's presence. "I fear we face mutiny, Geoffrey," Struan said softly. "There are those among our crew who relish not the prospect of going against Louis-bourg's guns . . . Ming Tsun, please strike a light. Jack Lacey holds the helm with Plaisted on the deck, so naught will take alarm at a candle. All the mischief is forward."

Frost sat up quickly on the edge of his berth, shedding night-shirt and reaching for breeches and shirt as Ming Tsun touched a smoldering fragment of tinder against a candle's wick in the day cabin. Frost glanced at the tell-tale compass above his berth, saw that the course was north-northeast, and from the slight heel to the deck knew the cat was steady on a starboard tack. A pale-faced Ezrah Green stood just inside the door, his eyes lost in deep sockets below his forehead.

"How grievous is the situation, Struan?" Frost plunged into his breeches and, ignoring shoes, drew on a shirt and stuffed the tails into his breeches.

"Three men, no more, but troublemakers of the first water, have been talking against ye. According to their likes, ye planned all along to rescue the American prisoners in Louisbourg. There are no British ships in harbor to take as prizes, so there's not a shilling's worth of profit in this venture, but cannon balls 'tween wind 'n' water—or more likely a noose, since the British are present in force in Louisbourg."

"Faith, I wish I had intelligence as good as those worthies seem to possess." Frost pulled his brace of Bass pistols from their box and began loading them, quickly but surely. Ming Tsun laid his brass-backed cutlass on the table. Frost thrust one freshly loaded pistol into his waist and grasped the cutlass in his left hand.

"How stand the rest of the men?"

"All the old *Salmon*s are with us, of course; it's difficult to say about the rest. I'm sure the ex-*Jaguar*s aren't very keen about fighting their countrymen. The ploughmen we shipped? Who knows?"

"All this is going on below? No one is on deck?"

"Aye, Hannibal Bowditch and Nathaniel Dance, each with one of my Strachan pistols, are athwart the mainmast, waiting to blow the first man who shows his head above the coaming to Kingdom Come."

"What about the rest of Caleb's woods-cruizers?"

"I've no idea," Struan said. "I was in my cabin—as I say, Slocum has the deck—when Hannibal and Nathaniel crept in to bring this distressing news. I loaded and gave them each a pistol and told them to take station at the mainmast until I fetched ye. I disliked leaving the good doctor a-sleeping un-awares, so I roused him along."

"Very good." Frost's eyes fell on Ezrah Green. "This is bad business, having to fight one's own neighbors, Ezrah. No one will harm you, regardless of what the next few minutes bring. But I'll thank you to remain in this cabin until I call for you."

Ezrah Green's very prominent Adam's apple bobbed several times up and down his throat, but no words came. Finally he nodded his head.

Frost beckoned to Ming Tsun, who extinguished the candle, seized his short halberd, and opened the cabin door. Frost led the way, not up the companionway to the quarterdeck but through the doorway that opened directly onto the larboard side of the main deck into a fair night, the faintest of crescent moons, and calm seas barely wrinkled by the wind. Over his shoulder Frost could see Jack Lacey, who had voyaged to China twice with Frost, and another man he did not recognize, at the helm, gripping the spokes of the steering wheel with greater force than necessary. The main deck was filmed with light dew, pleasantly cold to Frost's bare feet.

Slocum Plaisted was beside Frost in the dark, mouth close against his captain's ear. "No one's on deck save those known to you, and Will Simons, lookout in the main topmast cross-trees, Captain, a right man, as you know," Plaisted whispered.

Frost advanced warily across the deck, his gaze falling on the six-pounder ten feet to his left, then turned to whisper to Struan: "Where is Rawbone?"

"Snoring loud enough to wake Neptune himself. I couldn'a rouse him."

Frost speculated momentarily if he should unbowse a cannon, load it with langrage, and aim it along the ventilation gratings and access hatchways. No, all the powder had been secured below, there was not enough time. And even if powder were close to hand, and even if he could get a cannon loaded quickly, the noise of moving the gun into position would be ungodly, giving away his plan at the first squeal of trucks. Even if . . .

Frost continued forward, taking no notice of the easy roll of the ship, until he came up to two very wide-eyed and thoroughly frightened boys. He could hear loud, argumentative voices haranguing up through the gratings that ventilated the berthing deck. "These be not prime exemplars of mutineers," Frost reflected grimly, "arguing so foolishly and so openly." He paused to listen attentively to the babel of angry voices, attempting to identify their owners. "They must think this vessel has no ears but theirs."

Frost could not put faces to any of the snatches of voices he heard, so he edged closer to the gratings, Struan and Ming Tsun tucked in tightly behind him. Then he heard the one voice he immediately recognized.

"You surely have no complaint with Captain Frost."

"We have plenty of complaints about His Excellency Geoffrey Frost," a gruff voice sneered. "He's out to get us all killed, more-like, or taken prisoner by the Britishers. There be no prizes in Louisbourg harbor for the easy taking. This don't be no mutiny like, we just inform His Excellency as we leave to get back to Portsmouth and get ourselves berths on proper privateers, captains like Salter 'r Ayres who know how to winkle a prize fair as kiss my hand . . . our hands, which, by the way, are heavily blistered from all the labor he has charged us with, and for naught!"

"Assuming, which we cannot do, since Captain Frost's sources are scrupulous in their details, but assuming just a moment, for argument's sake, that no British vessels of any sort lie at anchor in Louisbourg harbor—surely the redemption of your fellow countrymen held captive under the foulest of conditions compel your arms to this enterprise."

A sneer and another voice, derisive. "Rescue's the business of the Continental Army, not privateers' men. Our business is bringing in prizes. His Excellency told us so hisself. Who knows how much British shipping has been snapped up already to south'ard by Salter, Manley, and schooners of their like, whilst we stand off Arcadia and play like we wus actual navy?"

Frost reached the edge of the grating midway between the main and foremasts and peered down into the berthing spaces, lighted only by two small lanterns hung from beams. But his eyes were quite adjusted to the dark: Joseph Frost stood with his back to the galley fire hearth, half-stooped rather from the lack of overhead in the berthing deck, flanked by two woods-cruisers on either side, the four nonchalantly holding their flintlock rifles, hammers at the half-cock, muzzles angled down so they seemingly threatened no one, but readily enough raised. And ranged beside the woods-cruisers, just to the right of the stove, was the entire ship's complement of newly manu-mitted black freemen, several of whom held billets of firewood.

Facing Joseph a scant six paces away and directly beneath the grating was a knot of five, no, six men. The rest of men on the berthing deck pressed back into the shadows or remained in their hammocks.

Geoffrey Frost immediately understood: three or four mal-contents were exhorting the crew to mutiny. Somehow Joseph had collected four woods-cruisers and the black freemen and confronted the ringleaders before they could incite the crew to rise. Frost recognized only one of the six, the burly lands-man who had tailed so poorly on the cannon drill at pierside on Rising Island. When had that been? Scarce a fortnight ago. He would have to act quickly before things got out of hand.

"We wus fools to ship with this captain who ain't naught but a chinee trader, not a Manley or Ayres, who've already swept up a dozen prizes between them . . ."

"And none of their crews have seen so much as one dollar of prize money," Joseph shot back quickly, "whereas this captain has vowed to advance prize money from his own account as soon as prizes are dockside in Portsmouth."

"To a favored few perhaps—not a captain who ships nigras as crew, never pay them and never pay us . . ."

"This captain keeps his word," Joseph said hotly, "on that you can depend."

"What do you know of this captain's ability to keep his word?" someone hooted. "You who came aboard in a coffin, how would you know of this captain?"

"He said he would bowsprit my brother, and he did . . ."

Frost gestured to Ming Tsun and Struan to lift the grating; they seized upon it firmly, wrenching it quickly from its frame, making a sudden racket. Frost dropped into the void as voices exclaimed and startled faces glared up in surprise. He landed lightly as a cat, bare feet stinging from contact with the deck, between Joseph and the knot of six men, knees flexing and cushioning the shock of the six-foot fall. He ignored the tear and stab of pain in his side: how long ago had he taken that wound, a month? Then instantly he was on his feet, the cutlass in his left hand smashing out, side of the blade, not cutting edge, smiting the nearest man above the ear and felling him instantly, then the point of the cutlass just above the Adam's apple of the man next behind him, while the Bass double-barreled pistol in Frost's right hand was leveled steadily on the chest of the man beside him.

"Half cocks! Steady!" he shouted, for he had heard the hammers of the woods-cruisers long rifles snick back, almost in unison. Frost raised the tip of his cutlass, forcing the man to come toward him a-tip-toe in the space under the open gratings where they could stand fully erect. Frost gave the cutlass a slight twitch, and a trickle of blood flowed down the man's neck.

"Please, Captain . . ."

Frost recognized the man now, the dullard who had exhibited absolutely no cannon handling skills the first day he set foot on the cat at Rising Island: the man he had chastised. "Shut your mouth except to tell me your name and where you hail from!"

"Campbell, Captain, Bob Campbell," the man at the tip of the cutlass said hurriedly, almost stammering, "originally from Philadelphia, Captain, but late of Portsmouth."

"You made a conscious decision to ship with me, Campbell, did you not, rather than Captains Manley or Ayres?"

The man said nothing. Frost twisted the cutlass slightly. More blood flowed down the man's neck. "I asked you a question, Campbell, and I expect an answer."

"Yesss, Captain."

"Therefore you bound yourself to my orders?"

"Yesss, Captain."

Frost tipped the cutlass higher and Campbell, sweating mightily, rose even higher on tip-toe.

"I have sworn to advance against prizes safely landed in Portsmouth until the prize agent's condemnations and sales. Doubt you that I'll do so for every man regardless of his skin color?"

"Nooo, Captain."

"Then agree you, Mister Campbell, that I be a man of my word, for as this man has just now testified, I indeed put his brother on the bowsprit." Frost twitched the cutlass again; Campbell's eyes bulged as he rose to full tip-toe, arms flailing to maintain balance. Frost pulled Campbell closer with the tip of the cutlass and stared directly into the man's venal eyes hued with the faded colors of a long ago yellow fever. Campbell began to babble, fat jowls shaking. "But know you this, Campbell; that brother was mine also, for behind me stands Joseph Frost, all three of us sons of the same mother. Think you that if I would not shrink from bowspriting my brother for cause I would shrink from killing you and the rest of these whores' sons who've risen 'gainst me, though I be but a chinee trader?"

"Nooo, Captain."

Frost thrust up suddenly with his cutlass, but not so quickly that Campbell was caught unprepared. The fat man started to rise even further, when Frost quickly lowered the cutlass and banged the flat of the blade against Campbell's skull. He let slip the cutlass from his hand and it struck point-first on the deck, where it stood upright, quivering slightly. Frost knelt by the fat man, who was now blubbering copiously, seized the man's lank, greasy hair in his left hand and tilted Campbell's head backward sharply.

"Bob Campbell, I expect that you and everyone aboard this vessel shall honor the commitments made to me, the colony of New Hampshire, and the United Colonies . . ."

Campbell nodded his head vigorously. "Yes, Captain Frost."

Frost pulled the man toward him and whispered sharply under his breath so that only Campbell could hear. "Campbell, next time you stand next to my servant, and you shall live to do so, depend on it, for I have your word and the prisoners in Louisbourg have need of you . . . but next time you stand next to my servant, mark that he has no tongue . . . and should I ever hear yours wrap itself around such mutinous, traitorous sentiments as I've just heard, so shall your tongue be wrenched out. Have we an understanding, Bob Campbell?"

Campbell nodded vigorously. Frost was suddenly aware that the man's bowels had loosened. "Say it loudly so all can hear you, Campbell."

"Yess, Captain Frost, we all know ye to be a man of yore word."

"And you shall do your duty before Louisbourg, for prizes and American prisoners, and the United Colonies?"

"Yess, Captain Frost."

Frost rose to his feet and gestured toward one of the shadowy figures trying desperately to disappear into the hull timbers to escape his attention. "You there! Does Campbell speak for you?"

"No sir," the man quavered, "I mean yes sir, I mean no sir . . . well, I mean, sir, he don't speak for me about turning back to Portsmouth, but I mean to do my duty before Louisbourg, by God, sir, that I do."

"Very well; bring some of your fellows and help these men to their hammocks, though one of you will have to assist Campbell to the roundhouse after he shifts his drawers. All of you, back to your hammocks, for tomorrow brings much work . . . and the opportunity for more money than any of you have ever dreamed."

Frost plucked his cutlass from the deck and nodded at his younger brother. "Obliged for the woods-cruizers' help, and yours, Joseph." He caught Darius' eye and winked. "And especially yours, Darius. It is a great comfort knowing you are here. Don't let a trifle like this upset you. Now and again it takes a little time to steady down a new crew at the beginning of a cruize." He moved toward the fore hatch ladder, the dozen or so men standing hear the base of the ladder moved out of his way with alacrity.

⤛ X X ⤜

IN THE LATE TWILIGHT OF A DAY IN THE THIRD WEEK OF MAY FROST BROUGHT THE CAT INSHORE UNDER EASY SAIL TO THE RENDEZVOUS POINT two leagues to the east of Lighthouse Point, on a course to bisect Landing Cove. A ship standing in so close to the land at midday could well be glimpsed by a sentry at Lighthouse Point, but with night closing rapidly the possibility of a sighting was remote; still, there was that chance. Frost had all cannons loaded and run out, and slow match in tubs smoldering well.

"Another reef in the main top'sl, Mister Ferguson," Frost said softly, "though not gusseted so tightly the sail cannot be dropped quickly."

Struan Ferguson dutifully repeated the order to Daniel O'Buck, who trotted forward to whisper the order for Nason and his foretop men to execute.

Frost could see the shoulders of the shadowy figure of the leadsman in the starsboard foremast chains flex as the man shot the sounding lead forward. Hannibal Bowditch stood ready to relay the depth halfway down the larboard side of the deck to Darius, who would relay the word to Frost while Cato Calite waited to fetch word of the next cast.

"I collect half a mile off the mouth of the cove will see us in twenty fathom of water, Captain," Struan said, closing his telescope with the soft pleasurable snick of brass sliding into brass.

"More like ten fathom, Struan," Frost replied. "The bottom comes up sharply on these coasts."

"We dare venture no further inshore than half a mile."

"Not a fathom more," Frost agreed.

"The signal Caleb and I agreed will be a small fire at the west point of the cove, quickly extinguished, then to blaze up again," Struan said nervously.

Frost smiled to himself. This was the fourth, possibly the fifth, time his first mate had repeated the signal.

"I have oft' wondered whether we heard musket shots after we landed Caleb, Libby and Clark."

"I doubt they were anything else," Frost said tersely.

"Four days is scant time to cover the ground we appointed to Caleb."

"If Caleb is not here by midnight, Struan, the very latest time I can allow, then we must divert to the second plan."

"Yes," Struan said, "as you have laid it out: HM *Jaguar* with its red ensign flying shall enter Louisbourg Harbor on the morning tide. No sooner will we take our anchor than we shall send as many men as we can ship in our small boats ashore."

"It's risky business, Struan, to go in blindly without knowing Louisbourg's strengths and disposition. I have been depending heavily on Caleb's intelligence."

"I am not among those who would call it folly," Struan Ferguson said mildly. "Though even with Caleb's intelligence, the task will be tricky—aye, but either plan has sufficient audacity to succeed."

Darius came padding up the companionway from the waist and self-consciously knuckled his forehead in a semblance of a salute. "We have fifteen fathom, Capt'n, with the last cast."

"Thank you, Darius. Mister Ferguson, pass the word to ease the bower. Once we hold bottom, let out just enough scope to bring us stern-to toward the land."

Struan hastened away to oversee the anchoring. Frost stared at the land, which was now invisible except for the faint outlines of pine tops silhouetted against the last faint remnants of an overcast sunset. "Tell me, Darius, if so far you have found the sea to your liking," Frost said, looking directly at the newly manumitted youth.

"Aye, Capt'n, much to my likin'." Darius essayed a small grin. "I much prefer the sea to workin' for Masta John."

Frost nodded absently. "To leave off wearing that foolish costume must be a vast relief."

The only sign of a smile in the darkness was the quick flash of white teeth. "I had prayed many times never to be forced to wear such a garment."

"You have a deity to whom you pray, Darius?"

"Yes, Capt'n, I do."

"Then pray especially well to your deity this night, Darius, because the morning will bring . . . ," Frost paused, "the morning will bring much uncertainty."

Darius knuckled his forehead again as he withdrew. "Every morning brings much uncertainty, Capt'n."

The cat snubbed to her short cable and swung stern-to toward the land. Frost paced his quarterdeck, twelve paces from starboard rail to larboard rail, and forty-eight paces before he would allow himself to face the land, urging a faint flash of light to glimmer. Then he waited ninety-six paces before facing the land; and then one hundred and fifty-four. And then one hundred and ninety-two careful, measured paces.

Frost guessed that the present eternity had lasted only two hours, and the time was close to half-nine. He stepped to the binnacle, shielding it with his body while he opened the shutter momentarily to verify the time with the watch his mother had given Jonathan. It took several seconds for his eyes to adjust to the soft lamp's red-filtered glow. Twenty minutes past eight. Frost shuttered the binnacle and resumed his pacing, conviction growing with every pace.

Hannibal Bowditch interrupted Frost's pacing with a small cough. "Yes, Mister Bowditch?"

"Sir, I believe Mister Mansfield is at the appointed place," Hannibal Bowditch said, his juvenile voice so low it almost squeaked.

"I am of that opinion also, Mister Bowditch."

"I believe he has good reason not to signal."

"We think alike on that, Mister Bowditch."

Hannibal Bowditch hid a small cough with his palm. "I would like to take the gig and find Mister Mansfield."

Frost weighed this option carefully. Hannibal Bowditch was volunteering to do something that, by rights, Frost should do himself, something he had already considered. He *knew* that Caleb was on the headland; he knew in the same way he had known that Joseph had smuggled himself aboard the cat in a coffin, in the same way Joseph knew that Frost was bound for Louisbourg to rescue Marcus Whipple. And both brothers knew that the matter was quixotic, possibly a brave gesture, nothing more, but were venturing it anyway. Great God, if only Jonathan had possessed that same fey insight . . .

Frost made himself pace the breadth of his quarterdeck twice, outwardly calm, his fingers writhing like snakes behind his back. He turned toward the young man, no, boy, that what Hannibal Bowditch was, a mere boy who had been innocently entrusted by his father to Frost's care. O Dios, O Senhor! Just show your wretched servant what to do! "You are not to go ashore, Mister Bowditch. Approach not further than a long musket shot from the beach. You may have the gig and O'Buck for your coxswain. My clock and best boat compass as well."

"Please, sir. Mister Dance wishes to accompany me as well."

O Dios, O Senhor! Not both of the lads! "The gig must take O'Buck as coxswain, four oars and yourself as navigator. If Mister Dance goes he shall have to pull his own weight on an oar."

"Oh, sir, capital, sir. Yes, sir." Young Bowditch fairly hopped in his excitement. "Mister Dance is a good oar, and coming back we'll have Mister Mansfield and his men to help with the rowing."

"Ashore under no circumstances, Mister Bowditch. Fifteen minutes to call in softest voice for Caleb. If he is there he will hear your oars, no matter how quietly you row. Fifteen minutes, then return to the cat, with or without Caleb Mansfield and his two woods-cruizers." Hannibal Bowditch knuckled his forehead self-consciously, turned, and was gone.

Frost resumed his slow, measured pacing, heard the gig clear away, strained to listen to the quiet creak and splash of oars, and satisfied himself that the gig was being propelled as quietly as possible.

"Geoff!" A soft voice.

Frost halted, startled, one foot poised for a step, then turned quickly and saw the slim shape of his brother, Joseph, two paces away. It was not so dark that Frost could not see the smile on Joseph's face. "You presume upon my good humor, landsman, venturing upon my quarterdeck without so much as by-your-leave." He put as much steel in his tone as he could.

"Geoff . . . I came to thank you for saving my life . . . and to ask to go ashore with your assault party."

Taken aback, and seeking frantically for appropriate words, Frost could only murmur: "You are too weak to be of value ashore."

"But it is a month, no more, since you took your wounds . . ." Joseph retorted softly.

Frost's two quick paces closed the gap between them. "You remain aboard this vessel, Joseph!" he hissed sharply, knowing full well that Slocum Plaisted and the two men at the wheel were hearing every word but trying not to. Dear God, where had Joseph found the impudence to dare transgress his quarterdeck! "You shall remain aboard this vessel," Frost repeated, this time in a lower voice, "because if I fall only one son remains to comfort Maman. You be that son."

"So! I then play the roles of three sons! That is too much to ask, Geoff!"

"You forget I command, Joseph," Frost reminded his brother bluntly.

"And will you bowsprit me for disobedience, Geoff?" Joseph shot back, face flushed visibly even in the dark.

"Not whilst you serve a gun, Joseph. Do not force me to chain you to a gun carriage. Your service with Knox has made you valuable as a cannoneer. I know well your gun laying was responsible for the shot which struck the flour cask that first exercise."

Joseph lowered his gaze, now less defiant, avoiding his brother's eyes. "Mister Rawbone is an excellent pedagogue of the cannon."

"Precisely, but he needs assistance. You are henceforth his assistant. Seek him out and make this desire of mine known to him. Follow his orders closely."

Frost saw the protest rising in his brother's face. "Enough, Joseph!" Frost said in as low a voice as possible, pulling his brother to the lee rail. "This may seem a lark to you . . . Damn it, why could you not have kept to casting cannon ball in Saugus? By morning this vessel may be a burning hulk, every man aboard her dead, or wounded and wishing he were dead! If you wish to give me peace to contemplate what I must, then serve Rawbone as you would me . . ."

"Geoff . . ."

"You are dismissed, landsman!"

Shocked and dismayed, Joseph's lips quivered; he was on the verge of crying. Great Buddha! It was hard to remember the lad was only eighteen. Eighteen! By that age Geoffrey Frost had been at sea almost half his life. Frost grasped his brother and hugged him. "There, Joseph, I spoke harshly because I must. Go now, and give me one less worry. Do that for our mother, lad."

Joseph suppressed a sniffle, drew himself up, and nodded, not trusting himself to speak.

"Thank you, Joseph." Frost patted Joseph awkwardly on the shoulder. His brother turned away toward the ladder to the waist.

"Joseph," Frost said, recalling another Portsmouth mother's son, "there is a man aboard named Quentin Fowle. He is assigned to one of the starboard cannons. When you report my orders to Mister Rawbone, say it is my wish that he seek out this Quentin Fowle and ensure this Quentin Fowle is kept aboard as a matross, not detailed as a member of the force going ashore. Do you understand me?"

Joseph nodded, "I know Quentin; I pulled him out of an alehouse at your bidding."

"Good lad, now go."

Joseph was two steps away when Frost called again, very softly: "Brother, that was a damned, damned stupid thing to do, hiding yourself aboard in that coffin . . . you courted your own death . . . and almost won it . . . but I love you for it." Joseph continued across the quarterdeck as if he had not heard. Perhaps he had not.

Frost resumed his pacing, shutting Joseph and all else out of his mind, reviewing his plan for taking the cat into Louisbourg Harbor without benefit of Caleb's intelligence. What would he likely find at Battery Island? Were the cannons at Battery Point manned? If he were a betting man . . . no, he was a betting man all right, his being two leagues east, north-east of Louisbourg Harbor at the present time proved that. He would bet that the British garrison commander would be short of men, with Howe in Halifax wanting every soldier he could winkle out of the British Army in North America. But short of men or not, a canny commander would still have prepared for an attack from the sea, no matter how unanticipated such an event might seem.

And given the choice of spreading his scarce cannoneers between Battery Island and Battery Point, the canny commander would concentrate his gunners on Battery Island in order to seal the harbor's mouth. To the west of Battery Island lay the shoals of Rochford Point; half a mile to the northeast lay Nag Head Point and Lighthouse Point. At low tide there was scarce ten fathoms in the channel between Battery Island and Lighthouse Point. Frost's money was on Battery Island.

No thought at all of landing a party west of Black Rock Point and attacking Louisbourg from the landward side. Frost had a crew of green hands, mostly landsmen, with less than three weeks aboard the cat learning how to function as a unit and fight the ship. A great deal of training remained to be done. Frost had no illusions about the capabilities of his crew; a trained amphibious force they were not. And yet, the assault had to come from the sea.

But it would be a nice piece of work to get past Battery Island. He would go in just before first light on the in-flowing tide, the Royal Navy's red ensign at the cat's mizzen peak, a signal with HM *Jaguar*'s number, though there was little chance the British had not early on learned of *Jaguar*'s capture from their numerous spies in the Ports of Piscataqua. Still, the cannons on Battery Island might not be charged, the cannoneers numbed and confused by their rouse from sleep, the identity of the ship uncertain . . . enough time to bring the cat within range and put enough iron on target to silence the cannons on Battery Island.

And then? Nothing but a calm, smooth sail of a mile or so right into Louisbourg Harbor, allowing the British garrison commander ample time to rouse his soldiers, prepare whatever cannons might be guarding the quay . . .

Frost's subconscious mind registered the faint swish of an oar through water; instantly his ruminations on the difficulties of getting past Battery Island and into the inner harbor were thrust aside with the speed of a Chinese fan's being folded. In the southern sky a faint crescent moon, eyelash thin, was barely visible a finger's width above the watery horizon. Frost's eyes were well accustomed to the dark, and to landward he glimpsed the small, vague smear of something grayish against the engloomed dark of the sea.

Frost stepped to the wheel and whispered to Slocum Plaisted and Darius, now stationed there as a messenger: "Pass the word, be ready to receive Mister Bowditch and Caleb Mansfield at the starboard waist entry." Darius departed on bare, silent cat's feet.

"I've heard nothing, Captain Frost," Slocum Plaisted demurred.

"I expect not, Slocum," Frost said. "That blow you took to your head scarce a month past left you with something like a cricket's chirp in your ears. It's as bad as the constant ringing caused by cannon fire I cannot shake from my ears. But there, you should hear it now." Indeed, the stroke-pause-pull of oars seeking to make speed, no matter how muffled, was there—just at the edge of audibility.

Frost heard the soft buzz of activity on the gun deck, a bit louder than he liked, but much softer than he would have heard four days earlier. Given time, he could weld this crew and the cat into a formidable weapon. Time: the one commodity scarcer than gun powder, and which he had wasted in prodigious quantities. Frost peered over the quarterdeck's starboard rail as the gig pulled into view in the faint light, O'Buck and Nathaniel Dance pulling oar with Hannibal Bowditch at the tiller and something in tow . . . no, it was O'Buck on one oar and Nathaniel Dance and Caleb Mansfield on the other, Hannibal Bowditch steering, surely enough, and towed behind the gig, the most disreputable birch bark canoe Frost had ever seen—with Paul Libby and Homer Clark clinging to its gunnels for dear life.

"⚙⚙⚙⚙ ORAGIN' PARTIES," CALEB MANSFIELD
⚙ F ⚙ SAID DISGUSTEDLY AS HE FOLLOWED
⚙   ⚙ STRUAN FERGUSON INTO FROST'S DAY
⚙⚙⚙⚙ CABIN. "FORAGIN' PARTIES AND FIRE-
wood parties. Coal mines ain't bein' worked, not enough men,
'n' gas in the shafts. The garrison's starvin', starvin' still they
be, even though four vessels with provisions arrived two days
ago—surprised ye didn't cross them. Precious little in the way
of provisions got ashore yet . . . and not much will, they be destined for Howe's army in Halifax. Only came to Louisbourg
because they wus separated from their convoy by a storm."

"Would a dram of rum take the edge off your choler, Caleb,"
Frost said, motioning Caleb Mansfield to the chair in front of
his desk as he unrolled his Uncle William Pepperrell's map of
Louisbourg Harbor.

"Appreciated mightily, Capt'n Frost, it's been a dry four
days." Caleb's face was wan and drawn, skin stretched tight
over cheekbones, eyes sunk far back in their sockets. Frost
knew that Caleb, Paul and Homer had not had an easy four
days. Frost nodded at Ming Tsun, who produced a cup and a
pitcher in which rum and water had already been blended in
equal proportions.

Caleb volunteered without urging: "Glad I be ye kept me
from swattin' that inoffensive ladybug. It were bad luck for
sure, 'n' we'd still be flailin' about in them muck holes, 'stead
of back here with ye and Mister Ming Tsun."

Frost ignored the digression. "Those were the three shots I heard after we set you ashore, a foraging party?"

"Three shots? Hell, Capt'n Frost, thar was a fusillade! Three redcoats and a renegade Mi'kmaq had been trackin' a cow moose since the day afore! They put more round ball into her than the poor critter's weight. Game's scarce around Louisbourg, I shouldn't wonder. Howe didn't give the garrison no provisions when he sent 'em packin' from Halifax."

"But there are still foraging parties out?" Frost asked, weighing down the map's edges with books and inkpot.

"Foragin' parties wus recalled when the little convoy sailed in, but thar be not much in the way of trees near Louisbourg, all's been cut! So it wus a woodcuttin' party bivouacked down the shore had Homer, Paul 'n' me 'fraid to show a light. 'Course, I knew ye wus offshore, so I went back to whar I had seen this canoe blow'd up on the beach and we set out to find ye. Would have got to ye 'fore them kids met up with me in mid-ocean, 'cept we had to carve paddles. Wusn't much for paddles."

Frost planted a forefinger on Battery Island. "Is there a garrison?"

"Yes, though it ain't much."

"Cannons?"

"Twenty. Thirty-six-pounders. Left by the French."

"How do you know?" Struan Ferguson asked as Ming Tsun poured another splash of watered rum into Caleb's cup.

"'Cause, Mister Ferguson, me and Paul swum out there night afore last, powerful cold the water wus, as you might guess. No more 'n thirty redcoats on the island; got a serjeant is all."

"And Battery Point, Caleb?" Frost asked as Nathaniel Dance, carrying a tray of bread, cold meat and cheese, entered the day cabin. Yes, he knew how cold the water was in these latitudes, less than fifty degrees; a mortal man would have succumbed to the cold within ten minutes. But Caleb Mansfield and his woods-cruisers were not mortal men.

"A few sickly soljers keepin' watch, but they couldn't get a cannon ready to fire in a week. No powder there, either. It's all in Louisbourg or on Battery Island."

"Strength of the garrison, Caleb?"

"Hundrit and ninety men, I reckon, a company about. A lot of 'em sick with the pluersey, but the crews of the vessels what came in two days afore be ashore. They ain't got their land legs yet, but they be fit."

"And the prisoners?" Frost asked the question he had saved for last. "With provisions scarce, how are they faring, and where are they?"

"In storehouses back from the waterfront. They be near some big stone gate."

"You are sure?" Frost asked, anxiously.

"I didn't see no reason to go inside, if that what ye be askin', but I used thet spy glass of yore Uncle Pepper's to good purpose when I winkled into the town at night 'n' spent a day in the bell tower of a church. Saw people let out 'n a little space less than the size of this vessel's maindeck, then marched back inside. All of 'em had skins the color of this her' bread, and at least a year's growth of beard. Prisoners, right enough. Saw 'em there!" Caleb plunged a dirty forefinger onto the map slightly southeast of the Dauphin Gate.

"Excellent, Caleb. If that glass served you well, please keep it, with the compliments of my Uncle Pepperrell. It could not be in better hands."

"Speakin' of glasses, Capt'n . . ."

Frost knew where Caleb was trending. "I know it's been a thirsty four days, but not presently, Caleb, for we have to silence those cannons on Battery Island." Frost stressed the "we."

Caleb nodded as he chewed a large mouthful of cheese and boiled meat. When he had swallowed the food, Caleb drained the last of his second glass of watered rum and wiped his mouth on the back of his hand. "Thet be a chore for my woods-cruizers. We'll need the loan of yore longboat and a few hands to help us row."

Frost consulted the Kendall chronometer, something that had become a simple but satisfying pleasure. "Lacking five minutes of ten. Gather your woods-cruizers. We'll turn seaward to avoid the lighthouse, then head for Battery Island in line with Rocky Island, which will conceal our hull. We can let the in-flowing tide take us close to Rocky Island with no sails visible on the yards. You will have less than half a land mile to pull."

On deck the thin rind of the crescent moon cast little light, but the men at the capstan had already raised the anchor, and top sails and jibs in light airs had laid the cat on a starboard tack, heading south-southwest. "Maintain our light discipline, Mister Ferguson," Frost said as he walked up to Struan Ferguson and two quartermasters at the helm. "We've done better than I thought with such a large crew, but we can't afford to grow lax now."

"I've charged a solid man from each mess to account for his mates, sir. Do ye think we can sleep the men by watches? I expect we shan't pull behind Rocky Island 'til near midnight."

"My thoughts also, Struan," Frost said, remembering all the sleepless nights he had spent in pirate waters, narrow straits and anxious negotiations, when his body and soul desperately craved rest. "Sleep is as much a weapon as a musket. Stand down your watch first and send them below, but quietly, quietly. Plaisted's and Nason's watches may send down for blankets and sleep next to their cannons. All topmen not needed for sail changes below also." Frost's eyes fell on Nathaniel Dance and Hannibal Bowditch standing at the break of the quarterdeck. "The youngsters below also."

Ming Tsun was beside Frost, holding out Frost's boat cloak. Frost threw it about his shoulders gratefully as he walked forward to the foremast larboard chains, Ming Tsun a silent pace behind. Caleb Mansfield materialized beside him, matching Frost step for step, though like Ming Tsun, a pace behind. "Ye got some bad 'uns in the crew, Capt'n Frost," Caleb said, employing an unseen porcupine-quill pick tooth inside his beard with deliberate, unseen and objectionable noises.

"Yes," Frost agreed. "A few men who've never amounted to anything in their lives because they haven't wanted to work hard enough to achieve anything, nay, who never knew what that 'anything' was, and who are envious of those who have worked hard. They are frustrated and jealous of those who have accomplished something. But such people can be useful, if you watch them closely."

"I nona', Capt'n Frost, some ther be who belike ther miseries, drawin' comfort from it so's they have sommon's to blame for ther miseries aside therselves." Caleb swore softly as his pick tooth broke. "Mighty fine job of preparin' meat yore Mister Ming Tsun did, Capt'n. Capital it were."

"You were hungry from four foodless days ashore in my service, Caleb," Frost said, smiling because he knew that in the darkness Caleb could not seen his smile. "To such a hungry man a piece of salt beef from the Royal Navy's commissariat would seem a feast indeed."

"Mayhep, but I tell ye true, Capt'n Frost, this Campbell, 'n' another named Sweeney, bear ye no great love."

"That I understand, Caleb, but they are hopeless as matrosses, so, hoping they will be better wielding a cutlass, I intend to set them in Mister Ferguson's party in hopes they can at least do our men some good by screaming and uttering blood curdling oaths to chill the ardor of Louisbourg's defenders."

Frost sensed, rather than saw, Caleb's shrug of resignation. "Wus it me, Capt'n, I'd have 'em chained to a staple sommers below decks, that I would."

"There are two hundred and twenty-eight men and boys aboard this cat, Caleb. But I can put ashore little more than a hundred and fifty. We go against a company of British regulars, though they may be the dregs of the British Army in North America. Every man aboard this vessel has his part to play." Frost, Caleb and Ming Tsun had reached the foremast larboard chains, where John Nason was listening to the quiet, rhythmic chant of the leadsman.

"Evenin', Captain Frost," Nason said, knuckling his forehead in unconscious imitation of the practice Nathanial Dance had unknowingly fostered aboard the cat. "We have twenty fathom hereabouts, but I'm concerned about a shoals I saw marked on your uncle's map of the Louisbourg approaches."

"I likewise, John, though the tide now is from the land, and raising us. We should pass over the shoals handily." Frost spoke with a conviction he desperately wanted everyone else to feel. "At the very ebb we shall sweep in, quietly, quietly, and mark you, we shall be in line with Rocky Island at midnight." Frost clapped a reassuring hand on John Nason's shoulder.

"Mister Ming Tsun wants to go ashore with my woods-cruizers on Battery Island, Capt'n Frost," Caleb said, somewhat deferentially.

Frost looked sharply at Caleb, then at Ming Tsun. "You know not our sign language, Caleb, nor is it light enough to communicate."

"Wal, ye must understand, Capt'n Frost, me 'n' Mister Ming Tsun, we've been together for some months now. Us woods-cruizers, we don't much speak, bein' by ourselves much, so when we meet up wit' a companion spirit, which is to say, Mister Ming Tsun and me have learn' we is, we kinda know what ta' other thinks."

"I forbid it, Caleb," Frost said sternly, turning on his heel and unexpectedly coming face to face with Darius. How long had Darius been following him?

"Capt'n Frost," Darius said quickly, "I wish to be with Master Mansfield when he goes to Battery Island."

"Call me Caleb or Mister Mansfield," Caleb retorted stiffly: "my only master be myself."

Frost quickly conjured up the mental image of Prosperous attending John Langdon and inwardly groaned. Prosperous' son! What if . . . "I forbid it! No more shall be said. Caleb! If you cannot subdue a mere thirty redcoats with a dozen woods-cruizers, then you are not fit to call yourselves New Hampshire men."

"Wal," Caleb said grudgingly, "that be true 'n' all, but I collect Mister Ming Tsun, he's godalmighty useful with thet ax o' his'n, and this young man, wal, anytime I hears a volunteer I mark him well, and as I told ye, Capt'n, we needs some crew to pull oar."

"Go from me, Caleb!" Frost said harshly, though in a low

voice to respect the quiet with which the cat was creeping down on the shoals at the entrance to Louisbourg Harbor. "These two I cannot spare," but he sensed, rather than saw, the hurt in Ming Tsun's eyes, and without turning toward Darius he knew the same hurt welled within that youth. "Caleb . . ." Frost began.

"But Capt'n, they be wantin' to get the New Hampshire men free," Caleb said mildly. "Volunteers, they be much preferable to pressed men."

Frost peered first at Ming Tsun, impassive in the darkness, then at Darius, seeing the youth's incongruous smile. "I've got my freedom, Capt'n, can't help but want to get Mister Whipple his freedom, too."

"You're a fool, Darius. Caleb, you're a fool also for encouraging them. Ming Tsun, after these years, you know better . . . all right, make it so!" Frost said savagely. For a moment he was tempted to draw the three of them into his embrace; but that would never do, and Frost was vexed that he had almost committed an unseemly display of emotion. Great God! Joseph! Earlier in the evening he had actually done so! Had he been observed by some of the cat's crew? Under what mystic spell had he fallen?

"But understand, no one comes back without the other two —and the rest of the woods-cruizers—or by the Great Buddha, not a one of you shall have a decent burial. Without a decent burial, your souls shall wander eternity . . . well, get you gone, Caleb. You have an assault to plan, whilst I have naught to do but retire to my cabin and wonder what move next I should make on the chessboard."

⤞ XXII ⤝

⚜⚜⚜⚜ TRUAN FERGUSON, LETTING HIMSELF
⚜   ⚜ INTO FROST'S DAY CABIN IN RESPONSE
⚜   S   ⚜ TO FROST'S COMMAND TO ENTER AT
⚜⚜⚜⚜ STRUAN'S KNOCK, FOUND FROST PRE-
tending an intense study of his chessboard by the light of two
lanterns, though Frost's every sense had been straining as he
had listened to the workings of his ship. "Caleb has cleared
away in the longboat. The men on my watch had gone below
and the other watches are resting easy at their cannons. We are
anchored with short scope in six fathom of water on the outgoing tide, and the sweeps have been shipped, all in accordance
with yer orders, Captain."

Struan took great pride in the fact that Frost had entrusted
him to perform a series of complicated maneuvers in shoal and
restricted waters while Frost had not been on deck. He had no
idea of the vast amounts of anxiety Frost had expended while
those complicated maneuvers were underway.

Frost nodded as nonchalantly as he could. "Pray, join me in
the last of this chocolate." Frost pulled a translucent porcelain
cup and saucer toward him and picked up the silver pot on the
desk. The exquisitely stark and simple Wedgewood cup and
saucer were from the stock selected by Hugh Stuart for the
Jaguar's dinner service; the plain silver pot was one that Frost
had purchased six years before from Boston silversmith Paul
Revere. "I fear it has gone cold, and Ming Tsun nowhere
around to warm it, but appreciated all the more for the invig-

oration of the cacao bean since, despite the advancement of the season, at this latitude the night is quite chill." Struan remained standing until bidden by Frost to take the chair across from Frost's desk. He looked at the chessboard with professional interest. "Ye have been playing exceptionally well of late, Geoffrey. Ye bested Ming Tsun and me on the game in play during the voyage out of Portsmouth. Now ye have the advantage of having captured our two bishops and one knight whilst we have won only two pawns and one bishop. The positions on the board are not auspicious for us."

Frost smiled inwardly, glad that his clandestine assistance from Nathaniel Dance had not been discovered. "I've been devoting more of my time to the study of the board, given my confidence in the abilities of this vessel's second-in-command. As a matter of fact, I'm thinking of playing *wei chi* with Ming Tsun again." He said the words sincerely, ungrudgingly, for Struan Ferguson was indeed an extremely competent mariner. Moreover, he was a brave man who stood to his duty unflinchingly. Every action of the man since Frost had shipped him at Batavia had proved Struan's worth. But Frost knew that he, or Struan, or both, might very well be dead within six hours, so Frost had paid Struan the supreme compliment a captain could give a subordinate, casually issuing several curt orders that involved critical maneuvers under dangerous conditions, then quitting the deck.

Struan took his cup of chocolate, cold though it was, and sipped it gratefully. "*Wei chi* is too complicated a game for me, Captain Frost. I have seen ye and Ming Tsun play it much, but its intent I cannot glean." Struan changed the subject. "What are we to do with those Campbell and Sweeney chaps?"

Frost sighed and lifted his cup. "I regret not having chained them to a staple on the cable tier as you did with Lieutenant Lithgow, immediately nipping the incipient mutiny. But I thought when Campbell soiled his trousers the point had been well made with his mates. Being the butt of his mates' scorn, that's always more effective in channeling behavior than clapping men in chains."

Struan had always thought his captain too generous by half in his estimation of his fellow man, but Struan kept those thoughts to himself. "But how shall we employ them in our endeavors at break of morning?"

"I beg you will forgive me, Struan, but I propose to place them in the landing party you command. Both men are no matrosses, but dangers to their mates when they serve cannons. It is my thought to issue them pikes and cutlasses, not muskets, and urge them sternly to present a fearsome countenance to the British we'll encounter."

Struan stroked his chin reflectively. "I shall have John Nason as my second. We've long agreed that Slocum Plaisted must remain with the ship. John can keep an eye on them to ensure they do their duty."

Frost shrugged. "They are landsmen. I've gotten the tenor of most of the men we've shipped this cruize. I've marked ten or eleven whom I intend to set ashore when we return to Portsmouth with Marcus and the other prisoners, not to mention enough spoil from the four transport vessels that entered Louisbourg two days ago to have all the Ports of Piscataqua agog and our prize-smitten crew ready to do battle with the entire British Navy in order to gain yet more wealth."

Struan raised his cup of chocolate again. "I toast Marcus Whipple, his fellows imprisoned in Louisbourg, and our success in liberating them on the morrow." Struan set his cup very carefully in its beautiful saucer. "Have ye calculated our chances of success, Geoffrey?" Only when they were absolutely alone would Struan presume to use Frost's Christian name.

"I have, Struan," Frost said wanly, "but perhaps you are better for not knowing."

"My duties shall be discharged strenuously, Geoffrey, whatever the chances of success, so long as my body still breathes."

"I know that truly," Frost said, unable to conceal a small grimace as he drank the last bitter dregs of the cold, cold chocolate. He turned the map of Louisbourg's inner harbor crosswise across his desk so that Struan Ferguson could see it equally. "You have heard my theory of forty and seventy before . . ."

"Enough to know it by heart," Struan assured him.

"I was prepared to violate it this time, Struan," Frost said as he scowled at the map, noting the depths marked, knowing that when he brought the cat to anchor in the inner harbor he would be lucky to have two feet of water beneath the cat's keel at mean low tide.

"Ye hold that anytime ye consider the probability of success to range between forty and seventy of percentages, the candle is worth the risk. Ye do not wait for assurance past the seventy because by the time ye have such assurance, the tide may have turned. Below the forty, ye have naught sufficient information upon which to hazard the venture."

Frost suppressed a half-smile as he glanced at some of the books, secure in their fiddled racks in his day cabin, that had been selected by Hugh Stuart, and sought out the folio of Shakespeare's dramas. He could just as well have illustrated his theory with Brutus' often quoted passage about the tide in the affairs of men being taken at the flood from *Julius Caesar*, but Struan was completely sour on anything and anybody English, even that greatest of playwrights. Both Frost and Struan Ferguson knew something about tides. "With Caleb's intelligence derived from four hard days and nights of diligent spying, I hold between forty and fifty. If Caleb and his woods-cruizers secure Battery Island without alerting the garrison, I hold near seventy. Yet had Caleb not been fetched back to us, Inshallah, I was committed to the attack in any event. And here is how I propose to lay our cannons and land our forces . . ."

Geoffrey Frost and Struan Ferguson earnestly and completely immersed themselves in the map of the southwest arm, the inner harbor of Louisbourg, formerly of New France, for the next two hours, revising and refining the lists of which men would be included in each of the landing parties Frost and Struan would lead; how to ferry one hundred twenty men ashore in two launches that could carry, at most, twenty-five men each; the men who would remain with the cat to serve her and her cannons, the instructions to be given to Roderick Rawbone, the instructions to be given to Slocum Plaisted . . .

But not so completely did they immerse themselves in their tasks of planning a complicated assault—on a fortress that had taken William Pepperrell and Commodore Peter Warren a siege of forty-eight days, over three thousand soldiers and militia, over a thousand sailors and five hundred marines, to reduce it in '45, while General Amherst and Admiral Boscowen required a force three times the garrison to reduce it in '58—that they did not hear, or sense, the quiet thump of wood against wood.

Frost and Struan, racing out of the day cabin and up the companionway, ran full tilt into Hannibal Bowditch, who announced in his loud juvenile tenor: "Sirs! Sirs! The longboat has returned!"

"That's obvious, Mister Bowditch," Frost said sharply, "though I see no need to announce its arrival in tones which are doubtlessly heard in Louisbourg." He led the way toward the starboard waist entry, where the woods-cruisers were climbing wearily aboard the cat.

"Yes, sir," Hannibal said meekly, and in a much lower voice.

Frost blundered into several obstacles before his eyes, adjusted to the lighted day cabin, accommodated to the dark. He came up to the waist entry as Caleb Mansfield, boosted from behind by Davis Cummings, threw himself wearily upon the deck. Another woods-cruiser, Jack Dawes, who had already gained the deck, was heaving and puking into the scuppers.

Struan Ferguson helped Caleb to his feet and nodded anxiously at the woods-cruiser who was convulsing in spasms. "What be the matter with him, Caleb?"

"Most likely the way Mister Ming Tsun dispatched three or four of the battery's defenders. Swiped off their heads neatly as a housewife nips peas, he did, with that great axe of his'n. Not to mention the soljers he potted with stick 'n' string. Then after the island wus took, he gathered up the heads and bodies of the English dead and said prayers to them."

"The battery is taken then?" Frost said quickly.

"Aye, Capt'n Frost, the battery be took, all our men returned safe, no hurt among them, less thar be a scratch or two, though nothin' thet a rub o' one of Mister Ming Tsun's allers won't make right. By my count thar be twenty-seven English souls gone to thar Maker in the hour past."

"No one is left to raise an alarm as we sail past?"

"We would not be har if thar wus," Caleb said with bleak satisfaction. "I twigged thar wus no need fur takin' prisoners. So we didn't."

"Inshallah," Frost said as a tiny bit of the tension within him eased. He thought momentarily, bitterly, of Lieutenant Barker's letter, he of the King's Own Regiment, in the *Gentleman's Quarterly*, the letter describing the British retreat from Lexington and Concord: *all that were found in the houses were put to death*. Where lay the difference between Lieutenant Barker's actions and his own? Frost shook his head to dispell the thought: "Ming Tsun . . . and Darius . . ."

"Safe, safe, Capt'n, though Darius be so pale he could pass for a white man on any street of Portsmouth, at all he seen this night."

Which observation was close to the truth, as Frost saw when Darius wearily hauled himself up the entry, followed by the inscrutable Ming Tsun. Frost noted that the quiver slung over Ming Tsun's shoulder was almost empty of arrows.

Darius avoided Frost's eyes. Frost laid a gentle hand on the young black man's shoulder. "Your watch is turned below to sleep. Do you likewise." Darius nodded and shuffled away, head low, shoulders hunched with the weight of the things he had seen.

Frost returned to his quarterdeck, pulled his watch from its pocket, unshuttered the binnacle, studied the watch's dial quickly in the small lamp's rosy illumination, shuttered it again and mentally computed the tide. Should he send sufficient men to Battery Island to garrison it and provide warning if any vessels appeared in the Louisbourg approaches? How many men should he detail? No, he could spare none from the assault on the town he had planned. He would have to take the terrible risk of leaving the Louisbourg approaches unguarded until he had settled the matter of investing the town.

Then, quietly, to the shadow at his side: "Mister Ferguson, whenever you wish you may weigh the anchor to cathead and tie off. Fore and main topsails, fore and main topgallants, mizzen topsail, jibsail and fore staysail. Leadsmen larboard and starboard sounding constantly. Please assure no word spoken from forward or aloft can be heard on this deck. Except for soundings, at this time silence is vastly preferred to speed. The ship's boats to be towed behind on ten fathoms' scope."

Struan issued the necessary orders to several runners with calm efficiency. Frost glanced aloft when he heard the soft rustle of canvas as the main topsail and topgallant were loosed. The thin rind of the crescent moon was directly overhead and the tide was setting in. He felt the ship gather beneath him, like a cat preparing to spring. *Cat. Cat. Jaguar. Jaguar.* Truly this vessel had been well named.

Frost moved to the stern counter. He was committed now, truly committed, sailing into an unfamiliar harbor while relying on an old French chart with soundings of a questionable nature added in his Uncle Pepperrell's spidery hand, and on his instincts as a mariner. No pilot, and compounding the sheer lunacy and madness of the endeavor, Frost was doing all this at night on a total run of slightly more than one league.

John Nason came aft to report sails set as ordered to Struan Ferguson at his station by the ship's wheel. He did not see Frost alone on his quarterdeck behind them; indeed, Frost, one hand clapped to the larboardmost swivel gun stanchion, was lost in his own thoughts and staring intently toward Rocky Island, where the wash of a wave cap against the rocks occasionally burst into a small dirty white splash just visible at the extreme edge of vision made possible by the faint crescent moon and starlight.

"Faith," John Nason said to Struan, as he blew on his cold hands to warm them, "how excellent that we have this slice of moon to give us warning of reef and rock, yet not so bright that we may be seen sailing so boldly into Louisbourg Harbor."

"Johnnie, Johnnie," Struan Ferguson said quietly, a chuckle in his rich brogue, reviewing in his mind the execution of the next set of orders he knew he would receive and equally forgetful of Frost's presence behind them on his quarterdeck. "Dinna ye no ken that what we be about this very night was planned weeks ago? Ken ye not why the captain drove the finishing of this vessel, her victualling and recruitment, so purposefully? He was fain to come to Louisbourg from the moment he learned prisoners had been removed to Louisbourg from Halifax. Reaching here on this moon, with this tide this night, was Captain Frost's plan from the time this vessel was warped to Langdon's dock yard."

"And how do you know that, Struan Ferguson?" John Nason said, disbelief in his voice.

"Because I know the man as no other except Ming Tsun, and our captain always sets about a task with the task's end first in mind." Struan stepped to the binnacles to check one compass, then the other, then dispatched John Nason to the foremast chains to listen to the soft chants of the leadsmen and relay their soundings.

Frost stood without moving for another fifteen minutes, until the surf line marking Rocky Island was well abaft the larboard quarter and the surf line of Battery Island's easternmost point was audible, though not visible. He had not noticed the cold until he bestirred himself and his stiffened muscles complained. He had long forgotten the exchange between his first mate and John Nason in his preoccupation with the husbandry of his ship as he moved up to stand with Struan Ferguson.

"No beacon from the lighthouse, Captain," Struan said as he glanced toward the north, where Lighthouse Point lay invisible in the darkness.

"Better that our crew not know how close we are to the breakers at the foot of the lighthouse, Struan; we have at most eight fathoms of water in the midst of the channel, and scarce three cable-lengths separate Battery Island and Lighthouse Point." In the calm night air, Frost could hear the sullen patter of surf heaving itself over the shoals south of Battery Island. "But as we round Battery Island I anticipate we shall see what lights there be in Louisbourg Town." Then, almost as an afterthought: "However, one hour before dawn we likely shall have a taste of fog."

Frost looked around for a messenger and, seeing acting bosun Daniel O'Buck, summoned him. "Please convey my compliments to Mister Rawbone and ask him to get the slow match alight. All crews muster by their cannons. And I'd enjoy Caleb Mansfield's company on my quarterdeck."

O'Buck murmured an "Aye, sir," and hurried away.

"Strike fore and main topgallants, quietly, quietly, Mister Ferguson, and loose the spritsail. We must coast in slowly, just enough sail to maintain steerage as this tide reaches its height and slows. We have little more than one sea mile to gain in two hours." Frost sought out the eyelash of moon in the southwestern sky and reckoned the time near enough half past the hour of two that he did not need to step to the binnacle and consult his watch.

"Caleb," Frost said as Caleb Mansfield appeared at the quarterdeck breast rail. "You have seen to the proper loading of all muskets to be issued to the landing parties?"

"Long betimes, Capt'n Frost, though no locks ain't to be primed until we hand each man his musket."

"Please ask Ming Tsun for the list of men to be divided between Mister Ferguson and me. Nathaniel and Hannibal will help gather the men and sort them into the proper party. Muster Mister Ferguson's party beneath the main hatch, the men with me beneath the fore hatch. We must divide the men in each party into halves again, since each launch can take only twenty-five men."

"Mister Ming Tsun give me yore list afore, Capt'n. Last I knew he wus puttin' a new edge on thet blade of his'n. I'll get the lads and we'll gather up yore parties."

"Good. Daniel O'Buck," Frost turned to the other man, "please ask Cook Barnes to begin serving those pots of coffee kept warm on his banked fire. Gun crews below by watches, ten minutes per watch, and any man who wishes it a ration of bread and cheese to bring back to his gun. But mind no light escapes."

⨝ XXIII ⨞

⚙⚙⚙⚙⚙ ATTERY ISLAND WAS ASTERN NOW,
⚙   ⚙ THE CAT STEADY ON A COURSE OF
⚙ **B** ⚙ NORTHWEST BY NORTH, THE MUR-
⚙⚙⚙⚙⚙ MUR OF THE SURF OVER THE SHOALS
still there at the edge of hearing. Having supervised the readying of the spritsail Struan Ferguson had returned to his post by
the helmsmen at the ship's wheel.

Frost looked around for another messenger, mentally reviewing the soundings marked on the old chart of Louisbourg
Harbor as he judged the weight of the fitful puffs of wind
stroking his right cheek. His eyes fell on the shadow of John
Nason. "Mister Nason, go forward please to mind the leadsmen's count. When we touch seven fathoms to starboard and
nine fathoms to larboard, advise me accordingly."

Frost judged that the cat's bowsprit was pointed directly at
Battery Point on the western shore of Louisbourg Harbor.
He trusted Caleb's intelligence that the cannons there were not
manned but was extremely mindful that five cable lengths to the
northwest lay the Battery Shoals, and just to starboard as the
channel narrowed were the shoals in front of Nag Head Point.
"Mister Ferguson, we shall touch our appointed depth in two
minutes or less, just time to broaden the leech on fore and main
tops'ls, flatten the jibsail and fore stays'l. Helm hard up to lay
the ship on a course of west-southwest when the call comes."

Frost saw the shadow of Hannibal Bowditch dart in front of
the quarterdeck breast rail, larboard to starboard, and up the

companionway to stand breathless before his captain. "Just touched nine fathoms to larboard, and the last cast on the starboard bow quarter fetched seven fathoms."

"Excellent, Mister Bowditch."

"By your leave, sir," Struan Ferguson said as he issued the sail change orders, and then, before the cat had progressed another hundred yards, ordered the helm hard up, then steady on west-southwest.

"Mister Bowditch," Frost said as Hannibal turned to scurry away, "how are Surgeon Green's preparations advanced?"

"Surgeon Green, sir?"

"Surgeon Green, Mister Bowditch. Has Surgeon Green settled himself in a lazarette well below the waterline, the implements of his craft and anything else Surgeon Green could wish ready to hand?" Frost said with exasperation he did not try to conceal.

"I don't know, sir," Hannibal said.

"Did I not appoint you assistant to the surgeon in preparing to receive our casualties?" Frost said sharply. "It went well enough when we were hurling our round shot at harmless flour casks two days past for you and Mister Dance to lollygag about the main deck like oriental potentates. But in less than two hours the targets we shall engage have the ability to kill and maim our people. Getting a wounded mate speedily to Surgeon Green's skills may mean the difference between a mate's living or dying."

"Yes, sir," Hannibal said dutifully, pushing aside his own hopes that he might join Nathaniel Dance as a powder monkey. Bringing cartridge up from the filling room to the cannons was infinitely more glamorous and exciting than assisting a surgeon in the swift paring away of shattered limbs. But he knew better than to remonstrate with his captain.

"Before seeing to the good doctor's needs, Mister Bowditch, please draw me a bucket of sea water. I would take it as a great favor if you could do so without any untoward noise."

"From over-side, sir?" Hannibal said, not certain he had heard his captain properly.

"That is where one usually finds sea water, Mister Bowditch," Frost said testily, though he was already speaking to the boy's rapidly retreating back.

Now the cat's bow was aligned with the South West Arm of Louisbourg Harbor and several lights were visible in the town and from the ships riding at anchor before the town. Inshallah! Hannibal Bowditch was scarce twelve, and Ezrah Green appeared much younger than his thirty years. But on Ezrah Green's surgeon's skills likely more than one man's life would balance before the sun was full up.

Ming Tsun had fetched Frost's night glass; Frost extended the tube and, braced against the breast rail, studied the inverted images of the anchored ships. Doubtlessly they would have chosen the greatest depths for themselves. And what had become of the hulks of the five, or was it six, warships burned or scuttled by the French defending the town from Wolfe and Boscawen in July of '58? Had those hulks been raised, or were they still resting in the prime anchoring grounds, waiting these eighteen years to embrace his ship into their deadly labyrinth?

Frost closed the night glass and exchanged it for the cup of tea that Ming Tsun extended to him. He drank the tea in two swift swallows. Por Dios, but this May night was cold, even for this latitude. The French could not really have had a long growing season, or could they? Only three degrees of latitude separated Louisbourg from Portsmouth.

Hannibal Bowditch came up the companionway to the quarterdeck, carefully cradling a wooden bucket in his arms, the contents of which had sloshed out to wet his clothes. Frost splashed several fingers in the four or so inches of cold water remaining in the bucket, and withdrew his hand to read the direction of the faint wind by which side of his fingers cooled first. How long could a man expect to live in these cold waters if his ship sank under him? Ten minutes? Fifteen? No more. Frost made a rough comparison of the difference between the seawater and the night air and estimated to the minute when fog would begin to form. "Thank you, Mister Bowditch. Please dispose of the water down the pissdale on your way to join Surgeon Green."

Frost dismissed the youth, then, remembering something, stopped Hannibal. "Mister Bowditch, before attending Surgeon Green, please find Ming Tsun and ask him to fetch the rattlesnake flag from my cabin."

He turned to Struan. "Mister Ferguson, we shall insert ourselves between the two vessels lying closest to the quay. Both vessels appear to be snows, though one may be a brig. The Dauphin Bastion to the west of the town is reported by Caleb to have no garrison, though discretion bids us stay out of musket shot. The British troops are quartered in private houses around the warehouse where our New Hampshire men are imprisoned."

"Shall we take the two vessels captive?"

"I misdoubt there will be more than an anchor watch and bosun's guard on each vessel, but Daniel O'Buck can tell off eight men to board the vessels. Their orders will be to keep any crew below decks and repel any reinforcements."

More lights were visible in the town now. Dawn was less than an hour away, and chances were good that someone might already be stirring. Sentries, there had to be sentries. And then the lights of Louisbourg Town began to dim as the phenomenon of fog Frost predicted began to form; the slight decrease of air temperature in the coldest moments just before dawn as its boundary met the slightly warmer water. Frost knew that the fog would form, but he did not know how thick it would be. A bit of early morning fog would be a fine thing, but not the deep, impenetrable fog that had cloaked the cat while putting Caleb Mansfield ashore.

And those sunken hulks! Frost stepped over to Struan and said quietly: "Mister Ferguson, the gathering fog will either confound or accommodate our entry. I would appreciate your telling off two men with sharp eyesight and proven vigilance and stationing them at the knighthead to look for buoyed wreckage. As we come between the vessels we've selected drop the starboard kedge with a cable spring passed through a starboard stern port. Let the tide take us past the vessels before dropping the larboard sheet anchor. Mister Rawbone will then oblige us with a demonstration of his excellent gunnery."

The fog was thickening now, though Frost could still make out the few fitful lights of Louisbourg Town. By the Golden Buddha, the paucity of lights confirmed Caleb's report that the commander of the Louisbourg garrison was miserly in his use of fuel, whether oil, wood or coal. Men moved about the cat nervously and hesitantly but with a tolerable amount of efficiency. An excited rustle of whispers brought the word that a can-buoy lay directly in their course some thirty fathoms distant, the limit at which something close on the water could be seen in this near darkness.

Frost ordered the helm hard up, and the cat answered her rudder obediently, but slowly, oh so slowly. The cat eased past to starboard of the crudely painted buoy, and Frost reckoned the distance remaining to the point off the quay where he intended to anchor at two cable lengths—barely a quarter of a land mile. The tide would sweep them there in five, at most six, minutes. Frost called Slocum Plaisted to his side.

"Mister Plaisted, as earlier agreed, you shall command this vessel whilst Mister Ferguson and I take our landing parties ashore. Our two launches can freight only twenty-five men, but since the harbor is calm, I shall freight each launch with thirty men, six told off to row back to this vessel as if all the dogs of Hell were nipping at their oars. You shall freight the remaining men in the launches and direct them where your judgment, aided by what you observe through your glass, causes you to believe reinforcements shall be most useful. Since most of the garrison is billeted in houses on the quay, where Mister Ferguson will be devoting his attentions, mayhap reinforcements there would be of greater use than reinforcing me."

"And the gig, sir? It can transport eight men." Slocum Plaisted accepted his role calmly. Good man! If Struan Ferguson was Frost's best bower anchor, then Slocum Plaisted was Frost's sheet anchor. Ming Tsun was . . . Ming Tsun was Ming Tsun. It was useless to compare Ming Tsun to anyone or anything.

"Those men will augment Mister Feguson's party. Please time the runs ashore. The launches' return should take less time. But it will be critical to get all our landing forces ashore quickly since we will be dealing with a garrison twice our numbers, and I know not what augmentation the garrison may have from the crews of the ships newly arrived in harbor."

Struan Ferguson was at his elbow. "Mister Ferguson, have the boats in tow brought alongside. Your division to embark on the starboard side, my division on the larboard. Caleb's men to prime and hand down muskets after our landing parties are properly seated. No muskets for the men told off to row back to this vessel. We'll pull away as soon as anchors have taken the ground."

Ming Tsun came up with Frost's Bass double-barreled pistols and brass-backed cutlass and a broad leather belt with a hanger for the cutlass. The rattlesnake flag was neatly folded over his fore arm. Struan Ferguson had already buckled on a similar belt into which were thrust the pair of Strachan pistols. He stooped to gather up his targe and basket-hilted backsword, lying at his feet on the quarterdeck, and flashed a furious grin at his captain. Frost motioned for Slocum Plaisted. "Mister Plaisted, please bend this flag to the mizzen topsail brace pendant." The cat was ghosting between the two vessels, which had now resolved themselves into a brig and a snow, each a half pistol shot on either side, and Frost could see a small light's glow, probably a candle, behind the small larboard quarter badge of the brig to starboard. Frost heard the rustle of the rattlesnake flag being hauled to the mizzen topsail and was strangely pleased.

First light was no more than thirty minutes away. The fog had not thickened, but the sky had long been obscured and Frost knew the day, the morning at least, would be overcast.

"Kedge a-trip, Captain," Struan whispered.

"Let go," Frost ordered, and he was gratified not to hear even the faintest splash as the kedge anchor was tripped, ran its short scope, took the ground, and the cat's stern began to swing slowly to larboard, passing the bowsprit of the brig to larboard with two fathoms to spare.

"Hey!" a sleepy but querulous voice hailed. "What ship?"

Startled, Frost, who was walking toward the larboard entry, turned quickly and saw the dim shadow of a man just rising from his interrupted toilet, breeches dropped to his knees, from the heads at the bow of the brig to larboard. "His Britannic Majesty's ship *Jaguar*," Frost said calmly in a voice he hoped would not carry to the quay. "From Sheerness, newly appointed to the North American Squadron."

"Hell ye be!" the man boomed back. "The *Jaguar* be tooken by the rebels!"

"Caleb!" Frost snapped, knowing the range was too long for Ming Tsun's bow but that Caleb would have Gideon in hand. "Kill me that fool." Hardly had he spoken when the long rifle cracked and the sailor dropped from sight. "Mister O'Buck, half your complement onto the brig to larboard, look to that man as you secure the ship. The rest of your men onto the snow to starboard. You know your duty."

Frost stood impassively at the larboard waist entry as the men in his landing party dropped into the launch. He caught a glimpse of Joseph and Darius crouched over a cannon as the last man in his landing party fell into the heavily burdened launch, and Frost followed, hearing the mutters and shouts from the quay but paying them no heed.

"Mister Rawbone," Frost shouted, "as soon as both launches are clear of your broadside you may salute the garrison." Then to the men bent desperately to their oars: "Pull, Pull! You can count your money from the sale of those fat prizes later." His launch flashed by the bowsprit, the jaguar perpetually crouched beneath it seeming to grin at him, and Rawbone's first broadside erupted in a deafening pulsating maelstrom of thunder and flame that rattled the teeth of the men in the launch scant yards from the cannons' muzzles. Frost did not look to judge the effect of the first broadside; employment of the cat's cannons was now a matter solely within the provenance of Roderick Rawbone. His only concern was getting his men ashore quickly.

A musket ball fired from who knew where raked across the larboard gunwale of the launch, plowing a trough that threw out several splinters and spent itself in the thigh of a sailor sitting two thwarts in front of Frost. The man yelped like a scalded puppy and attempted to stand up. His mates beside and behind him pulled him down. The man began to weep piteously. "Quiet!" Frost roared, "You've no more than a scratch. The ball was mostly spent. Surgeon Green will remove it later and you'll have a memento to give a sweetheart and tell your grandchildren about."

The fog was especially heavy right at the water, but the gray, suffused light had increased in intensity to the point that Frost could see the quay clearly, though not the buildings behind the quay. He saw a flight of stone steps, slippery with weed, twenty fathoms in front and slightly to the right of the launch's bow, and he gestured toward the steps. Jack Lacey, Frost's best quartermaster from the cat, who had the launch's tiller now that the anchored cat had no need of his particular services, saw Frost's gesture and shifted the tiller accordingly.

"Caleb! Two men with you to the top of the steps! Keep low at the top and tell me if we're opposed here." Caleb Mansfield had just reloaded one of his rifle barrels; he thrust the ramrod into its thimbles and nodded. By Frost's estimate slightly more than two minutes had passed since the launch had pulled away from the cat. He looked around for Struan Ferguson. Struan's launch had gone around the cat's stern and was pulling strongly for a squalid work barge bowsed against the quay two hundred yards to the right of the Dauphin Gate.

Jack Lacey put the tiller hard up as Frost ordered starboard oars shipped, and Caleb Mansfield and two of his woods-cruisers were out of the launch and scuttling crab-like up the stone steps before the launch bumped against the quay. Caleb lifted his head warily over the top step, brought his long rifle to shoulder, fired, leaped to his feet and motioned for Frost.

"Jack Lacey, give the tiller over to the wounded man. You

fellow! Direct this launch back to the cat in half the time for its second lading or every man in this crew shall have a piece of your guts to wrap as garters! With me!" Frost shouted, jumping for the steps, Ming Tsun a pace behind him, the men in his party, armed with cutlasses and muskets, swarming out of the launch reluctantly but drawn by Frost's decisiveness.

"Glad I be not to be with ye!" one of the told-off rowers hooted. Frost did not spare the launch a glance, but concentrated on maintaining his footing on the weed-slippery quay steps.

A dead British soldier lay sprawled on the quay twenty yards away as Frost cleared the steps, and the cat fired another broadside. A tendril of smoke was rising from one of the houses behind the quay that had been shattered by several of the six-pounders' cannon balls. To his left Frost could see Struan's landing party laying into a small knot of British soldiers with bayonets, cutlasses, and enthusiasm.

Ming Tsun caught Frost's arm and pointed. A squad of soldiers was trundling a small field piece, three men on the trail, one man each on a wheel and the sixth pushing on the barrel, barely in control of the ponderous metal, down a cobbled street from the direction of the citadel. The iron rims of the wheels thumped loudly against the cobbles, striking a small shower of sparks from one cobble. "We need that cannon more than the British," Frost snapped, turning sharply to his right and running up the street toward the squad, Ming Tsun, Caleb and the rest of his men pelting along behind.

The squad of soldiers saw the landing party and hastily braked to swing the field piece around, almost losing control of the piece as they did so. Caleb and two of his woods-cruisers dropped to their knees, their three shots coming almost as one. Two men in the squad fell, two men turned and fled, but two men stayed with the field piece, one of them blowing on a short length of match as the cannon's muzzle slewed, then stopped at belly level.

"Inshallah," Frost whispered to himself, running toward the gunners as hard as he could in the narrow, confined street, which was little more than an alley, "if that cannon be loaded with langrage, I have led these men to their deaths." Then he saw the brief flash of the arrow arcing down at the same time he heard the slap of bowstring against Ming Tsun's wrist guard. The soldier with the slow match saw the arrow also, throwing up his arms as if to ward off the vision, and then the arrow took him in the belly and he sprawled backwards on the cobbles. The remaining soldier snatched up the smoldering slow match.

Caleb fired the second barrel of his long rifle. The man's shoulders hunched as he took the shot, but he still tried to lay the match atop the touchhole. He missed his several attempts and Frost was on the man, sabering the dying soldier viciously in the throat, a great gout of blood following his blade as he wiggled it loose.

One of the men in his landing party cried out, even before Frost heard the fusillade of musket shots. Another knot of British soldiers, this one much larger, was advancing down the street from the citadel. This group of men was commanded by a sergeant who evidently knew his business, for he had divided his men into two ranks, and was calmly ordering the second rank three paces forward, halting the men and ordering the rank to present their pieces. Behind this squad, coming down the steep hill from the direction of the citadel, hustling as fast as they could in a crabbed, sideways scuttle, two soldiers were lugging a wooden chest.

"The cannon!" Frost shouted, dropping his bloody cutlass and grasping the trail of the field piece. Two sailors joined him with enthusiasm, but the field piece, though only a four- or six-pounder, was heavy and ponderous, and responded slowly, oh so slowly, to their exertions; Frost felt the pain stabbing anew along his spine and through his ribs. The front rank's muskets were already at shoulder . . . Ming Tsun had picked up the smoldering match and before the field piece had turned brought it down on the touchhole.

Frost saw the match descend and wondered for a moment if the field piece was actually charged . . . the men hastening to catch up to the squad of soldiers were bearing the shot locker.

Then the field piece crashed and bucked, the trail tucked into a joint between two large cobbles, the piece's wheels rearing six inches off the cobbles rather than rolling backward, both iron wheel rims throwing off sparks as they bounced on the stone, spewing a deadly blossom of case shot. Caleb bawled out his own command for such men among Frost's landing party who had shouldered muskets to fire. And in the street above them, the smell of fresh blood above the cloying sulfur smell of burnt gunpowder, the smell of struck pyrites like lightning striking near, and the sobs and shrieks of mortally wounded men.

✲ XXIV ✥

✲✲✲✲ND FROM THE QUAY THE FURIOUS,
✲ A ✲ DULL POP-POP-POP OF MUSKET FIRE
✲   ✲ INTERSPERSED AMONG THE SOUNDS
✲✲✲✲✲OF CANNON FIRING, NO LONGER IN
a coordinated broadside, but still the steady businesslike fire of
a cannon every thirty seconds or so. Frost called Caleb and
Lacey to him. "It's likely Mister Ferguson requires our assistance. That chest yonder is the shot locker for this gun . . . fetch
it and charge this gun. Mister Lacey, keep five men to trundle it
after me. Caleb, two of your men to guard the matrosses.
Gather up the muskets of those British lest there be one or two
among the wounded who can still cause us harm."

"But I see no rammer," Lacey remonstrated.

"Use a musket barrel, man! You can find many ways to pick
up a squalling cat when the devil is breathing down your neck!"
Frost snapped.

"But Captain, we need a swab sponge to damp smoldering wad."

"Piss on it, man!"

"Beg pardon, sir?" Lacey said, completely lost.

"Piss on it, like the Capt'n tells ye!" Caleb Mansfield shouted.
"Afore rammin' the powder with a musket, piss on a shirt—
take thet 'un from thet dead soljer . . . piss's good as water fer
swabbin' a barrel, cuts the foulin' too."

Lacey threw back his head and laughed, a nervous, high-
pitched laugh skirting close to hysteria. If he survived this day,

and he was not at all sure that he would, what tales he would have to tell his mates!

This interchange was lost on Frost, who gestured imperiously to the rest of the men in his landing party, furious that they were standing idly, few, if any, having seen to the reloading of their muskets. "And you men, whilst you stand lollygagging, paying no heed to what is happening around you, another troop of British could have encircled and killed us all!"

"We've never seen such like, Captain, not this dying and all . . ." one of the men in the landing party said haltingly.

Frost reached the man in two strides—no, not really a man, a youth, scarce older than Hannibal or Nathaniel. "It's William Chasse from York, is it not?" he said kindly, relieved that despite all that was happening around him he was still able to summon the man's name and home place. The youth nodded hesitantly, the pallor of his face making the scars of small-pox stand out like the craters on the moon's surface when Frost had occasion to study that heavenly orb through his telescope.

"I don't like this killing, William Chasse," Frost said quietly, "Great Christ, no sane man does! Those men lying there whimpering for their mothers, they feel the same as you do. God only knows why the corrupt ministerial government of England makes war on us. But war we have, and killing is part of war until the saints decree otherwise. Like as not, those British soldiers now tumbled in a midden of offal and rags would be feeling the same things you and your mates are feeling . . . but they would be feeling them. The only thing you would be feeling would be the lump of langrage in your guts that steals your life. Now, is your musket charged?"

William Chasse mumbled softly, "I don't know, Captain."

"Then inspect your musket. All you men do the same." Frost looked around. Caleb and Ming Tsun were staggering down the street with the heavy munition chest between them. He was pleased to see that the other woods-cruisers had formed a rough protective square around the knot of men, eyes vigilant, thumbs on rifle cocks.

"Is there naught we can do for those British, Captain?" someone asked.

Frost shook his head. "We cannot attend them whilst our mates need us sorely. Now, follow me." He turned, scooped up his cutlass, and broke into a trot down the street that his landing party had just come, confident that his men would follow. Despite what he had said, Frost knew that some men liked to kill. As long as his opponent was English, Struan Ferguson was one of those men. And from the shouts and musketry coming up from the quay, Struan was engaged in more killing that he could comfortably handle.

Struan Ferguson had indeed gotten himself into a hot corner, as Frost saw when he broke out onto the quay. The larger part of the British garrison must have been quartered in two or more of the houses behind the quay, and the cat's gunnery had done little more than infuriate them, much like a bear's overturning a hive of bees in an apple orchard to get at the honey would enrage the bees. The quay was one amorphous mass of men, with partially dressed British soldiers far more in evidence than Struan Ferguson and the cat's men.

Frost halted to gain his breath as much as to absorb the scene, heartened to see that both launches with the second complements of his landing parties were almost to the quay. One of the woods-cruisers was at his elbow. Frost spoke quickly. "Into that building, as many of your mates as you can muster. The second floor, shoot the British, but only when you have clear shots. Take no chances of hitting our men. If you can see officers or sergeants, shoot them first. Now go!"

Dios! He was sending men into a building to snipe at the British when at any moment Rawbone, thinking the building harbored British soldiers, could fire into it. Great Buddha, let Rawbone be studying the quay carefully, and let his glass be sharp enough to distinguish between the red coats of the British and the buckskins and lindsay-woolseys of Caleb's woods-cruisers.

"With me lads!" Yes, the blood lust was rising in him now, and Frost made no effort to temper it, for that blood lust might well mean the difference between his living and his dying in the next five minutes. That and the hope that Struan's drills of the crew in the techniques of cutting and thrusting with cutlasses had taught some men the rudiments of skills necessary to defend themselves while at the same time pressing their attack. He led his men into the melee, taking the bunched-up British soldiers from their rear and flanks, slashing with the brass-backed cutlass, two soldiers down and Frost was stepping on their still-living bodies to spit a third through the kidneys before the British realized they were being attacked from the rear.

A soldier, hatless, red tunic stained even deeper with blood, turned and attempted to raise his musket, but he was clear of any Americans and a ball fired from a woods-cruiser's long rifle smashed into the man's skull just above his left ear. The man's face distorted into a bloody caricature of a Chinese festival mask as he fell. Two soldiers, wielding their bayonets with dexterity, advanced relentlessly behind their bayonet-tipped muskets and pressed Frost against the wall of a house. Frost beat back one bayonet with a desperate parry, giving himself time, though barely, to pluck a pistol from his belt, cock it, and kill first one man and then the other.

O Senhor. Had he fired the other pistol? A touch to his belt reassured him that one pistol remained unfired. A musket fired, then another. Frost did not hear the shots, though one ball cut the upper sleeve of his coat, searing across the top of his right shoulder, ploughing a bloody furrow, though the ball touched only flesh, not bone. The second ball struck the stone doorway of the house against which Frost had been pressed, throwing off chips of granite, one of which laid open a two-inch gash across his right cheek, others of which struck his neck violently, momentarily stunning him.

Ming Tsun intervened with his halberd to parry a bayonet aimed at Frost's heart, and Frost thrust himself away from the doorway, slipping in a pool of blood and almost losing his cutlass, but regaining his feet and waving on the field piece that Lacey and five of his mates were trundling along the quay, quite as rapidly as a team of draft horses, Frost opined.

"Ming Tsun!" Frost cried, no time for signing, and he needed his hands for his weapons: "Get through to Struan! Tell him at my order to disengage . . . withdraw east toward the Dauphin Gate, quickly!" Frost sought out Caleb, and in a few curt words told Caleb to withdraw to the west as soon as Frost had maneuvered the field piece into position.

Then Frost ran to intercept the cannon, urging the men straining to move it fifteen yards further on, then ordering the gun stopped and swung round to face the quay. "Struan! Ming Tsun! Caleb!" Frost shouted as the top of his voice. "Disengage your men! Disengage your men!"

Struan Ferguson, Ming Tsun and Caleb heard and obeyed. A few of the cat's men were slow in disengaging. It could not be helped. Frost nodded, and young Chasse brought the match down on the cannon's touchhole. In an instant another mass of bodies lay tossed about in the killing field in front of the cannon. Frost knew he was going to be sick. A bare dozen, no more, British soldiers still stood, dazed, and they were dropping their arms. Behind Frost the launches bumped against the quay and the second complements began clambering onto the quay's stones.

"Struan, these men are yours! Secure the quay. Search every house. Collect all British and put them under guard."

Then to Jack Lacey: "Lacey, reload that piece, get some fresh men from those just landing to help you, and follow me." Frost trotted off toward the street down which he had so recently descended, breath rattling in his throat, pain stitching his sides, but anxious, so anxious to locate the warehouse that was the gaol of the New Hampshire men.

Caleb caught up to Frost easily. "Ye won't know the war'house les'n I show it to ye," Caleb grunted. Frost had no breath to speak; he nodded once and did his best to match Caleb's pace, though his legs were leaden, detached, without feeling. He staggered, braced himself against a wall and vomited, bringing up old, bitter tea and bile and nothing else.

Caleb paused at an intersection of the street with an alley, shielding himself against a building while he glanced around the corner. He waited until Frost, gasping like a foundered horse, joined him, then said companionably: "Bein' at sea so much don't give ye much call to use yore legs," Caleb said sympathetically. "Now me, I enjoyed a stroll through these yere evirons less'n two days afore."

"The warehouse, Caleb," Frost whispered with the last breath he had, pressing one hand sharply into his waist to stifle and keep the pain at bay.

"It be that 'un." Caleb pointed toward a massive door set in an even more massive brick wall built atop a solid stone foundation at the end of the alley. "Thar be a small field, the quality most like would call it a courtyard, a'hind thet door. Prisoners be let out, then taken back inside the war'house."

"Where would the sentries be?"

"At that gate if any thar be, but most like they joined the fightin' or they be run."

Hearing the metallic rumble of the field piece's ironbound wheels coming up fast, Frost pushed off from the wall he had clutched to catch his breath and ran toward the sally port set in the massive wooden door. Caleb followed more warily. As both Frost and Caleb expected, the sally port was securely barred from the other side.

"How is that cannon loaded?" Frost demanded of Lacey as soon as the field piece rumbled to a halt ten yards from the door and the six men pushing the cannon slumped to the cobbles in exhaustion.

"Case shot, Captain, that's all was in the shot locker."

Frost pointed to the cobbles. "Use a bayonet to prise up three stones which will fit in the bore. Train the cannon directly on the sally port." A sailor, Chasse, thrust among the stones with a bayonet, eyeing the stones and measuring them against the cannon's bore, until he selected three and prised them from their fellows. Without prompting, he thrust the three stones, each the size of a small fist, into the muzzle, ramming them atop the case shot with the musket's barrel after detaching the bayonet.

Frost nodded at Lacey. "At your command." The match

came down on the touchhole. The cannon roared and bucked, and the sally port door was rocked violently, sagging open on shattered hinges. Caleb Mansfield ordered William Chasse to push the sally port door fully open with the barrel of his musket.

"Looks clear, Capt'n," Caleb said. "Don't see no redcoats waitin' fer us in the yard." Caleb stepped through the sally port, followed closely by Frost. Behind him in the alley Ming Tsun and two sailors appeared, staggering under the weight of the shot and powder locker.

"Remove those bars and open the main gate," Frost directed Chasse. "Lacey, load that cannon again and follow me with it. It's almost as comforting a piece as Caleb's Gideon." Frost stepped quickly across the courtyard, searching carefully for any guards. A massive, iron, portcullis-like gate barred the entrance to the warehouse, but a foot-long key hung on a spike nearby. Caleb seized it, inserted it into the lock and gave a mighty heave. The lock mechanism protested mightily, but the key turned slowly, the bolt withdrew grudgingly, and the iron gate swung open.

"Lacey, train your cannon on the gate. William Chasse, you've become a remarkably able matross. You and the mate beside you shall tend the cannon with Jack Lacey. If any British soldiers appear, discourage them with case shot. The three of you," Frost said, pointing out three men, "with Ming Tsun and me."

Ming Tsun dragged the powder and shot locker to the field piece and unslung his halberd. Frost found a barrel of torches just inside the entrance to the warehouse. "Lacey, lend me your slow match," Frost said, holding out the oil-soaked spun oakum twisted around a stave. Jack Lacey blew on his slow match until he had a good ember, and applied it to the oakum, which ignited instantly.

Great Buddha, but he had forgotten to load his pistol. Well, he had Caleb at his back with his double-barreled long rifle, and Ming Tsun's terrible halberd. Frost gripped his cutlass in his left hand, the blazing torch in his right, and led the way into the warehouse.

"Captain, sir," William Chasse said, his self-confidence buoyed enough by his satisfactory performance under fire to encourage him to address his captain directly: "what is that most terrible odor?"

"It is our New Hampshire men," Frost said bleakly. "I fear the British have no high regard for cleanliness." They were in a short passageway of steep brick and rock walls that turned abruptly to the right. Something scurried out of the deep shadow of a stack of hogsheads to Frost's left and broke for the entrance. Ming Tsun tripped whatever it was with his halberd. And whatever it was bleated like a terrified sheep with its throat in a wolf's jaws.

Frost held his torch aloft, illuminating the features of a hunchback dressed in greasy black garments. The hunchback stared up, terror-stricken, at Frost. Frost put the tip of his cutlass beneath the hunchback's heavily whiskered chin. "Who are you and what are you?" he demanded.

"Slopsman," the hunchback stammered. "Cook's helper. I feed the prisoners."

"Where are the American prisoners?" Frost interrogated, never moving his cutlass. Dios, but this was the second time in little more than a week that he had questioned terrified men at cutlass point and he hated doing it.

"Big, big room, fifty steps along the passage," the miserable creature moaned. "I hid there in the barrels when I heard the shootin', had just taken half their morning vittles. Got more to bring. Prisoners need their breakfast."

Frost peered closely at the hunchback, who could have been a twin to Reedy Stalker, though much fatter, almost obese: the same close-set, protruding eyes, mostly bald head with a few strands of lank hair, rotted teeth and incredibly foul breath, sallow complexion, and total vacuous obsequiousness. The hunchback was plainly no guard, and plainly he was well fed, something to be expected of a slopsman.

"Fetch along their vittles, then." Frost beckoned to William Chasse who had forsaken his post at the cannon and had joined Frost's party: "Go along with him to the galley and bring all the food you find there." Frost started to turn away, thought better of it, and stared at the hunchback, who had crawled over against a wall and was clutching to it as he pulled himself slowly erect.

"Marcus Whipple is among your prisoners." Frost stated it as fact, not as a question.

The hunchback blinked his eyes in astonishment, but recovered quickly: "Captain Whipple is indeed one of the prisoners. He ain't been well, so I been givin' him an extra portion, though such don't set good with the commandant."

Frost turned and broke into a run, going as fast as he could without overracing the torch light, down a short flight of brick steps and around another corner until he glimpsed ahead a large room dimly lighted with small square windows high up in the brick walls just under the roof. Two tall, haggard figures waited like specters at the end of the passageway. Frost elevated his torch as high as he could. "Geoffrey Frost with men from Portsmouth! We've come to take you home!"

The two figures regarded Frost wordlessly, vacantly, then looked at each other, and back to Frost. "Who are you? Where are you from?" Frost demanded.

"Dick Kennedy, comin' from Newburyport," one apparition answered through a toothless mouth.

"I be Tom Anderson from Boston," the second apparition said.

"Where is Marcus Whipple?" Frost asked. Por Dios, but these two were little more than scarecrows, and the stench in the large room, urine, feces and putrefaction, made him gag.

Both apparitions turned and pointed toward the far side of the room that was lost in darkness.

"Ming Tsun, Caleb, get some more torches, lanterns, or candles in here, whatever you can find." Frost said hurriedly. Then he called out: "Marcus! Marcus Whipple! Where are you? Answer me!"

From across the room came the quaver of a dry, thin, disbelieving voice: "Geoffrey! Can that be? . . . Geoffrey Frost!"

"Marcus!" It seemed to Frost that it took forever for him to cross the evil-smelling room, pitifully illuminated in the small circle of light cast by his torch, until the light fell on a skeleton-like figure half-raised on elbow from a pile of mouldering straw. "Marcus!"

Frost dropped his cutlass and quickly knelt in straw so poor and foul that no self-respecting New Hampshire farmer would have considered it fit bedding for swine, and looked, disbelieving, on the wreckage of his brother-in-law, a man as close to him as a brother. Marcus Whipple, the husband of his sister, Charity, Jonathan's twin. Marcus seized Frost's left hand in both of his with a death grip and pulled Frost closer. Someone took the torch from Frost's right hand.

The skeleton's features contorted into something that Frost took to be a caricature of a smile, paper-thin flesh stretched tight over cheek bones, eyes invisible in deep sockets, mouth hidden somewhere inside a thick beard, lips hardly moving, the fingers of the hands that clasped his seemingly with no meat on them. "I trust I see you well, Geoffrey, though you seem to have more blood on your cheek than a dull razor can credit, and there's blood on your shoulder as well . . . and that you bring me good news of my wife and family . . ." Marcus' words ended abruptly in a spasm of coughing.

"Your beloved wife, Charity, waits for you, and she has given you two fine children, a boy and a girl."

"Aaah," Marcus said in a long, drawn-out whisper, one of great happiness, "Cinnamon had told Charity that she was carrying twins."

"Yes," reflected Frost, "the line repeats itself, and through the women, of course." For Charity had been the twin of Jonathan, and his mother, the Lady Thérèse, had a twin brother somewhere in the naval service of the French king, an uncle Frost had never met. Would he, Geoffrey Frost, celibate bachelor who had never paid court to, much less known, a woman, ever realize the joys of fatherhood for which he yearned?

He greatly envied his brother-in-law, but knew it was time to push such thoughts forcibly from his mind.

"Marcus," Frost said sharply. "We have stormed the town,

and taken it—taken it, that is, to the best of my knowledge. It did appear that way when I left Struan Ferguson not ten minutes past. But Allah alone knows how long we can hold the town, or when a British man-o-war may appear and bottle us in the harbor. We must quit this foul-smelling prison at once, so tell me, how many are there of you?"

Marcus Whipple started to answer but was prevented by another rack of coughing.

"If I may answer for Captain Whipple," a soft voice said, jerking Frost's attention upward to the person who had taken the torch from his hand. "Two hundred and seventy-two prisoners were removed from Halifax to this place. We are now between forty-seven or forty-eight, forty-seven more likely since I believe Thomas Hudson opened his eyes to the light of God this hour past."

"And who are you?" Frost demanded, rising to his feet so that he could see the man better.

"He is Ishmael Hymsinger," Marcus said hoarsely. "He has been both minister and physic to us . . . though more the former than the latter these two months we've been Mister Loring's guests." Marcus suddenly recognized Ming Tsun. "Why, dear Ming Tsun, I'm sorry not to have greeted you sooner. Our diet has affected my vision, and the light, of course, is poor."

"Marcus," Frost said urgently, "can you walk? There is food on the way, but it will savor better in the courtyard than this wretched dungeon."

"You talk of food, Geoffrey," Marcus said, a note of wonder in his voice. "Have you brought food with you?"

"No, Marcus, the cook's helper who fetched your morning rations has gone to obtain more . . ."

Marcus began laughing, a thin, keening laugh that skirted, then crossed over into the maniacal. "Geoffrey, no man here has had nourishment for . . . for . . . days."

"But the hunchback in the passageway . . ." Frost said hesitantly.

"Hunchback! A dirty little man who would pass for Reedy Stalker's brother?"

"Yes," Frost said, startled that Marcus had made the same comparison as Frost. "He . . ."

Marcus's laughter increased. "That was Whip Loring, our gaoler, who has starved us and beaten us, the same who cut the tendons in my heels to keep me from escaping again . . ."

Frost snatched up his cutlass. "Caleb, to the quay as quickly as ever you can. Surgeon Green is probably ashore by now; he is to come directly here once our wounded have been tended. Advise Struan that he is to order Rawbone and sufficient matrosses in one launch to Battery Island to ready the cannons there. Rawbone may wish to take my brother, Joseph, whose experience helping Henry Knox move great iron may be useful. Ming Tsun, you and these men," Frost indicated the three sailors who had accompanied him from the entrance where Jack Lacey and the field piece had been left, and who stood open-mouthed at the horrors they saw, "begin conveying these sick to the courtyard. Caleb! Once you have delivered my orders, bring back gruel, soup, small ale . . . these men can stomach nothing else."

"Geoffrey!" Marcus whispered urgently, instantly twigging Frost's intentions: "Exercise care, Loring has a brute of a dog even more fearsome than he . . ."

But Frost was already pelting away, leaving his torch behind, holding his breath as long as he could to avoid breathing the unwholesome air in the great room, which was little better than a charnel house. Up the short stairway of bricks, a sharp turn to the left, down the long passageway past the stack of hogsheads, the light of the entryway with its opened portcullis-gate scarce fifty yards away, when he tripped over something soft and barely yielding and fell heavily, bruising and skinning knees and elbows as he slid on the unforgiving stone.

But he was on his feet in an instant, bruises and abrasions unfelt, as he groped in the semi-darkness for what had tripped him, what he knew with dreaded certainty had tripped him, laying hands on the body of poor William Chasse, late of York in that portion of the colony of Massachusetts known as Maine, a place that William Chasse would never see again.

Frost looked at Chasse's body in the dim light, noted the protruding eyes and tongue. The young man from York, so promising a matross, had been strangled. Footsteps were pounding up from the entryway, torch light rippling on the ceiling of the passageway. "Captain Frost . . . God . . . ," horror in the voice of Jack Lacey, "it be Billy Chasse . . ."

Frost rose wearily to his feet and demanded of Jack Lacey: "Did a hunchback dressed in black clothes pass you at the entry?"

"No one came past, Captain . . ."

"Another passageway then! Your torch!"

Another torch flared on the scene from the direction Frost had come. Caleb!

"Stupid fool I! Loring the gaoler slipped by as easy as kiss my hand, and a fine man lost to my grievous error!"

"He's a bad 'un, Capt'n, but we kin smoke him."

"You've orders to deliver first, Caleb," Frost reminded, "but follow as quickly as you can." He looked around for his cutlass, saw it a long way off, and ran for it. "Take Billy Chasse to the entry, find a cloth to cover him." Frost walked swiftly toward the entry.

Aah, here was a narrow turning to the right he had not spied in the first headlong rush to locate the American prisoners. Frost paused for breath and to check the priming of his unfired Bass pistol. The priming powder in the right pan had fallen out, but the priming powder in the left pan under its sliding lid was intact. One barrel should be enough. Frost thrust the Bass pistol back in his belt and advanced cautiously down the dark passageway. How many minutes had elapsed since he had first encountered the hunchback? Less than five surely, more likely four, even a few seconds less.

The passageway contained archways into which doors were set, but quick inspection in what light filtered into the passageway through cracks in the roof slates showed their lintels thick with undisturbed dust. The passageway turned to the left and three paces away through an open door was the courtyard.

Billy Chasse had been armed with a musket. The musket had

not been with the body, so Loring must have it. But was it loaded? Frost eased to the door and peered into the courtyard of packed earth. There was a bricked well with a wooden bucket perched on the well's rim. Frost realized how thirsty he was; he had been fighting since dawn without water, and his lips were split and stuck together with gum. But he dared not approach the well.

To his left fifty yards away there was bustle and movement at the main entry caused by Jack Lacey's arrival there. Frost scanned the other wall of the courtyard and saw a flight of stone steps leading to the top of the wall, noting that the ground around the well was muddy and the first three or four steps of the stone staircase bore freshly deposited mud. Well, Billy Chasse had been using his musket as a rammer to load the field piece. So perhaps the musket was not loaded. Or perhaps the hunchback had British muskets close to hand.

Only one way to know. Where was the most likely place for the hunchback Loring to be lying in wait? There was a parapet at the top of the stone steps; anyone concealed behind the parapet would command the right half of the courtyard where the well was located. All right, fat Mister Whip Loring, far better at torturing American prisoners than feeding them, how good a shot are you?

Frost braced himself momentarily just inside the doorway, then hurled himself into the courtyard, running hard for five paces, then pivoting to his right and running three paces, then pivoting again, bending at the waist and running as fast as he could hunched-over, directly for the well, seeking to shelter behind it.

Nothing! Frost pivoted once again to his right and raced for the steps, clearing the first three in one leap, bending low still, using his right hand to balance and help climb the steps. He was halfway to the top of the steps when a small figure in black rose from behind the parapet and hurled the musket at him. Frost flattened himself against the steps, the musket tumbling over, missing him by an inch or less, then he was up and climbing again, to the top of the steps and onto the roofline of steep slate rooftops just in time to see Loring clamber through the window of a building thirty yards away.

Frost drew his pistol, then thrust it back in his belt. Too far to chance the one shot he had. He ran across the rooftops, stopped to peer into the interior of the room into which the window opened, saw nothing, and swung himself over the sill.

The hunchback charged Frost with a heavy iron floor candelabra, smashing down on his head and shoulders, then using the candelabra as a pitchfork, thrusting Frost back through the window, where he sprawled on the roof. Leaning out the window, Loring sought to use the candelabra to push Frost off the slippery slates. Frost caught one of the candelabra's arms with his free hand and thrust upward with his cutlass. Loring yelped in pain and released his grip on the candelabra. Frost felt himself slipping down the steep roof but arrested his slide by catching the roof's peak with the candelabra's heavy base.

Slowly, painfully, Frost pulled himself up to the roof peak. He was deathly tired, but he dared not pause. He threw the candelabra through the window base first and threw himself after it quick as thought, into a room that was fetid with the stench of ordure, but fatigue snagged a boot on the sill and he tripped. Still clutching his cutlass, Frost rolled to his feet in time to see Loring struggling to slip a chain from the iron spiked collar of the largest dog Frost had ever seen.

"Eat him!" Loring shouted, flinging the chain loose. The dog popped his teeth and gathered his haunches under him for a spring.

"Halt!" Frost commanded, dropping his cutlass hand. "Stop! Arrêt!" The dog did not spring, but paused, undecided.

Loring swung the chain and struck the dog a hard blow on the flanks. "Eat him, I said!"

"Stay!" Frost commanded. Loring turned on his heel and retreated through a door two feet behind him, pulling down and overturning a writing desk as a partial blockage of the door.

Frost held out his hand. "Come," he said softly. "It is all right, he can't torment you any more." Slowly, hesitatingly, the dog crept toward Frost. He recognized the breed now, a

Newfoundland, yes, the largest dog he had ever seen, but one of the most pitiful, hair thickly matted, a raw wound on the neck from the chafing of the collar, as gaunt almost as the American prisoners. Plainly, Whip Loring had been as sparing of food with this animal as with the men in his gaol.

Frost pulled a bench toward him and collapsed onto it. He held out his hand, palm up; the dog slowly advanced to sniff his hand. Frost reached behind the dog's left ear and began to scratch the ear. The dog bounded up, placed both forepaws on Frost's chest, tipping him and the bench over, and then lay down partially atop Frost, brushing Frost's weak, ineffectual hands aside with his huge head, licking Frost's face with his great, raspy tongue in happy abandon.

It was in this position that Caleb Mansfield and Davis Cummings found Geoffrey Frost and the gaunt Newfoundland dog a minute later when they clambered through the window.

❧ XXV ☙

⬡⬡⬡⬡⬡ EOFFREY FROST STOOD ON THE LOUIS-
⬡ **G** ⬡ BOURG QUAY, WRAPPED IN TENDRILS
⬡ ⬡ OF SMOKE FROM THE FIRES STARTED
⬡⬡⬡⬡⬡ BY THE CAT'S CANNONS THAT BURNED
in buildings along the quay, and regarded with distaste the
sullen British soldiers and sailors grouped in front of the Dauphin Gate, hemmed in by hastily strung cables, guarded by
most of Caleb Mansfield's woods-cruisers and all of the cat's
men Struan Ferguson had ordered ashore, saving only Slocum
Plaisted, Doctor Green, Cook Barnes, and Hannibal and
Nathaniel, who were assisting Doctor Green. More soldiers
and sailors were being added to the rough staging area by ones
and twos and threes, brought in by the cat's men, who were
combing the town with orders to bring in every able-bodied
man even remotely near serving age and wearing a stitch of
military clothing.

His surly mood was not helped by the deep draught of water
he had drunk at the well in the prison courtyard, nor by the rice
cakes Ming Tsun had given him to eat when Frost reached the
quay. Geoffrey Frost reread the butcher's bill Struan had given
him immediately upon reaching the quay. It was not an exorbi-
tant bill considering that the British garrison had surrendered
to him, and he held Louisbourg, all before nine of the morning clock. Five dead, including poor William Chasse, twelve
wounded, one seriously enough that his survival was extremely
problematic, and whose wounds were being tended by Doctor

Green aboard the cat just now; the rest, an assortment of wounds little worse than those Frost himself bore.

"And how did Campbell come to his end?" Frost asked Struan, his eyes lingering over the list of dead and wounded.

"Ming Tsun separated Campbell's head from his body with that thunderin' great halberd of his," Struan said. "Two of our lads confirmed that Campbell shot at ye with a musket he picked up from a dead British soldier whilst ye were fightin' two redcoats. When Ming Tsun came from the prison after removing our New England men to the courtyard, he walked up to Campbell and smote him."

"There were two shots, almost simultaneous, either of which would have been fatal but for execrable marksmanship," Frost said. "The odds that Campbell fired at me in conjunction or collaboration with a British soldier are extremely unlikely."

"No one can confirm that the second shot was fired by one of our men, else there would be two headless bodies on the quay," Struan said, "though I do not believe the second ball was fired by any of our ex-*Jaguar*s. They have been right men, harder even in the fightin' than our New Hampshire, Maine and Massachusetts men."

"Let it be for the present," Frost replied, turning the paper over to look at the list of British casualties Struan had also prepared. "You have counted seventy-and-four British soldiers killed, and sixty-two British soldiers unwounded. How many wounded?" Frost marveled at the efficiency of Rawbone's well-laid cannon fire, and the fierce execution of the field piece he had commandeered. Though he mourned each of his dead, yes, Campbell included, Frost's casualties had been incredibly light compared to the British casualties.

"In excess of thirty, most severely. As yet they have not been tended. The garrison lacks a surgeon, though one of the ships in the harbor boasts a surgeon's mate. And I'll warrant the number of British bearin' no wounds will increase substantially. I have men goin' house-to-house still ferretin' out redcoats and sailors, and as ye see the British bastards are poppin' up everywhere like flies on a carcass a week dead." Struan Ferguson cracked his knuckles angrily. "This particlar batch of British bastards don't know the how of fightin'; they surrendered too soon for my likin'."

Frost paced the quay, nibbling at a rice cake from the handkerchief of cakes supplied by Ming Tsun, who had also reloaded Frost's Bass pistols, and for several long seconds considered the disposition and employment of his crew. He could count almost two hundred effectives, but twenty-five men under Roderick Rawbone and Daniel O'Buck had been dispatched in one launch and the gig to take possession of Battery Island and man its cannons. Frost had earlier considered leaving his own garrison on Battery Island, but his need for Rawbone's gun-laying abilities in besieging the town, and storming it with every man he could muster, had mitigated against that plan. Once he had taken possession of Louisbourg, Frost had lost no time in sending Rawbone and O'Buck to ready the cannons guarding the harbor.

He had forty-seven weak and ill former prisoners now in his charge to prepare for a voyage, and there were four ships in the harbor with cargoes that would immeasurably benefit the American cause, though his crew had doubtlessly already calculated to the penny what the ships and their cargoes would bring in prize money besides. And at any time a fleet of British warships could appear from Halifax or England and effectively bottle him inside Louisbourg Harbor.

Something bumped his hand; Frost glanced down. The big Newfoundland dog had sought him out and was pacing beside him, waiting expectantly. Absently, Frost fed the dog a rice cake, then another, then the last one he had in the handkerchief. The dog shook himself violently, the spikes of the dog's collar tinkling against each other; one pricked Frost through his breeches. "You are as much in need of food and bathing as poor Marcus," Frost said to the dog.

Frost glanced several times at the five mounds that were American bodies Struan Ferguson had ordered covered with tarpaulins taken from a waterfront chandlery. He turned to the nearest cat's man, John Nason. "Mister Nason, there should be good hemp in that chandlery. Please cut me a ten fathom length and fashion a hangman's noose at one end." He continued to pace until John Nason hurried up with the coil of rope with its hangman's noose quickly but expertly fashioned.

Frost walked over to the sullen group of British soldiers and sailors. The Newfoundland dog kept step with him. "You will strip to your breeches," he ordered. "Do so now, or verily you shall be hanged."

"Now see here!" A corpulent British officer with a major's gorget at his throat pushed his way to the front of the group. A least one Britisher in Louisbourg besides Whip Loring was well fed. "You cannot order these men to undress. It's against all the laws of war to treat prisoners such wise. We surrendered, and there are conventions of treatment which must be observed."

"And who are you?" Frost demanded. The Newfoundland dog growled menacingly.

"I am Major Starkweather, the commander of the Louisbourg garrison." Major Starkweather looked nervously at the big dog.

"You took your time announcing your presence," Frost said evenly. "Your protests concerning lawful treatment of prisoners fall upon deaf ears to those whose eyes have just beheld the manner in which you British have gaoled, tortured and starved New England men."

"That was done by General Howe's orders," Starkweather said stiffly.

"The order to strip to your breeches is done by Geoffrey Frost of Portsmouth, New Hampshire. Speak one more word, and I shall have you hanged. Now strip!"

Starkweather paled; his mouth worked, but formed no words.

Frost turned to John Nason. "Toss your hemp over the arch of the Dauphin Gate, the noose around this British officer's neck."

As Nason stepped toward him, Starkweather fell back several paces quickly, seeking safety in the anonymity of the British prisoners. The Newfoundland dog barked, and the prisoners, all of them, backed away.

"Aah," Frost thought, "so they are afraid of the dog. Loring had done his work well." Now that he was reminded of the dog's vicious reputation, Marcus was very much afraid of the dog. He laid a restraining hand on the dog's head. "A choice for you, Starkweather; you can kick out your life at the end of a rope, or you can provide entertainment to this dog. A few rice cakes are a poor breakfast for an animal accustomed to the taste of human flesh." Frost did his best to put a sneer in his voice.

Starkweather did not answer. The British prisoners began undressing with a will. "Boots also," Frost said, when the soldier immediately in front of him appeared reluctant to remove his boots. "Stockings also."

When all the soldiers and sailors, including Major Starkweather, stood in their bare feet, Frost commanded them to pick up their wounded and march to the warehouse that had been the American prisoners' gaol, and that now would be theirs. He tarried on the quay to wait for Doctor Green, whom he saw putting out from the cat in a gig commandeered from one of the British transports and rowed by Nathaniel Dance and Hannibal Bowditch.

"Bad business, Captain Frost," Ezrah Green said, wiping his brow with a bloody handkerchief when he joined Frost on the quay. "Gary Clifford, a topman with Mister Ferguson's party, was struck in the lungs by a musket ball. I could do nothing but make his life's end as comfortable as possible. Both lads were of immense assistance to me, I assure you."

Frost looked at Hannibal and Nathaniel with interest; Hannibal carried Surgeon Green's bag of instruments, and Nathaniel had the surgeon's bloody apron folded over his arm. Both lads looked none the worse for the horrors they had undoubtedly witnessed in Ezrah Green's surgery. Indeed, both boys were looking at the big Newfoundland dog with great interest. "I thought you were happy enough being a powder monkey, Mister Dance. I knew not that your interests lay in surgery and physic."

"No, sir," Nathaniel protested quickly. "Knives and blood make me fair sick, but once Mister Rawbone ordered the cannons to stop firing, there weren't no more work for me in the magazine, so's I was off to assist the surgeon and Hannibal."

"Remarkable," Frost said, as he began following the remnants of British prisoners painfully picking their way barefoot over the cold cobbles. "You should know that I have in mind making you both sous-officers."

"Oh, sir, ye can't do that," Nathaniel Dance immediately remonstrated. "That would mean I'd have to learn to read an' cypher, and man will grow wings and fly like a bird 'fore I can do such."

"Then we shall soon see able-bodied seamen matching the gulls wingbeat for wingbeat, Mister Dance," Frost responded. "The mind is a wondrous instrument, especially so when it is constantly engaged in productive thought. Your next task, both of you, will be to give this dog a bath and comb out its hair. Now that I consider it, the both of you can stand a bath."

"A bath, sir?" both lads said in incredulous unison.

"A bath," Frost said firmly. "A bath for you and the dog as soon as we reach the courtyard, where the most piteous sight I have ever seen in this life awaits us. Perhaps the good surgeon can spare a spoonful of salve to rub on the sore caused by the collar's chaffing. And unbuckle that heavy collar."

Both lads reached out hesitantly to stroke and pet the Newfoundland dog, who was almost as tall as they. The Newfoundland responded by nuzzling playfully first Nathaniel and then Hannibal. By the time the five of them reached the courtyard, the dog and the lads had made friends of each other.

Frost was pleasantly surprised by the activity that had occurred since he had left the courtyard after a hurried drink from the well. All the American prisoners had been removed from the warehouse and made comfortable on pallets of straw covered with sailcloth brought up from the chandlery. More sailcloth had been stretched as awnings to provide shade from the fitful May sun now that the morning fog had mostly burned off. Several large pots were beginning to bubble over fires stoked with wood from doors and furniture hauled from adjacent buildings and broken up. As he watched, two of the woods-cruisers came in with sailcloth bags stuffed with fern leaves that they showed to Ishmael Hymsinger.

Hymsinger nodded his approval, and the woods-cruisers dumped the contents of their sacks into one of the pots. This was the first occasion Frost had for a good look at Hymsinger, and Frost studied the man keenly. He was Frost's height, but emaciated, extremely emaciated. He had removed what was left of his shirt and his back, chest and arms were thickly covered with old scars as if he had once been hideously scourged. His face, except for his eyes, was hidden in a beard of truly biblical proportions, and his hair was plaited, indian-like, in two long braids.

Ezrah Green walked over to the pots and examined the fern leaves. "Fiddlehead ferns!" he exclaimed. "A most excellent regimen for the scorbutic."

"I have ever found it so," Hymsinger said gravely. "I think with the exception of Captain Whipple, who has grievously borne the malicious torture of a worm unfit to stand in his shadow, the ills of the remaining men can be remedied with adequate nourishment and cleanliness."

Ezrah Green bristled: "Are you a physician, sir?"

Hymsinger gestured deprecatingly. "I have neither pretension nor desire to claim such profession, sir. I have some slight knowledge of remedies gleaned from the Indian tribes among whom I have lived. Their knowledge is ancient, and effacious."

Ezrah Green nodded curtly. "Where is Captain Whipple, that I might examine him?"

Frost, recognizing the onset of professional jealously, quickly took Ezrah Green by the elbow. Ezrah Green had earned Frost's respect as an excellent surgeon, but Hymsinger's ministrations had physicked the prisoners during their long privation, and by his lights Hymsinger could continue. Betimes, he wished for enough time to enjoy a bait of fiddlehead ferns. "Ezrah, I had not considered assisting them at all, so hardened was my heart against all people British, but there are a multitude of wounded soldiers as a result of this morning's fighting. They have been carried inside to lodge in the same wretched conditions which were our men's lot. Decency counsels me to forsake my bitterness and ask that your medical skills succor them."

"Of course!" Ezrah Green said. "So bound up in the care of our wounded brought back to me aboard our vessel have I been that it never occurred to me the British sustained casualties. But from below decks Mister Rawbone's bombardment sounded most horrific; I cannot imagine what injuries were inflicted."

"You'll soon see for yourself, Ezrah," Frost said grimly. "Do you wish the British wounded fetched out? I must warn you that conditions where our men were late captives will turn the strongest stomach."

"Fetch them out, by all means. I've had full measure of operating by lantern's light."

"May I arrange some hay and sailcloth, Doctor?" Ishmael Hymsinger said diffidently. "There is plenty of hay in a barn nearby, and as you can see, Captain Frost's men have provided ample sailcloth."

"That's most kind of you," Ezrah Green said, relenting slightly. "I trust some of that water you have a-boil can be offered up for my purposes."

"Pots and water we have a-plenty," Hymsinger said. "Firewood may be scarce, but these men," indicating the woodscruisers, "are finding a ready supply of furniture . . ."

All this talk had gone on much too long for Frost. "Mister Hymsinger," he said testily, "Doctor Green, you must have your physic finished by noon. I intend to embark our New England men aboard the cat, and sail, with the ships in harbor as our prizes, on the afternoon tide."

Frost could not see the harbor from the courtyard, but he could see and smell the smoke rising from the houses on the quay set afire by the cat's cannon. That would not do; the smoke would be a beacon visible to any British warship cruising off the Acadian coast. He left the courtyard and walked hurriedly toward the quay. Was no one attempting to douse the fires? All of the soldiers and sailors his men could find had been apprehended and herded into the warehouse, but there had to be some town's people, surely, who would be acting to save their property.

Caleb Mansfield fell into step beside him. "'Bout thet Lorin' fella, he won't be tormentin' any more New Hampshire men."

Frost did not pause, nor even look at Caleb, because he knew Caleb would explain without any prompting from him.

"Ol' Davis lit out atter Mister Lorin' when ye got almighty bollixed up with thet big dawg them boys be tryin' to bath right now. Ketched up to him right enough, 'bout half a mile south of the town, bein' Mister Lorin' so fat and all." Caleb took a pick tooth from his cap and employed it industriously.

Frost said nothing, but focused on the smoke and the quay, which he could see clearly now. His gig was approaching rapidly from the direction of Battery Island. That prompted him to quicken his pace.

"Dang it, Capt'n, ain't ye wantin' to know what Davis did when he ketched up to Lorin'?"

"You can't wait to tell me, Caleb, so out with it." There could be only one reason why Rawbone had dispatched the gig in such a hurry. Frost could see that the coxswain in the stern sheets was Daniel O'Buck.

"Wall, seein's how this Lorin' fella cut Capt'n Whipple's feet, and how he was starvin' and tormentin' like he wus Satan hisself, Davis shot him in a knee-cap. A right shot, ol' Davis is, not as good as me 'n' Gideon, but a right shot. Brought him down whilst he wus runnin', so Davis had a-plenty time to stroll over and put another ball in Lorin's other knee-cap. Fella wus takin' on so thet if thar be any Mi'kmaqs about they've been drawed to him like flies to a cow-flop by now."

"Are there any town's people?" Frost demanded. Loring's fate did not interest him. "With their homes burning the town's people should be out with fire buckets."

"What few thar be bolted theirselves inside the citadel when the fightin' started," Caleb said.

Frost briefly considered releasing a party of redcoats to fight the fires, but he could not trust British soldiers or sailors even with a guard detail that he could ill afford to spare, particularly if Daniel O'Buck brought the intelligence he was dreading. Inshallah. Dios Mio. The houses would have to burn unchecked.

The gig touched the quay, setting off a skirr of protesting herring gulls, and Daniel O'Buck bounded up the stone steps. Among the rowers Frost saw his brother and Darius. "Mister Rawbone's compliments, Captain . . ."

But Frost, guessing the import that had brought O'Buck at such a rate, broke in before the man could speak further: "How many sail and what does a sailor like you make of them?"

"Two sail. One looks to be a brigantine, or perhaps a topsail schooner . . . we had no glass with us . . . but the other looks to be a British man-o-war, not a frigate, mind, but a vessel at least the size of the cat."

"Thank you, Mister O'Buck," Frost said formally, "for your timely intelligence. Captain Whipple is alive, but he and the rest of the men we came to rescue have been sorely abused. If you were to go up to the courtyard, straight up this street and the first turning to your right, I know the sight of you would cheer him immensely."

Daniel O'Buck knuckled his forehead: "Thank'ee kindly, Captain Frost. I'll be back soon as I've shaked Captain Whipple's hand and congratulated him on a fine son and daughter." He broke into a quick trot up the street, but Frost did not watch him out of sight.

Frost stepped down into the gig and took the tiller. "Row me to the British vessel yonder, number fifty-two," he commanded, gesturing toward the largest of the vessels anchored in Louisbourg Harbor; the convoy number was painted prominently on her hull just abaft her starboard main channel board. Frost permitted himself a brief moment of grim satisfaction; that same convoy number had been entered in *Lloyd's Register* against the vessel's name, cargo and insured value. He reflected upon the consternation, shock and alarm that would be felt among the underwriters when word of the small convoy's loss reached London. Bleed the British merchants of their profits; raise the cargo insurance rates to the point they became prohibitive. That was the way to bring reason to the people who could pressure the ministerial government to cease this useless war. Frost checked himself abruptly. He was as bad as the most venal member of his crew, exultingly calculating his gain, when Frost, the cat, his crew, the newly freed prisoners and the four prize vessels were still hundreds of leagues from the Ports of Piscataqua. Number fifty-two was also the brig that had numbered among its crew the unfortunate sailor whose toilet had been untimely interrupted by the cat's arrival.

"Joseph, please come with me," Frost said, heaving himself aboard the brig at the larboard waist entry as soon as the gig bumped against the main wales. "Darius, please take charge of the gig; return to the quay and collect as many of the red coats you'll find there as you can fit into the gig. There is a major's gorget, a large oval piece of metal hung on a short chain, which I particularly covet. Bring as many hats as you bring coats. As you pass our vessel, call out for Cook Barnes to gather a sack of bread, cheese and meat, any victuals ready to his hand and hook, to swing down to you on your return for me."

Frost led the way down the aft companionway to the captain's cabin. "I am looking for the captain's or master's book of signals," he said to his brother. "As I cypher it, these vessels were part of a larger convoy to resupply Howe in Halifax. They became separated . . . ," Frost waved his arm dismissively at his brother's look of amazement, "I'm not conjecturing too baldly; Caleb's reconnaissance of Louisbourg turned up the fact that these brigs and snows entered Louisbourg two days ago . . . we most likely passed within a league of each other the night prior. If these vessels were part of a larger convoy, there must be a book of signals on board in order for the sheep to read the shepherd's orders."

"I would have thought you had sequestered the signals book aboard HM *Jaguar*," Joseph said. "You captured it quick enough."

Frost shook his head, remembering the surprised, desperate fight off the Isles of Shoals. "Gracias a Dios, the capture was quick enough, I warrant, but Hugh Stuart had his logs and signals book properly wrapped and weighed. They went overside as soon as we got men aboard. Besides, the fact that *Jaguar* was taken has spread wide. Portsmouth, nay, all of New England, leaks information like a stove-in boat. If you collect, the man we surprised at his ablutions this morning knew of *Jaguar*'s capture. All codes would have been changed immediately."

"Why not bring out this vessel's captain and demand that he produce the signal book?" Joseph asked.

Frost hardly paused in his rapid examination of the small cabin. "Suppose that you had somehow gotten separated from Knox during your Moses-like wandering in the wilderness, and you fell in with a troop of British soldiers who demanded that you lead them to Knox . . . would you have done so?"

"Of course not," Joseph retorted hotly.

"Once your thumbs had been pressed to jelly in a musket cock's jaw screw, you would tell them anything they wanted to know," Frost said matter-of-factly. "Entertain no illusions on that score." He thought fleetingly of Major Starkweather and his threat to have the British officer hanged. It was a good thing the man had not defied him. Frost did not know if he would have been able to carry out his threat. It was better that he did not know; he devoutly hoped that he never would know all that he might be capable of doing.

"Since I'm adverse to cracking anyone's thumbs to ascertain truth, I'd have to assume that any British officer I asked for information would either mislead me or spit in my eye. Both are results best avoided. Nothing here," Frost said, slamming closed with more than a mild degree of frustration the last drawer in the captain's clothes-press, and irritated that his brother had been standing idly, hunched over due to the low overhead in the cabin. "You search the mate's cabin; most likely the book of signals will be close to a rack of signal flags. I'll look in the common room."

"Would perhaps this be the object of your search?" Joseph stepped over to the captain's night cuddy and fished a sailcloth bag off the bunk. "I smoked it once you mentioned signal flags. Here appears to be a flag protruding from the bag."

And so it was, a bag of signal flags that would have passed

unnoticed as a bag of soiled clothes except for the one flag that had been carelessly not-quite-thrust into it and left a bright, tell-tale splash of color against the bleached gray of the sailcloth.

Frost seized the bag quickly, tore open the wrapping at the neck, upended it on the bunk, and grunted with satisfaction when a canvas-bound book tumbled out. "Yes," he said simply, thrusting the book into his belt and the flags back into the bag. He picked up a telescope that was a paperweight to a stack of bills of lading and stores lists on the captain's desk and was back on the brig's deck in an instant to find Darius just returning in the gig.

"Excellent, Darius," Frost said as he quickly surveyed the red coats and soldiers' tricorne hats piled in the gig. He jumped down into the small boat. "Can you swim?"

"No sir," Darius said.

"Joseph can," Frost said, over-balancing his brother, who was backing down the waist entry, and throwing him into the water in a fine geyser of spray. Joseph came to the surface and spluttered salt water, instantly chilled.

"Joseph," Frost said calmly, "I haven't time to deposit you on the quay, so please make your way ashore. Find Struan Ferguson; my orders to him are to secure the British prisoners in the warehouse where our New Hampshire men were late prisoners. He is to use as few of our men for guards as possible . . . a barrel of gun powder at the portcullis-gate, a short fuse and the field piece loaded with case shot should command the Britishers' concentration wondrously . . . all other men of ours back to the cat, slip her anchors and sail or sweep up to Battery Island, depending upon the wind, where we shall most likely be exchanging pleasantries with a British warship."

Joseph spewed water at his brother derisively.

"And Joseph, once ashore, the faster you run to find Struan, the warmer you shall be." Frost settled himself in the stern sheets, took the tiller, and smiled pleasantly at Darius. "Darius, I don't think there is any way you and your crew can land me at Battery Island in fifteen minutes, but I do expect you to split your guts trying."

XXVI

HE PULL TO BATTERY ISLAND, SLIGHTLY OVER A MILE INTO A BUILDING WIND, WAS AT LEAST MADE ON AN OUTGOING TIDE, THOUGH THE CREW OF THE GIG was tired from their run to the Louisbourg quay. Despite their tiredness, Frost timed the run at a respectable seventeen minutes, time that he put to profitable use by studying the signals book.

The gig's keel grated on the shingle at the small beach on the southwestern point of Battery Island, sending two harbor seals barking in protest, wiggling off the rocks where they had been sunning themselves, as Frost hopped nimbly ashore. "Bring all the British uniforms and victuals, smartly now," he commanded, running up the narrow path that led to the rear of the battery of ten thirty-six-pounder cannons that commanded the narrow channel leading into Louisbourg Harbor from the open Atlantic.

Roderick Rawbone and the men who had gone out in the launch to take possession of Battery Island were obviously relieved at Frost's arrival. Rawbone's homely face actually wore a semblance of a grin.

"Are these cannons ready to fire, Mister Rawbone?" Frost demanded, striding over to a vantage point and snapping open the telescope he had taken from the brig. Two ships all right, standing in strongly with a decent breeze from the northeast, a little over two miles to the east. Frost estimated they would fetch the channel in half an hour, perhaps less, depending upon how closely they skirted the Harbor Shoal. The cat could never beat up the harbor against such a head wind in anything less than a good hour.

"Their charges have been drawn and they are loaded with powder fresh from the magazine, Captain Frost."

"Well done, Mister Rawbone. As soon as your hands have had something to eat, please order the cannons double-shotted. Whilst they are eating they can rig themselves into these British coats and hats." Frost spied the signal staff and noted that the halyard was missing, but thankfully the spar pivoted on a tabernacle.

"Lay that staff over," Frost commanded the nearest man. When the thirty-five feet of old pine spar lay on the ground, he began tying on the various flags he had selected from the signals bag. Frost handed the signals book to Rawbone.

"Confirm your reading of this signal, Mister Rawbone, if you please." Frost shrugged out of his bloody and tattered coat and searched in the pile of scarlet British tunics to find one that would fit him.

"Well," Rawbone said hesitantly, "well, I ain't what you'd call an educated man, Captain Frost, all I be is a simple matross. But I believe you have spelled out m-u-t-i-n-y, if I cypher the meaning of these topmost flags, but I do not ken the meaning of the last three flags."

"Mutiny: immediate aid, I trust" Frost said. "The last three flags so grouped mean 'succor,' the closest I could come to 'immediate aid' with the signals in the bag. Please raise the staff; you'll need someone to help you," he ordered the man who was standing by, "then find yourself a crimson coat." He handed Rawbone the major's gorget and pointed to a coat with fringed bullion at the shoulders.

"That coat yonder and this symbol of insufferable arrogance were but recently worn by a British Army major, about your size and build, I collect. They should add mightily to your stature, Mister Rawbone, when viewed through the glass of the captain of that British man-o-war. Now please fire number six cannon and mark the plunge of shot. I would prefer the shot strike within one cable or less."

Frost winced at the heavy crack of the cannon's firing but watched the shot geyser with satisfaction. "Reload. Double shot. Handsomely!" He drew Jonathan's watch from his pocket, set it on the breech of a cannon, then focused the telescope on the approaching vessels, both bearing up smartly under as much sail as they could carry; the vessel in the lead was definitely a warship, probably of slightly greater tonnage than the cat. A sixth-rate for sure, possessed of at least twenty cannons.

Frost glanced at the bright bunting standing out clearly from the slender spar. "There should be no difficulty reading those signals," he thought to himself, hoping that he had translated the numerous multi-colored, triangular, square and rectangular flags depicted in the codebook correctly. Though from what he had seen of British merchant captains in the North Atlantic trade, Frost did not consider them nearly as competent as the captains in the employ of the East India Company. It was in an East Indiaman that he had first visited China. He knew the qualities of the East India Company and her people well.

Frost saw that all of the matrosses were donning British Army scarlet uniform coats that more or less fitted them, including Darius, though some of the matrosses were squeamish at the sight and feel of blood on the tunics, and reluctant. He addressed them: "I would appreciate your considering yourselves fortunate to have escaped the bloody mutiny now raging in the town, and your entreating your reinforcements to hasten here as quickly as wind can bring them." With a start, Frost recognized the tattoo of a mermaid on the forearm of the last matross to find a coat: Quintin Fowle. So, Quintin and Darius, two of the cat's crew he had tried so hard to protect, along with Joseph, Nathaniel and Hannibal, were thrust now into the thick of a desperate fight.

"In this dangerous, topsy-turvy world, I either must leave them safe home or teach them to fight as best I can," Frost told himself grimly, thinking of how he had presumed young Roger Green safe below decks of the old *Salmon*. "Able seaman Quintin Fowle!" he called out. "If you wish to see the inside of the Widow Crockett's tavern ever again, I suggest you express yourself with utmost vigor."

Frost beckoned to Darius. "Take this glass and run back to the gig landing. Apprise me if the cat has made sail."

Darius looked at the telescope apprehensively. "I know not its function, Captain Frost . . . I've never been shown."

Of course! A house slave would hardly have been exposed to a telescope's mysteries! And Darius had been just another land's man in the crew during the cruise from Portsmouth, struggling to learn how to reef and hand and steer, and tend his cannon. Frost smiled: "Come here please, and I'll show you."

The cannon that had fired was reloaded now; Frost swept Jonathan's watch into a trouser pocket. Not quite four minutes. Not a very good showing, but Frost very much doubted if the coming engagement would consume a great amount of time before the outcome was determined. One way or the other. A glance at the two vessels to the east told Frost that he might have fifteen minutes, no more, before the warship was in the channel.

Frost stood behind Darius, balanced the long cylinder on the metal of a thirty-six-pounder, and showed the young black man how to hold the telescope and move the ferrules back and forth until the magical point when the object in the lens resolved into sharp focus. Darius exclaimed in amazement and pleasure: "Most wondrous indeed, Captain Frost, this, this . . . device."

"A telescope, or more commonly called a glass by those who follow the sea. And you have decided the sea is your calling, have you not, Darius?"

"Well, Captain," Darius said impishly, "I be presently with you on this small bit of land, but 'tis true we came here by sea."

"And by the sea we shall return to Portsmouth," Frost said, "though we doubtless must exchange compliments with this British. I believe you have the knack of it, so speed you to the gig landing, and use your newfound knowledge to apprise me of the cat's movements." Darius smiled and turned to go. Frost watched him away.

"Conceal that slow match, Mister Rawbone. The British captain must think that we fired a cannon only to attract his attention. Lively there, able seaman Fowle! I'll warrant if your mother had you by the ear you could demonstrate exceedingly great enthusiasm . . . that's it, that's it, admirably, seaman Fowle! The rest of you, emulate seaman Fowle, who is so anxious for succor from the British that he fain would run out to embrace yonder warship's bowsprit!"

Darius came running back: "Captain Frost, it appears through the glass," he fairly beamed as he said the word, "that our ship has not left anchorage. I could not be sure, for it was very faint, but I thought I heard the sound of muskets firing. And there is much smoke over the town."

"Very good; it's as I expected." Frost held out his hand for the telescope and turned eastward to the enemy. Struan must have encountered some difficulties with the British prisoners. Significant difficulties if he had not gotten the cat underway. So be it. He would deal with the present threat. "Have you ever noticed, Mister Rawbone," he said conversationally, "that time is the Almighty's way of ensuring that not everything happens at once?"

Rawbone scratched his ear and blew his nose noisily between thumb and forefinger to give himself time for proper reflection before answering: "Can't say that I've ever had occasion to remark upon that, sir. Sounds right enough, as you say, sir." He looked at Frost dubiously from the corner of his eye, unsure if Frost was making sport of him.

"That scarlet coat becomes you, Mister Rawbone, but I trust you shan't become too attached to it. To disguise oneself in a British uniform is to be considered a spy by the ministerial government, and to be found out is to dance with a British hangman. If taken in the garb of a British Army major, your dance would be the first one on the card. Hello! What's this?" Frost leaned against the thirty-six-pounder and made minute adjustments with the tube of the glass he had taken from Darius. "Mister Rawbone, it appears that the schooner has run aground on Harbor Shoals! Her foretop has come unstepped!"

Indeed, the schooner's foretop, captured boldly in the glass's circle, oscillated wildly, then took on a pronounced lean, whipped backward, then fell forward. Even at the distance of three quarters of a mile, Frost could see the mainmast swaying back and forth as the energy captured in the schooner's sails drove the vessel deeper into the shoals.

Through the glass Frost could see the consternation register on the British sloop-o-war; then a parade of flags rose on her signal halyard. Frost consulted the book of codes, though he could not glean the exact sense of the signals. "Something about the tide, Mister Rawbone. I trust the British commander is advising the schooner to survey her damage and wait for a tide to float her." Which, since she had struck just after the crest of the current tide, meant that the schooner would spend the better part of the afternoon on its perch. No danger from that quarter, at least for a while.

Frost watched the British warship charging up, spray purling away from its cutwater, a fine, brave sight indeed, and for a few moments he wondered if her commander intended to check her before bringing her into the restricted channel between Rocky Island and Lighthouse Point; a very risky maneuver unless the commander, or a pilot aboard, knew the channel and its currents intimately. He doubted the former, but if a local pilot was aboard . . . well, a local pilot would likely twig that something was amiss on Battery Island.

But now the warship's courses were being shortened, topmen on the main and fore yards fisting in great handfuls of canvas, way coming off the vessel perceptibly, the vessel more sedate, purposeful, though losing none of her martial appearance. Frost wished that he had been able to interrogate the ships' masters in Louisbourg Harbor as to the identity of the convoy ship and its commander. "I expect we shall know all this soon enough," he told himself.

Indeed, the masters of the convoy transports had been conspicuous in their absences. "Mister Rawbone, I suggest we greet her warmly when she is two hundred yards off . . . a full broadside of these ten thirty-six-pounders. I doubt if the British can effectively train a gun on us before we have reloaded, and I desire each gun to be aimed and fired independently once reloaded."

"Aye, Captain Frost," Rawbone said, only too pleased that Frost was making the decisions for him. "And shall we be trying to hull her, or . . ."

"Concentrate on her main deck, Mister Rawbone. We must destroy her ability and desire to fight, and that can be done only by killing her people and wrecking her cannons." Frost had a good view of the British vessel now, barely half a mile away and closing; twenty guns, each of six pounds, a true sixth-rate of the British line, the type of vessel the Admiralty would have selected to shepherd a reluctant convoy across the North Atlantic.

"Where are the muskets of the battery's garrison?" Frost asked Rawbone. He knew that the launch of men he had ordered to Battery Island had taken only a few muskets, but Caleb had reported a store of muskets when he had returned from the bloody work of silencing the garrison. The entire garrison.

"Just inside the magazine, Captain Frost. I've not had a chance to look to them, being concentrated on these great heathern cannons and all."

"Quite right you were, Mister Rawbone, to concentrate on these heathern cannons, as you style them. You are a matross, not a grenadier, and there's a world of difference between the two. Darius," Frost commanded, "you and Fowle please fetch the muskets . . . belay that! Fowle is indeed expressing exceedingly great joy at the prospect of succor freighted in yonder British man-o-war. His animation is truly wondrous to behold! Like Walton the fisherman's dexterity with his minnows, the manner of Fowle's movements will surely draw the British more rapidly to our bait! Darius, assist me!" Frost raced to the magazine, Darius close at his heels. "Mister Rawbone," he called as he ran, "be so good as to advise me when the British warship has turned Rocky Island."

There was a satisfying rack of muskets ranged along one wall of the cool, dank magazine. Frost seized the nearest one to inspect it, a musket of the short land pattern of 1768, marked on the lock's tail with the stamp of the Royal Proof House at the Tower of London. This musket, and the others he could see in the magazine, were of recent manufacture and must just have arrived in North America. They smelled wonderfully of oil and stock varnish and bore none of the scars and scrapes that inevitably would have been their lot immediately upon first handling by His Britannic Majesty's troops. The flints were held snugly in their muskets' jaw screws with thin strips of lead. These muskets were straight from an arsenal, and Frost resolved to bear them away when he quit Battery Island.

Frost pulled out the metal ramrod, reversed it, and let it fall down the barrel. He was rewarded by the thunk of iron against solid paper. He pinched the ramrod at the muzzle to mark its length, withdrew the ramrod, then held the ramrod as a rough measuring stick against the barrel. He nodded in satisfaction; the distance from the breech to the point where the ramrod had come to rest in the barrel indicated the musket was loaded.

"I ken you probably have never loaded a musket, much less shot one, Darius," Frost said as he picked up another musket.

"You say true, Captain." Darius replied with a small moue and a deprecating laugh. "The tending of muskets was not on the list of necessaries Master John had me learn."

"Learn now—there is a leather bucket of cartridges, and this musket contains no charge." Frost showed Darius how to set the lock to half cock, prick the vent, bite off the end of the twisted paper cartridge, pour the powder down the barrel, follow the powder with the ball, then wad the cartridge paper and thrust it down the barrel with the ramrod, tamping the load solidly. There were exactly twenty muskets in the rack, and loading or ensuring that all twenty contained a charge took five minutes of exceedingly valuable time in which the British man-o-war came that much closer to Battery Island.

When the hail came that the British vessel was turning Rocky Island, Frost was expecting the call. "There are other requirements to prepare the muskets for firing, but we'll learn those presently. Take up as many muskets as you can and come with me." Frost seized a candle from a lantern, thrust it into his coat pocket and snatched up an armful of muskets, carrying them like a turn of firewood. He turned left outside the powder magazine and jumped down into the partially brick-lined trench in front of the low, heavy stone parapet above and behind which the thirty-six-pounders so ominously squatted.

Frost propped a musket every ten feet along the channel face of the trench, which had been little used and was heavily silted, the firing steps filled with debris. "Bring the rest of the muskets and the bucket of cartridges, place them here," he instructed Darius as he left the trench and ran, stooping low, to where Rawbone stood, bleak and stolid as one of his cannons, watching the British man-o-war, under topsails and staysails only, standing cautiously into the channel. The vessel was less than two hundred yards from the easternmost point of Battery Island.

"Would you care for some wax, Mister Rawbone?" Frost said conversationally, struggling to keep his voice calm after all his exertions.

"Wax, Captain Frost?" Rawbone said disbelievingly, not taking his eyes from the British vessel.

"Wax, Mister Rawbone. Darius and I shall be keeping up as hot a fire as we can with muskets from the firing trench below. Your cannons booming overhead will make quite a racket. Wax to plug your ears to block out sound, as Ulysses did for the ears of his crew so they could not hear the sirens' song. You know the story from the *Odyssey*, of course."

"If it be not in the Holy Book I've marked it not, Captain, and all matrosses be destined for deaf."

"You may open fire whenever this Britisher closes to half a cable's length. Your matrosses must continue their joyous capering until the instant before you loose your broadside directed against her main deck."

"Aye sir, double shot or single shot?" Now that Frost was near, Rawbone plainly wanted him to make the decisions, but Frost knew that once the firing commenced Rawbone would come right.

"Independent fire, Mister Rawbone. Concentrating on her main deck, cannons and crew. As much iron on target as you can, as quick as you can. That would rule out double shot after the first broadside, would it not?"

"Quite, Captain Frost . . . I would beg a piece of wax from you after all, sir."

Frost's lean and haggard face broke into a wolfish grin: "Excellent, Mister Rawbone, only those who expect to live to use them later think to protect their ears." He snapped the candle in two, giving Rawbone the larger portion. "Share this out with the men." Frost saw Darius scurry past with his second armload of muskets, turned, grabbing up two red coats as he did so, and followed Darius to the firing trench, kneading and rolling a pinch of wax between his fingers.

Once in the trench Frost plugged Darius' ears with wax, then his own. Bending low in the firing trench, Frost bit off the end of a cartridge, opened the frizzen of the closest musket, and poured just enough of the powder into the pan to come to the level of the touchhole. He primed another musket, then indicated to Darius that he was to prime the rest. Frost wished for an instant that he had Caleb Mansfield and Caleb's entire complement of woods-cruisers in the trench with him, but that was a forlorn wish, and it was up to Darius and him to make the British think that at least a dozen or more highly disciplined marksmen occupied the firing trench.

Frost was detached, standing outside himself as he folded the two coats on the channel edge of the firing trench to make a rest. His trench was ten feet above the water, and there was nothing between the firing trench and the water save for several large boulders. The bows of the British vessel began to swing toward him as her helm came up to set her southwest by south in the middle of the restricted channel. Her larboard bow was half a cable's length, one hundred yards away. The men standing to her larboard cannons were plainly visible, as were the topmen standing in the stirrups below the fore topgallant yard and rapidly gathering in weather-worn canvas.

"She is long between refits," Frost told himself, sizing up the sails, well-frayed at their leeches, the much-mended running rigging, an incongruously shortened bowsprit, and long, bleeding sores of rust streaking the hull beneath her chains. Still the vessel came on as quickly as a prudent commander would permit in the restricted channel. The larboard bow of the British vessel breasted a line drawn from Frost to Nag Head Point, then slowly passed through that line.

Several of the topmen waved their tarpaulin hats at the cheering men in red coats cavorting in front of their cannons on Battery Island. Frost focused on the quarterdeck now plainly in view, gliding by eighty yards distant. Why had Rawbone not opened fire? Frost scanned the quarterdeck, seeking the man he would try to kill first, hating himself for what he was about to do but knowing that joss had left him no choice, wishing that he had a rifle like Caleb's Gideon rather than these Tower muskets with no rear sights, only rudimentary front sights, and unpredictably inaccurate smooth bores. But he had what he had, and what he had would have to do. Then the grounds around him shook and quivered, and a fast-moving wall of hot, sulfurous air threw him sharply, face first, into the dirt of the firing trench.

Frost looked first for Darius, saw the concussion of the broadside had sprawled him across the bucket of cartridges, spilling a quantity of them, but he was getting to his feet. Frost raised himself cautiously above the firing trench and saw the British vessel's smashed deck, mainmast beginning to topple, at least two cannons overturned. Rawbone's broadside had struck true, every ball, but it would be a good three minutes, perhaps longer, before one of the thirty-six-pounders would fire again.

Frost picked up the nearest musket, eared back the heavy cock until the sear engaged, and rested the musket on the piled coats. He had his target now, a figure in an officer's frock on the quarterdeck. He held a good foot over the man's head, drew in a breath, let out half, and squeezed the trigger as gently as he could while holding the musket as still as possible. The cock snapped forward and downward, the flint, held tight by the jaw screw, scrapped a shower of sparks from the steel frizzen that fell onto the priming powder in the opened pan. The priming powder sputtered, burned, and flame leaped through the touchhole to ignite the main powder charge, instantly generating a choking pall of blackish-gray smoke.

The iron buttplate recoiled brutally against his shoulder. Without pausing to check his shot, Frost dropped the musket and moved to the next musket in the line propped against the channel wall of the firing trench. Cock, select a target, concentrate always on the quarterdeck, hold over to allow for the bullet's drop at this distance, squeeze the trigger, wait for the recoil to bruise his shoulder, then drop that musket and move to the next.

Frost shot off ten muskets before the British man-o-war got its first cannons into action. He had been concentrating on the men on the quarterdeck and had not watched the British gunners. Two cannon balls struck just in front of the firing trench, throwing up great gouts of dirt and stone. Frost picked up the next musket and turned his attention to the gunners. Gracias a Dios! Was Rawbone ever going to get those thirty-six-pounders of his reloaded and back into action?

This time Frost watched to observe the effect of his shot, noting with grim, morbid satisfaction that one gunner standing behind a cannon ready to fire spun around, then fell backward onto the deck. Frost glanced down the trench. A very shaken and quite frightened Darius was nevertheless methodically going about his duties of reloading the discharged muskets. The next musket: forget about the men on the quarterdeck, the gunners at the cannons were the muscles and sinews flexing the British warship's claws and fangs.

Another cannon from the British man-o-war fired; Frost had no idea where that ball struck, and then, mercifully, Inshallah, first one of Rawbone's thirty-six-pounders, then another, fired. A knot of gunners clustered around two upright cannons forward from the waist entry simply disappeared in a cloud of splinters and sawdust. Frost turned back to the quarterdeck and saw only three people standing, but his gaze was too unfocused to determine if they worn officers' frocks or not; he aimed carefully, as always, and was pleased, yet sickened at the same time, to see his target slump to the deck.

Two more muskets and he had fired away all twenty of the pre-positioned muskets. Frost raced back to the other end of the firing trench, vaulting over Darius, who was gamely tamping a load down a musket's barrel with its ramrod. He reached the first musket, thumbed the steel frizzen forward to see that the pan was primed: good. Darius was learning his trade. Cock back, aim, this time at a gunner, down with the musket and on to the next. Another thirty-six-pounder on the parapet above roared, again the rush of superheated air that seemed to draw all breath from his lungs, the vain attempt to hawk spittle against the clot of acrid smoke in Frost's throat. Gracias a Dios! Another direct hit against a cannon on the British sloop-o-war! Rawbone had mastered his trade extremely well.

Bring the next musket to shoulder, cock back, select a target, squeeze . . . and a violent concussion threw Frost backward, his eyes dazzled by the burst of light, left cheek lacerated, left side seemingly paralyzed, no feeling at all in his left arm, the world reeling and tottering around him, sickness, nausea vile and retching in his stomach, his eyes completely unfocused. Great God! Had a cannon ball struck him directly? Why then was he not dead?

Darius was hauling Frost to his feet by the lapels of his ill-treated, unkempt British coat, fear and anxiety writ large on his broad, shocked face. "Captain Frost, Captain Frost!" he shouted, words Frost dimly heard through the barriers of wax in his ears: "Be you all right?"

The world's lurching abated somewhat: Frost fought the nausea and willed his eyes to focus. The first thing he saw was the Tower musket lying on the lip of the firing trench, half its butt stock split away. "Darius, damn you, you double, nay, most likely triple-charged the musket!" Frost flung off the young man's arms, and Darius, fear whitening his lips, dropped to his knees and cringed against the dirty brick wall of the firing trench, mutely awaiting the blows that would punish him.

Frost burst out laughing, a hoarse laugh breaking into something more like a mule's bray—so foul was the air in the firing trench from the sulfurous stench of smoke that his throat had constricted involuntarily. He willed his left hand to move and seized Darius under one arm, drawing the youth to his feet as Darius had set him upright seconds earlier. Frost brushed his coat's sleeve across his face, smelling in its cloth the sulfur impregnated in the very threads of the fabric. "There's a good lad! I hope you learn from this that a musket prefers to be fed only one cartridge at a time. Any more produces indigestion, with the consequences you have just seen."

Something below them caught his eye. "Hello! What's this?" Frost spun Darius around so the young man could see through a rent in the pall of powder smoke what had engaged Frost's attention. The British warship, now completely dismasted, had grounded on the far side of the channel, and someone was lustily waving a white shirt tied to an oar. "Darius, the British have surrendered! Your triple-charged musket won the day," Frost said jocularly, to shake the youth out of his fear and apprehension.

"Come on, man!" Frost shouted, digging the wax out of his ears as he ran from the firing trench. "Mister Rawbone! Cease firing! The British are surrendering! No more firing!" One thirty-six-pounder fired as Frost burst onto the stone floor behind the smoke-shrouded parapet on which the cannons were emplaced. Another was preparing to fire, the linstock slowly descending. Frost knocked it away. "No more firing! The British are surrendered, can you not see!"

A breeze, and the fact that no cannons were firing, dissipated the fog of smoke enough for the matrosses to see for themselves the waving flag of surrender. "Quintin Fowle! Take a dozen men, row out in the launch and order whoever commands to abandon yonder vessel, using boat, cask, spar, grating—anything which will float a man. The British are to take their wounded and dead, leaving no soul aboard, and gather on the shore in front of the Nag's Head. They are my prisoners and are to remain there until I come over to deal with them. Assure them that these cannons can easily reach to that shore. Nor is anyone to take a weapon ashore, not even a dirk, not even a marlinespike, or a fid, or a belaying pin!" Frost thought hard about his next command before giving it. "Then, Quintin Fowle, row out to the topsail schooner impaled on the Harbor Shoals and take its surrender. Get the schooner's men into whatever boats the vessel possesses and order them to join their fellows."

"Aye, Captain Frost," Quintin Fowle said, grinning. With a sinking heart, Frost watched the young sailor tell off a dozen matrosses, exactly half of Rawbone's complement, and order them down to the small cove where the gig and launch were beached.

"Quintin Fowle, remove those red tunics before shipping oars!" Frost shouted at his disappearing men. Frost expected the surviving senior officers of the British man-o-war had had enough of fighting and would follow his orders grudgingly. But the schooner . . . perhaps her captain would fire upon the launch. "If they do," Frost promised himself, "neither British vessel nor any crew aboard shall live past sundown this day." Shocked, he reflected upon that promise. What treachery would be vile enough to cause him to execute so callously? Frost hoped the British on both vessels had truly had enough of fighting.

Rawbone handed Frost the telescope and Frost focused it quickly on the British man-o-war less than one cable length away: the main deck of the Britisher came into sharp focus. She was completely dismasted, and the British warship resembled nothing so much as the poor, mauled old *Salmon* following her battle with HM *Jaguar*. Frost felt a sharp stab of pity for the British crew and the ship they were being forced to abandon. Frost stripped off the British Army tunic he had donned and shrugged into his own much-abused trader's coat.

"Mister Rawbone, stand by your cannons. I would appreciate a ranging shot as soon as the British begin to go ashore,

right into the rocks beneath the Nag's Head, if you please."
Frost swept the glass half a mile seaward and scrutinized the
topsail schooner for a moment. He made a mental note of her
convoy number. More gloom and consternation at Lloyd's
Coffee House when news of the schooner's loss was reported.
"And Mister Rawbone, yonder schooner bears watching, particularly as our men row out to order her surrender. To enhance your matrosses' gunlaying, you might find it convenient
to pivot one of these cannons around and try skipping a ball
toward her."

Frost ran to the clearing above the beach where the gig had
been hauled ashore and focused the telescope on Louisbourg.
The cat still lay to her anchors, a heavy pall of smoke over the
town, and half a mile from the quay was a longboat pulling
mightily toward him.

Frost turned and walked tiredly back to the cannon em-
placements. "Mister Rawbone, I must temporarily levy from
you several hands to row me ashore to the town in the gig, or
actually just to meet a longboat that is even now pulling out
from the town. Please take this glass and keep it trained on the
schooner. If she hauls her colors leave off firing; otherwise,
keep your matrosses skipping balls at her."

XXVII

ING TSUN WAS SETTING THE FIERCE DOUBLE STROKE FOR THE LONGBOAT FROM HIS THWART AT THE STAR- BOARD BOW OAR. FROST ORDERED the gig's crew to rest on their oars and let the longboat approach. He leaped for the longboat, fatigue making him clumsy, but Ming Tsun caught him easily. Frost called over his shoulder: "Darius, please organize a crew to move all the powder out of the magazine to the cove where we beached the gig and launch. Keep the barrels above high water. We'll sail up in the cat presently to take off the powder. And Darius, collect all the muskets from the firing trench and bring them along as well. Those muskets will be of far greater use and value to us than the British."

"I'm . . . I'm to organize a crew, Captain Frost?" queried an astonished Darius.

"Of course, man!" Frost snapped. "Communicate my desires to Mister Rawbone and tell him how many men you'll need."

"But . . . but . . ."

Frost promptly forgot about Darius once he had given his order and clambered over the thwarts toward the stern sheets, where Struan Ferguson sat at the tiller. Larboard oars were already stroking the water as the longboat reversed course in the southwest arm of Louisbourg Harbor. Frost scooped water from overside and splashed his face, the cold water temporarily shocking away the drowsiness that threatened at any moment to overcome him. A cormorant popped to the surface of the South West Arm a dozen feet from Frost, shot a quick, startled glance at the longboat, and dived again.

"There was another entrance to the prison, Captain, or an exit if ye prefer that word. One which our prisoners, for all the time kept there, knew not existed, though the British obviously did." Struan's tone was filled with bitter self-reproach. "No sooner had we left Jack Lacey and his crew with the artillery piece to guard the portal aside where Doctor Green and this Hymsinger fellow were physicking our prisoners, and were returning to the quay, than the British fell upon us unexpectedly from a side street with pitchforks, scythes, cobbles, of such close press we had no time to defend ourselves except by individual fighting of the most fierce kind."

"We lost men." Frost voiced a statement, not a question.

"Yes, Captain." Struan Ferguson avoided Frost's eyes. "Another five brave young men who shall never see New England again. And muckle a grievous wound inflicted, which our Doctor Green and the half-Indian with a beard that Moses himself would covet are solicitiously dressing."

"I should have hanged that Starkweather on the quay some hours ago," Frost said bleakly, "and had done with him. Name me the men I have lost."

Struan Ferguson named the dead, and Frost heard the names without visible emotion: Briggs Belmont from Exeter; Gary Hudson from Dover; Pettis Fisher from York; Charles Garrick from Wellfleet, down on the arm of Cape Cod; and Richard Wiggin from Roxbury, both of the latter named from Massachusetts, farmers who had journeyed overland to join the cat's complement. Landsmen all, though Pettis Fisher had displayed some talent for the foretop. Another five men who had walked through the wall between life and death for Geoffrey Frost.

"As for the British Army's Major Starkweather, Captain, he's consigned to the devil in any event, for I ran my own good backsword through his breast." Struan said, with evident satisfaction. "Knowing that I could not move the cat against the tide, as soon as the Britishers were once again in hand I freighted this longboat with every man who could be spared and sped to render such aid . . . ," Struan Ferguson smiled his peculiar Scot's half-smile, "aid that it would appear ye did not require."

Frost lifted his gaze and squinted against the sun's glare, muted through the haze of cloud. "The tide shall outflow in two hours, Mister Ferguson. At that time our cat and the four prize vessels in the harbor must be sailing up this arm. I shall be at the helm of the cat. You shall command the larger brig. Slocum Plaisted the next. I fancy Jack Lacey, in addition to being an excellent matross, and having served as our quarter-master, is fit to command the larger snow. Daniel O'Buck, who was bosun to Marcus Whipple aboard the *Trout*, I have every confidence is fit to command the last snow. I shall leave the decisions as to allocation of crews for each vessel to you."

Frost looked at the town that the longboat was fast nearing. "It appears the smoke is abating, Mister Ferguson. Is someone fighting the fires?"

"Yes, Captain, yer brother, at the specific request of Marcus Whipple, has attacked the flames nobly and diligently. Captain Whipple confided to me that he dinna wish the citizens of Louisbourg to curse us for the burning o' their town as the good people of Falmouth shall forever curse Lieutenant Mowat of the *Canceaux*."

Frost nodded his understanding. Secure in the knowledge that his brother was safe and that nothing could be demanded of him for the next fifteen minutes, he lay down on a scrap of canvas in the bottom of the longboat at Struan's feet and went instantly asleep.

He was as instantly awake and marvelously refreshed when the longboat bumped against the stone steps at the quay. The tide was at its maximum ebb, he saw as he nimbly climbed the steps, only to be brought up short at the sight of six additional silent shapes ranged beneath canvas in the community of dead he had seen when he left the quay earlier. Young Billy Chasse's body had been brought down earlier as one of the five men Frost had lost in the initial fighting, so he knew the severely wounded seaman attended by Doctor Green had succumbed. Frost wracked his brain to recall the name: Gary Clifford, mild, unassuming topman, a Massachusetts man from Salem. Probably knew young Bowditch's family. Clifford had a large family, Frost recalled. Then he remembered that Ezrah Green had informed him of Clifford's death when Ezrah had first come ashore from the cat. When had that been? Years earlier it seemed, though it could not have been more than two hours earlier that day.

A knot of British soldiers sat, backs against the walls of houses fronting the quay near the Dauphin Gate, hands and feet bound. Frost approached them. "Is there an officer among you?" he demanded sharply, expecting an answer.

A blonde-haired man of twenty-five years or so, the entire right side of his head discolored by a nasty bruise, lifted his head defiantly, insolently. "I be Lieutenant Basehart. If Major Starkweather be dead, I be next in command of the Louisbourg garrison."

Frost signed to Ming Tsun, and the knife hidden in the sheath bound to Ming Tsun's left arm appeared miraculously in his hand. "I trust you know the way to the cemetery, Lieutenant," Frost said coldly as Ming Tsun severed the man's bounds.

"That I do, and I expect your design is to march us there, bid us dig our own graves, and then murder us . . ."

"Lieutenant Basehart, I hope you do not live up to your name," Frost snapped. "I mean to bury my dead in your cemetery. These dead of mine be farmers, ploughmen who would rest far easier in earth than on the sea floor. Mark you, Lieutenant Basehart, my intention is to show you where I shall bury my dead in your cemetery and charge you strictly under no account to disturb their rest. One day this current stupidity shall be ended, and I shall return to raise them proper monument." Frost reached down and drew the British officer to his feet, thrust him backward against the stone wall of the house behind, and stared him calmly in the eye until the British officer averted his gaze.

"I tell you true, Lieutenant Basehart of the British Army in North America. One day this stupidity, this obscenity of war between cousins, shall be over. Upon my return to Louisbourg Town, should I find the graves of my dead disturbed, the men who have walked through the wall between life and the hereafter on my account, I shall hold you culpable. If you be alive and in any corner, crevice, crack or cranny of this green earth created by a benevolent deity, I shall find you, depend on it, and upon finding you, your own death will be something you shall eminently desire."

The British officer stiffened and stared back at Frost with disdain. "My name, despite your aspersions, sir, is an honorable one, and well known to our King. Your men are rebels, defying your lawful sovereign. Nevertheless, all dead men are entitled to lie easy in their graves. They'll not be disturbed by me, that I'll grant. You have my word as a British officer."

"The word of a British officer, Lieutenant Basehart," Frost said flatly and coldly, "is as worthless as a flagon of spittle. I shall take your word as a gentleman of honor that you will permit no disturbances of my dead, and you already have mine. Please wait whilst I organize a burial party." Frost looked around and caught sight of a very tired and begrimed Joseph and a bedraggled skein of cat's men bearing buckets and shovels emerging from an alley.

"Joseph!" Frost commanded. "Be done with your quenching duties. Your shovels and yonder barrows are needed to pay final tribute to our gallant dead." Frost continued to search the quay and saw, to his immense satisfaction, Nathaniel Dance and Hannibal Bowditch. "Mister Dance! Mister Bowditch! How good of you gentlemen to join us!" Frost managed to put a slightly mocking tone in his voice. "Have you any idea where John Nason may be found?"

"Attended by Doctor Green, Captain sir," both boys chirruped in unison. "He received a broken arm in the fighting now ended."

"Very well. Mister Bowditch, off to the cat and fetch my Bible. Within the hour eleven of our mates shall be consigned to the earth. I had wished Mister Nason, who aspires to be a minister, and who uttered gracious words to speed our departed mates buried this month past in Portsmouth, to repeat those words for our mates who must repose in foreign soil. I shall . . ."

"If ye please, Captain sir," Nathaniel Dance said, breaking into his captain's sentence without thinking, "there be an equal holy man in Mister Hymsinger, don't doubt it. He was marvelous comfortin' for the Britishers who died as Doctor Green sought to preserve their lives. By yer leave, sir, Mister Hymsinger knows some words as sweet to the ear as any Mister Nason . . ."

"Very well," Frost said abruptly. "Mister Dance, fetch Mister Hymsinger along to the cemetery. Mister Bowditch, be good enough to remind Doctor Green that he must have all our ill and wounded aboard the cat within the hour. Captain Whipple is to be placed in my cabin. Beg Ming Tsun attend Captain Whipple. Then attach yourself to Mister Ferguson. Mister Dance, after bringing Hymsinger to the cemetery, please attach yourself to Mister Plaisted. The two of you must help ready our vessels for departure with the tide . . . inform Mister Ferguson that each prize vessel's captain shall enship twenty men as crew."

Eighty men divided evenly as hands among the four brigs and snows; that would leave him a crew of ninety-five, of which perhaps a third of that number would be pressed into service as nurses for the freed prisoners. Great Buddha, grant that no occasion arose for him to have to fight his ship en route to Portsmouth. "Mister Dance, count seventy-five men into my crew. Herbert Collingwood advanced from helmsman to bosun. All the woods-cruizers in my crew. I shall take off our men on Battery Island. And Mister Bowditch, belay fetching my Bible, but please nip down to my cabin en route to taking up your duties with Mister Ferguson; I collect it is past time to wind the Kendall chronometer. Make the appropriate notation in the log."

Frost curtly nodded to Lieutenant Basehart: "Please to lead me to your cemetery, Lieutenant."

⤳ XXVIII ⤳

HE GRAVES WERE DUG QUICKLY BY
TWENTY MEN CONGREGATED BY JOSEPH,
TO PROPER DEPTH AND LAID OUT SYM-
METRICALLY AND EVENLY SPACED IN
the soft, fragrant, yielding earth of a Cape Breton late Spring.
The sailcloth-wrapped bodies—Frost would have preferred
coffins but dared not take the time for their construction—
were lowered gently, ceremoniously, though with care taken to
place Campbell, who had tried but failed to murder Frost, in
the grave furthest from the massive granite cross erected in the
center of the cemetery. Frost did not spare that strangely trun-
cated shape a second glance; nor did he speculate on the identity of the other man whose bullet had joined with Campbell's
in a failed effort to remove him from this life.

Then he concentrated, with proper gravity, upon the prayers
for the dead, united now in terrestrial democracy, which Ishmael Hymsinger offered up so eloquently. The man's lilting,
sonorous voice and choice of words fitted well with his name.
It was, Frost reckoned, as much as could be done until he returned after the war. After the war—and how long would that
be, and how would it end, and would he be alive to see the end
of it? Well, if he did not survive until the end of the war, Inshallah; and if George the Third was victorious, Inshallah. Frost
would leave instructions and sufficient money in an account
designated for the erection of a fitting memorial for the New
England men whose bodies would shortly be absorbed into the

soil of a land about which they probably had known nothing, in a town they had never known existed until they answered the recruiting broadside penned by Struan Ferguson.

After the last sonorous prayer had been sent heavenward by Ishmael Hymsinger, Frost ordered the burial party back to the quay. A glance at Jonathan's timepiece showed less than thirty minutes remaining before he would have to be under weigh. He stopped to exchange a final word with Lieutenant Basehart, who was standing at the cemetery's ornate iron gate. The British officer was decently outfitted since his coat and boots, fortunately not among the garments appropriated by Darius, had been located and brought to the cemetery at Frost's order. The British officer stared straight ahead past Frost with a glance as stony as the slate markers in the cemetery as Frost stopped in front of him.

"A waste of prime cemetery space, rebel," Lieutenant Basehart said in a voice as stony as his glance. "British soldiers expect nothing more than a mass grave, and happy indeed are they to get that."

Frost glanced back once at the freshly spaded earth. He quickly reflected upon the number of British dead in Louisbourg proper, as augmented by the number of dead from the British warship battered now into a hulk aground in front of Battery Island. He could not reckon their butcher's bill. "Then you best engage your burial party to open quite a large grave, though perhaps that task may wait whilst you command your men to battle the fires yet in the town," Frost said, feeling no need to remind Lieutenant Basehart of his oath. Then, accompanied only by his own thoughts, Frost followed the cat's burial party back to the harbor.

The first person Frost saw when he gained the quay was his brother, who had returned to supervising the filling of yet more leather fire buckets from a pump let down into the harbor. The air still floated the acrid reek of smoke, and dirty tendrils of smoke still escaped from several houses near the waterfront, one of which had already collapsed into charred timbers and tumbled slate. "Joseph!" Frost bellowed, "Your efforts as a bomberiro are commendable to the point that if the good folk of this town are unable to quench the embers remaining, they deserve not to sleep this night beneath intact roofs! The tide is making, and we are away to Portsmouth."

Joseph looked up from his task with dismay, but the look on his brother's face told him that argument would be futile. Frost noted with satisfaction that the artillery piece that Jack Lacey had employed so ably, as well as bundles of muskets and military stores, were being swayed up the side of the snow Lacey had been given to command. Frost had no doubt but that Lacey would govern his vessel as well as he had governed the crew serving the artillery piece. Frost wished that Billy Chasse were among the hands swaying up the cannon instead of being pressed under a ton or so of earth in the Louisbourg cemetery. Damn all perfidious British for their black, hellish souls.

Ming Tsun stood impassively at the head of the steps. Though it was invisible below the stone of the quay, Frost knew that some form of watercraft waited for him and his men below. Frost waited until no cat's man was left on the quay, all carefully enumerated and annotated against the crew's roster book cradled in Ming Tsun's hands. Ming Tsun nodded and closed the book.

"We should be short eleven men," Frost signed.

"But we have forty-seven additional men," Ming Tsun signed. "Their names are written as Captain Whipple spoke them to me."

Frost stepped down into a battered wherry, most likely commandeered from a chandler's, and the boat pushed away from the quay. Frost concentrated on his vessel as it loomed larger in his sight, thinking of the orders he must give to bring her to life, to break free her anchors, deciding on what sails to spread, how best to maneuver out of the harbor. One of the men missed his stroke and used his oar to thrust at something in the water. "No, you devil! Begone!"

Frost roused from his thoughts and looked around quickly, seeing the oar's blade come down brutally on the Newfoundland dog, pushing the dog underwater. "Belay that, Pickering!"

Frost snapped. "The poor beast wishes to quit this place as fervently as any man who has enjoyed Whip Loring's hospitality. Bring him aboard, smartly now."

The look on Pickering's face told Frost that he feared the dog mightily, but he feared Frost more, so Pickering leaned far out, a mate holding him by his belt, to bury both hands into the fur of the Newfoundland dog and heave the struggling animal into the wherry. The men at the oars fell away as the dog gained its feet, rolling precariously as the wherry bounced about, shook itself furiously, showering them all liberally with harbor water, then dispossessed the two men from the thwart in front of the stern sheets as the dog curled up contentedly at Frost's feet, filling the space and more.

Once anchors had been weighed and topsails and jibs spread to catch the afternoon breeze springing from the south, Frost surveyed his little fleet with more than a touch of satisfaction. He knew Struan Ferguson's and Slocum Plaisted's competencies as mariners, but Jack Lacey and Daniel O'Buck had never commanded any vessel larger than a launch. Frost was gratified that neither Lacey nor O'Buck lagged behind. Thirty minutes after the flukes of the cat's anchors had broken the surface of Louisbourg Harbor, Frost stood to the northeast of Battery Island a cable's length away from the shattered hulk of the British man-o-war and watched his little flotilla tack in succession through the narrow channel.

"Mister Ferguson!" Frost shouted through his speaking trumpet as Struan, in the brig he commanded, passed. "Sail down to the schooner newly risen off the harbor shoals. You have fifteen minutes to remove anything of value from her before fetching her here."

Frost turned to his brother: "Joseph, the launch alongside, then ashore. I know you would prefer to gift those thirty-six-pounders Mister Rawbone has so well employed to Henry Knox, but alas, such cannot be. Your Knox and His Excellency General Washington must be content with the powder remaining in the magazine that you'll bring away. You and Mister Rawbone calculate how best to destroy all the cannons. Do not content yourselves with their spiking. The British must never be able to use those cannons again."

"Mister Collingwood," Frost ordered his newly rated bosun, "away in the gig to the British hulk, if you please. Have a care! All were ordered to leave, and bear away their wounded and dead, but loaded pistols would not go amiss. Pay the anchor cable into the gig and send the cable to the island. Fasten the bitter end to a substantial boulder and break the hulk loose from the ground with her windlass—I expect she has shipped a goodly amount of water betime. It is my intention to sink her in the channel, the schooner as well."

Herbert Collingwood had made two voyages to China with Frost, and he was a quick study. "Should I send over any powder from her magazine, sir?"

"Commendable thought, Mister Collingwood, powder is the currency of revolution." Frost glanced around his decks and saw Caleb Mansfield scrutinizing the British sailors ashore at the Nag's Head through the Pepperrell glass Frost had given him.

"Caleb Mansfield!" Frost shouted through his speaking trumpet, "A word with you if you please." Yes, powder was indeed both currency and lifeblood of revolution.

"The allowance of time is short, Mister Collingwood, but I'll send Caleb Mansfield and some of his woods-cruizers with you to fetch away as many barrels of powder as can be, whilst yet running a fuse. But mark you, when the schooner joins you in mid-channel, five minutes will be your time allotted to cross to the cat."

In a few sparse words Frost told Caleb what he desired of Caleb's woods-cruizers. "Waal, this be a task for a proper fuse, Capt'n Frost, not a flintcock a-layin' in a barrel of powder . . ." Seeing Frost's sharp glance, Caleb broke off, then said soothingly: "Now, Capt'n, Struan never told me, 'course Mister Ming Tsun never would. I saw Mister Ming Tsun go below with that Frenchy aproveit and surmised the rest. Waal, had ye not them precautions, I had plans to blow the old *Salmon* on my own. Woods-cruizers like me can't abide gaols. What wus thar in Loo-e-burg, waal, this ol' goose ain't ne'r goin' inta one, ye twig what I say?"

Frost nodded curtly. "I believe Ming Tsun can locate some fast burning fuse for you, Caleb. He'll bring it over when the gig returns with the first burthen of powder. But mark, long ere nightfall our little squadron must have lost sight of this Cape Briton coast."

Frost calmly paced his quarterdeck, masking his anxiety and his tiredness as he watched his brother, Herbert Collingwood and Ming Tsun go about their ordered tasks. Ming Tsun had brought up Frost's best telescope before going off in search of fuse, and Frost focused his glass on the gaggle of forlorn men ashore beneath Nag Head just as Caleb had done. The cat was within a long musket shot of the shore, and he trusted no one who wore a British uniform.

He refocused the glass on the schooner and the brig Struan commanded, which lay alongside the schooner even as both vessels made their way toward the cat. Boxes and bales were being transferred at a furious pace into the brig. Frost nodded in satisfaction as he saw swivel guns dismounted from the schooner's planksheer and fife rails passed over. Frost turned to survey the men aboard his vessel, his eye lighting first on the helmsmen Collingwood had left at the wheel, one of whom was Roland Pickering, the man he had earlier admonished for attempting to keep the Newfoundland dog from following the wherry. But Pickering was a foretop man, and a good one, Frost collected.

"Roland Pickering! Against the return of Mister Collingwood I mark you as next senior about this vessel. Count out the men into three watches. Once Mister Collingwood starts back from the hulk, let go and brace round the main course. Name another to the wheel." Frost would have to see about getting his men and vessel organized for the run back to Portsmouth.

The launch was returning from Battery Island, barrels of powder piled haphazardly in the bilges and balanced atop thwarts, and a prodigiously smiling Darius was handling the tiller with aplomb. He saluted Frost as the launch drew along-side the cat. "Mister Rawbone's compliments, Captain Frost, sir! Cannons will be blown in two minutes! I'm ordered back to the island by Mister Rawbone to take off our men and the remaining powder!" Darius gestured at the stern sheets where lay a pile of muskets. "I've fetched away all the muskets!"

Frost smiled down at the deliriously happy youth. "Even the one with the broken stock, I trust, Mister Langdon. I'm certain we can find a gunsmith in New Hampshire who can mend it. But have a care when next you lade cargo for its proper distri-bution." He counted the barrels quickly, as only a trader can count wares quickly. Sixty barrels, with ninety pounds of pow-der in each. Nearly three tons! And here was the gig being rowed strongly from the hulk, and fairly burdened with powder barrels also. When John Langdon saw this cargo, Frost imag-ined his cousin would fairly dance with joy.

Frost focused his glass on the parapet where the thirty-six-pounders were emplaced, or had been emplaced, since the can-non were no longer in view. He picked out Rawbone, then Joseph, and they were pelting madly toward the blockhouse. Barely had they reached it when the parapet dissolved, pushed outward by a grand explosion, bricks and stones hurling every which way high into the air, and then an ugly, squat, dense col-umn of blackish-gray smoke formed over the remnants of the parapet.

The brig veered away from the schooner. Through his tele-scope Frost could see Struan Ferguson at the whip staff of the schooner, fighting her way against the tide with main and fore gaff sails and headsails. The schooner came on until she was barely thirty yards from the hulk of the British man-o-war; then Struan ordered both anchors dropped. The schooner's headway in the channel fell off sharply once her anchors bit into the chan-nel's bottom and held, though she still bore down on the hulk. Four men in the schooner's bows hurled grapples that snaked out to engage the shattered bulwarks of the British warship. The two hulls bumped and ground together, and Struan ordered his men into the gig that had been towing behind the schooner.

The launch was returning from Battery Island; Frost counted the men in the boat, Joseph and Rawbone among them, sitting happily among a dozen or so barrels of powder. Frost looked at Ming Tsun, who reassured him by signing "All are returned."

Frost scrutinized the two vessels knit tightly against each other with the grapples; the hulk of the vanquished sixth-rater was held in mid-channel by the hawsers run to Battery Island. The two vessels swung half a hundred yards southward until snubbed up short by the schooner's anchors.

The cat's backed sails were keeping her a cable's length off Lighthouse Point. Frost raised his speaking trumpet: "Mister Collingwood! Light the fuse and pull away!" Then to Pickering: "Let go and haul!"

The launch was alongside the starboard waist entry, and barrels of powder were being lifted and rolled onto the cat's main deck. Frost was beside the entry in a twinkling. "Joseph Frost!" he shouted at his brother: "Aboard this instant! Take charge of securing all powder barrels into the middle hold! Mister Rawbone! As soon as you come aboard verify the condition of all cannons ready to give immediate fire!" Aye, scarce two hours south of Louisbourg were the main sea routes to Halifax. Frost must have the cat ready to fight long before his little squadron cleared sight of land.

The gig was abreast the starboard entry and Herbert Collingwood was first aboard, followed closely by Caleb Mansfield. Frost had been mentally counting down the minutes, though he knew that fuses were notoriously fickle. He reckoned the time in excess of six minutes since the fuse had been set alight. Frost was watching the brig Struan Ferguson commanded grow fine on his larboard bow when he heard the sullen boom that marked the death of the British hulk, and the schooner held captive against it, turning quickly to catch the momentary reddish cancer twinkling from the hulk's waterline, breaking the hull asunder at rough mid-point. The hulk rolled ponderously over on her larboard side, the concussion of exploding powder throwing up a tremendous wave that rose over the schooner.

Had the schooner not been held back by her anchors, she likely could have risen against the wave that poured over her, but tethered as she was, without scope to add buoyancy, the schooner filled with water and settled quickly, coming to rest on an upright keel, the top twenty feet of her mainmast protruding above the channel. The hulk was settling now in a vast seething hiss of foam and protesting timbers.

Collingwood proffered a sailcloth-wrapped bundle to Frost. "Her log, codebook and sextant, Captain. Yonder British warship went by the name of *Scimitar*."

Frost signed for Ming Tsun to take the bundle. "His Britannic Majesty's sixth-rate man-o-war *Scimitar*. Did you learn the name of her commander, Mister Collingwood?" He was very, very tired, and wanted nothing more than to retire to his cabin and sleep.

"I twig the name was Mortimer, judging from the page of the log I saw open when I found it, sir."

"Most likely he is dead then," Frost said, almost too tired to think, but knowing that had the *Scimitar*'s commander lived, nay, even a junior officer, perhaps even a midshipman, the log and codebook would have been over side. The carnage aboard the *Scimitar* must have been horrific.

Judging the larger brig now within the range of his voice, Frost stepped to the larboard rail and shouted through his speaking trumpet: "Mister Ferguson! The after guard if you please! Ensure none straggles! Presently our course will be due south. Pass the word! Expect a course change shortly after sunrise!"

"Aye, sir!" Struan's words came faintly across to Frost. "Course directly south. Course change at sunrise. None shall straggle, my word on it!"

Frost turned to Herbert Collingwood: "You have an apt pupil in Roland Pickering, Mister Collingwood. I must beg you take the first watch, he the second; I shall take the third." Frost was experiencing difficulty speaking, and his voice seemed to come from a great distance.

He turned sternward just as a long swell rose under the cat, lifting her, glad that Ming Tsun was beside him so that a hand on the man's shoulder for steadiness did not look amiss. "You are to maintain a watch from the main crosstrees the night; I am to be called upon the sighting of any sail other than our own."

"Yes, sir. Course is due south, sir." Collingwood knuckled his forehead.

"Your sails?" Frost queried, longing to seek out his cabin, though not his berth, because Marcus would be there, but afraid to quit his quarterdeck until he knew Collingwood could serve.

But Collingwood had been with Frost on two voyages to the Orient, and he was, after all, a quick study. "Courses and top sails on this starboard tack, Captain Frost, whilst I study the brigs and snows and see how they hold course. Have no fear, sir. The four vessels pressing us now shall be with us at first light."

"Thank you, Mister Collingwood," Frost said, and let Ming Tsun accompany him to the companionway that descended to his cabin, but not so close that anyone could have thought Ming Tsun was supporting him. Good Ming Tsun, who, if anyone, had exerted himself more than Frost this day, though quite begrimed from the day's and the previous night's fighting yet showed no fatigue.

One lantern had already been lighted in the main cabin when Frost entered. The gaunt Hymsinger looked up from where he sat on a low stool beside Marcus Whipple lying in Frost's berth in the night cabin, then rose to his feet.

"Your most excellent man, whose name I have yet to learn, brought some broth which nourished Captain Whipple marvelously. The forgotten luxury of clean linen, following the cleansing bath ashore . . . now he sleeps like a babe."

Somewhat unsteadily, Frost paced across the main cabin to look down at his brother-in-law's serene features. "Divinum est opus, sedare dolorem," Frost said, smiling down at Marcus.

"Why, yes," Hymsinger said, startled, looking in amazement at Frost, the equally gaunt, unshaven, hollow-eyed Frost with the mussed, bedraggled, powder-stained hair, the massive raisin-colored bruise on his left cheek caused by the vicious recoil of the triple-charged musket, the caked blood over his right eye, "why yes, to relieve pain is a divine task."

Ming Tsun guided Frost to the desk, where a pannikin of warm water awaited. Frost let Ming Tsun bathe his wounds and bind crushed aloe against his bruises, particularly the bruise to his left cheek caused by the over-charged musket, the other cuts and scrapes, and bullet furrow on his right shoulder. He drank something bitter, something he had drunk only once before, off the Madagascar Coast when he had had a raging fever, one of the strange concoctions known only to Ming Tsun. Ming Tsun had rigged a pallet along the starboard bulkhead. Ming Tsun helped Frost out of his ruined, blood-spattered coat, and Frost sank down upon the pallet, not protesting as Ming Tsun relieved him of his shoes, murmuring faintly as Ming Tsun covered him with a blanket. Frost heard from a great distance the familiar, comforting sounds of the taut creak and twang of the tiller ropes through the cabin sole beneath him, and then he knew no more until late that night, when something exceedingly hairy and warm crowded in beside him, and Frost raised a hand in protest, drowsily trying to fend off the Newfoundland dog, who snuggled against him. When the dog settled down, Frost slept again.

HISTORICAL NOTE

On 5 January 1776 the Naval Committee of the Continental Congress ordered Commodore Esek Hopkins to sortie "with the utmost diligence" the eight ships of the fledgling Continental Navy and destroy the flotilla of Lord Dunmore, former royal governor of Virginia, then cruising in the Chesapeake. After destroying Dunmore, Hopkins was directed to cruise off the Carolinas and clear the fledging United States' southern coasts of British warships.

Instead, after being icebound in Delaware Bay for six weeks (during which time the First Lieutenant of Hopkins' flagship *Alfred*, a Scot named Jones, stood constant anchor watch to prevent desertions), Hopkins read his orders exhorting him to "distress the Enemy by all means in your power" as sufficient authority to mount an amphibious assault on New Providence in the Bahamas to capture cannons and powder for the Continental Army. Hopkins' dilatory tactics made the invasion on *opéra bouffe*. He captured a large number of cannons, but that lifeblood of revolution, gunpowder, was strangely lacking: the governor of New Providence had sufficient time to spirit away one hundred and fifty barrels. However sound his military reasoning for descending upon New Providence, for his dereliction of duty and tepid ardor in failing to subdue off Block Island HMS *Glasgow* with the overwhelming firepower of five vessels, Hopkins was subsequently censured by the Congress, and dismissed from service.

In Portsmouth, New Hampshire, Continental Agent John Langdon was desperately seeking cannons for his thirty-two gun frigate *Raleigh*, scheduled for launching in May 1776. It would have made perfect sense for Langdon to contract with his cousin, Geoffrey Frost, to fetch New Providence cannons home to Portsmouth. (In a revolutionary society nepotism is natural—a result of the desire to work with trustworthy people during a time of crisis: in our Revolution only Washington refrained from practicing nepotism.) Sadly, it took Langdon another year to collect the hodgepodge of cannons to outfit *Raleigh*. Even more sadly, *Raleigh*, under the command of John Barry, was captured by HMS *Experiment* and *Unicorn* after Barry was forced to run her aground in Penobscot Bay. But that's another story altogether.

Maintaining discipline on a privateer or Continental Navy vessel during the Revolutionary Era was not easy. Mutinies were common: J. P. Jones crushed his share, and that great privateer captain of Washington's Schooners, and subsequently second in seniority on the first list of Continental Navy officers, John Manley, once resolved a mutiny amicably—and single-handedly—by brandishing a cutlass under the chins of the would-be mutineers. He doubtlessly learned this tactic from his colleague, Geoffrey Frost.

Americans taken prisoner-of-war by the British—and there were thousands—were in perilous situations. The British, obviously, did not recognize their rebellious colonies as a co-belligerent, therefore prisoners-of-war were embarrassments. Consequently, their captivities were brutal. A soldier in the Continental Army might legitimately hope for eventual exchange via a cartel. American seamen could not. They were confined aboard hulks in New York and Halifax—or transported to England's Forton or Mill Prisons. In mid-1776 several dozen American prisoners-of-war in the Halifax hulks were removed to Sydney, Nova Scotia, to be forced laborers in the Sydney coal mines.

In October 1776, J. P. Jones was ordered by Commodore Hopkins on his second independent cruise to the waters of the Gulf of Saint Lawrence. In addition to raiding commerce, Jones was instructed to attack Sydney and free the captive American seamen. Unlike the American seamen turned New Hampshire militia under Marcus Whipple at Breed's Hill, who were languishing in Louisbourg when Geoffrey Frost freed them, the American seamen in Sydney, disdaining to labor in the coal mines, gained their freedom by enlisting in the Royal Navy.

Our Revolution was an exceedingly complex affair: the great wonder is we won it at all. The rôles played by Geoffrey Frost, Ming Tsun, Struan Ferguson, Darius Langdon, Hannibal Bowditch, Nathaniel Dance, Caleb Mansfield and his woods-cruisers, and the crew of ex-*Jaguar* are difficult to sort out, but no less important than the rôles played by Adams (John Adams really should be recognized as the father of the United States Navy), Hancock, Hopkins, Jones, Langdon, Manley, and Washington.

ABOUT THIS BOOK

Military orders took me to New England in 1976, when the Bicentennial of the American Revolution rekindled my interest in our nation's unique origins. My small library of Revolutionary era materials grew to several hundred volumes (with more being added monthly); biographies; interpretive texts on economics, diplomacy, and geo-politics; and critical analyses of battles. Employment in the Portsmouth Naval Shipyard, the U.S. Navy's oldest and preeminent shipyard, placed me within half a mile of the yards where USS *Raleigh* and USS *Ranger* were  built and increased my appreciation of all facets of U.S. nautical history. Membership in the Portsmouth Athenaeum brought an understanding of the daily life of a great port in the middle of the eighteenth century and of the rôles crucial to the success of the American Revolution played by all the people of the Ports of Piscataqua.

Into this amalgam at a propitious moment came the Ming Tsun Chronicles, glimpses into the life and times of Portsmouth mariner and trader Geoffrey Frost, who willingly wagered his life, fortune and honor pursuing freedom for all his countrymen. There are fragmentary, tantalizingly vague, apocryphal references in Revolutionary Era documents to an unnamed privateer captain sharing certain similarities with the ascetic, austere, enigmatic Frost. Had he been a naval officer, or not universally condemned for his brother's death and his mother's dementia, Frost undoubtedly would be much better known today. Those desiring to learn of Frost's contributions to our Revolutionary Era history must do so through Ming Tsun as amanuensis, and me as interpreter.